My Favorite Sin

Playing Favorites, book 1

SKYLA SUMMERS

My Favorite Sin
Copyright © 2024 by Eliza Luckey

Contact Information: www.skylasummers.com

ISBN: 978-0-6455663-7-6

Cover Designer: Books and Moods
Editor: MK Books Editing

BOOKS BY SKYLA SUMMERS

Celebrity Fake Dating series

Fake Dating Adrian Hunter

Fake Dating Zac Delavin

Fake Dating Daxton Hawk

Playing Favorites series

My Favorite Girl (Prequel novella)

My Favorite Sin (Book 1)

A WORD FROM SKYLA

My Favorite Sin is **book 1** in the Playing Favorites series. It is a standalone novel with a happy ever after for Dan and Ally. For the most immersive reading experience it is recommended to read the **prequel novella** first, **My Favorite Girl**.

Sensitive topics in My Favorite Sin include but are not limited to: social anxiety and panic attacks; mention of domestic violence, bullying, and parental death. For a more detailed list, visit www.skylasummers.com

Happy reading!
Skyla xoxo

For all the good girls who want to be naughty and fuck the one guy they know they shouldn't.

CHAPTER ONE

DAN

I lost five hundred thousand dollars playing poker earlier today because all I could think about during the game was that time Ally fingered herself in front of me.

I think about that night often, among others which never should have happened between us. She was always so caught up on being a good girl in front of our parents and the public's eyes. Behind closed doors she was *my* good girl.

The things she did in front of me were filthy. And yet the one time I kissed her, she ran scared, fleeing from New York to Paris for a year without saying goodbye to me.

She thought a hand-written letter would be an adequate goodbye. While I wait in the terminal for her flight to disembark, I read Ally's letter again. The paper is crumpled from how many times I've studied her words.

I'm in love with you, Dan.

I can't be in love with you. Our relationship is wrong in every sense.

Fuck. I was in love with her too but never got the chance to tell her.

Who am I kidding, I'm *still* in love with her. I thought I could stay angry with Ally for leaving the way she did. I thought I could get over her. But this year apart has changed nothing for me. I'm more obsessed with her now than ever. Unlike Ally, I don't care that her mother and my father are married.

When I return from Paris, I promise I'll return as your friend and nothing more.

Passengers start trickling out of the arrivals gate. I tuck Ally's letter into the inside pocket of my jacket and rest one shoulder against the wall while waiting for my girl to appear.

My mind wanders to curiosities about Ally and all the ways she'll have changed from the girl I knew. Will she have moved on from me like she intended to? Is there someone new in her life? Is she still a virgin?

That last question... My jaw clenches at the thought of anyone touching Ally. Perhaps it's best I don't find out the answer.

It's not long before I spot her among the crowd of passengers. My pulse is thumping so fucking loud in my ears I can't hear a damn thing inside this airport. The sight of her has me burning up like I'm a teenager again and about to have sex for the first time. How the fuck is Ally more beautiful than the last time I saw her?

How am I supposed to act like nothing happened between us?

Some guy—another passenger, I assume—is chatting her up as they walk with the flow of people. I can't blame him for being interested in her. She has this alluring presence like she's not even from this world. The first time I saw Ally she was fifteen, I was a year older, and she looked like some creature that had stepped out of a mythical story. A nymph or a fairy. So incredibly gorgeous.

The Ally in front of me still has that vibe. Her hair is the palest blond, slung over one shoulder and trailing down to her waist. Her complexion matches, as though she's never stepped foot in the sun. She has the prettiest lips. And those goddamn eyes that constantly say *fuck me*... I swear they're the brightest blue any eyes have ever been.

Her fashion hasn't changed. Always pastels and whites and like she belongs in a country garden. She's wearing a yellow dress with a delicate pink flower pattern and sleeves that fall off her shoulders. The bodice hugs her tits, which I shouldn't take notice of, but there's no ignoring how incredible her cleavage is. A pink satin ribbon sits in her hair. Always the ribbons and bows, like she's a little girl instead of twenty.

The urge to announce myself is strong. I want to wrap Ally in my arms. Lift her off her toes and spin her in circles. I need to see her smile at me and hear her sweet voice.

I hold off, unsure of our dynamic. I'm not certain she'll be pleased to see I'm the one picking her up from the airport.

Remaining in my spot, I lean against the wall and watch Ally walk with this guy. He looks to be the same age as us, clean cut and with a smile that lets me know he's into her. They come to a standstill. As I've seen so many times before, Ally starts fidgeting with her hair and shifts back and forth on her feet. Her shoulders grow tight. Her smile is strained. The guy makes eye contact with Ally and her gaze drops to the floor.

She's still awkward around new people, that much hasn't changed.

Ally holds her hand out to shake, forcing an end to their

interaction. The guy looks down at her palm, a little confused, then shakes it and leaves. I can't help but laugh over how adorably awkward Ally can be sometimes. I shouldn't feel so relieved by the guy's dismissal. It's not like I can have Ally for myself.

Ally scans the terminal for our parents. My heart pounds so heavily I can feel it as her gaze grows closer and closer to my direction until... Those blue eyes pause on me. We're staring at each other for what feels like a lifetime. I can't move. I can't seem to make myself do anything.

Her cheeks turn rosy beneath my gaze. Then suddenly she's... *smiling* at me. It's small, but the smile is there, and I'm so relieved that she's pleased to see me.

Ally steps up to me and lowers her carry-on luggage to the ground before wrapping her arms around my neck. The hug is guarded. She doesn't get too close and keeps distance between our bodies.

I should follow Ally's lead, but this moment feels surreal, too good to be true, and I pull her close, afraid she'll disappear. Ally laughs softly, caught off guard by my actions, but doesn't pull away. The sound of her voice is heaven. I breathe in Ally's floral scent and hug her tighter. I want to feel her lips beneath mine so fucking badly and remember what she tastes like.

I notice something else that makes me frown. She's tiny in my arms. Tinier than I remember. Ally hasn't been taking care of herself. What about her panic attacks? I've often worried about her mental health, being alone in a foreign country.

With reluctance, I end the hug, not knowing how to greet her.

I missed you.

I've thought about you every day.

You broke my heart, leaving the way you did.

None of those options seem appropriate. "How was your flight?"

"Fine." Her voice is cautious. She stands in silence, her gaze roaming my face, her expression troubled. "You look really different, like you've been hanging around Felix too much."

In other words, I've lost the boyish look of jeans and hoodies and replaced them with suits. I *have* been hanging around my oldest brother a lot, ever since Ally left. The parties are non-stop. So are the poker games and visits to his speakeasy. Felix was bound to rub off on me.

"What are you doing here?" Ally asks. "I thought our parents were picking me up."

"They had a last-minute work thing to take care of and called me to be here instead."

"Okay. No problem. Should we get out of here?"

"Sure." I pick up Ally's carry-on luggage and sling it over my shoulder.

"I can carry that." There's apprehension in her voice. Perhaps I shouldn't be carrying her belongings; it's something a boyfriend would do.

As I pass the bag back to Ally, a camera flash goes off nearby, making her jolt. Several more flashes light up our surroundings. Neither of us bother searching for the photographer. It's been ingrained in us as offspring of a high-profile marriage to ignore paparazzi. But Ally still hates it.

Our parents are known for their philanthropic ways and five years ago, when they got engaged, they founded Forever Families, a charity to assist families in need. They've thrown it upon our family that we're to be the face of the foundation, portraying how a blended family can be a strong unit. I think it's great they're so passionate about helping others. I just don't want to be a part of it, not when my father has been absent for the majority of my life, and all I ever want to do is get Ally naked. Nor do I want to live my life walking around on eggshells to aid the family image.

"Best part about Paris—no one took my photo."

"Walk on this side of me," I tell Ally, placing myself between her and the camera.

I've never cared about the public attention as much as she has. When I was younger, sometimes I enjoyed it. But I can't say I'm looking forward to today's poker loss hitting the news. Ally, on the other hand, stresses over what the tabloids say about her, always wanting to uphold a good reputation for our parents and Forever Families.

Of course, she never does anything scandalous for the tabloids to report on. At least, nothing anyone knows of, except me. A relationship with me would definitely not be accepted by the public. The last I heard, the media were praising Ally for how talented and dedicated she is to her piano studies at the Paris Conservatoire.

"So, what's the plan for tonight?" Ally asks as we follow the stream of people heading for the luggage collection area. "Mom told me she and Josh are still living in the beach house. You're not driving me to The Hamptons at this hour, are you?"

"I thought you could spend a couple of days with me in the city before I take you to our parents."

Her cheeks darken and she licks her lips, keeping her eyes straight ahead of us. "Sure, that sounds like fun."

My suggestion makes her uncomfortable. The invitation to stay at my place is innocent. Despite still being in love with this girl, I've missed having her as my friend this last year. Friendship was the start of our relationship, five years ago when our parents introduced us. From the color in Ally's cheeks right now, I can tell she's thinking about all the times we were more than just friends and that staying at my place will be dangerous.

"I can take you to our parents straight away, if you prefer," I tell her as we step onto the escalator, descending to the ground floor.

"No, don't hassle yourself. It will be good to spend some time in the city."

"If you're sure."

Our conversation is stilted and unnatural. She's being awkward around me, and I hate it. One of the things I love most about Ally is how she's shy around most people except me. She has to be nervous over the way things ended with us. I don't know how to broach the topic or if I even should. Maybe it's best I don't mention the past.

Ally and I rarely spoke about the inappropriate things we used to do. The silence gave her a sense of comfort. It was her way of pretending like she wasn't doing anything wrong. Is she going to run away all over again if I ask to talk about the past? I can't risk that, not when I've just got her back.

"So, tell me everything about Paris."

She smiles again, and this time when she talks, the Ally I used to know reappears—the girl who used to talk my ear off for hours on end about her passion for music. Her voice rises in pitch and speed as she launches into a recap of her year abroad. "DeLacroix was such a phenomenal piano teacher. I learned the most amazing things from him. Performed in the most amazing cathedrals. I got to visit so many incredible historical places. Dan, I stood where

Debussy stood. It was so surreal to be where these famous composers once were. A dream come true."

"Did you visit the Catacombs?"

She rolls her eyes at my teasing and gives a laugh of disapproval as we arrive at the baggage collection. "You know that's illegal."

"Wouldn't have stopped me."

"I visited Saint-Saëns's grave and Chopin's tomb. Does that count? It was so beautiful but also sad. I shed a few tears."

Of course she did. I chuckle at the information, relieved that some sense of normality has returned between us.

"I'm being weird, aren't I? Sorry," she says. "You probably don't care about any of these details."

I have no interest in this classical music stuff whatsoever, aside from the fact that Ally loves it. So, naturally, it's become a passion of mine too.

"You *know* I care about these details. I want to hear everything. Ally..." A confession sits on the tip of my tongue. Against the warning in my head, I say the words out loud. "I missed you. I thought about you a lot—"

"Oh, there's my suitcase." Ally points to the conveyor belt and leaves my side.

She heard me. I know she did. She's setting a precedent. Ally has moved on from me, just like she promised in her letter.

I'm the only one between us who is still plagued with this obsession.

CHAPTER TWO

ALLY

"Nice place you've got here." My fingers trail along the industrial-style brick wall as I walk through Dan's living room for the first time.

It's a one-bedroom in Soho he bought a few months back and every inch of it spells out Dan Blackwood. He's always had a thing for dark rooms lit by neon lights. I swear that's the only way I ever saw his bedroom back at our parents' penthouse. We're standing in dull red light right now, curtesy of the neon strip skirting the ceiling.

I don't know what it is about the neon lights, but they always evoke a sinful feeling, like it's two a.m. in a dive bar where nothing good ever happens. They make me think of sex, secrets, danger and.... all the times I was alone with Dan in his bedroom when I shouldn't have been. I'm tempted to ask that we turn on the regular lights, but can't seem to make myself say the words, shamefully comforted by the return of this sinful feeling I haven't felt in a year.

I continue scanning the apartment, attempting to distract myself from thoughts of sex. On the coffee table, there are a few towers of poker chips and a mess of playing cards, along with a bottle of whiskey and five crystal tumblers.

"Did you win big?"

When Dan doesn't answer, I glance over my shoulder, catching his gaze flick up from my ass to make eye contact. Heat pools in my cheeks which I'm thankful can't be seen in this red light. My breath catches at the way he's looking at me. This silence between us. The sexual tension has been thick since we locked eyes at the airport.

Regardless of whether Dan has moved on from me, I know he's thinking about all the times I got undressed in front of him and... performed. I've been thinking about them too. Non-stop. As a twenty-year-old virgin, I didn't think it was possible I could think about sex more. But since the moment I stepped off the plane tonight and saw Dan, my mind is in overdrive. My skin is constantly tingling with a nervous state of arousal, being with him again. Hearing his deep voice. I forgot how intoxicating it is to have Dan Blackwood simply look at me. To be in his presence. Be the girl he's thinking about.

A lock of dark hair falls in his eyes. I want to reach out and touch that piece of hair and trace the shape of his lips with my fingers. He has a thin layer of stubble and my fingers crave to brush against his jaw to feel the coarse hair.

In the year we've been apart, he's changed so much and is all... *man* now. His shoulders have broadened. He's taller. More muscular. I feel so tiny beside him, like a little girl. I don't think I've changed much at all. Paris was meant to be a reset. A chance to meet new guys and forget about my feelings for Dan.

Paris changed nothing at all.

I didn't meet any new guys. I didn't make any lasting friendships. I'm still the same awkward girl from a year ago who can't hold a conversation with anyone outside of my family.

I always wonder if talking to guys and finding a boyfriend would be easier for me if my mom hadn't sent me to an all-girls school, or if I'd grown up knowing my father instead of the violence I was exposed to from Mom's ex-boyfriend. The trust issues would be fewer. I'd have more confidence in social settings. More friends. Maybe I wouldn't have been bullied for being so quiet. Maybe I wouldn't have panic attacks or have needed to see a therapist for years.

Dan doesn't need to know how stagnant my year abroad was. Let him think I've moved on from him. It's for the best. I can't risk people finding out about us. Our parents would be disgusted in me. Forever Families' reputation would be disgraced and never recover.

"I should go to sleep. It's late," I say, needing some way to break this spell between us, though I'm not the least bit tired. I didn't expect to feel this instant overwhelming need for Dan, and if I don't distance myself from him immediately, I know I'll cave in and do something with him tonight I regret.

"Of course. Take my bedroom. I'll sleep on the fold-out couch in the living room."

My stomach clenches, thinking about being in Dan's bed again. He sees the apprehension on my face, and I swear a flash of annoyance crosses his eyes.

"The sheets are fresh, if that's what you're worried about."

That's the *last* thing I'm worried about. "I can't take your bedroom. That would be rude."

"Ally, you know I don't give a shit about you taking my room. You've been on a long flight and are bound to get jetlag. It's easier if you take the bedroom so I don't disturb you."

Dan opens the door to his room and places my luggage inside. It too is dark in there, soaked in neon blue light.

"Okay, um, thanks." I step into the room, staring at his king-sized bed, imagining the two of us— No. I shut down that trail of thought. "I suppose... goodnight, then."

"Ease the fuck up, okay? We're not like this." Dan jabs my ribs as he walks by, and I squeal at the sharp poke. A smug grin tugs at his lips and he shuts the door on his way out, leaving me alone in his bedroom. "Night, sis."

I spin around, staring at the door he left through, my eyes wide and my cheeks hot all over again at his parting words. There was a tone to them I can't figure out. Slightly sharp and sarcastic. Also suggestive. Sexual.

Overall, Dan has been nice to me in the few hours I've been back in the country. I wonder how much of his behavior is genuine, considering how things ended between us. If Dan is furious with me, I won't hold it against him. What I did was harsh but necessary.

After I graduated from high school, Dan secretly sent an audition tape to the Paris Conservatoire of me playing the piano. I didn't have confidence to apply to the institute myself, due to my anxiety around auditions. When I received my acceptance letter, it was the tipping point that made me realize I'm in love with him. He'd done something so incredibly thoughtful for me and we kissed for the first time ever, which sounds bizarre considering everything we'd done prior.

We never engaged in sex together. It was always one-sided. Me, stripping out of my clothes, the innocent virgin eager to be taught about my body and how to give myself an orgasm. Though what we did was wrong, the physical barrier between us was a comfort, making me feel like I hadn't technically done anything with Dan.

The kiss was different. It broke that barrier. In came a rush of emotions that made me realize I was in too deep and I couldn't resist my feelings for him any longer. Sooner or later, someone would have found out about us, and I was so addicted to Dan that there was no other option than a clean break.

I accepted the scholarship and fled town. I should have said a proper goodbye to him in person instead of through the letter, but I couldn't go through with it. I knew he would find some way to convince me we should be together. I would have given into him too.

Trying to forget those memories and that Dan is sleeping on the other side of the wall from me tonight, I take in my surroundings, scanning his bedroom—the built-in closet with a mirror sliding door; the massive windows that give a jaw dropping view of the Manhattan skyline.

I sit on the edge of the bed to remove my shoes, my attention snagging on the bedside table to a photo of Dan and our three older brothers at a black-tie event. They're all very handsome men but don't have anything on Dan, in my opinion. I have a normal, healthy relationship with my other stepbrothers, and it will be nice to see them again.

Behind the photo of Dan and his brothers is one of the two of us. There are no faces, thank God. The photo is from the waist down. But I know it's us. I remember the exact moment. We're sitting together on a couch. My legs are draped over Dan's and his hand is high on my leg, between my thighs in such a possessive way.

A thrill runs through me, traveling to that same spot between my legs where he held me. The feeling turns into

an ache, one I'm all too familiar with whenever I think of
Dan touching me.

In the next room over, the shower turns on. My eyes
flick to the sound, finding light seeping beneath what I
assume is a second bathroom door. It only deepens the ache
low in my core.

In an attempt to not think about Dan in the shower, I
change into my pajamas and crawl between his black satin
sheets, needing to sleep this night away, along with the
growing pulse in my groin.

But sleeping through this tension, this urge for release,
is near impossible.

My eyes snap to the bathroom at the sound of something deep. A... groan?

My body flushes with even more heat. The pulsing
between my thighs gets heavier. Outright painful. It was
only a small groan. Maybe not even a groan at all. Maybe
I'm imagining the whole thing. Surely Dan isn't...

The shower turns off. I hear him leave the bathroom.

My God. I just heard Dan jerking off. I know I did.

An image comes to mind of what he'd look like with his
hand wrapped around his cock. Of all the things that
happened between us, I never saw Dan without his clothes
on. I never got to see him come.

Jesus. I should *not* be thinking about Dan jerking off.

Or what he would sound like having sex.

Or how his muscles would flex when he thrusts.

I told myself this obsession would stop in Paris. I
promised myself—I even promised Dan in the letter I left
him—that I would be returning as a friend.

I'm going to keep that promise.

But not right now.

Not while I'm in Dan's bed. It won't hurt if I give in just one more time.

I squeeze my thighs, teasing the ache. I'm sure Dan has brought many girls back to this bed. We never spoke in depth about his sex life, but I know he's experienced. Girls have always flocked to him, and not only because he's a Blackwood, though his father's wealth never hurt. Dan is the kind of guy who gets invited to every party, has countless friends, and fits in everywhere he goes. He doesn't do girlfriends, just fucks girls, and never the same one twice. He hasn't mentioned any girlfriend since my return, so I assume not much has changed.

Right now, *I'm* the girl in Dan's bed, and it's a thrill I haven't felt in the longest time. I squeeze my legs tighter, intensifying the throbbing ache in my muscles. A rush of flutters travels through me, down to my clit, and draws out a tiny moan from my lips. A little voice in my mind tells me I *definitely* shouldn't be doing this, not in Dan's bed.

My thighs squeeze tighter.

I love defying that little voice. It's fucked up that this is what gets me off—doing the wrong thing. Being the good girl everyone thinks I am, but secretly a slut for Dan. For him and only him. I like that I shouldn't be doing this in Dan's bed.

"You've never had an orgasm?" I hear the memory of Dan's smooth, deep voice from one of the most intense nights of my life. The night he walked in on me touching myself.

"No. I've tried. I can never get myself there unless I think of..." I wouldn't say his name aloud, but he knew I was referring to him. *"It feels... wrong."*

"That's the whole fun of it, Ally. The more wrong it is, the better it feels. Let me teach you how to take care of yourself."

My hand slips beneath my panties, into the wet heat as I replay that night, remembering Dan's praise as he stood back watching me naked on my bed and telling me what a good girl I was while instructing me how to give myself an orgasm. He corrupted me and I loved every second of it, especially the excitement that came with doing something I shouldn't. Doing something wrong for once in my life.

Another time, I let him teach me how to use a dildo.

It was by far the most erotic moment of my life. *So* fucking wrong to be doing with Dan, of all people. Again, he didn't touch me, yet from the way his eyes lay on me and the soft praise of his voice, the way he took care of me afterward, it felt like we'd had sex.

I was so confused after that night, riding a wave of both empowerment and shame. I'd lost all dignity, desperate to find my orgasm. Fucking that dildo in front of Dan was the hardest I've ever come. I let the memory take over my body as I lay in his bed now, with mind-blowing pleasure unravelling through me as I hit my peak.

Another intense orgasm, given to me by the thought of Dan.

Something is seriously wrong with me.

CHAPTER THREE

ALLY

Ally,
I didn't want to wake you. I'm playing poker at Club Noir
tonight. Meet me there when you wake and we'll get
dinner together after my game.
Dan

I fold the note and return it to my pocket, peering up at the street entrance to Club Noir. I slept most of the day, recovering from my long day in transit yesterday, and woke early evening to find Dan's letter on the pillow beside me. My skin tingled when I first read the note, thinking about Dan being in the room with me while I slept.

I was tempted to give some reason as to why I can't attend dinner, but things have to stop being awkward between us. We were friends before anything sexual happened. I want us to be friends again.

ALLY

> Hey, I'm waiting on the street in front of
> Club Noir.

DAN

Come inside. My game hasn't finished.

You know I'm not old enough to get inside.

Tell security you know me. They'll let you in.

I don't want to get in trouble. I'll wait on the street till you're finished.

I might be a while. Just come inside. No one will care that you're underage.

I'm waiting outside. End of discussion.

I bury both hands inside my coat pockets, shivering as a cool breeze sweeps by me. Summertime is still here. We're at the end of August, but there's a dampness to the evening air along with the dewy smell of approaching rain. It's just my luck that I'm stuck on the street with bad weather. But I'm not going inside. The last thing I need is for photos to hit the media of me entering a burlesque club.

I don't even know how Dan is playing poker here. I doubt Club Noir has a gambling license. Which means... Ugh. Honestly, it would not surprise me in the least if Dan is playing underground poker. Even more reason for me to keep clear of this place.

I rock back and forth on my feet, glancing around every few seconds to keep my wits about me. A few people are scattered throughout the street, some entering nearby venues, but overall the night is quiet. Dark too, with only the sign of Club Noir glowing around me.

A drop of rain falls on my forehead. And then another and another until this light pitter-pattering of rain suddenly intensifies, gushing down. Swearing, I run beneath the tiny entrance canopy of Club Noir.

"Are you coming inside, madame?" Crammed beside me is a tall and broad man dressed in a suit, guarding the door.

I clutch my arms for warmth. "Oh, no. My... brother is inside. I'm waiting for him."

The wind picks up, the rain slanting beneath the canopy. I step back, pressing against the door, but it's not shelter enough and my coat quickly becomes drenched, the moisture seeping through to my dress beneath.

"Madame, I must insist you come inside."

"I... uh... okay."

The suited man opens the door and I shuffle in, out of the dark, wet, and windy night, and into a small entrance room. "Please, make yourself comfortable while you wait." And with that, he steps back outside, leaving me alone.

I brush the wet hair off my face, shivering as the cold a/c hits my damp skin. Great, just great. How am I supposed to go out to dinner in a wet dress?

I let out a long sigh, scoping out my surroundings. A moment ago, I thought I was about to step inside some seedy establishment, but Club Noir is the opposite. Luxurious and sensual and...it's like I'm standing inside a boudoir. Everything is silk and velvet. The walls are draped with red curtains and large mirrors framed with gold embellishments. There are plush couches and ottomans.

Ahead of me, a doorway is concealed by a velvet curtain, leading to the club, I assume. Within that doorway is the distant music of a live band—beautifully eerie and mystical music, like something I'd expect to hear at a circus. There are voices, too, and intermittent applause.

Temptation pulls at my chest. I lick my lips, wanting to step forward and peek through the curtain. A nearby thud distracts me. I turn around, expecting to find someone in the room with me.

But I'm all alone.

Thud.

Muffled laughter.

My eyes dart to the source, finding a wooden door near the street entrance. A cloak room, I suppose. Someone's in there?

I raise a skeptical eyebrow and grab my phone to text Dan, wanting to get out of here as fast as possible.

ALLY

> It's raining so I'm waiting for you inside the front entrance.

A third *thud* draws my attention back to the cloak room. This time, the sound is louder. There's a moan. The door slides open a fraction, just enough for me to see a man and woman making out.

My stomach does a little flip at the realization. Heat sweeps through me, gathering low in my tummy. Lower and lower. Although my dress and coat are soaked from the rain, I'm no longer cold.

I should look away, but I don't.

My head tilts to the side, trying to gain more of a view. From what little I can see, the guy is handsome and clean-cut. The woman's hands knot through his dark hair, ruffling it into a mess. His white dress shirt is untucked from his belt and the collar is unbuttoned. Behind them are a bunch of clothing racks. They're in a cloak room, like I first guessed.

The woman giggles as he kisses her neck. His hands hike up her dress, grabbing her panties and sliding them down her legs. My lips part with anticipation and my groin is suddenly hot. Are they seriously about to have sex in such a public setting?

Next, the man is unbuckling his belt. My eyes remain pinned to the area, never having seen a man's dick in real life. The angle doesn't allow me to see it now either, but I keep watching as he grabs the woman's thigh—his fingers dig into her flesh, that's how much he wants her—and wraps it around his waist.

The two of them make a loud moan as his hips thrust against hers. I clench my legs, feeling a slickness between them as I watch these two strangers having sex. Another thrust. Grunting. The man's jaw clenches like he's straining, like the pleasure almost hurts. The desire I see in his eyes as he watches her... It makes me... *jealous*.

Never have I wanted to be another woman so badly in my life. To have a man desire me so deeply that he has to fuck me in public because he can't wait for privacy.

The man's breathing becomes more labored as his thrusting intensifies. There's a glisten of sweat on his forehead. His groaning is so primal, it sends another wave of arousal through me. I touched myself only last night, yet the ache is back between my legs, needing release.

My breath turns heavy as I continue to watch, wondering what sounds the couple will make when they come.

"Ally—"

I gasp, my entire body suddenly stiff and flushed with embarrassment as I turn and see Dan. His gaze switches from me to the couple having sex through the crack in the door. A second later, the tiniest smirk pulls at the left corner of his lips.

The woman murmurs, "Babe, is someone out there?"

The man peers out, seeing me and Dan, yet that doesn't stop him from working his dick into the woman while sliding the door shut.

"I... uh..." I try to explain myself to Dan, but all that comes out of my mouth is a bunch of stutters.

"Voyeurism, huh?" He chuckles, the soft laugh smug. "Come on, my game hasn't finished yet. Wanna watch?"

My face burns hotter at the pun in his question. I'm so humiliated and need to shake this moment off that I follow him through the velvet curtains and into the club, ignoring the underage factor.

Just like Club Noir's entrance, the entertainment area is sensual and classy and is filled with an audience of patrons lounging on couches in front of a stage. I'm no prude, but considering the embarrassment that is still fresh in my system, the strip tease on stage does nothing to calm me down.

"You got caught in the rain. Take my jacket," Dan offers.

It's an offer I want to accept. The wet fabric of my coat clinging to my body isn't pleasant and I'm sure I'll start shivering again as soon as this embarrassment wears off. But the act of wearing Dan's jacket feels too intimate. "I'm fine."

"You sure?"

No. I would love to wear his jacket and be surrounded by his scent, which is exactly why I shake my head.

"Suit yourself."

Dan places a hand on my upper back, guiding me through the venue. The contact sends a warm shiver down my spine. Unable to function with Dan touching me, especially after he walked in on me watching two people having sex, I shrug his hand off. He glances at me curiously as we walk side by side, examining me, and that damn smirk returns. I can only imagine what he's thinking right now.

"Through here." Dan nods to a door, holding it open for me.

I step inside the dark room, finding a single light hanging over a poker green, a card dealer, and a group of suited men sitting at the table with rivulets of cigar smoke swirling around them.

I glare at Dan. "Is this even a legal poker game?"

"Legal enough. Don't worry, you're safe with me."

He brings me up to the table with him and takes a seat.

"Baby sis, you made it." I recognize the sly tone of my oldest stepbrother's voice before I see him. He sits to the other side of Dan, spinning a poker chip between two fingers.

I should have known Dan would be playing with Felix tonight. Dan is the youngest of my four stepbrothers, and even though there's five years between him and Felix, they're the closest out of all them. Felix is the one who got Dan into poker, teaching him about the game when he was only fifteen. Dan and Felix have tried to teach me too, but I've never been any good.

I give Felix a hug. He always smells like whiskey, and right now is no different. He looks a lot like Dan, but where Dan has more charm to him, Felix is a little intimidating. There's a sharp and cunning manner about the way he holds himself. His blond hair is always slicked back like something from the 1920s, and ink peeks above his suit collar and over the backs of his hands.

"Good to have you back. How was Paris?" Felix squeezes my waist. His warmth spreads into me, and as soon as he drops his arm, my shoulders clench with a new wave of shivers from the a/c. He gives me a once over, raising a brow. "You get caught in the rain or something? You look cold."

"I already offered her my jacket," Dan says. "She wouldn't take it."

"I'll warm up soon. Finish your game so we can get dinner." I take my wet coat off and step back from the game, draping it over a chair against the far wall.

The game continues. A female member of the bar staff arrives with a tray of crystal glasses and whiskey. There's chatter among the men and laughter. But overall, the game has a serious tone, and I can't help feeling nervous being in this room, being part of this "legal enough" game. Whatever that means. I swear, I am going to kill Dan after this.

As for Felix, I'm not fond of him being involved in this stuff either. His morals are worse than Dan's but at least he's secretive about it and keeps me out of his business. He's not the one who dragged me along tonight.

When I think about it, the two brothers aren't so different. Dan makes a living off winning poker games, many of them illegal; Felix makes his money through owning an illegal speakeasy here in Manhattan called The Scarlet Mirage.

I'm not supposed to know about the speakeasy. Not even Mom and Josh know about it. They think he sets a fine example for the family name by owning a cocktail lounge. I'm only aware of The Scarlet Mirage because Dan told me a few years back and swore me to secrecy.

Within a minute or two, Dan glances over his shoulder, finding me over by the couch. His gaze trails down my body in concern, and I realize it's because I'm clinging to myself, shivering in my wet outfit.

"Come here. I need to tell you something."

"Yeah?" I step beside him and go rigid the second his arm wraps around my waist, pulling me tight to his side.

"Nothing. I just want to keep you warm since you're too stubborn to take my jacket."

When he doesn't release his hand from my waist, my temperature climbs higher and the shivering stops. I keep thinking about his smirk from when he caught me watching that couple having sex, and how he shouldn't be touching me after that experience. I shouldn't have fingered myself in his bed last night, no matter how much seeing Dan again made me in desperate need for an orgasm.

Too caught up in my sordid thoughts, only now do I notice each player has revealed their cards and Dan has won.

Felix pats Dan's shoulder. "Damn, you're good, bro."

The dealer rakes several towers of poker chips toward Dan.

"Seems like you're my lucky charm." Dan winks at me. "I might have to start bringing you to more of these games."

"How much money did you win?" I ask.

"Five hundred grand."

I clap a hand to my mouth, smiling in disbelief. "Oh my God, Dan." I knew he was good at poker, but I didn't know he was *this* good.

Felix twirls a poker chip between his fingers again. "Don't be too impressed. He's only breaking even. Lost five hundred in a game yesterday."

"You *what*?" I scold Dan.

"Win some, lose some," Dan says without the least of worries. "That's the fun of it."

An older man sitting across from Felix raises his voice for Dan to hear, while nodding at me. "Seems like you're winning a lot more than just money tonight. You're a lucky man. Your girlfriend is beautiful."

Felix smothers a laugh by lifting his drink to his mouth. I can feel my cheeks growing hot again over the label.

"She is gorgeous, isn't she?" Dan says.

I press my lips together. *That's* the part Dan chooses to comment on? Not correcting the girlfriend title?

Dan stands from his seat with his hand still at my waist. "Come on, sis, you ready for dinner?"

CHAPTER FOUR

DAN

That fucking ribbon sits so sweetly in her hair. I want to rip it from her head and wrap it around her tiny wrists, shackling her to my bed.

"Dan?"

I blink away the fantasy, finding Ally waiting for an answer to a question I never heard because I was too busy thinking about her naked. It's all I've been able to think about this entire weekend.

"You're staying for dinner, right?" Ally peers up at me from the passenger seat of my Aston Martin with this soft look in her eyes that pushes blood to my cock. The sun is low in the sky as we sit idle in the driveway of Dad and Amabella's beach house in The Hamptons. Beethoven's *Funeral March* plays quietly from the speakers. I take it as a warning sign to turn down the dinner invitation.

"Why, so I can get into a fight with my father? No thanks. I'm dropping you off and heading straight back to the city."

"There won't be any fighting. Josh will be happy to see you. Mom says you haven't spoken to him since I left."

"That's not true. My father and I have lovely chats every time my name lands in the media and gets him in trouble."

She smiles at my joke. I can see she wants to retort with some speech about how my father is a good man and that family is important. It sounds like something that would come out of his mouth too.

"Oh my God, there's Mom!" Ally jumps out of the car and races toward Amabella standing on the front porch of the house.

Ally's mom I have no issue with. She's lovely and oftentimes I've felt like she's my own mother. Despite the broken relationship between me and my father, I lived at home with him, Amabella, and Ally right up until she left for Paris, because Ally and Amabella made it bearable. Even though I've kept my distance this last year, Amabella always phones to check up on me.

I grab Ally's luggage from my trunk and carry it to the front door, by which time Amabella has her daughter wrapped in a hug.

"Sweetheart." Amabella wipes the tears of joy from her eyes. "My goodness, look at you. So beautiful. I've missed you so much."

Dad really did get lucky landing Amabella as a wife. He's in his early fifties. She's still in her thirties and is stunningly beautiful like her daughter. Long, blond hair, and always dresses in designer labels. Even with all the hardship she's been through—a teen mom and losing Ally's father to sickness when Ally was only a baby, then the physical abuse from her next partner—she still had the courage to open her heart to my father, along with all four of his sons.

"Dan, you're not escaping a hug." She lets go of Ally and draws me into her arms. "Come here, darling."

"It's good to see you again," I tell her, and it's the truth.

She's the only mother figure I've ever known and has always been good to me. Too good, considering what I've done with her daughter. The whole family is under the impression that Ally and I are just really close friends and I'm a protective older brother due to the bullying and social struggles she's dealt with. Fuck. If only they knew. I'd lose any credibility I have with Amabella. She's a big part of the reason why I never took things further with Ally.

"Please tell me we'll be seeing more of you now that Ally is back from Paris," she says.

Before I can answer, the front door opens and my father steps out, all smiles for Ally. My jaw works, tensing at his presence. The sight of him in his casual attire, willowy cotton shirt and long pants, takes me a moment to adjust to. I'm used to the city version of Josh Blackwood. The version of him that's always in the media. Business suits every day of the year and gelled, black hair.

"Ally, I thought I heard your voice." He tucks Ally beneath one arm. Beneath the other, Dad draws Amabella into a group hug. I stand on the outskirts of the reunion, observing this happy family I've never fit into.

Felix was only five when Mom died giving birth to me, but he tells stories from that time and the following years, of how distraught our father was over her death. Understandably so, but his coping mechanism was the issue. Our father threw himself into work, focusing on his hotel development projects that brought in the big money, and hired full-time staff to take care of me and my three brothers. Maybe he thought the best way to be a father was to give us financial stability, opportunities, and an education. He did give us all those things, but at the cost of no relationship with his sons.

Most of my childhood memories of my father are of seeing him on TV in a press conference or an image of him in the tabloids. He'd leave early in the morning and return late at night. Some days I wouldn't see him at all.

I spent my early years trying to impress him with academics, believing I could earn his affection that way. He never seemed proud, so I stopped trying. I always got the sense I wasn't good enough, and that every time he looked at me, he was reminded of my mother's death.

He went through women like crazy. Never any girlfriends and he never brought them home to meet us. But I'd hear all about it in the media. When he started dating Amabella, he was suddenly a changed man. He was all about us being a family. He insisted we all spend quality time together and take family vacations. But the effort was too late for me and my brothers. The damage had been done. Tyler and Felix had already moved out of our home and were lucky enough to escape the forced family time. Killian and I were still finishing high school.

"Dan, join the family hug," Amabella urges.

I force a smile. She tries to fix the tension between me and my father, but that's a task she's not capable of. "I'm fine where I am."

Finally, after the initial reunion is over, my father steps back and looks at me for the first time. He offers me a firm nod. "Son. It's good to see you. Thank you for dropping Ally off."

"Actually, Dan is staying for dinner since he hasn't seen you two in a while."

My eyes dart to Ally as soon as she says the words. She sees the frustration in my eyes and responds with an innocent smile. The sweet girl act she loves to pull. It's what makes me feral for this girl, knowing I'm the only one who sees the real Ally and that there's nothing sweet and inno-cent about her. She knows what that smile does to me, and she has the nerve to use it on me right now. The fucking little brat.

"You're staying, Dan? Excellent," Amabella says. "I'll add an extra place setting to the table."

Staying for dinner hasn't turned out to be such a bad idea. With all the focus on Ally as she retells her time in Paris, I'm barely a part of the conversation. Amabella's cooking is delicious, and the beach views from where we're dining on the back veranda are nice. The house is right on the water with every luxury you'd expect to find in a Hamptons mansion.

When Dad and Amabella started dating, we made proper use of this beach house for the first time and migrated here as a family every summer. Those vacations weren't so bad, considering how massive this place is and the freedom we had. I basically never saw my father except at mealtimes. I was always doing something with Ally and my brothers, whether it be lounging around the pool, using the tennis courts, wandering the gardens and hedge maze, even playing secret games of poker in the library. The list of things we got up to was endless.

"Oh, Ally, honey, there's something I need to ask of you." Amabella finishes her meal, dabbing the corners of her mouth with a napkin. "Forever Families has a benefit next Saturday night. I'd love if you could play a few songs on the piano as a little entertainment. Can I count you in?"

"Of course. I'll happily perform. Where is the event held at?"

"Thank you, sweetie. Here in The Hamptons."

Great. I guess I'm not seeing Ally next weekend if she's busy up here.

"We really appreciate you playing at the benefit," Dad tells Ally. "Since you've been gone, your mother has been suffering from empty-nest syndrome and has been pouring all her energy into Forever Families. It's her new baby."

"Yes, and my baby is thriving." Amabella laughs, then switches her focus to me. "Dan, what have you been up to lately?"

I lean back in my chair, having finished my meal too. "Same old." No point on elaborating. It won't get me anywhere good.

The sound is quiet, but I swear my father scoffs in response. He swirls a glass of red wine and clasps his other hand with Amabella's in the chair beside him. "Now that you're back from Paris, Ally, your mother and I would like to organize a family lunch to officially welcome you home. Dan, I hope you'll be here for it. Your brothers have confirmed. We're planning on hosting it here in a couple of weekends once Daxton and Jordan have returned from a work trip."

Daxton is Amabella's cousin and one of Ally's closest relationships. He helped raise Ally and took care of them both when he learned how bad things were with Amabella's ex. Being a big name in hotel development, he also worked alongside my father, back before Dad decided to focus solely on Forever Families, which is how Amabella and Dad met. Jordan is Dax's fiancée and also extremely close with Ally. I know she'd love to see both of them.

"That sounds really nice," Ally says.

"Dan, can we expect you at the lunch?" my father asks. "We'd like to see you more."

I don't believe that statement. He's only saying it to look good in front of Amabella. The man thinks I'm more hassle than I'm worth. He cut me off from receiving my trust fund when I turned eighteen, insisting my life choices didn't warrant the reward and that I was a disappointment. If it was a parenting tactic, he failed yet again. I've never wanted his money.

Any event where I have to interact with my father sounds like a nightmare, but if the lunch is for Ally and my brothers will be here, chances are I won't have much to do with him. "Sure, I'll be at the lunch."

This lunch can't be too far off if they're hosting it at the beach house. Summer is about to end, which means my father and Amabella will be returning to their penthouse on the Upper East Side.

"When do you two plan on returning to the city?" I speak up at a lull in conversation.

Amabella pours herself a glass of water, smiling excitedly at Ally. "Actually, we're thinking about staying here."

"Really?" Ally gasps, matching her mother's enthusiasm. "Oh my God, I love that. You'll be here with me?"

Dad laughs, pleased at Ally's response. "We haven't seen you in so long and thought it would be nice if we were all under one roof again. Your mom and I can both work remotely and travel to the city when needed."

"Absolutely," Amabella adds. "We also thought living here would be a nice way to help you settle in with your new job, seeing how busy you're about to become. I'll cook all your meals. Do your washing."

"Mom, I've been living away from home for a year. I know how to do all those things," Ally laughs. Apparently, her year abroad has done nothing toward helping Dad and Amabella view her as an adult.

"I know, darling. But I'm your mother and I've missed taking care of you."

I seem to be the only one confused by the conversation. Ally will be living in this beach house permanently? I enter a downward spiral of thoughts, trying to figure out Ally's motives for wanting to live here, as the three of them continue sharing their excitement for being a reunited family. Call me selfish but I thought now that Ally has returned from Paris, she'd be in the city and I'd actually get to see her again.

Is that why she's moving here, to keep her distance from me?

"Dessert time." Amabella stands from her chair. "Josh, honey, can you help me in the kitchen?"

"Certainly."

The two of them leave Ally and me alone on the veranda. I keep my mouth shut until they're out of earshot. Perhaps I shouldn't say anything at all, but frustration gets the best of me and I need to know the truth.

"If you're moving to The Hamptons to get away from me because of what happened—"

"Dan," she hisses, her eyes shooting to the door with panic that this conversation isn't private. "I got a job here, okay. This has nothing to do with you."

I'm not convinced. "What kind of job?"

"Killian got me a job at the school he teaches at. I'll be a private piano teacher."

My brows narrow in confusion. "Is this job a temporary thing until you get accepted into Juilliard?"

She scoffs and looks away from me, out at the ocean. "Juilliard isn't going to accept me."

"That's fucking bullshit and you know it. You got

accepted out of thousands of applicants for that scholarship in Paris."

"Juilliard is more competitive. The only reason I received that scholarship was because you filmed me playing the piano without me realizing, then secretly sent off the application. I can't do auditions. The panic attacks haven't gone anywhere."

"What's your point? See a therapist and work on overcoming your anxiety of auditions. That was your plan all along because you wanted Juilliard so badly."

She looks back at me, her voice just as sharp as mine has turned. "Why are you so worked up over this?"

"Uh, maybe because I fucking care about you. Since when have you ever wanted to be a piano teacher?" I ask, right as I hear the door open behind us.

"Don't discourage Ally," my father reprimands, placing a stack of dessert plates on the table. Here we go.

Amabella is right beside him holding a lemon tart with concern etched on her face. For her sake, along with Ally's, I hold back a groan and maintain my calm. "I'm trying to encourage Ally to chase her dreams."

"Ally is on her own path. At least she is making sensible, adult decisions that don't publicly humiliate and disgrace this family and all the good we are trying to do in this world."

Fuck this. I push my chair out, the legs scraping loudly against the ground, and stand from the table with my car keys. It's always about the Blackwood name and his goddamn Forever Families, but where the fuck has he been for the majority of my life?

Ally stands too, clutching my wrist. "Dan, don't leave like this. Please."

"Ally, I'd like you to stay out of this," my father says,

then directs his anger at me. "I didn't want to say anything during this dinner, but you've pushed my buttons too far. Five hundred thousand dollars? Where is your brain, because it's certainly not in your head."

Shit. So, *that* news hit the media at some point since I checked my phone in the last few hours. "I've explained this to you before. The money I gamble with is all money I've won from poker. I never go into debt. Why does it matter what I do with it?"

"Dan," Amabella interjects with a calm voice of reason. "It doesn't matter where the money comes from. It's about the image the gambling presents to the public."

"Exactly," Dad agrees, yet with none of the patience. "Money is money, and you make Amabella and me look like frauds and scammers when we are running a non-profit organization. How do you think your actions look in the public eye when we're trying to raise money for a good cause, yet our son is throwing money down the toilet?"

"I'm leaving."

I head for the door. Before I make it off the veranda, Dad raises his voice again. "And how dare you bring Ally into your mess."

"What are you talking about?" Ally's voice is timid. I hate hearing her like that.

Instead of responding to Ally's question, Dad directs the answer at me. "Ally's name is in the media too. Underage at a strip club. Entering a private room filled with several men. I don't know what's going on but that is not in line with Ally's behavior. She would have only been placed in such a compromising situation because of you."

Ally's cheeks turn red and her shoulders rise, clenching into her neck. "It wasn't a strip club. And the room I entered was to watch a poker game."

"Honey, you don't need to explain yourself to me," Dad says. "I understand. None of this is about you."

For fuck's sake. I head back inside, making an exit before the man has a chance to finish speaking.

"Daniel, do not walk out of this conversation."

I don't look behind me but I take a guess that the footsteps running after me don't belong to my dad or Amabella.

She grabs my hand but I slip out of her grasp and continue through the house, out the front door and down the front steps to my car.

"Dan, wait," Ally begs.

"Ally, don't. There's nothing you can say or do."

She catches up to me and steps in front of the driver's side door, barricading it with her body. "Don't leave. Not like this. Please."

"Why? So I can argue with both you and my father more?"

"No. I'm sorry. I hate it when we fight. I know you were just trying to help me. I planned to tell you about my new job and living in The Hamptons. It just hadn't come up in conversation yet. Please don't drive when you're angry. Just... stay until you've calmed down."

"There's no chance of calming down when I'm anywhere near my father. This is why I have no relationship with him. It was a mistake agreeing to this dinner."

I try to move around Ally to open the car door, but she grabs my wrist. "Stay for me, because I'm asking you to."

"Ally..."

"Stay because... you're my person."

The history behind those words hits me hard in the chest. The way I spoke them to her for the first time right after my seventeenth birthday, begging for her forgiveness. I'd gotten drunk on my birthday—an annual habit—to forget how my mere existence in this world was the cause of my mother's death, and how it feels like my father blames me for her death. I wanted to stop feeling guilt over how I'm the reason my brothers lost their mother.

It was the first year I'd known Ally and had asked for privacy on that day. I didn't even want her to acknowledge my birthday. Of course, she didn't listen, gifting me a deck of cards. The present was small and understated. Perfect, really. She said she cared too much about me to completely ignore my birthday. We got into a fight about it, and I later realized I'd been a complete dick. She wouldn't talk to me, so I surprised her after school the next day, waiting at the gates with a bouquet of red roses.

"I'm sorry." It was the fourth time I'd said the words that day, begging for her forgiveness. *"You have to forgive me because you're my person and I don't know what I'll do if you stay angry at me."*

"Your person?"

"My favorite person." I was young. I didn't know how to express such intense feelings to a girl, especially a girl who was about to become family and I shouldn't have had feelings for at all. In hindsight, the words were my way of saying I love you.

"You're my person too." Finally, she accepted the roses and smiled at me, and I knew the words were just as meaningful leaving Ally's mouth.

The words took on even more meaning the following year when I brought Ally to a party which ended in her having a panic attack because she felt so uncomfortable.

I remember the explanation for her anxiety once I finally managed to calm her down. *"I'm not like you or any of the people here. I'm boring. I sit in my room and play the piano all day. I don't party. I don't even have friends outside of the family. But you thrive in this setting, and it's easy to forget that there's a whole other side of you I don't know about. It makes me feel pathetic."*

Her feelings took me by surprise, that she didn't realize how much I adored her. *"Ally... you have no fucking clue, do you?"*

"About what?"

"You're my person, remember? You get the real me. You're the only person who does." I reached into my pocket and retrieved the deck of cards she'd bought me for my birthday. It had become a habit to carry them on me and mindlessly shuffle them whenever I had an issue on my mind. I'd think of Ally and it would calm me. Standing before her, I searched through the deck, stopping at the Queen of Hearts, and handed it to Ally for safe keeping. *"This belongs to you. You're my Queen of Hearts. Never forget it."*

Another love confession.

She told me she wouldn't let go of the card.

That turned out to be a lie.

Along with the letter she wrote me when leaving for Paris, she slipped the Queen of Hearts into the envelope, returning it to me with the words written across it: *You'll always be my person.*

"Ally..." My eyes shut tight, the pain of all those memories returning to me. "Don't pull that bullshit on me right now."

"It's not bullshit. And..." Her gaze drops to the ground, her voice lowering. "I missed you too, okay. More than I want to admit. I also thought about you a lot. You know I did."

I take her chin in my hand, tilting her head up so she can't escape my eyes. She's nervous but sincere. The touch of her smooth skin is electric on my palm. I notice the quickening pulse in her neck. The flush of her cheeks. Her lips open to suck in a quick breath.

She steps back from me, out of my grip. "You can't touch me like that, Dan. I just... want things to go back to the way they were, when we were just friends."

My hand flexes by my side, the skin on my palm tingling from the high of touching Ally's face. "You know we were never just friends. And don't tell me I'm your person if you don't mean it."

"I do mean it. Just... as friends."

I rake a hand through my hair and groan. "Always so fucking ashamed of your feelings. I need to get out of here."

CHAPTER FIVE

ALLY

"Last, but not least, I would like to welcome Alexandra Hastings to the Performing Arts faculty." Headmistress Sinclair speaks into her microphone, addressing all staff in a rigid manner.

She's on the elderly side of middle-aged and has a grey bob. I've been sitting in this auditorium for an hour, listening to her welcome all staff back for the new school year and our preparatory week before students return, and not once has she smiled, which does nothing for my nerves.

"Alexandra will be filling the position of Sacred Heart's piano teacher."

I stand from my chair in the auditorium—as every other new member of staff has during this meeting—and try not to turn red in the face as everyone looks at me. Mission failed. I can feel how hot my cheeks are. The knowledge that I'm turning red makes me even hotter. I smile, give an awkward wave, and quickly sit back down.

"We're very lucky to have Alexandra. She's just completed the DeLacroix Scholarship in Paris. A fun fact about Alexandra—" Her bland tone leads me to believe there is nothing fun about to leave her mouth, and I swear, I've never heard my full name spoken so many times in the space of a minute. "She's also Killian Blackwood's sister. So, she'll fit in nicely here. Please do introduce yourself and make her feel at home."

"*Alexandra*, you're red," Killian whispers from beside me, holding in a laugh.

I draw my hair forward to shield my cheeks. "You're not helping the situation."

The headmistress says a few final words, wishing us luck for the upcoming academic year, then the welcome meeting is over and staff begin to disperse from the auditorium.

Sacred Heart is the exact type of high school I was sent to. A private, Catholic, all-girls school, with many students who board, teachers who wear suits to work and drive expensive cars, and parents who pay upward of 100K for their daughter's education. Coming from no money, my uncle Daxton paid for my education until Mom met Josh, of course.

Killian has been at Sacred Heart for one year, working as an athletics coach, and when he told me the school was looking for a private piano teacher, I knew it was a good opportunity. No education degree is needed for my particular role. Sacred Heart offered me a teaching position as soon as Killian mentioned the DeLacroix scholarship.

The argument that took place between me and Dan last night at dinner plays on my mind, about me throwing away my dreams of studying the piano at Juilliard. My anxiety of auditions is definitely a deterrent. The panic attacks started when I was a kid and lived through the violence that Mom's boyfriend brought into our home. He never touched me, but I witnessed a lot of physical abuse against my mother.

I learned from my childhood therapist that I'm triggered by stressful environments where I feel trapped and have a loss of control. In my senior year of high school, I auditioned for Juilliard and couldn't get through my performance without seizing up.

Juilliard is a dream I'm sad to give up on, but it's not just auditioning that's standing in my way anymore. The truth is, I don't think I'm cut out for Juilliard. Though I was studying alongside college students at the Conservatoire, the course I completed wasn't a degree. It was a preparatory year for students who have promising potential and was an eye-opening experience, emphasizing how I'm a small fish in a big pond.

My studies in Paris were taxing and pushed some real-world sense into me. Teaching is a safer option. Yes, I could work on my fear of auditioning and rejection, but I don't see the point when barely any college graduates go on to be successful musicians.

I follow Killian's lead as he moves into the aisle of the auditorium. Anyone would think I'd be at ease entering a new job where I already have an established relationship with one colleague. Perhaps Killian's presence does help a little, but I still feel out of sorts. Everywhere I look, staff are at least twenty years my senior. They all have an expression on their faces as though they're frustrated and stressed, and like anything I say to them will be a burden.

This is the first job I've ever had, and I feel so inexperienced. Even appearance wise, I look too young to be teaching here when I could pass for a student myself. I don't possess the authoritative nature that all teachers should have. There's no way I can control a bunch of students, which makes me nervous for the extra-curricular orchestras I'll be conducting. Thankfully, the majority of my role at Sacred Heart is to teach one-on-one piano lessons.

But the icing on the top of the cake—what makes me feel like even more of a child—is that Mom insisted on driving me to work this morning, like it was my first day of school and she was proud of her big girl. I don't have my driver's license. Mom and Josh said they'll organize a car service to deliver me to and from work each day, but I'd rather just walk.

"Hey, you didn't meet me for that morning jog we planned," Killian says.

"Sorry, it slipped my mind. I didn't get any sleep last night. You know, stressing over my first day here."

"No worries. You think you'll be up for tomorrow morning?"

"Yeah, tomorrow should be fine," I tell Killian, even though waking up at five a.m. every weekday to go jogging on the beach isn't my idea of fun. But I made a promise to be his jogging partner and I'll keep it.

He's only one year older than Dan, so we get along well. I get along well with Felix and Tyler, too, but they'd already moved out of home by the time Mom and Josh started dating, so I haven't spent as much time with them.

"Hey, Killian," a feminine voice calls out over the hum of staff greeting each other after their summer break.

I turn in the voice's direction, finding the only other young person in this auditorium. She wears a nice smile on her face and looks to be in her early twenties. She's slender, with brown hair in a tight bun, a black pencil skirt, white blouse, and heels.

"Violet, hey." Killian greets her with a hug. "Ally, this is one of the dance teachers. You two will be in the same staff room."

"Hi, it's nice to meet you." My voice wobbles mid-sentence.

"You too. It will be nice to have another young person to work with."

"You two might get along well," Killian says. "Violet is an ex-ballerina. She's an incredible dancer. Used to dance for the New York City Ballet."

She rolls her eyes and nudges him. "Stop being embarrassing. I *was* an incredible dancer. Career-ending injury. So, teaching it is." She grimaces and laughs.

A career-ending injury would be devastating. I want to offer Violet my apologies, but perhaps the topic is inappropriate to talk about, seeing as we don't know each other. I could ask her what ballets she's danced in. I've never been to a live ballet before but I've always loved music from *Swan Lake* and *The Nutcracker*. Maybe I should mention that Tyler's girlfriend dances in the New York City Ballet and they probably know each other.

"Hey, I went on a date on Saturday night," Violet says to Killian.

Crap, I missed my chance to say something. This is what it's always like for me around new people. Overthinking and planning what to say. I have this constant inner dialogue critiquing every tiny detail about our interaction and how the other person perceives me. It's exhausting. I wish I could speak freely but my brain freezes up.

"The date was terrible," Violet continues. "I can't wait to tell you about it. You'll laugh."

Killian is already laughing. "I look forward to this story. You want to catch up for drinks tonight after work?"

"Yes! That sounds great. Ally, you'll come too, right?"

"I, um... Yeah, okay." A burst of unease hits me in the chest at the thought of more socializing. I try to convince myself the outing won't be that bad, not with Killian to carry the conversation.

"Great," Violet says. "I have to do some work in the library now but I'll see you two tonight."

As Violet walks toward the exit, I notice Killian's eyes trail after her.

"You into Violet or something?" I ask, low enough for only Killian's ears. Surely she's into him too. Killian is charismatic. He has dark hair, like Dan, and a friendly face. I'm sure half the students here have a crush on him.

Killian looks back at me and shakes his head. "She's attractive but I wouldn't go there."

"Why not?"

"One thing you'll learn about working at Sacred Heart is that you're always on show and one step out of line will get you in deep shit. Staff relationships are highly frowned upon. *Anything* that isn't the utmost respectable behavior is frowned upon." He leans in, lowering his voice. "Listen, you didn't hear this from me, but last year one of the female staff got pregnant and it was rumored she'd been having an affair with a married teacher in the math department."

"Was it true?"

He shrugs. "I don't know. But they both lost their jobs over the rumor."

"How is that allowed?"

"When parents are paying as much as they do for an education at Sacred Heart, the school does anything to keep them happy. Staff reputation is everything here."

I gulp, intimidated by Killian's story.

He laughs. "Don't look so worried. You have the cleanest record of anyone on this planet."

"Yeah, aside from being caught at a strip club."

Someone steps up behind me, and a cold chill runs

down my spine. "Yes, I heard about your weekend fun, Alexandra."

My stomach tightens as I turn around and see Headmistress Sinclair. "I can explain. It was a complete misunderstanding. I wasn't—"

"I do hope so," she cuts me off. I try to maintain my confidence, like an adult should. But her reprimand makes me feel like I'm one of the students at Sacred Heart. "Alexandra, I am quite aware the media makes incorrect reports. What I have no tolerance for is when a staff member's name brings a bad reputation upon the school. Make sure you are not placing yourself in a position where misinformation can spread. This will not happen again, will it?"

"No. It won't."

"I'm glad we have an understanding. We're very pleased to have such an esteemed musician such as yourself teaching at Sacred Heart."

I nod. I'm so nervous the gesture almost turns into a bow. "I'm very grateful to be working here."

"Killian, I trust you can show Alexandra to the Performing Arts staff room."

"Yes, I'll take care of her."

"Very well." Headmistress Sinclair walks off without another word, and I feel about two feet tall.

The comforting smell of garlic and rosemary fills the house as soon as I step through the front door. Josh is right behind me, having picked me up from work in his car. I planned on walking home, but when the hour grew late due to new staff induction meetings, Josh insisted I get a lift with him, worrying about my safety walking alone at night.

My mother's high heels click on the marble floor and she appears from the kitchen wearing a Chanel dress and cooking apron, along with pearl earrings. "Honey, how was your first day of work?"

She looks so excited for me. I fake a smile to please her. "Amazing."

"They've got you working hard, staying back till seven-thirty. I can't wait to hear all about it over dinner. I've made your favorite, garlic chicken."

"Thanks. Do you mind if we eat a little later? It's been a long day and I need a moment to myself."

"Of course. Take your time." She places a kiss on my cheek, then takes Josh's hand, leading him into the kitchen.

I climb the stairs to my bedroom, each step a struggle, being drained of energy. Killian and Violet are meeting up for drinks right this minute but I can't find it within myself to join them. I enter my room, not bothering to turn the light on, and send Killian a quick apology text before collapsing onto my bed.

A moment later, my phone starts buzzing with an incoming call. I press the phone to my ear. "Killian, I'm sorry. I'm so exhausted—"

"Wrong brother."

My eyes flash open at the smooth sound of Dan's voice. A flicker of nerves coil deep within me in places Dan should have no impact over.

If I'd taken any notice of the caller ID and known Dan was calling, I probably wouldn't have answered. After the way things were left between us yesterday, I have a feeling this conversation will take a lot of effort that I don't currently have the capacity for. I don't even know how he feels about the way I left for Paris, but he can't be pleased.

"Everything okay?" I ask.

"Yeah. I won't keep you long if you're tired. I just wanted to tell you I've been thinking about our argument from last night. And, look, I don't want things to be weird between us. I'm glad you're back from Paris. I've missed having you around this last year as a friend. I don't want what happened in the past to ruin things for us... as friends."

The way he clarifies the friends part twice makes me hopeful. We can't have repeats of what happened before Paris, especially when more is at stake now. If two teachers got fired from Sacred Heart due to the *rumor* of an affair, I'd for sure lose my job if it ever leaked that I'm involved with Dan.

"Now that we've got that sorted, how was your first day of work?"

"Tough," I sigh. "I'm sure you don't want to hear the boring details of my life."

"Oh, come on." There's a trace of amusement in his voice. I visualize Dan on the other end of this phone call, maybe in bed like me, with a lazy grin sitting on his lips and his body drenched in that neon blue light. "I need a rundown of the scandalous shit Ally Hastings gets up to when I'm not around. What did they make you do at work today—get a staff badge, sign up for playground duty?"

I laugh at the way he teases me. Of course, only Dan can make me laugh after a day like today. I've missed this side of him and it's so nice to finally get it back. When Dan and I first met, I was awkward around him but he had a way of breaking down my barriers. He took an interest in my music, so far as to request I give him piano lessons. I told him about the bullying and my lack of friends, so he took it upon himself to walk me home from school every day so I wouldn't feel so lonely. We bonded over the sadness of how we both have a deceased parent we've never known. With our parents dating, Dan was always around, and I grew attached to him quickly.

Everyone always assumes I hung around him so much because I had no other friends, not because I had inappropriate feelings for him.

Have inappropriate feelings. They're still here and I hate that they are. I just wish I was normal. A normal girl with normal friends and a normal boyfriend.

"Okay, what scandalous shit did I get up to at work today?" I roll onto my elbows, my feet gently kicking in the air as I think about a response. "Well, this isn't work related but Killian and I have started a thing. Five a.m. jogging sessions."

"You have a thing with Killian? I'm jealous. You and I need a thing."

The deep sound of Dan's voice gives me butterflies, his tone amused, even teasing, like he's flirting with me. Maybe he is. I don't know. It's hard to distinguish between what is normal, friendly behavior with me and Dan since he's always spoken to me like this, even before anything sexual happened between us.

"Okay, fine. What do you want our thing to be?" I ask.

"We talk on the phone every night."

My eyes widen. My legs stop kicking. "Isn't that a bit excessive?" Like something a boyfriend and girlfriend would do.

"This is us, Ally. Nothing is excessive."

Us.

Why does that word have to sound so good coming out of his mouth?

When I don't reply, Dan speaks again, his voice low and intimate but with a firmness to it. "You ran away from me for a year and it fucking hurt, Ally. I understand why you did it, but now that you're back, we don't just continue as strangers. You and I used to talk all the time, even before you started getting off on being naked in front of me."

"Dan," I gasp, trying to ignore how my inner thigh muscles clench. "Don't speak about that—"

"I know, sis. Relax," he chuckles. "Clean slate between us. No weirdness. We're just friends now. Brother and sister."

"You're kind of being a jerk right now."

"I'll call you tomorrow."

"I won't answer." I end the call without saying goodbye, annoyed at the buzz of excitement that's swarming through me, pooling in my groin. Annoyed that despite what I say, I know myself and I'll most definitely be answering Dan's phone call tomorrow night.

CHAPTER SIX

ALLY

My fingers press the final keys of Chopin's *Fantaisie-Impromptu*, the music fades, and a gentle applause spreads through the audience of the Forever Families benefit. I gaze around the art gallery, at everyone dressed in their sparkling gowns and tuxedos, and find a room full of smiles directed at me.

Cameras flash. My photo will be in the news tomorrow, but I don't mind the attention when it's for a good cause. Plus, I love performing. For me, it's nothing like an audition. There's no stress involved nor do I feel trapped. Performing doesn't come with rejection and disappointment. My skill pleases people and makes them happy. They praise me and I feel accepted, even if only for a short period.

I stand and bow, soaking up their approval. The weekend is here and giving this piano performance is the first time since starting work at Sacred Heart that I've felt some sense of normality. The preparatory week has been a huge adjustment. I'm not sleeping properly because of the stress. Each day at school, I walk around on eggshells trying to act professional and impress the staff. At night, I arrive home late due to the overwhelming workload. I haven't had a single moment to myself where I can practice my music. I'm constantly tired and hating on life except for that moment each night when I see Dan's incoming call appear on my phone.

To my surprise and relief, he behaves himself on the phone. We tell each other about our day. We laugh and vent about our issues. It feels good to have him as a friend and brother again even though things are still a little weird between us. I keep using those labels, hoping they'll ward off this never-ending attraction I have for him. Each night, when I lie in bed and listen to his deep voice through the speaker, I try to block out the memories of our past. I fail every time. There is no blocking out the way Dan makes me feel.

When our calls end, my hand finds its way beneath my panties and I fuck my fingers, just like Dan taught me to. Maybe that's the base of the issue. I'll never get over Dan if I keep giving myself orgasms to the thought of him. But when I get in those moods, I'm so desperate and worked up over him, I'll do anything to find release.

Once the applause for my piano performance fades, the evening continues with wait staff handing out champagne to the guests. Polite chatter takes place among the crowd, and there's gentle background music.

"Honey, that was wonderful." Mom joins my side as I fold down the piano lid. "Thank you so much for playing. Everyone loved it."

"I'm always happy to help out at these events."

"Careful. I might hold you to your word. We have a lot of upcoming events over the next few months."

"I'll perform at all of them." They'll be the only performance opportunities I have from now on.

"Wonderful, honey. Okay, I have to run through my speech one more time. Wish me luck. How do I look?"

Absolutely stunning. She's both sophisticated and powerful in a gown the color of lilac flowers. I helped Mom choose her outfit. She picked out a dress for me too. It's pastel pink with a large bow at the back, short puffy princess sleeves, and knee-length tulle for the skirt. The dress is girly and a little flirty and I love it. We spent the afternoon getting dressed together, curling each other's hair and doing our makeup.

As for this speech she's giving tonight, I listened to her rehearse at home, recounting all the struggles she went through with her ex, how she was a young, single mom without much of an income and didn't know how to leave their toxic relationship, but how she found the strength for me. She didn't believe there was a man she could ever open her heart to again, but her love for Josh and his sons proved her wrong. She speaks about how she was fortunate to have the support of family members when she left her ex but that many victims of domestic violence don't have support, and that's why Forever Families has opened a shelter for victims seeking refuge. The speech is so inspiring it made me teary.

"You look incredible, Mom. Strong and like no one would dare lay a hand on you."

She holds my shoulder, smiling at me with sentiment.

"What's that look for?" I ask.

"Nothing. You've just grown into such a beautiful young lady. Though, you'll always be my little girl. Your father would be proud."

"Thanks. That means a lot."

She babies me too much, but I let Mom do her thing, knowing it makes her happy. I'm surprised she let me live in Paris for a year, though I didn't go without almost daily phone calls from her checking up on me.

My whole life, I've strived to please my mother and be the perfect daughter for her. When we lived with her ex, she was always so sad, and I quickly learned the best way to bring life back to her eyes and a smile on her face was if I excelled at school and performed well on the piano. I was her only happiness during that dark period. When Josh entered my life, my desire to please Mom spread to him too, and he was more than receptive, proud to have a role model child.

In a depressing way, sometimes it feels like Mom and Josh only like me when I act in a certain manner. It's not just them, but the public too. The media. Everyone here tonight. They all praise me when I'm the picture-perfect daughter. The talented musician.

Not Dan.

He likes me however I am.

The more fucked up I am, the more he likes me.

A tightness coils low within me just thinking about my most depraved moments with him. The moments when I feel most alive. I wish those moments didn't feel so wrong.

I brush my hair back from my shoulders, attempting to cool myself down from thoughts of Dan, and return my focus to Mom. "Speaking of my dad, did you ever find that photo of him?" The only photo we have of the three of us, taken in the hospital when I was born. It used to sit in our living room and I'd look at it every day. When we moved in with Josh, the photo somehow got misplaced and we haven't seen it in years. We don't speak about my father a whole lot, but the last time he was mentioned, Mom said she was going to do a deep clean through our home in the city to find it.

"Honey, I don't know where that photo has gone. But I promise you we will find it. Okay, I really need to practice this speech one last time. Killian is around here somewhere if you want someone to talk to."

He catches my eye in the distance, talking to a girl. From the way they're smiling at each other, I'll take a guess that he's chatting her up, which I have no plans to interrupt.

"I'm fine. I'd like to step outside for some fresh air."

We part ways and I head out to the balcony where the lights are dim and the ocean waves drown out the voices of everyone inside the gallery. After a deep breath of the salty sea breeze, I step up to the railing and rest my forearms on the banister, gazing out at the night and feeling so... lonely and miserable, even while being surrounded by hundreds of people at this evening's event.

Within a few moments, my vision adjusts to the night and I gaze out at the moon's shimmering reflection on the dark sea. Below me, on the shoreline, a bunch of people are on the beach. They're young, perhaps younger than me, all scattered along the sand and heading to the left. I follow their trail with my eyes, finding a bonfire party farther down the beach.

People are dancing around the flames. They're drinking and making out. A guy strips out of his clothes, completely naked, and people cheer as he runs into the water for what looks like a dare.

This is the exact kind of party Dan would always be at back in high school. I went along with him once and it was horrible. I didn't fit in, and it felt like Dan was babysitting me, making sure I had someone to talk to. While we were socializing in a group, he was bringing up topics that I'm interested in but that no one else cared for. I could tell none of the girls actually wanted to talk to me. It was Dan they were after, and it made me feel even more pathetic than I am.

I can't blame Dan when he was only trying to take care of me. But knowing how awkward I am, that I needed someone to hold my hand at a party, made me freeze up and be even less able to talk, and ended with a panic attack. I hated that I was a burden to Dan.

After that, I never attended one of those parties again.

I thought I would grow out of this inability to socialize. That Paris would change something within me. But here we are. Still as awkward as ever.

I've been so focused on music as a means for dealing with the loneliness, but looking out at the beach party, I can't lie to myself. I'm jealous. I want everything I see on that beach. The friends. The physical intimacy. The fun. All of it. Being a reckless teenager feels like a rite of passage I missed out on.

I want... Dan. More than anything. But that's not going to happen. I can't allow it to happen.

None of these things can happen while I'm kept under such close scrutiny by Sacred Heart and have a reputation to uphold for Forever Families.

"Hey, Ally, you were incredible on that piano."

The voice makes me jolt. It's male, young, and vaguely familiar. I turn around, finding a guy with a friendly smile, dressed in a suit, and with blond hair. I recognize him a second later—the guy from the plane. The one I'd been sitting next to, and who had walked with me into the terminal. We parted ways right before I saw Dan.

The two of us barely exchanged any details on the flight. Despite thinking he was attractive and wanting to have a proper discussion with him, the conversation consisted of awkward chit-chat on my behalf about the in-flight entertainment and how the airplane food tasted decent for once. I assumed I'd never see him again, especially after the awkward handshake I initiated at the end, and I haven't thought about him since.

But now he's here. What are the chances.

The guy's name is Ben George, if my memory is correct.

"George, hi."

His smile broadens. "It's Ben. My last name is George."

"I knew that. Sorry." I cringe on the inside. I'm off to a real great start with this conversation.

"So, you're like an amazing pianist. That performance inside was incredible."

"Thank you. My mother is a founder of Forever Families. She asked me to play tonight."

"Yeah," he laughs. "I figured from the introduction she gave for your performance."

Of course he knew that. Everyone here knows that.

"She said you studied music in Paris?"

"Yes. Do you... live in The Hamptons?"

"Yeah, I was vacationing in Paris for the summer. Back to work now."

"What do you do?" I ask.

"I'm a chef at a restaurant my parents own. And you? You must be a concert pianist or something incredible."

"Oh, no. I just started a new job at Sacred Heart. It's... teaching. I'm a piano teacher. Uh... obviously. Sorry."

He smiles with this look in his eyes, similar to how he looked at me on the plane, like he thinks I'm being endearing. "You know, ever since we had that good chat about airplane food, I've regretted not asking for your number."

It takes me a second too long to realize he's making a joke about the food conversation. As for the part about my number, he seems genuine. I try to think of a reply, but I'm so shocked that he's interested in me, nothing leaves my mouth.

"You're very pretty," he says. "Would you like to hang out some time?"

Like, as a date? My stomach flutters with a mixture of excitement but also fear. The one time a guy ever asked if I'd like to hang out, I was fourteen and eager, until it turned out to be a dare from one of the girls at school. Ask the loser girl on a date. Kiss her, catch it on camera, and spread the video around school for everyone to laugh over.

"Um… sure. Yes. That would be nice." Maybe it's wrong of me to agree when I'm so caught up in my feelings for Dan. But how will I ever get over Dan if I don't at least try to be with another guy?

Ben retrieves his phone from his pocket. "What are your digits?"

I tell him my phone number, then a moment later my phone buzzes. "Ah, sorry, someone is calling me. Excuse me."

He laughs again. "Yeah, it's me."

My neck prickles. Wow. Kill me now. This is worse than the awkward handshake. "Oh, okay. Thanks."

"Are you free next weekend?"

"Yes."

"Great. I'll text you and we'll set something up."

"That will be good." I need to end this interaction before saying anything else embarrassing. "I, um… I should see if my mom needs help with her speech. She's… a founder of Forever Families." Shit. I already said that. The nervous talking is shining through.

Another laugh. "Okay. See you later, Ally."

"Bye, George. I mean Ben." Oh my God. I need to get out of here right this second.

As soon as I'm out of sight, I run for the ladies' restroom and lock myself in a stall, burying my hands through my hair as I cringe something shocking.

A text message beeps on my phone.

NO CALLER ID

Hey, it's George :P You're pretty cute and funny. I'm looking forward to hanging out with you next weekend.

Ben wasn't frightened off? He actually thinks I'm cute and funny and wants to see me after that disastrous encounter?

What on earth am I supposed to do? I need help. *Expert* help because I have no clue what I'm doing.

CHAPTER SEVEN

ALLY

I have a date tonight. The first real date I've been asked on and my nerves are out of control. One minute, I was hiding in a toilet stall, reading Ben's message that we should get dinner the following Friday night. The next, my entire week has flown by in the blink of an eye.

I've finished my first official teaching week at Sacred Heart. It was also another week of no piano practice and disjointed sleep, of me waking at five a.m. each morning to go jogging with Killian, and awkward chit-chat with Violet each time we crossed paths in the staff room despite wanting to befriend her and have a real conversation.

I spoke to Dan every night on the phone but didn't mention anything about this date, not wanting to make things weird between us. He asked to see me this weekend. I would have invited him to the beach house if it weren't for this date, and instead gave him some excuse about being busy with work.

Now, here I am, standing in front of my bedroom mirror while fidgeting with the belt buckle on my dress and readjusting my headband for the tenth time in five minutes, wanting to look perfect for Ben.

I left work at a reasonable hour today so I had time to freshen up. Being Friday, it wasn't such a big deal. Ben said he'd pick me up tonight at six and we'd get dinner at Ocean Breeze Grill.

I check the time on my phone. Ten past six. His lateness doesn't help my nerves, but I try to maintain positive energy. Ben could be a guy I really like. Maybe I'll like him so much that I get over Dan. Ten minutes isn't terrible. He may be stuck in traffic.

I grab my purse and head downstairs, out to the front porch to wait for Ben. On the way, Mom catches sight of me from the living room where she sits curled up on the couch with Josh, watching a movie.

"You look nice, honey. You're going out?" she asks.

"Oh, yeah. I made a friend at work. We're having dinner." I haven't mentioned the date to either of them, knowing they'd make a fuss and ask me a million questions. They'd probably want to meet Ben and insist he come inside for a chat. "I'm not sure what time I'll be back. Don't wait up for me, okay?"

They both wish me a great night. I head out the front door and sit on the porch swing with my legs jittering as I wait for Ben's arrival.

Another ten minutes pass, and then another. There's a pain in my jaw from how hard my teeth are grinding. My skin is prickling with an unpleasant heat. I don't want to think the worst of Ben, but past traumas resurface, and even after all these years I can't help but think back to my fourteen-year-old self and Jackson Phillips who kissed me as a joke, or the girls who invited me to the mall and ran off while I was in the changing room.

I gulp down my fear, telling myself Ben doesn't have any motivation to hurt me. Maybe he's lost or stuck at the property gates, unable to access the driveway.

Trying to be mature about this, I dial Ben's number.

A feminine voice answers. "Hello?"

"Ah, hi. Is this Ben's phone?"

"Yes. I'll get him for you."

There's a muffled sound of someone passing the phone, then Ben speaks into the receiver. "Hello?"

"Ben, hi, it's Ally."

"Ally? Oh... shit." Silence lingers from his end of the phone and I know this can't be anything good. "Ally, I'm so sorry. I forgot all about tonight."

The prickling in my skin amplifies, stinging deep, so deep that I feel it in the core of my stomach. "Um, that's... okay."

I don't know why I tell Ben the situation is okay. Nothing about the way I'm feeling is okay, but I'm so desperate for people to like me that I'm willing to give him another chance, as pathetic as that sounds.

"No, really, I am sorry. The thing is..." He sighs, then curses under his breath. "Look, I'm back with my ex. It happened a couple of days ago. Tonight slipped my mind."

I'm surprised I don't burst into tears. Ben's reason is perhaps worse than being tricked like I have been in the past. What he's saying is I'm so unmemorable he forgot all about me.

Of course he forgot about me. It makes sense. I'm the quiet girl no one notices. This is my life.

Instead of those tears I expected, the emotions implode into numbness. A dark void inside me.

"I understand," I tell Ben. "I'm... pleased for you."

"Ah... thanks?"

I hang up the phone and stare into the distance, rocking slowly on the porch swing and hating myself.

CHAPTER EIGHT

DAN

The Scarlet Mirage—Felix's speakeasy, hidden beneath the streets of Manhattan. Every time I enter this place, it's like being transported back to the 1920s.

Art Deco paintings line the mahogany walls. The dim chandelier casts a faint glow on the venue, leaving the perimeter in shadows. A wooden bar stretches across one side of the speakeasy with all kinds of alcohol shelved on the wall behind. Along the back wall of the venue is a row of booths, each one concealed with velvet curtains, allowing God knows what to happen inside.

Illegal gambling.

Sex.

None of it would surprise me.

That's the appeal of this place: it's not legal at all. The Scarlet Mirage brings people back to the seduction of the Prohibition era. Entry is by invitation only, and it's a risk for any patron to walk through the doors. Dad would lose his shit if he found out about this place.

Tonight, it's busy down here, as Saturdays always are. The air is heavy with a mixture of cigar smoke and liquor.

Everyone has their eyes set on the stage where a strip tease feather dance is unfolding. The audience applauds as the dancer unclips her bra, hiding her breasts behind the feathers.

While I can admit she's putting on a good show, I seem to be the only audience member disinterested in seeing what's hidden behind the feathers. It's been two weeks since I've seen Ally and she's all I can think about. We've formed a habit of speaking on the phone every night, but it's not the same as being with her in person. Last night was the first time she didn't answer my call. I assume it's because I called late, after my poker game, and she'd gone to sleep early due to a long week at work.

While the dancer shimmies out of her thong, I pull out the deck of cards Ally bought me for my seventeenth birthday—the cards I used to carry with me everywhere until she left for Paris. I've stored them in my bedside drawer for the last year, ignoring the deck until earlier this evening because the memory of these cards was too painful. As I sit in this armchair, bored by the entertainment, my fingers fall into a familiar pattern, shuffling the cards for relaxation like I used to.

The deck is exquisite, each card black and embossed with the neon artwork of skulls. My shuffling stops when I see the Queen of Hearts, and a tightness forms in my chest. I trace my thumb over the card I once gave to Ally, reading her handwriting from when she returned it to me before Paris. *You'll always be my person.*

Those words... My jaw clenches, angered over how she willingly threw us away. I'm still caught up on how she left for Paris without saying goodbye and how we haven't discussed it yet. How badly she fucked me up. If she thinks

I'll let her get away with her little Paris stunt and life will carry on as if we never happened, she's wrong.

Ally is mine. She's always been mine and she always will be.

What we had was the most meaningful connection I've ever experienced. Deeper than just lust. We were everything to each other on an emotional level. We were each other's safe place.

Feelings like that don't just disappear, I don't care what she claims.

Our physical need for each other... Fuck. I never even got to indulge in her body. The day will come when this good girl persona snaps and I have Ally bouncing up and down on my cock.

The audience cheers, drawing my attention away from the Queen of Hearts. I glance back at the stage, seeing the feathers have lowered and the dancer's breasts are on full display. Again, I can't seem to make myself care. Her tits are good and she's pretty. Almost as pretty as the redhead sitting at the bar who's been sending me smiles all through this act. I don't care much about her tonight either.

The dancer steps into her final pose and the audience applauds. "You up for another game of blackjack?" Felix asks, occupying the armchair beside me.

I'm already up twenty K tonight from our previous game. It's only ten p.m. and I have a lot more stamina.

"Or are you keen to get your dick wet?" He nods at the redhead by the bar. "From the way she's been watching you, I'd say she's down for more than a friendly chat."

I could fuck her. I should at least try to do the right thing by seeing other women in an attempt to get over Ally. That was my tactic when she first ditched me for Paris. I was so

angry at her that I spent the first few months crashing at
Felix's apartment where there were constant parties and I
was rarely sober, fucking countless women to get Ally out of
my system. It didn't do shit for breaking my obsession with
her. Sleeping with this redhead tonight won't do shit either.

Besides, I don't want to get over Ally. She's had me in a
chokehold since the day I first met her five years ago. I let
her run from me once. I won't let it happen twice.

If I don't play this right, she'll be frightened off again.
I haven't yet figured out how, but I'm going to own Ally
in every way. I'll make her drop this good girl act and
return to the desperate little slut who fucked that dildo in
front of me. She'll embrace this raw side of her instead of
being filled with shame. I want her to admit with pride
how fucked up she is for wanting me, then ride my cock
and own every part of the decision. I'm going to make her
do the most messed up shit that pushes every boundary
she has because I know that's what turns her on the
most.

She's my slut. My Queen of Hearts. I'll make her see
how perfect we are together. Ally Hastings will be so
addicted to me that she begs for my dick every day and
can't fathom the thought of running away from me ever
again.

"The redhead isn't my type." I return the deck of cards
to the inside of my suit jacket, deciding it's time to duck
away for my nightly phone call with Ally.

Felix laughs. "Everyone is your type."

At least I've got him fooled.

My phone vibrates with an incoming call just as I reach
for it. I pause before answering, seeing Amabella's name on
the screen. There's a mood-killer, reminding me of what a
shitty person I am for all the things I want to do to her

daughter, when Amabella has been nothing but good to me.

Aside from that, the phone call is odd. We speak regularly enough on the phone that a call from her shouldn't be alarming. But she never calls me at ten p.m.

I raise the phone to my ear. "Amabella, everything all right?"

My suspicion is confirmed when I hear the concern in her voice. "Dan, Ally hasn't come out of her bedroom all day. She won't tell me what's upset her. She's not speaking to me at all. I asked if she'd speak to you but she said she wants to be alone. I don't think she's had a panic attack. She doesn't normally hide those issues from me. But I'm very worried. I'm hoping you can help. Do you know what's upset her?"

I'm already grabbing my car keys, standing from the armchair. "No clue. I'm on my way." In the past, I've been the only one who can ease Ally's panic attacks. Amabella doesn't think there's been a panic attack this time, but whatever the issue is, I need to be there for Ally.

"You're coming here right now? Honey, I don't want you driving at nighttime."

"I'll be fine on the road. See you soon." I hang up the call before Amabella can try to talk me out of driving.

"Everything okay?" Felix asks.

"No. That was Amabella. There's some issue with Ally. I need to go to her." I work hard to keep my voice casual, not letting him sense the protective side in me that's just flared over Ally.

"Shit. A panic attack?"

"Maybe. I don't know." I shrug, playing down the situation. "She won't speak to anyone. I'll see if she talks to me."

"You want me to drive?" There it is, the protective

instinct in Felix too. Except for him, it's brotherly concern, which is a large part of why I don't want Felix discovering my feelings for Ally. We're close as brothers. His morals are in the dirt, yet I don't think even he would accept this thing between me and Ally.

"I'll handle Ally. Stay here and enjoy the night."

"If you're sure. Keep me updated."

"Will do." I head for the exit, concerned for Ally but taking any opportunity I can to get in close with my girl again.

CHAPTER NINE

DAN

It's midnight when I arrive at the beach house. I kill the engine on my car and race up to the house. The front door opens before I have a chance to knock.

"Thanks for coming, Dan," my father says, with Amabella right beside him in the doorway. They're both in their dressing gowns, looking as worried as the other.

"It's no issue at all. Where's Ally?" I ask as Amabella greets me with a hug.

"Still in her room," she says. "I'm not sure she'll answer you. I told her you were coming and I got no response."

"It's okay. I'll take it from here."

I jog up the main flight of stairs, taking two at a time, and catch my breath before knocking on Ally's bedroom door. "Ally, it's me."

No response. It's late, and while she could be asleep, instincts tell me otherwise.

"I'm picking the lock if you don't answer in ten seconds."

Soft footsteps pad across the floor, the lock clicks, then the footsteps retreat. I poke my head inside, finding Ally in the dark, sitting on the window seat in her pajamas and staring out at the night. There's no emotion on her face, and that's what worries me the most. I can deal with tears and anger and even her panic attacks. But the girl in front of me is completely withdrawn.

I sit with her in the bay window. "What's going on?"

No answer.

"Did something happen at work—"

"I was supposed to go on a date last night." Her voice is lifeless as she continues staring out at the black sky.

My chest turns hollow, not having known anything about this date. I understand why she didn't tell me; as much as she insists we're just friends, she knows that's a lie.

This date restates how little I know about Ally's past year, and I feel so... jealous, being kept in the dark about the intimate details of her life, when this girl used to sleep in my arms every night. Did she date guys in Paris? Did she have sex? Who was this guy from last night? I wish I had answers, but right now, all I want is to make Ally feel better.

"What happened with this date?"

"I spent hours doing my hair and makeup. I was nervous but excited. I waited for him on the front porch. When he didn't show up, I called him." She laughs, but there's nothing humorous about the sound. "He told me he's back with his ex and forgot all about me." She speaks the words with such a blank voice that it sounds eerie. My chest flares with anger that someone would hurt Ally like this. "I guess that's a fair point. I'm not memorable. There's nothing special about me."

"Ally, stop. When your mom called me and said you're upset, I raced here. That's how special you are to me."

Her brows pinch. "You shouldn't have done that."

"It's worth it, to be with you when you're upset."

"I'm not upset. I'm... numb." She looks at me for the first time since my arrival. "You want to know what I said to the guy? I told him I understood and that I wish him and his girlfriend all the best. I didn't stand up for myself. I didn't get angry at him. I acted like I was pleased for him. Pathetic, huh?"

"You're not pathetic." I grab her hands and slide closer, urging her to believe my words. "You're perfect, Ally, just the way you are. If some jerk can't see that, then it's his loss."

She looks down at her hands in mine and withdraws them. "You're the only one who likes me. I don't have any friends."

"You run with Killian every morning. Felix loves you. So does Tyler. Daxton and Jordan—"

"Family doesn't count. I didn't make lasting friendships in Paris. I was too shy. Killian encouraged me to be friends with a girl at work. She's nice and I'd like to be her friend, but I've been too awkward. Now, I've probably left a bad impression on her."

"You can mend that relationship—"

"I've never been on a date." Her blank tone continues as she stares out the window. "I didn't meet any guys in Paris. I'm twenty years old and I'm still a virgin."

There's my answer to the question about her virginity. I'm pleased for my own selfish reasons but not that it causes so much grief for her.

"You're barely a virgin after what we did—"

"*Don't* talk about that," she snaps, still not looking at me. I know I shouldn't have mentioned it, but at least it brought out an emotion in her.

"Ally, there are plenty of people your age and older who haven't had sex. None of this means anything."

"You don't get it," she whispers, back to the lifeless canvas. "I'm sick of being like this. I'm sick of being me. Something has to change."

"Ally..."

She stands up and heads for her bed. "I'm going to sleep. I'm sorry you wasted your time coming here tonight."

I watch as she draws back her bedspread and climbs beneath the sheets. She should know better than to believe I'll follow her words and leave. I slide my shoes off and lay on the bed with her, on top of the sheets and with plenty of space between us.

"Dan..." I can hear the warning in her voice.

"You're my person, Ally. I'm not going anywhere."

CHAPTER TEN
ALLY

Warmth encompasses me. My eyes slowly blink open to the morning light, and I realize someone's arm is around my waist. There's a wall of muscle pressed to my back. Hot breath caresses the nape of my neck.

My heart rate picks up and I'm instantly wide awake, aware of every inch of Dan's body that touches mine and loving it. Memories flood back to me of how I used to sleep in his bed most nights with the two of us in this exact position. I was fifteen the first time it happened. Though I wouldn't have wanted Mom and Josh to find us like that, those nights were innocent, the two of us just hugging. As we grew older, Dan's hand would slide beneath my shirt and cup my breasts. His fingers would brush against my nipples. I'd go to sleep every night with wet panties. He never shied away from letting me feel his erection pressed to my back. As I gained confidence, I even grinded my ass against his dick and loved whenever I heard him groan.

I remain still in Dan's arms, wanting this moment to linger and not wake him. Being wrapped in his embrace is the only thing in this world that feels right, and after being stood up two nights ago, I'll cling to anything that makes me feel good.

A moment later, I remind myself how wrong it is to give in to my feelings for Dan, and gently attempt to remove myself from his arms.

His grip tightens around my waist, pulling me closer. My stomach flutters with excitement.

"Uh... Dan?" I whisper.

He stirs slightly. Without seeing his face, I pinpoint the exact moment he wakes and realizes the intimate position we're in. Dan's muscles stiffen and he releases me.

"Shit, sorry." He sits up against the headboard, rubbing both hands over his face and through his hair to wake up. "How are you feeling?"

"Oh, you know, amazing after my date forgot I exist."

The left corner of his mouth slants upward as he looks me over, his gaze warming my cheeks.

I sit up beside Dan. "What's that look for?"

"Your voice is back to normal."

"What was wrong with my voice?"

"Last night you sounded so... defeated. You had me worried."

I shrug because he's right, being forgotten about was defeating. And humiliating.

But I have a new sense of direction this morning.

After I went to bed, I spent the whole night tossing and turning while reflecting on my situation and found clarity. My life started going downhill when I was a young girl and lived in a toxic household with my mom and her ex. Everything always seems to link back to that one period of my life —my lack of confidence, my difficulties meeting new people and socializing, the panic attacks, the inability to audition.

But I'm tired of blaming everything on Mom's ex. The abuse happened. It fucked me up, but I need to move on with my life. I can't keep sitting around feeling sorry for myself. I want a boyfriend and proper friends who aren't family. I want to have sex, to let loose for once and not have the pressure of always being on my best behavior. I want to step out of my comfort zone and experience life instead of being the good little daughter of Amabella and Josh Blackwood. None of these things are going to happen unless I start making drastic changes to myself.

What I want most in this world is Dan, but those desires are messed up and maybe I only want him because I've never been around other guys much.

I climb out of bed and brush my fingers through my hair. "Hey, would you like to take a walk on the beach with me? There's something I'd like to discuss with you."

"So, I've been thinking about my dating situation," I say as the tide washes over my feet. The early morning sea breeze rustles my hair and sand squishes between my toes with each step I take along the shore. Dan and I slipped out the back of the house before our parents knew we were awake.

"You know, you could have told me you had a date. It didn't need to be a secret." I can feel Dan's eyes on me as he speaks those words. His tone is gentle. He's been treading carefully around me since arriving at the beach house last night, like he thinks I'm about to break, when in fact, determination is all that runs through my veins right now.

"I thought me going on a date might be weird for you to hear. Definitely not as weird as what I'm about to tell you.

But I've gotten to the stage of desperation and I'm not sure what else to do."

"Okay," he says with caution. "I'm listening."

I take a deep breath, nervous, but force myself to speak the plan out loud. "I'm going to hire a... teacher."

His brow furrows with suspicion. "What kind of teacher?"

"Someone who can help me fix... you know, my issues."

Dan stops short, staring at me with confusion. "As in a therapist?"

I continue walking along the beach, trying to keep the conversation light. "No. A guy to teach me about men and dating and how to be confident so I can meet people. Have friends, a boyfriend, and be normal."

"Ally, you *are* normal. And what the fuck? You're not hiring some random guy to teach you about dating."

Rolling my eyes, I turn around to face him. "You're always wearing rose-colored glasses around me. It's not normal to have no friends or that the only guy I've ever been interested in is my—" I stop mid-sentence, agitated with myself.

"Stepbrother?"

My lips part with embarrassment. He's challenging me but I stand my ground. "Yes. And I hate it."

"Believe me, I don't need any reminding." Dan gives an irritated laugh, the wind whipping through his dark hair.

I brush off his comment, getting back on topic. "I need help. Otherwise, I'm going to remain lonely and untouched for life."

"I don't like this."

"Well, then, it's a good thing I don't need your approval."

A frustrated sound comes from deep within his throat. "So, why are you telling me any of this?"

"Because my plan needs to be discreet. I can't risk the public finding out that I'm hiring someone to teach me about men and... dating."

"Sex—that's what you really want to say, isn't it?"

I sigh, both humiliated and annoyed. "Do you have to be so blunt?"

"Yes. I need to understand exactly what you're trying to achieve with this ridiculous idea. Do you plan to sleep with this guy?"

"Of course not. I would never pay someone for sex." My hair flaps with a gust of wind and I brush it back from my face. "As I was saying, this needs to be a secret. Reporters would probably twist the story and make it look like I'm hiring an escort. I'm asking you for help—to speak to Felix on my behalf since he owns an illegal venue and is the king of keeping its existence hidden. Without mentioning my name to him, of course. I thought maybe he'd have the means of hooking me up with someone appropriate and who he can trust will keep this private."

Dan glares at me. "I'm not speaking to Felix for you. *None* of this is happening."

"Fine. I'll go to Felix myself. I was only hoping to avoid embarrassment by having you as the middleman." I leave his side, picking up my pace along the shore.

Dan's footsteps pound in the sand as he runs after me, until he steps in front of me, blocking my path. He's so close that I almost bump into his chest and need to take a step back to look at his face.

"Felix is the last person you should be involving in this," Dan says, his tone scolding. "The crowd he hangs around with have less than questionable morals. I wouldn't trust any of them around you. How do I know the guy would be honorable? That he wouldn't take advantage of you? Knowing Felix, especially if you don't want your name mentioned to him, you probably *would* end up with an escort."

"Well, so be it. If the escort is discreet, I'll take my chances. That's how dire my situation is."

A tormented look sits in Dan's eyes, like he's running through a list of things to say that will change my mind. Finally, he rakes both hands through his hair and groans. "Don't do this. If you're so adamant about needing a boyfriend, I'll... Fuck, I'll find a guy to set you up with."

"I don't want to be set up. I want the skills to meet men myself. And besides, that would be strange if you found me a boyfriend, considering our past. If you want to help, just talk to Felix for me. Otherwise, I'm heading to the city today to meet with him."

I step around Dan and continue walking along the beach.

"Fuck, Ally," he calls after me. "*I* will help you, okay? I'll teach you whatever shit you think you need to learn. No one else is getting involved in this."

I pivot on my heels, my face burning up when I see how serious he is. "There's no way. That would be awkward for both of us."

Dan's voice lowers into something almost pained as he steps up to me, looking me directly in the eyes. "You returned from Paris as my friend and sister, right?"

Oh, gosh. My throat tightens. He's quoting the letter I wrote him. "I... Yes."

"Then there's no awkwardness." His gaze upon me is so intense, so penetrative, that it makes me blush and shift my gaze to the ocean. "There's no guarantee Felix could keep all of this from the public once someone else gets involved, and I know how precious you are about maintaining a good reputation for yourself and the family. Do this with me instead, the safe way."

Despite not liking his words, he makes a solid case. Dan would be a safer option as far as publicity is concerned, for sure, and I do trust him.

He says this won't be weird between us. I don't know if that's true, but some part of me thinks accepting Dan's offer could be good for both of us if he plays an active role in helping me move on with another guy, solidifying the past as the past.

Dan grips my jaw. My body quivers from how much I like his touch. He guides my face back from the ocean to look at him. "Promise me you'll leave Felix out of this."

I huff out a breath. "Fine. I won't hire anyone. You can help me instead."

CHAPTER ELEVEN

DAN

We walk back to the beach house in silence, with Ally a step ahead of me the entire way. My eyes never stray from her petite body. A pink ribbon is tangled through the ends of her blond hair, a mess from the ocean breeze. The bottom of her dress flaps in the wind, high around her thighs, revealing a glimpse of white lace panties every so often. I'll jerk off to the sight of it later.

My gaze flicks to her hand. I want to grab it and tug her back to me, then shove Ally against the side of the house and hold her there with the weight of my body as my lips slam into hers. I want to rip those white panties off and sink my dick into that tight virgin pussy.

Most of all, I want to be enough for her. *I* want to be the one who makes her happy.

She climbs the steps to the front door and turns the handle, stepping inside. The impulse to tell her all these things takes over and I reach for her hand—

"Ally, honey, how are you feeling?" Amabella's right there, along with my dad, the two of them walking down the main staircase in the entryway.

My hand shoots back to my side.

"Much better. I'm sorry if I frightened you yesterday."

They meet us on the marbled floor and Amabella strokes a hand through Ally's hair. "What had you so upset, darling?"

"We'll talk about it later, okay? I need to shower and freshen up."

"Of course. We'll be in the living room when you're ready to talk."

Amabella and Dad exit the main entryway, leaving me alone with Ally. I watch as she heads for her room upstairs, scolding myself for losing control a moment ago with my need for her. Before Ally climbs the first step, I catch her peering over her shoulder at me and smiling.

"You all good?" I ask.

Her smile breaks into a soft laugh. "Yeah. I'm just happy. You're a good guy. Thanks for helping me."

Jesus fuck. If she knew my real motives, she'd be furious. "Go take your shower, Ally."

She climbs the rest of the stairs, disappearing out of sight. I'll work hard to boost her confidence because I want her to be happy and feel comfortable in her skin. She deserves friends. As for a boyfriend, I'm keeping her for myself. Agreeing to help her find a boyfriend is only a means of stalling until she realizes how good we are together.

"Thank you for being such an amazing brother," Amabella calls out from the next room over. "How is she?"

I enter the living room, finding Dad and Amabella with a cup of coffee and sitting on the couch. "Boy issues. She'll survive."

Amabella places a hand at the base of her neck. "Oh, the poor thing."

My father nods at me. "Thank you for taking care of her. Will you be staying the day? I'd like us to chat."

Aside from his quick greeting last night, this is the first contact we've had since our argument two weeks ago. He called me once, but I ignored it, knowing the conversation would end in a fight, as it always does with him.

"I don't have much spare time." It's not a lie. I have the whole day free but no time for my father's shit. "I'll see you two later."

Leaving him and Amabella alone, I head out back to the pool, slumping onto a sun lounger with my eyes closed and listening to the ocean while contemplating how best to approach this teaching thing with Ally. We'll start with getting her a friend. Make it a guy too. That will give her practice talking to the opposite sex. The thought of helping Ally meet a guy who is intended for friendship only is a whole lot easier for me to stomach than helping her find a date.

I run through a mental list of who could be a good friend for Ally. The selection of guys I know isn't appealing. The majority only view women as opportunities for sex. The remaining guys are in committed relationships whose partner would be suspicious of their man getting friendly with a girl as beautiful as Ally.

One guy comes to mind.

I dial Theo Wilson's number. He's a couple years older than me and frequents poker games at The Scarlet Mirage. He's friends with Felix and I've learned a lot about poker from him too. We have a few drinks every time we cross paths but rarely play together anymore since I know all his tricks.

Theo answers my call right away. "Blackwood, good to hear from you."

"Hey, man, I've got a random question for you."

"Hit me."

"Your brother, Liam, the jazz musician, he'd be about twenty, right?"

I've met Liam a couple times in passing when his band has performed at The Scarlet Mirage. We've had a few casual conversations and he's a friendly guy. Average in looks. Respects women and isn't fucking everything in sight from what I can tell. Perhaps Ally and Liam can bond over music.

"Yeah, Liam is twenty-one. Why?"

"My... sister—" Fuck, that label never stops feeling dirty on my lips. I never stop liking it. "Ally is back from a year abroad. She's looking to meet some new people and make friends. Do you think Liam would be interested in getting to know her? They're both musicians. I thought it could be a good match."

"I'll text him about it now and get back to you."

"All right, man. Good talking to you."

No sooner than I end the call, Ally enters the pool area with a bowl of fruit and is wearing nothing but a white bikini. What the actual fuck. Is she trying to kill me? Or is she that adamant about us being friends and siblings that she has no care factor of me seeing her half-naked?

"You're going for a swim right after a shower?"

"I skipped the shower," she says. "Thought a cold swim would be more refreshing."

Ally places the bowl on the sun lounger beside me and I get a glimpse of her from behind, of the fabric that barely covers her ass. My cock is more than aware of her body too. With the little amount of fabric covering Ally, I'm reminded of all the times I saw her naked. She's thinner than I remember. Too thin, but I can picture what her body would look like beneath the bikini. The perfect shape of her tits. Her smooth pussy. I can hear her breathy moans from the time she teased me by leaving the bathroom door open while showering, giving herself an orgasm with the showerhead.

Ally dives into the water, surfacing with her hair slicked back. She places her forearms on the pool ledge, resting her chin on the backs of her hands. "Do you mind passing me an apple?"

Not with the situation that's going on in my pants. I toss her the apple instead, hoping she doesn't clue onto my reason for staying seated. Luckily, she catches it.

"Why are you glaring at me?" she asks, biting into the flesh.

I only realize the harsh look on my face once she points it out. "You're too thin. Did you even eat in Paris?"

She frowns. "I told you last night, Paris was rough. I was lonely and... the panic attacks were an issue. I guess I didn't take care of myself as well as I could have but it wasn't on purpose."

"Fuck, Ally. I wish you would have—" I don't let myself finish that sentence. It will be no use. What am I going to say, that I wish she would have reached out to me for help? Or that she should have let me be with her in Paris, which had been my plan all along when I applied to that scholarship for her. Speaking those words won't achieve anything.

"It's not as bad as it sounds. I got through the panic attacks like you taught me to." There's a quietness to her voice but I can hear the shame. I understand everything her words don't say.

That night at the party when she was sixteen and I was able to calm her panic attack by holding her hands and telling her to focus on my eyes as I instructed her through breathing exercises. Afterward, giving her the Queen of Hearts card. Over the following years, Ally told me she always thinks back to that moment when needing to calm herself during a panic attack.

From the current shame in her eyes, it's clear she still uses that intimate memory to calm herself. I realize I'm staring at her when she blushes and drops her gaze.

"Ally…"

"So, what's my first lesson going to be?" She takes another bite from the apple.

My God, she's infuriating how she avoids speaking about… *us*. We're *not* a thing of the past. I can see it so clearly in her eyes. She just doesn't want to have feelings for me.

Before I can say anything more, I get a text from Theo.

Theo: Liam is interested in chatting with Ally. What's her number? I'll send it to him.

A sour taste rises in my mouth. I send Theo a quick response, clarifying the friendship part and omitting Ally's number.

"You know you're an attractive girl," I say, answering Ally's question. "You have an amazing personality too. But only your most trusted people get to see that side of you. You need to learn how to relax and feel comfortable around a guy without the pressure of trying to impress him. We need a guy for you to become friends with before any romantic relationship is considered. If you end up being attracted to him, we'll discuss what the next step is. If there's no chemistry, at least you've made a friend. I know a guy I think you'd get along with."

"Okay, I like your thinking. Who is he?"

"His name is Liam. He's my age and is a jazz musician."

She pretends to blanch at the jazz part and laughs,

being classically trained. My dick twitches from that laugh. Jesus fucking Christ. Can she do anything that won't turn me on?

"I suppose beggars can't be choosers. Do you have a photo of him?" she asks.

I pull up my web browser and search for an image of Liam's band, joining Ally at the ledge of the pool.

She studies the image on my phone, her expression indiscernible. "Not really my type but maybe that will help with my nerves."

I resist groaning. "He's not a date, remember."

"True. How should I approach this guy?"

"We could organize something for next weekend."

"We? As in you'd be there too, right?"

"No. I'm abandoning you and setting you up for failure." I flick her with water.

"Dan," Ally laughs, the sound making me desperate to kiss her. She flicks water back.

"Of course I'll be there with you." Queen.

I don't speak the name out loud. After I gave Ally the Queen of Hearts, I started calling her my queen. She used to love it. One day, I'll speak the name out loud to her again.

"Good. Maybe I'll be able to relax with you by my side and Liam will see this amazing personality you keep insisting I have."

I return to the sun lounger, muttering under my breath, "He'll see it, but he's not having you."

CHAPTER TWELVE

ALLY

Sunday night dinner, I eat all my food plus dessert because Dan thinks I'm too thin. There was no judgment in his voice when commenting on my weight. Instead, concern and protectiveness. Even something possessive. I shouldn't have liked it so much. Nor should I have felt so sad when he left late afternoon and returned to the city.

After dinner, I'm lying in bed, sorting through my work emails and preparing for the upcoming teaching week, when a No Caller ID rings me.

"Hello, Ally speaking."

"Hey, Ally," a guy says. "This is Liam Wilson. Your brother gave me your phone number. I hope it's okay that I'm calling you."

I sit up in an instant. Dan gave Liam my number? When was that ever part of the plan? Panic rushes through me. I'm not ready for this conversation. What do I say to him?

A moment later, I manage to talk myself down from the ledge, telling myself I can handle a phone conversation with this guy. After my Friday night date forgot I exist, being pushed out of my comfort zone is exactly what I decided I need. Just act cool. Dan said I'm supposed to think of Liam as a friend, not a date.

"Hey, Liam. Thanks for calling." Ugh, *thanks for calling*? Way too formal. Before I realize it, I'm pacing in circles on my bedroom floor. What happened to my little pep talk from a moment ago? I force my pacing to stop and take a deep breath, trying to calm myself and focus on the friend analogy. "Yeah, Dan mentioned you. I didn't realize he'd already given you my number."

"It was actually Felix who gave me your number."

Felix? I thought he wasn't supposed to get involved in any of this.

"I hope you don't mind," Liam continues. "I asked Dan for your number but never heard back from him. So, I asked another Blackwood brother."

"I, um... no, that's fine. How do you know Felix?"

"My brother is friends with him. My band also plays at The Scarlet Mirage on occasion."

There's a moment of silence between us, broken by Liam's laughter. It's a friendly laugh, handsome in nature. Not as deep as Dan's voice but still charming. I think back to the photo I saw of Liam, of him with short, blond hair and dark skin, and imagine what he would look like laughing. In the photo, he was wearing a fedora, along with a white suit and a bow tie. He looked like a jazz musician from the 1920s, which really isn't my type. But maybe he only dresses like that when performing.

I groan internally, reminding myself Liam isn't supposed to be my type. Honestly, I'm going to have a hard time finding anyone who is my type unless they're a replica of Dan. Maybe I'll form an attraction to Liam if we become friends.

"I'm totally freaking you out right now by calling, aren't I?" Liam says, the laugh lingering in his voice.

"No. Of course not. I'm still processing the Felix part."

"I should have waited for Dan to give me your number, but at the risk of coming on too strong, I got impatient and wanted to talk to you now. Felix sent a photo of you, and I have to tell you how beautiful you are. Then he started talking you up. Said you're a talented classical pianist."

"Oh, um, thank you." My pulse is racing. How am I meant to relax and think of Liam as a potential friend when it doesn't sound like he has friendship in mind at all? "You're not coming on too strong. I'm probably the one who looks like a creep needing my brothers to introduce me to guys." I cringe as soon as I speak the words, wondering if it was a weird thing to say.

He laughs. "No complaints here. You sound great and I'm just excited to talk to you because I don't know many female musicians."

"That's so nice. Um…" My brain draws a blank, not knowing how to carry the conversation. I cough to prolong my thinking time, then tell myself to imagine this conversation is taking place with someone I'm comfortable around. Think of him like Dan. "Sorry, I had a tickle in my throat. Dan told me you're into jazz. What instrument do you play?"

"The double bass. My band is based in the city, but we play all around the place in jazz clubs."

"Wow, that must be really fun." The pounding in my chest eases as the Dan pretense continues. *I'm talking to my best friend*, a little voice plays on repeat in my head. I return to my bed, lie back, and gaze at the ceiling. "I must admit, I don't know a thing about jazz except that it all sounds like clutter to me."

"Don't most people say that about classical music too?" he teases.

"Yeah, people with no taste."

We both laugh at the joke. And jeez, are we... flirting?

"Seriously, though, I appreciate the skill required to play jazz," I tell him. "I can't wrap my head around how it works. I don't know the first thing about improvisation."

"Improv is what I do best. But I have mad respect for classical musicians. Do you perform anywhere?"

And that's how the rest of the night progresses, with back-and-forth questions, discussions about music, our families, jobs, and interests we have. By some miracle, I don't have any more awkward moments where I blurt out something stupid or can't think of anything to say. The conversation flows because I imagine I'm... talking to Dan.

That could be a bit of a problem. I try to not let it faze me.

For the first time, I have hope that maybe I can grow a connection with Liam and stop being in love with a guy I can never have.

I cancel my morning jog with Killian due to the late hour I stayed up till last night on the phone with Liam. And now, as I sit at my dressing table, brushing my hair for work, a text message arrives from Liam, making me smile.

Until I read the actual words.

LIAM

Good morning. I had fun talking to you last night. Do you want to meet up in person? I'd like to take you on a date Saturday night, if you're interested.

I chew on my bottom lip, both nervous and excited, beyond pleased that Liam enjoyed our conversation enough to want to date me. A date isn't part of the plan, though. At least, not yet anyway. And I had in my head that Dan would be with me during my first meeting with Liam as moral support. I didn't need Dan's help during the phone call last night, but a phone call is different to a face-to-face meeting.

I call Dan for advice on how to respond to the text, my knees jittering as I wait for him to answer. The line rings out, which doesn't surprise me at this hour. Dan isn't a morning person, always staying out late playing poker or drinking with Felix or whatever it is he gets up to when I'm not around. He's probably fast asleep. I'm on my own with this situation, needing to figure out for myself how to reply to Liam's message.

I type a draft response to Liam in my notes app, trying to find the right wording to explain that I only want us to meet up as friends and with Dan to join us. Nothing I write sounds flattering. The inclusion of Dan's name even comes across as weird. Liam will get the impression that I'm trying to let him down easily and don't want to ever go on a date with him.

After ten minutes of attempting to construct the perfect message, an idea comes to me. It's the only solution I can think of that will lessen the pressure of a date and make our first meeting feel like more of a social outing.

ALLY

Sure. Would you like to go on a double date?

LIAM

Sounds fun. Let's do it.

Our messages are replaced with an incoming call from Dan. I answer him immediately. "Did you know Felix gave Liam my number? Liam called me last night and—"

"Shit." Dan clears his throat, his voice deeper than usual, like he's just woken up. He swears again, the word low and spoken to himself, sounding furious. "How did the phone call go?"

"It went surprisingly well. I tried to forget about Liam being a potential date. But this morning he texted, asking to take me on a date Saturday night."

"No." The word is firm. "Tell him a date is moving too fast and you want to know him as a friend first."

"Okay, but here's the thing. You weren't answering your phone, so I already replied. I didn't know how to get out of the date without sounding disinterested in him. So... I thought of the next best thing. We're going on a double date."

Dan takes a moment to register my words, and when he speaks again, he's just as pissed off as when he first answered the phone. "We? As in, you want me to bring a date too?"

"Yeah, I guess."

"Fuck, Ally. I don't date."

"Surely there's someone you can bring."

He groans. "I wish you would have waited to respond so we could discuss a better solution. This is not at all how I envisioned this would go."

"I couldn't just leave Liam's message on 'read.' And this isn't what I envisioned either, but I think I did pretty good coming up with this plan. What would you have done differently?"

"Left him on read and spoken to me first." Another groan. "Shit. Now I have to find a date."

"Oh, yeah, like you'll have a real problem with that. Okay, I need to get to work. Call me tonight."

"Not happening. Sorry. I'll be too busy trying to find a date I have no interest in."

"Dan," I laugh. "I thought nightly phone calls are our thing. Are you stopping our thing?"

"Don't be all cute. You're in my bad books right now."

Dan hangs up and a rush of heat spreads through my chest, my clit, at how he called me cute and scolded me. My hips grind against the chair, seeking out pleasure. Jesus, what is wrong with me? I just agreed to go on a date with another guy. I'm trying to move on from Dan.

I force myself to continue getting dressed for work, fixing my hair and applying a little makeup. This date should hopefully be a success. I'm pleased with how I took charge, pushing myself out of my comfort zone while still molding the circumstances of the night into something that will create the least amount of anxiety for me.

No one-on-one situations. It will be me, Liam, Dan, and... Dan's date.

I let out a breath of annoyance. I've never liked seeing him with other girls. Maybe I didn't think this plan through properly.

My pen taps against my work diary with speed as I try to psych myself up. I survived a phone conversation with Liam; how hard can it be to talk to Violet?

I stare at her back, the two of us sitting at our desks on opposite sides of the staffroom. It's five p.m. Monday afternoon and we're the only ones in here, finishing up work for the day.

Tap. Tap. Tap.

There's got to be something I can say to Violet that will help bridge the gap and help us become friends.

"I have a date this weekend," I say into the silence of the staffroom, hoping she won't think this topic is inappropriate at work.

My pen taps faster at her lack of response. My teeth grind. Did I not speak loud enough?

Violet glances over her shoulder, peering around the staffroom. "Are you talking to me?"

"Yeah."

She swivels around on her chair to face me and smiles. "That's exciting. Who's the guy?"

The pen stops. "My brother, Dan, knows the guy through a friend. We're going on a double date."

"Oh, a set up? Interesting. How are you feeling about the date?"

"I've never been on a date before so I'm nervous. But I spoke to the guy on the phone, and it went well. Fingers crossed the date is a success."

"Have you decided on what to wear?"

"Not yet."

Her eyes light up with intrigue. "Oh, you *have* to let me help."

My mouth opens and closes, unable to form a reply. The girls from my teenage years and their cruel ways are my first thought, and a vision enters my mind of Violet purposefully choosing an unattractive outfit for my date.

I shake the thought away, telling myself to stop projecting my fears upon other people. This is why I have no friends, because I've closed myself off.

"Thank you. That would be nice," I say. "Maybe I can

take some photos of my clothes and bring them to work tomorrow."

"Tomorrow is too long to wait. I've mentally checked out of work for the day now that I've heard about your date. Do you live nearby? We can head to your place now and choose an outfit."

"Um, yeah, okay. Let's go." I'll take this as a win too.

CHAPTER THIRTEEN

DAN

"Do I look all right?"

"Yes, for the hundredth time. You look amazing," I tell Ally as we arrive at the front of an Italian restaurant in Hell's Kitchen for the double date.

Her appearance is *more* than amazing. I can't even look at her without my mind turning to filth. Thank fuck she hasn't caught me staring. My gaze keeps traveling to the gap of skin between her pink plaid skirt and thigh-high white socks with pink satin bows at the tops. When I'm not looking at that soft strip of skin, it's at her breasts beneath that tight white shirt.

Ally once told me she only wears clothes she thinks I'll like. I used to get off on seeing what outfit she chose each day, knowing it was for me. Of course, Ally could have worn a sack and I'd have still thought she was the most beautiful girl in the room, but the clothes were a symbol when around our family and in public that she was secretly mine.

"Sorry. I'm nervous about this date," she says. "I want to look nice."

I'm fucking pissed, hearing Ally speak like that and

knowing she spent the lead up to this evening prettying herself for Liam. I've tried talking Ally out of this date multiple times, reminding her that she's meant to build a friendship with Liam first. But she's impatient. She says they've been texting throughout the week and things are progressing well.

I hold open the restaurant door for Ally. As she steps inside, her phone buzzes and she's quick to check it.

"Oh, that's Liam." She reads the message and laughs, then types something back to him. My teeth clench. I've never seen her like this with a guy before and it's taking everything in me to act happy for her.

"Welcome to Dolce Trattoria," a waiter greets us. "Do you have a reservation?"

"Yes. Blackwood," I answer.

While the waiter checks the reservations book, a female calls out to me. "Hey, Dan."

Both Ally and I turn, finding Chelsea walking toward us —my date for the night. She's a model who frequents The Scarlett Mirage and is one of the many women who can often be seen hanging off Felix's arm. After I got pissed at Felix for giving Liam Ally's number and explained how I now needed to find a date without leading a girl on, he offered up Chelsea, saying he'd fill her in on my situation and she'd do this favor for him.

I thought having Chelsea as a date would be effortless. In hindsight, I fucked up, considering what she's wearing. The woman looks like she's modelling a BDSM lingerie line, with a leather skirt that does little to cover her ass, fishnet stockings, a sheer bra that reveals the outline of her nipples, and a black choker. Her lipstick is a bright pop of red, and her black hair is tied in a knot on top of her head. I know Chelsea is eclectic with her fashion; each time I've seen her, she looks drastically different, but how the fuck does this outfit match the friendly vibes of the date I described to her?

Chelsea slinks her arms around my neck, pressing her breasts to me. "It's so good to see you again, Dan."

She speaks as if we're more than just acquaintances. I act polite and return the hug for Felix's sake. As far as I can tell, the two of them are just fucking and not exclusively, but I'm not about to be rude and comment that her attire is inappropriate, making this situation more awkward than it already is.

"Thanks for coming tonight," I say after she hugs me.

She looks me over and playfully pushes my arm. "Don't you look handsome."

"Hi," Ally intercepts, offering no smile.

"This is your little sister?" Chelsea nods at Ally. "She's adorable. It's so cute that you're setting her up."

Ally's cheeks are a dark shade of embarrassment and from her rigid stance it's clear she's not pleased with my choice in date.

"Chelsea, do you mind giving me and Ally a moment alone?"

"Sure. Don't be too long, though, or I might get lonely." She winks at me.

Jesus. I thought Felix explained to her she's not a real date. Chelsea better just be a flirt and not actually want anything sexual from me tonight.

I place a hand on Ally's upper back and guide her to the side of the restaurant entrance, out of earshot. "I'm sorry. I didn't realize she'd be dressed like this."

Ally shrugs away from my touch and scoffs. "I just hope Liam isn't staring at your date's nipples all night long. You could have picked better. This was supposed to be a casual and fun night. Now we all have sex shoved in our faces."

"I'll give Chelsea my jacket."

Ally's gaze flicks behind me and a grin wipes away the scowl on her face.

"Hey, stranger," a guy says.

I turn and find Liam. He's wearing jeans and has a black hoodie pulled over his head. He pushes the hood back and scoops Ally into a hug, lifting her off her toes. I can barely believe what I'm witnessing and hate the way he's touching her. What I hate even more is the laugh she gives, and that when he places her back on her feet, she's a blushing mess. There's no nervous avoidance of eye contact like I've so often seen from Ally when she's around new people. Her shoulders aren't tensing up. She's into him and not just as a friend. That must have been some amazing phone conversation between them. This is all a fucking mess and was never meant to play out this way.

"Wow, you look stunning," Liam tells her.

"Thank you." She takes the compliment with another shy laugh. "Ah... you know Dan. And this is his date, Chelsea."

Liam shakes my hand. He says a polite hello to Chelsea, disinterested in her lack of clothing, then addresses all of us. "All right, are we ready to head through to the table? I've eaten here before. The food is really good."

"Dan, should the two of us share a pizza?"

I barely hear Chelsea's question, even though she's sitting right beside me in this booth. All I can focus on is the display in front of me, of Ally sending Liam the most gorgeous smiles she only ever reserves for me. The two of them haven't stopped chatting in the ten minutes we've been seated. It's like they're on their own date and no one else exists.

"Dan?" Chelsea repeats.

"What? Oh, yes, the pizza is fine." As soon as I answer the question, my focus returns to Ally and Liam.

They're reading one menu together. Neither one of them are paying much attention to the food selection, continuously stopping to exchange words. "I'm going to order a pasta," Ally tells him. "So, who are your favorite musicians?"

"That's an easy one." Liam closes the menu and drapes an arm over the backrest behind Ally, angling his body into their conversation. He's not touching her, but any onlooker could tell they're on a date.

My blood boils, watching such a simple yet intimate gesture. I can't recall having ever felt this jealous over something so minor. I've never been able to show affection to Ally in public. I even need to be careful how I *look* at her in public, otherwise people will catch on to this secret between us. If she weren't my stepsister, I know without doubt she'd be my girlfriend. I'd have her sleeping in my bed every night, naked and satiated and filled with my cum.

"My favorites are Louis Armstrong, Duke Ellington, Ella Fitzgerald, and Miles Davis," Liam says. "You probably aren't familiar with them. They're all jazz."

"I can't name any of their music, but I know their names. This is kind of nerdy but there's this coin set I've been collecting. It consists of famous musicians in history, and those artists you mentioned are in the collection."

Liam's eyebrows rise with disbelief. "Don't tell me you're referring to The Greats of Music coin collection."

Ally gives a surprised laugh. "Yes. How do you know about it?"

"I've been collecting those coins too. Wow, this is fate, I swear. I've never met anyone my age who collects them. My brother always teases me. Says it's for grandparents."

Ally licks her lips—another small gesture that fucks me up completely. Poker has made me well attuned to reading body language. She likes Liam. She's even thinking about kissing him.

Chelsea's hand slides to my inner thigh beneath the table. I push it away, but she gets the wrong idea and thinks I'm trying to hold her hand and weaves our fingers. She's got some kink for brothers? I'm going to kill Felix the next time I see him.

I break free from her grip by waving the waitress over. "I assume we're all ready to order?" I ask the group.

Ally and Liam give me a quick yes before returning to their conversation about coins. I shove my fists into my pockets to avoid any more hand holding. Something pointed grazes against my right hand, and it takes me less than a second to realize what it is—a corner of the deck of cards I've started carrying around again. The neon cards Ally bought me. I pull them out and start shuffling, needing to calm down.

"How many of the coins do you have?" Ally asks Liam. Her gaze flicks to my shuffling, not seeming the least bit fazed until she recognizes the neon cards.

Her smile drops and she's staring at them, in a world of her own while Liam answers her question, perhaps remembering everything the cards symbolize between us. Ally glares at me, as if I pulled the cards out on purpose to sabotage her date, then returns her focus to Liam.

"The coins are expensive, so I've been prioritizing the

jazz composers," Liam says. "I have all of them except George Gershwin."

"Oh, I have him!" Ally gasps. "It took me five years to track him down and ten thousand dollars. It was an eighteenth birthday present from my parents."

"You're serious? There are only ten of George Gershwin in the world. You *have* to show me sometime."

"Yeah, of course I will."

"Wait, so you were collecting these coins when you were thirteen?"

She gives a shy smile and chews on her bottom lip. "Yeah, weird, huh?"

Liam smiles right back at her. "Definitely weird, but I like it."

Oh, fuck off. I've never seen anyone geek out over this stuff as much as Ally. I picked well for her when thinking of Liam. Perhaps a little too well. But there's no way I'll stand back and let him take her from me.

The waitress steps up to the table and asks for our order. As Liam lists off the items he'd like, Ally looks at Chelsea, at the sheer bra she's wearing, and scowls. I said I'd give Chelsea my jacket but never did. I shrug out of my jacket and drape it across Chelsea's shoulders.

"Thanks, handsome." Chelsea kisses me on the cheek.

Ally groans, and when I look back at her, she's throwing daggers at me with her eyes. The anger in her expression pleases me. Perhaps I'm not the only one of us who feels possessive.

I try not to smirk, but seeing Ally like this is fucking hot, igniting so much anger in her, all from offering another girl my jacket. She's told me before she doesn't like seeing me with other girls—it was the first time I walked in on Ally touching herself, and I asked what she thinks about to get turned on.

"You, fucking me. Only me. You want me and no one else. No other girl turns you on."

I wipe a hand over my mouth, covering the smirk I worked hard to keep at bay. My sweet little stepsister was the jealous type before Paris. Apparently, not much has changed. She's trying real hard to move on from me, but my queen is still in there.

CHAPTER FOURTEEN

ALLY

"Can I come back to your place?" Chelsea asks Dan as the four of us exit the restaurant, stepping out to the cool night.

Traffic is dense. There are many people on the sidewalk, but it all blurs out of existence as I fixate on Chelsea's question. She's been looking at Dan all night like she can't wait to sink her claws into him. I don't know what kind of sex Dan is into but given the nature of Chelsea's outfit and that Dan asked a woman like her to be his date, he's probably into BDSM. It wouldn't surprise me, given the dynamic we used to have. Each time I got naked for him, he took a more dominant role, instructing me on what to do with my body. I enjoyed submitting to him.

Those moments felt so uniquely us. I can't imagine doing the same thing with anyone else and it makes me sick to think that Dan would. Somehow, I have to try and act like none of this bothers me.

"Rain check," Dan tells her. "Ally is staying at my place tonight."

My gaze whips to Dan. We never discussed me staying

at his apartment. He knows there's a car service waiting at his place to drive me back to The Hamptons tonight.

"Too bad." Chelsea pretends to pout, her voice all sex. "We'll arrange something for another night." She pecks Dan's cheek and heads for the subway without saying goodbye to me or Liam.

"Kind of rude," Liam mutters to me, watching her leave. We look at each other and laugh a little. Though my laugh is forced.

"You ready to go home?" Dan asks me.

"To your place?" I clarify.

"Yeah. I'll drive you back to the beach tomorrow."

"Um… Okay. Let me say goodbye to Liam." My answer feels dangerous. The last time I was at Dan's apartment, my resolve to treat him as a brother weakened and I ended up giving myself an orgasm in his bed. After seeing him with Chelsea, my insides are purring that he's chosen me over her.

Dan leans one shoulder against the restaurant's brick wall, once again shuffling the neon cards as he waits for me to say goodbye to Liam. The purring grows stronger. I'm desperate to ask whether the deck still holds the same sentiment for Dan, but that would entail opening the door to our past which I'm working so hard to shut.

"So, Ally." Liam lowers his voice, though I'm not sure how private this conversation is with Dan only a few feet away. "I had a really good time with you tonight."

"I did too."

"If you're free next Saturday night, I'd like to take you out on a proper date. Just the two of us."

"Yeah, I'd like that," I tell him, and it's the truth, regardless of how much effort it's taking to be present with Liam, distracted by those cards. Liam and I got along well tonight —when does that ever happen for me? I'd like to get to know him better. Regarding Liam's appearance, he's more my type than I originally thought. Liam could be the guy that helps me let go of this obsession with Dan.

"There's something I should first tell you." His tone shifts to serious. "And look, perhaps I should have mentioned this the first time we spoke, but I wanted to meet you and see if we got along."

The deck of cards vanishes from my mind, replaced with a red flag alert. "Wow, great way to make a girl nervous. You're a serial killer or something?"

He laughs. "No, nothing like that. I just want to let you know that I only do open relationships."

"Oh."

The red flag intensifies. This is just my luck—I meet a guy I could genuinely see as my future boyfriend, and yet he doesn't do monogamous commitment. By the wall, Dan's shuffling comes to an abrupt stop.

"I know open relationships can be a deal breaker for some people," Liam says. "I understand if it's not your thing. I just want to be transparent with you."

"Um..." A nervous laugh leaves my mouth. I don't know how I'm meant to answer him. "It's something for me to think about. Are you currently seeing other people?"

"Not currently, and if that were to change, I'll tell you. This is just a lifestyle that works best for me."

I shift back and forth on my feet. My fingers find the end of my hair and start twisting. "Um... thank you for being honest."

"You don't need to say anything right now. Just know I had fun with you tonight, and I hope to see you again." He scoops me into a hug and kisses my cheek. "I'll call you, okay?"

Liam releases me from his arms and I'm too speechless to say anything other than goodbye.

Dan and I don't exchange words for the entire drive back to his apartment, partly because I'm still seething over Chelsea and that Dan thought she would be an appropriate date. The deck of cards also keeps plaguing me, reminding me of the connection Dan and I had before Paris, how intoxicating and all-consuming we were together, and that the past is fighting hard to not be buried. Then there's the curveball Liam threw at me at the end of our date.

Whenever we stop at a set of traffic lights, I feel Dan's eyes lingering on me. I pretend not to notice, occupying myself with my phone, but there's no denying the thrill that runs through me, tightening my tummy. I'm questioning my sanity and why I agreed to spend the night at his place. Nothing good will come of it, not when the anticipation of us being alone together already has me aroused.

When Dan pulls up in front of his apartment, I spot the car service I hired waiting in front of us. I can still return to The Hamptons tonight as originally planned. Going home would be a far safer option than spending the night with Dan.

The engine switches off and I make a move to exit the car, reaching for the door handle and gasping when Dan's hand slips into mine.

"Tell me what's going on."

"With what?" I ask, peering back at him in the dark car, lit only by the surrounding streetlights.

"You've been quiet the entire drive."

I gulp, gazing down at my hand that Dan still holds. The heat of his touch spreads through me. I never want him to let go, which is exactly why I pull my hand free. But his grip tightens. His free hand tilts my chin up so that I have nowhere to hide. I don't know why it excites me so much when he handles me like this, controlling my body. His breath brushes against my face, he's so close. My mind swirls and I can't think straight, intoxicated by the thought of him leaning forward and kissing me.

"Are you seeing Chelsea again?" I answer his question, reminding myself why I'm frustrated with him.

"What's it to you?"

"General curiosity." I shrug, trying to sound more confident than I am. "I feel pathetic beside her, considering how much sex appeal she has. That's the kind of woman you're into?"

He raises an eyebrow. "This is what's got you upset?"

"Yes. It makes me feel differently about our past. Inadequate. I thought what we had was intimate and intense. Now, I'm realizing it was probably all very amateur to you. I never really knew anything about your sexual desires. You always watched me, but I never saw you do anything."

His gaze drops to my lips and remains there as he speaks slow and deep. "Don't you think that tells you what kind of sex I'm into—watching my stepsister do things I *definitely* shouldn't be asking you to do. Teaching you about sex. Corrupting your sweet virgin ways and turning you into a desperate little slut for me and only me. Since telling me you're still a virgin, all I can think about is teaching you how to ride my cock." His eyes return to mine, boring into me, making my pussy clench. "That's not quite true. Taking your virginity is all I've *ever* been able to think about. So, you don't question for another second whether I have any fucking care factor for Chelsea. Or any other woman."

Every inch of me is burning up. My clit is aching, begging to be taken care of. I press my hips firm to the car seat and grind a little. Just once. The movement isn't as subtle as I thought, and the slightest smirk rises on Dan's lips.

"Ally, are you rubbing your pussy on my car seat?"

My breath hitches. I nod, too embarrassed to speak the truth. Common sense tells me I should have just lied. But when Dan gets me in these moods, I can barely think straight.

"That's my girl. My sweet little sister. Don't stop."

Everything in me wants to follow his command. The times I've been vulnerable like this in front of Dan were the most intense moments of my life. But they were also wrong.

"I... can't," I whisper, lowering Dan's hand from my chin and reaching for my purse. "What you want with me is the exact thing I've been running from. It scares me."

"It scares you, but you want it. Admit it."

I weave my arm through the purse strap, trying to occupy myself with a task, any task, so long as it distracts me from Dan. "I can't stay at your place tonight. I don't trust myself alone with you. Maybe we shouldn't continue this teaching thing either. Lines are being crossed. I think I could have something good with Liam."

"Yeah, I can see you two really hit it off." His words are bitter. Dan leans back against his door, watching me rummage through my purse. "You don't care about the open relationship policy?"

"It's different from what I expected but I'll see how

things go with him. He seems like a really good guy, and we got along well tonight. I made a commitment to myself that I'd stop being so timid and start seeking out life experiences. I don't need exclusivity."

"Ally, any guy who is happy to share you is a fucking idiot. You deserve to be treated like a queen."

My eyes pop open wide and I freeze, hearing the word *queen* leave his mouth, remembering all the times he called me Queen, symbolizing exactly what I meant to him. It's not right how much I want to hear that pet name leave Dan's lips again.

"I should go. The car service is waiting for me."

"I'll let you go if you answer one question for me." He takes my hand and pulls me in close again, whispering, "Are you wet right now?"

I swallow hard, my breath heavy. "Yes."

"All from a little conversation about riding my cock." He's so smug about the effect he has on me, and I hate that I find it so hot.

"It won't ever happen." I speak with confidence, trying to throw him off his game. "I'm not precious about my virginity. Maybe Liam will take it next weekend on our date."

My words only intensify his smug demeanor. "You get off on teasing me? You always have, rubbing your ass against my cock each time you snuck into my bed. Leaving the bathroom door open so I could watch you with the showerhead pressed to your pussy. You're mine, Ally, and I'm not letting anyone else fuck you."

The ache between my legs is so intense, hearing him claim ownership of me. I fight against the urge to grind against the car seat again. "You don't get to tell me what to do." I pull free of Dan's grip and exit onto the sidewalk before he can stop me, knowing if I spend another moment with him, I'll cave in and do something I shouldn't.

"Ally." Dan's car door slams shut as he calls after me.

His footsteps approach but I don't look behind me. Instead, I slip into the backseat of the car service, telling the driver to take off immediately.

CHAPTER FIFTEEN

ALLY

"Time out. I can't breathe," I struggle to say.

"No time for slow pokes," Killian teases, running ahead of me with Violet.

Monday morning and I'm breathless, jogging on the beach with Killian and Violet before work starts. After Violet came to my house last week to help me choose an outfit for the double date, I took things a step further and asked her to join the morning runs.

Both she and Killian look like they should be in an active wear ad campaign; they've barely broken a sweat and somehow manage to look good while exercising. Meanwhile, my shirt is soaked, and I need to bend over, bracing my elbows to my knees in order to catch my breath.

Killian glances over his shoulder at me. "Fine. A quick break."

They circle back to me, jogging on the spot while waiting for my recovery.

"Hey, how was your date on the weekend?" Violet asks me.

Killian stops jogging and grins. "You went on a date, baby sis? I *have* to hear about this."

I'm surprised he hasn't heard about it from Dan. The two of them aren't as close as Dan and Felix, but they still talk regularly. Tyler is the brother who is always left out of the loop.

"Yeah. Dan set me up with a friend's brother. Liam. It went well. I really like him."

Mention of Dan forms a shameful swell of arousal low within me, remembering the conversation that took place Saturday night in his car. I've lost count of how many orgasms I've given myself since that night, hearing him talk about wanting my virginity. The tension between us in that car... It was the most alive I've felt since our kiss right before Paris. It would have been so easy to slip back into old patterns. I nearly did, grinding against the car seat in front of him.

But it was wrong and a distraction I don't need, not when I have an upcoming date with another man. Dan called me as soon as I left him. I didn't answer, for self-preservation. I haven't answered any of his texts or phone calls, and I don't plan to, at least not until I can think straight regarding him.

"Liam?" Killian lifts a confused brow. "As in Theo's brother?"

"Yeah. You know him?" Killian sometimes plays poker with Dan and Felix. I suppose that would explain the connection.

"Barely. But enough to know Liam only does open relationships."

"Girl, *what*?" Violet gasps, giving up the jogging too.

I stand tall, finally having a better hold on my breathing. "It's not that big a deal."

"You sure?" Killian asks, the protective big brother tone thick in his voice. "You don't seem like an open relationship kind of girl."

"I've never had *any* relationship. How do I know what I like without experimenting?"

"Okay, if you're sure. When are you seeing him again?" Violet asks, not sounding overly convinced.

"I have a solo date with Liam this weekend."

It feels weird going on a date with Liam when Dan is so hard to shake from my mind. But if Liam is all about open relationships, then I suppose I'm not doing anything wrong. Plus, it's not like Liam and I are even in a relationship yet. We're testing the waters and getting to know each other.

"He's taking me to a jazz club," I continue, then change the subject to clothes, attempting to form more of a friendship with Violet. "I could use your help picking an outfit again if you're available."

"Sure," she says, but with none of the enthusiasm she showed last week toward my date. "Does this afternoon work?"

LIAM

I'll be at your place in 5 minutes. Can't wait to see you, beautiful.

I adjust the ribbon in my hair, smiling at Liam's message. Our Saturday night date has arrived and I'm excited, though nervous. Fears keep entering my mind, that perhaps the double date only went well because I had Dan by my side keeping me calm. What if tonight is a disaster and I freeze up, unable to talk?

Someone knocks on my bedroom door. It could only be Mom or Josh, so I call out for them to enter, still fixated on the position of my hair ribbon.

"Wow."

I spin around at the sound of Dan's voice, his unexpected presence sending my stomach into an even tighter ball of nerves. I'm both excited and scared to see him. He's standing so casually at the entrance to my room, leaning one shoulder against the doorframe and with both hands in his suit pockets. There's a look in his eyes, complete obsession, as his gaze rakes over me. I'm addicted to how desired he always makes me feel.

I gulp, my voice quiet. "Is that a good wow?"

"Yes." His answer is coarse and a little pained. "You look beautiful. You always do, but especially tonight."

"I... um... What are you doing here?"

"You haven't answered any of my phone calls over the last week. I thought phone calls were our thing."

"They were until... that conversation in your car. You shouldn't be here. You know I have a date." I turn to my mirror and continue fixing my hair ribbon, trying to shift my attention to Liam and looking nice for him. But my fingers are suddenly jittery, knowing that Dan is watching me.

"That's exactly why I'm here. I'm glad I caught you in time. I contemplated keeping my distance. Clearly, I'm not very good at staying away from you."

I hear Dan close the door behind himself and his footsteps slowly approaching. My breath quickens. I'm achingly hot beneath my panties, the feeling intensifying with each step closer Dan takes. He stops behind me, with his chest pressed to my back and our eyes locked onto one another in the mirror. I'm pinned beneath his gaze, both scared and loving every second of it. Dan takes the ribbon from me and weaves it through my hair, tying it in a perfect bow.

"I love this dress on you, Ally."

A shiver runs through me when Dan speaks my name and how intimate it sounds on his lips. His hands lower from the ribbon, creating gooseflesh on my skin as they trail down the length of my arms. Dan's right hand links with mine, and despite my inner voice shouting at me to retrieve my hand, I don't.

"Tell me to leave," he whispers.

I shake my head, words evading me as I watch him in the mirror.

The left corner of Dan's mouth slants up, his voice so velvety smooth. "I've been going out of my mind, not able to hear your voice this week. Your laugh. I've been thinking about you non-stop."

"You think of me?"

"You know I do." His lips rest beside my ear, his breath hot against my skin as he whispers, "Multiple times a day with my hand wrapped around my cock."

A tiny moan escapes me and I shiver, wishing I could watch him during those moments. "What do you think about?"

"That you never ran off to Paris. That you stop fighting this thing between us and give in to what you want. Those are the thoughts I start off with. What makes me finish is the thought of you coming on my cock."

My chest rises heavily with each breath, and I lick my lips.

"You like that thought too, don't you?"

I nod, unable to break the intensity of our eye contact in the mirror.

In my peripheral, headlights pan across the trees outside my bedroom, interrupting the moment between us. I duck my head, trying to shake off this trance Dan has me in. "Liam is here. I need to leave," I mutter, slipping out from my position between Dan and the mirror.

His arm darts out, wrapping around my waist. Dan's lips are even faster, crushing down upon mine. His mouth is hot and desperate, and it takes me only a second to match the urgency. My fingers tangle through Dan's hair as I press my body to his. I can't think straight. I can't think at all, except that I need this. Him. I've needed Dan for the longest time. I've *never* stopped needing him.

"Fuck, Ally," Dan groans during the slightest break in our kisses, his lips trailing down my neck, across my collarbone. His hands are on my thighs, working their way up beneath my dress.

"Kiss me again, Dan. *Please*," I beg. "Don't stop."

Dan's mouth returns to mine, his tongue pushing past my lips and claiming me. I moan as his palms explore my body, working over my waist and up to my breasts. Our breathing is the only thing I can hear, so loud and rapid, becoming one with each other's. With Dan's chest pressed against mine, I feel his heart pounding as heavy as mine. Dan's hips pin me to the wall, and I let out a tiny gasp when feeling that he's hard. My pussy tightens, aching to be filled with that hardness.

The sound of someone knocking on my bedroom door shocks me back to reality. "Darling, your date has arrived."

Panic shoots through me, hearing my mother's voice. I'm kissing my stepbrother. Our parents could walk in on us at any second. I'm about to go on a date with a different man. What the fuck am I doing right now?

Dan and I quickly step apart from each other. I examine myself in the mirror while catching my breath. No lipstick smudges, thank goodness.

"Don't go on the date," Dan says.

More knocking. "Ally?"

Shit. There's no time to even think. "Ah... come in, Mom."

"Everything all right in here?" Mom enters and sees the two of us. "Oh, Dan, honey, I didn't realize you were here. How lovely to see you. Ally looks stunning for her date, don't you think?"

"Most beautiful girl I've ever seen." He looks directly at me as he says those words. My God, this is an absolute disaster. I can't be back here, sneaking around with Dan once again. I've moved on from this. Liam and I can be good together if I just get a chance to be with him.

"Dan, before I forget," Mom starts. "Your father and I have organized a family lunch here next Saturday with the entire family as an official welcome home for Ally. It's the first chance everyone is available at the same time. I know the situation between you and your father is tense, but he cares about you and wants you around. We'd would love to have all the family together. It will be casual and if the weather is nice, we'll turn it into a pool party."

"Sure. I'll be here," he says, still watching me.

I pretend to search for something in my purse, afraid that if Mom sees the way I look at Dan, she'll read everything that just happened between us.

"Okay, sweetie, we won't keep you from your date," Mom says. "Stay safe, please. Always watch your drink. And if this boy doesn't treat you right, I'm just a phone call away. I'll drive to you immediately."

"Thanks." I don't comment on Mom being overbearing. Let her have her way if it gets me out of this house faster.

Dan clears his throat. "Ally was telling me something important about her job. I'm sure Liam won't mind waiting a moment."

I can read between the lines. Dan is giving me an opportunity to stay back so we can continue where we left off. He even asked me to not go on the date, which I can't do. I shouldn't have kissed him. I need to get as far away from Dan as possible, right this second.

"Actually..." I sling my purse over my shoulder. "I finished telling you the thing about work. I'll see you both later."

CHAPTER SIXTEEN

DAN

I shuffle my deck of cards on the front porch of the beach house, perched on the railing as I wait for Ally to return from her date. The hour is closing in on midnight. The night is dark, with my father and Amabella asleep and only the inside hall light casting a dim glow where I sit. Waves roll into the shore, but their gentle sound does nothing to calm me. I grow more impatient for Ally's return by the second, with one thing tormenting me.

That damn kiss.

No matter how much I enjoyed the way she clung to me and rubbed against my cock, the kiss was a mistake. A decision acted out of jealousy and some prior claim to Ally I convinced myself of. I drove all the way from the city to ask Ally not to go on her date. To be with me instead. Yet she still chose to leave me.

The fucking irony of history repeating itself and how I never learn.

She *always* runs away from me.

I'm so fucking furious with myself. I knew the moment she returned from Paris that if I didn't play my cards right,

I'd frighten her off again. And that's exactly what I've done.

I check the time again. Past midnight. Ally won't be pleased to see me waiting for her when she returns from her date. But I can't leave without trying to fix this situation.

My shuffling grows more impatient. Surely she's coming home. My stomach churns over the possibility that she's gone home with Liam instead—

Headlights appear in the distance, traveling up the long driveway. I sit up straight, my spine stiffening when a pickup truck comes into view, parking in front of the house. The engine turns off, along with the headlights, but my eyes are adjusted to the night, and I can still see inside the vehicle.

Ally and Liam talk for a minute. He makes her laugh, then my shuffling stops and I'm full of bitterness as he leans in and kisses Ally on the lips.

Kiss me again, Dan. Please. Don't stop.

She's clearly moved on quick.

Her kiss with Liam is long and slow. His hand bunches through Ally's neat hair. Hair that I had my hands in only a few hours ago. Liam unbuckles his seatbelt and leans across the center console—

She smiles and pulls back, saying something I can't hear. Ally steps out of the truck and closes the door behind herself. The engine turns on and Liam calls out to her. "Miss you already."

They both laugh, and she watches him return down the driveway.

As soon as Ally steps onto the veranda, her eyes flick to me, sitting on the railing, and she gasps. "Dan, you scared me."

An awkward silence lingers between us, and I hate it. But I don't know how to start an honest conversation about the kiss we shared tonight, not when I'm so fucking scared that this is the absolute end for us.

Her gaze drops to my hands and the tiniest smile tugs at her lips. I follow Ally's gaze, surprised to find she's smiling at the neon cards when there's so much intimacy attached to them for both of us.

"I like that you still carry them with you," she says.

"I *can* control myself around you, Ally. I promise. I'm sorry about earlier in your bedroom. I shouldn't have kissed you. It won't happen again."

"It's okay—"

"It's not okay."

She looks at me, standing in silence with such an innocent, doe-eyed expression. There's no shame like I expect to see. She appears to even be... happy. About what, I don't know. The date with Liam went well, I suppose.

"I want to tell you something about my date. Can we... talk somewhere more private? Our parents could wake up and hear us. Can we sit in your car?"

My jaw clenches and I shake my head, trying to keep a level tone, but the frustration is clear. "No, Ally. I hate seeing you with him. I hate that you can be with me one minute then him the next. The worst part is I can't even blame you for the way you act because I never should have kissed you in the first place."

She glances at the front door, with her lips pressed into a concerned line. "Please stop saying that. You never know who could be listening."

I sigh, tucking the deck of cards into my pocket and stepping down from my seat on the railing. "Fine. We'll talk in my car."

The two of us leave the veranda and walk in silence along the driveway, across to the far side of the house where my car is parked.

We slip into the front seats and the doors shut behind us with a *thud*, blocking out all noise of the ocean and sheltering us in a world of tense silence and darkness, all but for the moonlight and a couple of garden lanterns. My awareness of Ally's presence multiplies in here. Her sweet perfume fills the air. I can hear her breath, soft but fast. She's nervous about something.

My gaze trails over her tiny body. My chest tightens by the sight of her slender legs and her cleavage in that purple dress. The way her breasts swell with each breath. Her pretty lips, parted slightly. Her eyes that are already on me. An instinct creeps over me, that being alone in this car with Ally is the last place I should be right now. Last time we were alone in here, I started talking about all kinds of inappropriate things.

Ally swivels side-on in her seat to face me with her body. "I want to talk about... us. About everything that's happened between us. I've never wanted to have this conversation because there should be no us. But there is. You know how much you mean to me. I wish we weren't family and I could be with you."

I grip the steering wheel tight, frustration getting the best of me due to the mixed signals this girl gives. A year's worth of unresolved anger pours out of me. "You want to talk about something real, Ally? I spent months being angry with you, *hating* you, for leaving the way you did. I got you accepted into an elite scholarship. I even told you I'd move to France with you if you needed support. Then you did me dirty by accepting the scholarship and leaving the country without saying goodbye. I felt like I'd been used and disposed of. How could you not even give me the decency of a goodbye after everything we'd been through? How could you return to the country and act as if our past never happened?"

"I'm sorry," she mutters, submitting to me and lowering her gaze to her lap. "Everything was so intense between us. I'd... fallen in love with you and... I had to snap myself out of those feelings. If I said goodbye in person, I wouldn't have left and gotten the space from you I needed. I didn't know what else to do."

"You broke my fucking heart, Ally. I was in love with you too."

Her eyes dart back to me. "You were?"

"How could you not realize that?"

She watches me for a long moment with sadness in those beautiful blue eyes. "I'm sorry I hurt you so much. What we had was too intense. It still is. I went to Paris to forget about you." She pauses, letting out a long sigh. "It didn't work."

"So, what's the point of this conversation? You're still convinced our feelings for each other are wrong."

"I'm trying to move on by meeting other people," she says. "I like Liam and want to keep seeing him. I had a really good time with him tonight, but overall, you ruined my date by kissing me. During every second of the date, I was thinking about you. When he kissed me at the end, I was wishing I was back in my bedroom with you and that Mom had never interrupted us. See my problem? I can't get you out of my head."

I let out an annoyed laugh, running my hands through my hair. "You're describing the dilemma I face with every girl I hook up with."

"How often do you... sleep with girls?" She treads carefully, knowing she lost the right long ago to ask me such a personal question.

"I haven't slept with anyone in months because you're all I think about."

Ally smiles to herself, matched with a look in her eyes like she's contemplating something. A moment later, she leans into me a little closer, her voice soft and inviting. "I like the way you look at me when we're alone, in ways a brother shouldn't. I like how you used to let me sleep in your bed with you. How you don't correct people when they think I'm your girlfriend."

Ally's hair hangs over one shoulder. She brushes it back, the movement drawing attention to her breasts. I get caught in the act of looking at her cleavage. From the way she's talking, I hardly think she minds.

She leans even closer to my side of the car. "That first weekend when I got back from Paris, you let me sleep in your room. I did something bad in your bed that I shouldn't have."

My cock strains against my pants, hearing the words out of this girl's mouth. Every inch of my skin is lit up with heat. I can't tear my gaze away from her. This is what I live for—this side of Ally that has no shame. Yet I can't figure out why she's showing this sudden change in behavior.

"Tell me what you did in my bed." My words are a low rasp.

"Exactly what you taught me to do with my fingers. I made myself feel good while imagining what you would look like when jerking off. What you'd sound like. You're always on my mind, Dan. I came to a realization tonight. I'm thinking... The only way we can get over each other is if we have sex."

My blood feels like it's boiling. I'm hard and catch Ally looking at the tent in my pants.

Before I can form an answer, she continues with her reasoning. "I know it's wrong. But we can keep it a secret. No one will know but us if we just do it once. We can get this attraction for each other out of our systems and move on with our lives, never speaking about this moment again."

I swallow hard and stare out the windshield, barely believing what I'm hearing. For years, the two of us worked hard to not act on this attraction between us. Since returning from Paris, Ally has been adamant nothing will happen between us. Now *she's* the one, little miss perfect, suggesting we give in. *She's* the one begging, all in an attempt to block out the side of her that is a freak for her stepbrother. To make herself feel normal because she's so goddamn ashamed of who she is and what she wants.

Fuck. Is this the only way I'm ever going to have her?

After we have sex, what happens next? She gets what she wants, to move on with Liam or whoever the next guy is, all while I'm still jerking off to the thought of her because I won't ever get Ally out of my system.

"This plan only serves your interest," I say. "One time may be enough for you but I'm not ever getting over us."

"You don't know that."

"I do."

"Maybe once you've had me and the chase is over, you'll..."

"I'll what? Lose interest? Not going to happen."

She sighs. "Dan, be reasonable about us. What do you expect for us, that we become a couple? No one would accept us. Our parents—"

"I know. I feel guilt toward your mom, but I can't live

my life to please her. I've stopped caring what other people will think. We can keep us a secret."

"How? We nearly got caught kissing."

She has an answer for everything. There's always a reason as to why we can't be together. No matter what I say, there's no winning with this girl. She irritates the fuck out of me with her righteousness.

Fine. We'll do this Ally's way, but I won't make it easy for her. She'll suffer. I'll break her down. She *will* be mine. I won't fucking let her get over me.

I glance back at her, keeping my calm. "You really think one time is enough for you?"

"I…" She swallows, nervous. "Yes. It has to be."

It won't be. But I can humor her. "I'll agree to this on one condition. I get your first time."

"Yes," she says within an instant, not even thinking through my words.

Eager little virgin. So naïve. So eager to take my dick.

I slide my tongue along my teeth, staring out the windshield again. "It's getting late. You should go inside. I have a long drive back to the city."

"What?" she asks with a rude shock. "We're not going to have sex right now?"

My mouth works hard to resist the smirk tugging at it. "I'm not fucking you in the backseat of my car."

"When do you want to do it?"

"I haven't decided yet. Not any time soon."

"Dan—" she groans my name. "I have a date with Liam next Saturday."

"I've given my one condition. If you're not happy with it, you're free to back out of the deal."

"It would feel wrong seeing him when I've promised myself to someone else."

"You two aren't exclusive," I point out. "Liam told you he's available to other people. I'm sure he's getting plenty of sex elsewhere. If he's so into you, he'll be happy to wait."

"I'm trying to do the right thing and move on from you," she argues.

Finally, I match her temperament, my voice low but harsh. "You leave me high and dry for Paris, then you leave me again tonight after begging me to kiss you. Now you're asking me to sleep with you, not for the purpose of wanting me but to get over me—"

"You know I want you—"

"I'm not done talking. You're a fucking brat, Ally. If you want me to get over you, a quickie in the back of my car isn't the way to go. When the time comes, I'm going to enjoy your body for an entire day and night. I'm going to fuck you in every hole. Fill you with my cum till it's dripping out of you. I am going to degrade the fuck out of your body with my dick and I won't be gentle."

A moan slips from Ally's lips. Her eyes widen and her breath grows more audible. That's my girl, turned on from my words despite not wanting to be. "My God, you're infuriating," she mutters, dropping her head.

"You don't know the definition of infuriating, Ally." I grab her chin, drawing her face toward mine. "I have a constant fucking hard-on from this whole good girl persona you show the world. The cute little dresses you wear. The pretty ribbons in your hair. Yet I'm the only one who knows beneath it all you just want to get fucked by your stepbrother. You've been hiding that side from me since returning to the country. I want to see the real you again. The needy girl who is a slut for me and only me."

She stares at me in shock for the longest moment, her lips parted, her breath heavy. I've never spoken to her in such a harsh manner before and expect her to pull away from my hand. Instead, she launches forward, slamming her lips to mine.

My hands grip the back of Ally's head, tangling in her hair as I match the aggression of her kiss. Needing her closer, I pull her onto my lap, grip her ass and shove her onto my cock, wishing there was no barrier of clothes between us. She moans into my mouth, kissing me harder, grinding her pussy against my erection.

"That's it. Good girl, getting yourself off on my dick and taking what you want."

I lean back from the kiss to soak in the image of Ally above me. It doesn't feel real, having always wanted this ethereal creature who is constantly just out of arm's reach. Then, the pain I felt when she vanished a year ago. I never thought I'd get her back.

Her hips roll in a consistent pattern as she works herself toward an orgasm. My Queen of Hearts.

"Look at you," I murmur. "I want all your clothes off so I can watch you just like this."

Ally reaches for the zip on the side of her dress, her hips moving with a little too much enthusiasm, and her ass hits the car horn.

She freezes, glancing at the house with fright. "Do you think our parents heard?"

"Perhaps. Get in the back seat so you don't bump the horn again."

She does as I say and climbs between the two front seats, making her way to the back. I follow her, taking the risk of us being caught. Dad and Amabella are in bed. Even if they woke from the horn, chances are they'll go straight back to sleep.

Once I'm in the back seat, I get Ally beneath me and

hook her legs around my waist. She lets out the sweetest sigh I've ever heard as I thrust against her. The friction sends a wave of pleasure all through my cock and to the rest of my body. I thrust again and her back bows off the seat as she moans my name. My breath shakes, hearing Ally like this and seeing what I do to her.

"When the time comes, you're going to take my dick so well. I can tell," I say while gliding a hand up the length of Ally's body, savoring the sensation of her soft, warm skin beneath my palm.

She nods, tightening her legs around my waist, making my cock press firmer against her pussy. My kisses find her neck, trailing a line down her collarbone and enjoying the sounds my touch draws from her pretty lips. I tug Ally's sleeve down her shoulder, the fabric ripping from my urgency, exposing her bra. She doesn't seem to care about the damage to her dress. Her hands are too busy sliding beneath my shirt and exploring the planes of my torso.

I push one cup of her bra down, nearly coming in my pants when I bring her nipple into my mouth for the first time ever. She cries out my name again, her hands burrowing through my hair.

My fingers hook beneath her panties and slide them down her legs. They're white lace and I tuck them in my pocket for later when I'm alone, all while staring down at her pussy. The inside of the car is dark, but I can still see how wet and smooth she is. I've never wanted anything more than to feel her wrapped around my cock right this second. There are so many things I want to do to her. Fuck her in every position. Command her. Fuck her *hard*, like no virgin should ever be fucked.

She reaches for my fly, but I grasp her wrist. "If I don't keep it in my pants, I'll end up fucking you. And I told you not tonight." I lower her wrist, guiding her hand between her legs. "I want to see you touch yourself. It's been so long since I've watched you please yourself and I've missed the sight."

She moans. I look down and realize she's already rubbing her clit. Pre-cum leaks from my dick.

"Such a needy little thing, aren't you?" I say, unable to tear my gaze from between her legs.

"This is what you've turned me into."

"No, this is who you've always been and I fucking love it."

She rubs herself faster, moaning softly. The wet sounds of Ally's hand moving against her pussy fills the car. Her fingers glide up and down, alternating between teasing her clit and plunging into her opening. There's a rhythmic tension in her muscles, tightening and releasing to build an orgasm.

"You still do it just like I taught you. You've gotten better."

She gives another desperate nod, then her head tilts back with pleasure. "I do this most days, thinking about you."

My dick throbs, begging to be inside her. "Take your clothes off. I want to see all of you."

Ally pulls the dress over her head and unclasps her bra. I'm groaning at the sight of her naked body, splayed out on my car seat as she continues touching herself. My hands grasp onto the headrests either side of us, knowing if I touch any part of Ally's body, I'll cave in, we'll have sex, and we'll be over for good. But I can't stop myself from imagining her wet pussy clenched around me, milking my cock as I thrust into her.

"Dan," she pants as her free hand plays with her peaked

nipples. Her hips arch off the seat, her breasts rising and falling with the intensity of her arousal. "You make this feel too good."

"I'm not even touching you. Just wait till you're coming on my cock."

Ally's eyes roll back into her head and her breathing becomes more ragged. She's working herself toward the edge. Her legs tremble. I can see the beads of sweat on her forehead, the flush of her skin, and the way her body is begging for release.

"You're about to come, aren't you?"

"Yes." She winces.

This is the moment I've waited for, but something greedy takes over me. I love that I'm the only one who has ever seen this side of Ally. Her upcoming date with Liam enters my mind, and jealousy rages through me at the thought of Ally acting like this for him. Ally promised me her virginity, but there are other ways to engage in sex on her date, and I can't stand the thought of her being with anyone but me.

Her moans grow louder, and I know she's right on the brink of an intense climax. I steal the orgasm from her, gripping both her wrists and pinning them above her head. She looks up at me hovering above her, shocked and confused. Her mouth opens in protest. She even struggles to free herself from my grip, but I hold her tight and keep her quiet with a *hush*, pressing my finger on her lips.

"You want to come?" I murmur.

She nods desperately.

"I'll let you come if you promise me something."

"What is it?" Her words are thick with impatience.

"That's not how this works. You make the promise first.

I tell you the agreement after you come. Otherwise, you don't come and I drive away."

For the first time in our relationship, there's a look in her eyes as though she's afraid of me. Like she's about to make a deal with the Devil. I'm not at all opposed to it, wanting to see how far Ally will take this. If I know anything about my girl, she won't disappoint when in this desperate mood.

"I promise."

A smile curls at my lips. I release her wrists and climb off her. "That's my girl. Now, let me watch you make your pussy feel good."

Ally's fingers resume their work, plunging and stroking, bringing her right back to the edge of her orgasm. A sheen of sweat covers her skin. Her eyes clench shut, and her hips buck against her hand. Then her body tenses and she shudders with the force of her orgasm. I don't know what gets me off more—the pleasure on her face, her pussy clenching around her fingers, or the way she moans my name while coming.

Ally collapses onto the car seat beneath me, satiated and her eyes glazed over with pleasure.

I sit back, rubbing a hand over my mouth as I glare out the window. One time—how the fuck am I meant to have sex with her only one time?

"Did I... do something wrong?" Her voice is small. "You're angry."

I look back at Ally, finding her with her bra back on and attempting to cover up with her dress. She has moments of acting with such sexual confidence that it's easy to forget how inexperienced and vulnerable she can be.

I pull her onto my lap before she gets the dress on and

kiss her softly. "You're perfection, Ally. You didn't do a thing wrong."

I search her eyes, but she drops her head, refusing to look at me, just like after the kiss in her bedroom.

"Are you going to hate yourself after I fuck you too?" I ask.

"What do you mean?"

"You're regretting what we just did. I won't have sex with you if you're going to end up regretting it."

She keeps her gaze down. "I don't regret anything that happened tonight. I feel ashamed for how much I liked it. There's a difference. How can you not feel the same way? We shouldn't be doing any of this."

"I'm in too deep to care."

She shakes her head. "You don't mean that. You're keeping us a secret too."

"Because I know our parents would keep you away from me if they found out. They treat you like a child and you let them. You're their precious little girl. Regardless, if people found out about us..." My throat works, despising the truth of what I'm about to say. "*You'd* stay away from me out of your own choosing."

She presses her lips together, her silence speaking for itself. I hate that she can so easily shut me out of her life. She's done it once before. She'd do it again.

"We were perfect, Ally. You ruined us."

"I know."

"You were a fool for thinking running away from me would work."

Her gaze remains lowered, cowered, and she murmurs, "Can I find out what promise I agreed to keep?"

I place a finger beneath her chin, raising her head till she meets my gaze. "This deal between us seems a little short-lived. I want to make the most of it and your virginity isn't enough for me," I tell her, my voice low but sharp. "I'm taking all your firsts. I'll do whatever I want to you, whenever I want, and you'll let me because you're a fucking slut for me and want it. I own you, Ally. You won't let anyone touch your pussy until I've fingered it, licked it, and fucked it myself. Likewise, you won't jerk off a man unless it's me. Your lips won't wrap around anyone's cock unless it's mine. Understand?"

She sucks in a sharp breath, the look behind those blue eyes equal parts aroused and angered. "You're being unreasonable. I told you I have a date—"

"Exactly. Guess you won't be doing much on this date."

"Are you trying to keep me untouched for the rest of my life?" Now she's just straight up furious with me, but I don't care.

"Oh, please," I laugh, releasing her chin. "I have good self-restraint but I'm not that good."

"Dan..."

"You agreed."

"You... manipulated me. You knew I'd say yes to anything when I was so close to..."

"Coming? Don't start acting shy, beautiful."

"You're being a jerk right now, you know that?" Ally slides her dress back over her head then opens the door to leave.

Right as she climbs off me, I grab her hips, shoving them back to my lap, and bring her lips to mine.

She kisses me. Hard.

Her entire body clings to me and the hottest little moans leave her mouth.

"That's better," I tell her. "Admit it, you're just as fucked up as I am and like this new arrangement between us. It's been your deepest hidden fantasy for years to be owned in every way by me."

"Are you this dominant with other girls?"

"You know I'm not. None of them have a hold on me like you do."

Ally grinds against my dick, her breath heavy. "Then yes, I like being your property. You wanted me to be a needy slut for you. Here I am." And then she's gone from my arms, stepping out of the car and glaring at me over her shoulder. "Doesn't mean I'm not angry with you right now."

CHAPTER SEVENTEEN

ALLY

I used to think I was a little fucked in the head, enjoying the thrill of sneaking around with my stepbrother behind our parents' back. Now, I realize I'm a whole lot fucked in the head. Dan called me a slut and instead of being repulsed, my pussy fluttered like it was a compliment. When he took advantage of me by tricking me into that promise, I found it hot he would resort to such measures to keep me for himself.

I'll do whatever I want to you, whenever I want, and you'll let me.

My God, I am seriously fucked up for being turned on by whatever leaves this man's mouth. He's punishing me for how I fled to Paris, and I'm embarrassed to admit how much I like my punishment. He's already started taking advantage of this arrangement between us, video-calling me every night this past week, telling me to pleasure myself while he watches and instructs me through it. I obey without hesitation and enjoy it to no end.

Each day after, I feel guilty and struggle to look at Mom,

especially Josh, knowing the performance I've given their son. How am I supposed to face any of the family today at this welcome home lunch Mom and Josh are throwing for me?

My earphones are in, playing Mahler's *Symphony Number 1* as a means to soothe my nerves while getting dressed for lunch. It's wrong of me, but I keep applying makeup Dan has previously complimented me on. Now that I know how much my "cutesy" fashion gets under Dan's skin, I've styled my hair in soft curls for him and tied it half-up with a ribbon he bought me. I'm wearing a baby pink dress with a large bow that sits over my ass.

From the corner of my eye, I catch sight of a Porsche parking in the driveway. Removing my earphones, I step up to my bedroom window, noticing a whole bunch of cars are parked in the driveway, including Dan's Aston Martin. My chest hollows. He's here already yet hasn't come upstairs to greet me.

Daxton steps out of the Porsche, looking fit for the beach in flowing pants and a shirt half-buttoned, showing off his tattoos. "Hey, Uncle Dax!" I shout down to him as he opens the front passenger door.

He lifts the sunglasses off his face, props them on top of his dark head of hair, and smiles up at me. "Hey, kid."

Daxton might be the one person in this family I can face without embarrassment. Well, him and his fiancée. It's kind of pathetic, but Daxton—fifteen years my senior—was my best friend before Dan came along. Without a father, Daxton has always been a big part of my life, taking care of me and my mom when she needed help escaping her ex. We video called a lot when I was in Paris. In middle school, when I struggled most with the bullying, he took it upon himself to learn the piano and would challenge me to who could play piano scales faster. He always lost, of course. But it was fun, and I always enjoyed his company.

His fiancée, Jordan, exits the car and greets me too. She's the most stunning woman I've ever seen, a famous burlesque dancer and looks like a pinup model from the 1950s. Her hair is always styled in long, black, finger waves. I don't think I've ever caught Jordan without red lipstick and cat eyeliner. She has a sleeve of colorful tattoos. Together, Jordan and Daxton make one attractive couple, both in their thirties.

They head inside the house. I count seven cars, which means everyone is here and I need to find the courage to face the family.

With a deep breath, I adjust the top of my dress and leave my room. Downstairs, everyone is mingling in the living room. I instantly spot Dan with his shoulder slanted against the far wall, mid-conversation with Felix.

His eyes flick to me despite no one else noticing my arrival. He checks me out, his gaze dipping down the length of my body for a split second, then he glances back at Felix with the slightest traces of a smirk. Heat creeps up my neck, pleased that he likes what he sees but nervous over being in the same room as him and our family.

"Here she is," Josh says, and everyone turns to face me —the good little daughter I am, sister, and niece. Yet I have this secret none of them know about except Dan, and it makes my skin itch.

Felix rolls his eyes and mutters something to Dan. Whatever he's said, I know it's a comment about Josh and not me. The dynamics between Josh and his sons is always a bit tense at these events, but they generally all manage to behave.

Daxton and Jordan are the first to greet me, each giving

me a hug. I say a quick hello to Killian. Our morning runs have been awkward this week, with him and Violet asking about the date I went on with Liam, and me trying to focus on something other than how I got naked in front of our brother.

Next, I move onto Tyler and his girlfriend Harper. They're a year younger than Felix, twenty-five, and have been dating since forever. They'll get married one day, I'm sure of it.

"Hey, Ally." Tyler gives me a quick hug.

Out of all my stepbrothers, he's the one I've spent the least amount of time with. We've never lived together. When Josh stepped down from developing luxury hotels, he passed the reins to Tyler. For as long as I've known Tyler, he's worked like a dog, trying to fill the shoes of his father, and is constantly stressed. He doesn't have the same easy-going nature as his brothers. There's also some issue between him and Felix I don't understand. Harper has some issue with Felix too. I asked Dan about it once and he didn't have an answer for me other than a personality clash. The pair stay away from Felix, and considering Dan and Killian are closer with Felix, they rarely get the chance to see Tyler.

"How have you been?" I ask.

"Oh, you know. Same old. And you?"

"Oh, you know. Same old."

"Funny." He says the word without humor. I can tell it's not out of rudeness. This is just Tyler. I never see him smile or crack a joke. He looks older than his years from all the stress of his job. More like his father than the youth of his brothers.

I hug Harper next.

"Love the dress, Ally. You look gorgeous."

"So do you." Harper is always stunning with her strawberry blond hair and pale complexion. She's friendlier than Tyler, though I haven't spent much time with her either, due to her busy dance schedule in the New York City Ballet.

Once we've shared a few words, I'm left with only Felix and Dan to greet. Neither of them approaches me. Felix, I understand, considering his issues with Tyler and Harper and how I'm standing right beside them. As for Dan not greeting me, perhaps he's trying to keep our public interactions limited so no one suspects anything of us. But everyone knows we're close. Staying away from him today isn't an option.

"Baby sis." Felix winks at me, nodding me over.

I press my lips together, bracing myself and decide to just get this greeting over with. While everyone continues chatting among themselves, I hug my oldest stepbrother. Before letting go of Felix, I catch Dan staring at the ribbon in my hair. We make eye contact, and I see a glimpse of the heat within him I witnessed in the backseat of his car. Satisfaction ripples through me, though this is hardly the time or place to be pleased about toying with Dan.

"Hey," I say to Dan as soon as I've let go of Felix, not sure how to approach him.

Amusement plays in Dan's eyes and on his lips as he watches me, making my stomach do a somersault. "What, everyone gets a hug except me?"

"Of course you get a hug. I just haven't gotten the chance to hug you yet."

I lift up onto my toes and wrap my arms around his neck, planning to make this a quick encounter. But Dan's arms slip around my waist, pulling me flush to his warm body and holding me for a beat longer than socially acceptable.

"Cute dress. You wear it for me?" he whispers.

I squirm out of his arms, praying no one saw the hug.

"Good week?" he asks, still with a hint of something smug in his voice. It takes me a beat too long to realize the meaning behind his tone, that he's referring to the phone sex, and I go completely red.

"What? Oh, um, yeah. Busy week." I angle my body away from Dan, scanning the living room for onlooking eyes. Felix is occupied with his phone. Everyone else is in deep conversation. Thank God. "And you?"

Dan chuckles behind me but gives no answer. His finger hooks around my pinkie, the contact so understated and hidden in plain sight for the entire family to see. Gooseflesh rises on the back of my neck at his warm touch. I shake my hand free and fold my arms, earning another soft laugh from Dan.

Jordan steps up to me with a glass of champagne. "Hey, gorgeous. You look a little off. Everything all right?"

Crap. She's noticed. Has *everyone* noticed?

I blurt out the first thing that comes to mind. "I... have a date tonight that I'm nervous about."

"A date. That's so exciting. Who's the guy?"

Though I can't see Dan where he stands behind me, I hear the slightest groan in response to mention of my date.

"Ah... it's... this guy called Liam," I tell her.

"Nice. What does he do?"

"He's a jazz musician."

"Extra nice. And what kind of date is he taking you on?"

It's not unusual for Jordan to ask me such personal questions. From the moment we met, when she first started dating Daxton, she's treated me like one of her girlfriends, despite the ten-year age gap between us. She's always felt like more of a friend than an aunt to me, and I suppose she feels the same way since I'm one of her bridesmaids. What *would* be unusual is for me to *not* share details with Jordan. So, I tell her the truth, all while Dan listens to every word.

"He's making me dinner at his place."

"So romantic."

Thankfully, Mom *dings* a knife against her champagne glass, gathering everyone's attention. "Lunch is about to be served on the back veranda. Let's all make our way out there."

I make a move to follow the flow of everyone, eager to get away from Dan, but he holds me back, behind all the family, and whispers in my ear. "Did you not understand the rules? You're mine. Or are you just being a brat, trying to make me jealous? Trust me, you'll be punished." He grabs my ass and I work hard to not yelp.

"I understood perfectly," I whisper in return, pushing his hand away from my backside. "No form of sex with Liam. I can still kiss him and go on a date with him. I can let him watch me please myself, just like you taught me to."

"Sounds like you want to be punished." He walks ahead of me before I can ask what his idea of punishment is. I swallow hard, a little fearful, mostly turned on.

A long table, decorated with floral centerpieces, awaits me as I join everyone out in the back of the house.

"Mom, this is beautiful," I tell her. "You shouldn't have gone to this much effort just for me. I thought this was supposed to be a casual lunch. You've got the fundraiser tomorrow night you're meant to be focusing on."

Both she and Josh have been running around like mad

all week, organizing the next benefit for Forever Families, held in the gardens of this beach house.

"Don't be ridiculous. We're all so excited to have you back from Paris. It's worth celebrating." She speaks up for the family to hear. "There are name tags on your assigned seat."

Everyone spreads around the table, searching for their name.

I wait behind with Mom. "Isn't a seating plan a little intense for a family lunch?"

Her voice drops to a whisper. "I didn't want to risk Josh and Dan sitting next to each other and getting into an argument. I wanted Felix away from Tyler and Harper too."

Fair point.

"Ally," Dan calls out. I look in the direction of his voice, finding him already seated in the middle of the table. "You're next to me."

Mom places a hand on my back, guiding me toward Dan. "Yes, I've got you two kids next to each other since you're always attached at the hip."

I suck in a breath of embarrassment over her words. Dan laughs under his breath as I obediently take my seat.

"Bro, you down for a game tonight?" Felix asks Dan from across the table.

"Yeah, count me in." Beneath the tablecloth, Dan's hand slides to the inside of my thigh, brushing against my panties and making a statement—a claim on his territory in front of our family and a reminder that I belong to him, regardless of my date.

I'm instantly rigid. His hand should *not* be there while we're surrounded by family, yet I can't make myself push it away. Dan side-eyes me, doesn't speak a word, but from the smug expression, I can tell he's felt how wet my panties already are.

"Killian, you keen?" He continues conversation with our brothers like it's nothing unusual to have his hand between my legs.

I'm out of my mind when I tilt my hips forward into his hand, adding pressure to my clit.

CHAPTER EIGHTEEN

ALLY

"How many months until the wedding?" I strip down to my bikini and step into the water, feeling the heat of Dan's eyes from where he sits with Felix and Killian across the pool.

When I don't receive an immediate answer from Daxton and Jordan, I realize I've interrupted an intimate moment. The water skews visibility, but I can see Daxton has Jordan's legs wrapped around his waist. He whispers something against her lips, the two of them laughing through kisses. Everyone has relocated to the pool area after lunch, dressed in swimwear, though the three of us are the only ones currently in the water.

"Just under four months," Daxton says, ending the kiss and swimming closer to me with Jordan still in his arms. "We'll fly the wedding party to California a few days earlier, so make sure you get time off work."

"Sure. No problem." The wedding will be held at Daxton's family vineyard where he grew up. I've spent a bit of time there as a kid. It will be nice to return.

"Oh, before I forget," Jordan says to me. "We need to organize a time to get your bridesmaid dress fitted."

"Sacred Heart has this massive five-day weekend starting Wednesday night. Some religious holiday. Can we find some time over the weekend?"

"Sounds great."

"So, kid, how's the new job treating you?" Daxton asks.

"It's a big adjustment." I plunge into the water, fully submerged, and push my hair back from my face as I resurface. The water is borderline too cold, being the first week of October. If I'm being honest, I'm only swimming today because I want Dan to see me in my bikini.

As for my answer to Daxton's question about my job, I don't have much more to add. Nothing positive, at least. The staff stress me out. Appearance wise, it still feels like I could pass as one of the students and none of the staff take me seriously for that reason. I barely have time to practice the piano anymore. I'm always staying late due to meetings or to complete administrative tasks. It's not enjoyable at all. But I suppose a job isn't intended to be enjoyable. Thank God there haven't been any more mentions of my name in the media since the start of term when I allegedly walked into a strip club.

The one benefit of working at Sacred Heart is that it's brought me closer to Killian and I'm forming somewhat of a friendship with Violet. I suppose my students are nice too.

"You don't enjoy teaching?" Daxton asks, always perceptive.

"I didn't say that."

"Juilliard is waiting for you, kid."

"No, it's not," I mutter with a sense of melancholy dampening my mood.

He gets the hint, dropping the subject. "I've been practicing my piano scales in preparation for your return from Paris."

Finally, a topic of conversation I don't feel the need to brush off. I splash him with water. "You seriously think you can beat me?"

"The competition takes place this afternoon."

"Okay, you're on." We shake hands, laughing.

Jordan releases herself from Daxton's arms. "I'm getting pruney fingers from the water. You two stay talking. I'm going to lay in the sun for a bit."

"My skin is heading the same way," Daxton says. "I'll join you."

"Oh, hey, one last thing," Jordan says to me. "Your birthday is coming up soon. The big twenty-one. How are we celebrating?"

I shrug. "I'm not sure. I haven't had a chance to think about it."

The question makes me feel kind of bad. Dan's birthday is before mine—Sunday, one week from now. Yet no one ever mentions it because it's the same date as his mother's death. We'd all like to celebrate his birthday but Dan is the one who set the precedent many years ago that everyone ignore the day.

Dan and I rarely speak about the loss of his mom and my dad anymore, but it was a big bonding point between us when first meeting. I know the guilt of her death still gets to him, even after all these years. He blames himself for his brothers growing up without their mom. Josh lost his wife and Dan always felt resented by him throughout his childhood.

Perhaps Josh did struggle with resentment. I don't know. The two men have a complicated history I'm not a part of. But the Josh I know today doesn't harbor those feelings toward Dan. He wants a relationship with Dan and to celebrate his birthday. The two of them just don't know how to communicate.

As for Dan's brothers, Felix told me they were all too young to remember much of their mother and don't blame him for her death. Nothing anyone says changes Dan's mind. He insists on spending the day alone every year and without a single *happy birthday* or present from anyone.

I've learned to respect his wishes, but it never stops feeling strange to ignore his birthday, more so this year than others, considering we'll be celebrating such a significant birthday of mine.

"I'll talk to your mom and see what we can organize for your twenty-first," Jordan says, stepping out of the water with Daxton right behind her.

Alone in the pool, I dip my head back beneath the surface and stay down here for a long moment, holding my breath and ruminating on the birthday situation. When I'm out of breath, I pop back up in time to see Dan dive into the water.

He surfaces right in front of me, with that same amused spark he's held in his eyes for me all day. I'm suddenly hot within the cold water.

"Hey." It's a pathetic greeting but is all I can think to say.

He smirks, swimming closer to me. Far closer than he should. "Hey? You've barely spoken to me all day. Stop acting so nervous. People will notice."

I swim backward, trying to create an acceptable distance between us. "You're purposely trying to make me nervous."

"Maybe. Cute bikini." He swims closer, lowering his voice. "You, swimming in October? Come on, sis. If you want my eyes on you, there are easier ways that don't involve any clothes at all."

My legs squeeze together at the instant flurry of arousal that travels through me. My breath quickens. My back bumps into the pool wall. "Dan," I whisper in panic as he swims even closer. "What are you doing?"

I glance around, hoping no one sees us like this. Felix and Killian are busy chatting. Mom and Josh are lounging on daybeds, drinking cocktails with Tyler and Harper, now with the addition of Daxton and Jordan. But one look in our direction and they'll see a brother and sister far too close.

Catching onto my concerns, Dan grabs a nearby pool float—a giant swan—and positions it between us and the rest of the family, acting as a shield. It barely puts me at ease. With a tilt of someone's head or a couple steps to the side, we'll be caught.

"So, big date tonight," he says. "Don't you think we should talk about what will happen? I mean, as your teacher."

"I thought the teaching thing was off."

"You thought wrong. I still have lots of things to teach you," he whispers, the sound filthy.

My heart thumps so hard I can feel it all throughout myself. All I can do is breathe. No words come out of my mouth. All week, I've been desperate to feel Dan's hands on my body. Now that he's so close, the desire is intensified. Yet at the same time, I'm panicked someone will catch us like this.

"An hour ago, you wanted to punish me for this date. Now you're encouraging me to go on it?"

"Yes. All part of my teaching. You'll see. And don't worry, you'll still be punished."

Dan places both hands on the pool ledge, either side of

my head, and pulls himself closer, till his body is pressed against mine. I muffle a gasp at the feel of his cock against my stomach. He grabs my thighs and hooks them around his waist, pushing the head of his erection to my opening.

My legs tighten around him for a blissful moment, drawing us closer, until common sense snaps me out of it and I push space between us. "What has gotten into you, acting this way in front of the family when we could so easily get caught."

"That's half the fun of it. You've been such a good girl your entire life. I know how much it turns you on, doing the wrong thing."

"But—"

"No buts. I'll do whatever I want to you, whenever I want. Remember?"

I search Dan's eyes, trying to read what's happening between us. The way he looks at me is with the same depravity I witnessed in the backseat of his car. Utter obsession, and I love it. It's a look I haven't been able to get out of my head all week. I want to see him look at me like this again when it's just the two of us and I'm naked. Not when we're in public.

His antics suddenly make sense and my stomach twists with fear. "This is my punishment—submitting and letting you do what you want with me right in front of our family?"

"Yes, Queen."

The fear is replaced with shock, hearing that name leave his lips. My heart squeezes and I work hard to prevent my chin from trembling. "You haven't called me that name since before Paris—"

"You never stopped being my queen, even after how badly you fucked up by leaving me the way you did."

I lick my lips, thinking about all the years we lived

together and how much I miss what we had. "What do you want me to do?" I murmur.

"Go to the outdoor shower and wait for me there."

My muscles throb between my legs, *needing* to be relieved no matter what fucked up situation I'm about to get myself in. I follow Dan's instructions without question and climb out of the pool, wringing my hair.

"Are you heading inside, honey?" Mom calls to me from her sun lounger, mid-conversation with Jordan.

"Yeah, I need to start preparing for my date tonight."

I walk past the group, around the corner of the pool house and out of sight to its exterior shower. Cold water trickles down my body once I turn the faucet on, but it does nothing to lower the heat building in my core. I rest my back against the shower wall and close my eyes, trying to find some stability within myself while waiting for Dan and whatever he has in mind for me.

"I'm so happy for Ally. Have you met Liam?" Jordan's voice travels around the corner, emphasizing the short distance to the family.

"No," my mother responds. "I'm hoping she'll introduce us when he picks her up tonight."

When I open my eyes again, Dan is standing at the edge of the pool house, just out of everyone's view, staring at my body. He steps up to the shower, joining me beneath the downpour, and washes himself in silence. The way his abs move has me imagining what they would look like flexing during sex. Would he make the same deep and desperate groans from last weekend in his car too?

"I'm pleased she's found someone she likes," my mother continues. "It's also a big adjustment for me, seeing my little girl grow up and date someone."

Dan laughs, whispering into my ear, "If only your mother knew what her little girl is really like."

His words send a mixture of shame and desire through me. Dan stops washing himself and places a hand high up on the wall above my head. He's so tall and broad, towering over me. His gaze travels all the way down my body and slowly back up.

"As your teacher... brother... whatever title you prefer, I should let you know your date will try to touch you here tonight." Dan strokes a finger up the front of my bikini bottoms, the heat of his finger penetrating the material. I moan, my reaction drawing a deep sound of approval from Dan's chest.

His lips graze my ear again, his hot breath making me shiver. "You must be so wound up, rubbing against my hand all throughout lunch."

I can't bring myself to answer him. All I know is I don't want him to stop touching me down there. When Dan leans back and sees the desperation in my eyes, he gets the message loud and clear and slowly pulls on the string that ties my bikini bottoms together. I gasp as they come undone and drop to the ground, leaving me naked from the waist down. There's a splash wall on one side of the shower that I could duck behind for shelter if anyone walked this way, but it's narrow and would barely hide me.

"Dan—"

"I could fuck you right here." His finger strokes a languid line from my opening all the way up to my clit.

My hand claps to my mouth, smothering the cry of pleasure that bursts out of me. I'm the only one who has ever touched such an intimate place on my body. This is the first time Dan has ever truly indulged in taking my body for himself, and I've waited so long to feel him between my legs.

He groans, like this moment is just as intense for him. "Look how wet you are for me. Fucking little slut. You'd let me fuck you right here, right now, with everyone so close by, wouldn't you?"

I nod, my hips arching into Dan's hand, chasing the feeling of his touch.

"So impatient, aren't you."

I send him a pleading look, willing him to continue stroking me. Instead, he pulls at the string of my bikini top, until I'm completely naked, out in the open for anyone to see. I have no idea what excuse I'll give if caught, but I'm too deep in the moment to care.

Dan glares at my chest. Water trickles over my nipples, my breasts rising and falling with each heavy breath I take. "Your body is fucking perfection, you know that, right?"

"I thought I was too thin?"

"You're taking better care of yourself." He strokes a piece of hair behind my ear, his fingers following the direction of water down to my breast where his thumb brushes against my nipple.

My eyelids flutter shut at the pleasure. "Lower," I plead.

His fingers trace the curve of my hip, finding their way between my thighs and giving one painfully slow stroke to my clit. A whimper leaves my mouth.

"So, you like this, huh?" he says, his voice rough and low. "You like when your brother touches you here?"

Dan's thumb swirls around my clit this time. I nod, too lost in the sensation to form a coherent reply. My God, I am so fucked up for liking how he refers to himself as my brother.

"Trust me when I say you have no idea how much I

think about this little body of yours and everything I want to do to it." His finger slides inside my pussy, slick and hot, and I moan, unable to suppress the sound. It feels like he's reached a part of me I never knew existed, and I don't dare close my eyes, needing to see the way he looks at me, as though he's struggling to maintain control.

But then it dawns on me that my moan may have been too loud.

I glance back to the pool area, sweating with panic that someone could walk around the corner any moment and see me naked, with Dan's fingers inside me.

"You want me to stop?" he taunts.

I bite my bottom lip, holding back a moan, and shake my head. I'll take the risk. The public setting is frightening, but Dan knows me too well, how doing the wrong thing always gets me off. I need to feel Dan's hands on me. *In* me. I want *him* to give me an orgasm for once, instead of always standing back to watch.

Dan's eyes never leave mine as he pulls out and slowly inserts a second finger, eliciting another gasp from deep within me that I race to cover with my hand. His other hand gets busy, cupping my breast and teasing the hardened peak of my nipple.

"I thought you'd hold out on me for longer," I manage to say through the pleasure, being a brat and hoping to trigger that cruel, possessive look in his eyes from last Saturday night when he pinned my wrists above my head and delayed my orgasm. "You get all my firsts. Guess this means I can let Liam finger me tonight."

"Exactly."

Confusion fills me. His answer is not at all what I was expecting. Before either of us can say another word, my mother speaks.

"I need another cocktail. Anyone want a refill?"

Every muscle in my body stiffens with panic when I hear her footsteps approach. Dan swears under his breath and shoves the two of us behind the narrow shower splash wall, out of view, but barely.

His fingers continue to work my pussy, in and out repeatedly, the heel of his palm rubbing against my clit with each thrust.

"Dan, we can't keep—"

He covers my mouth with his other hand. "I don't stop until you're coming on my fingers. Understand?"

He adds a third finger, and I bite his hand to stop myself from moaning at the delicious stretch.

He smirks, his hand picking up speed. "You're being such a good girl for me. Now, tighten your pussy. Build your orgasm."

He's so bossy, yet I love it. I squeeze tight, the pleasure climbing within me, aching for release when I hear my mother's footsteps right on the other side of the splash wall. This might be the most fucked up thing I've ever done, the most fucked up thing I've ever been turned on by—the fear of my mother catching me, naked and with Dan's fingers in me.

"That's it," Dan purrs in my ear, lowering his hand from my mouth. "Fuck, you're such a slut and I love it."

My body is at his mercy, being this vulnerable in front of Dan. It's both terrifying and exhilarating, this loss of control. I want him to use me for his pleasure in every way possible.

His thrusting is rough. Rougher than I've ever been with myself. His fingers are both an instrument of pleasure and punishment, almost to the point where it hurts, but in the most addictive way. I look into Dan's eyes, seeing darkness and obsession. Jealousy. It only drives me closer to the edge, knowing how territorial he is over me.

"Dan, please," I beg, my brows pinching together. What I'm asking for, I don't know. Definitely not to stop. I'll be tender afterward, but I don't care.

"Please, what?" he taunts. "Make you come? Your mother is right around the corner. You want her to find me fucking you with my fingers?"

My pussy clenches at his words. A guttural sound leaves Dan's chest and his erection presses against my leg. The feeling of his cock pushes me to my peak. Pure, white heat radiates throughout my body as my pussy grips his fingers, pulling them in deeper. I'm gasping, choking on air, my entire body shaking with the force of the orgasm. Dan covers my mouth once more with his palm, muffling the scream of pleasure I have no control over.

As the last vibrations of my orgasm subside, Dan tilts his head around the corner of the splash wall, then releases his hand from my mouth. "Your mother is gone."

I collapse against the wall, weak and with Dan's arm around my waist being the only thing holding me up. I'm panting, my throat raw from screaming into his hand. My heart is pounding and I'm lightheaded.

"Fuck," Dan whispers as I catch my breath, watching me with awe. "Fuck, Ally. You have no clue, do you?"

"About what?"

"The power you have over me. I would do anything for you."

His words are both everything I want to hear and everything I *shouldn't* hear. "Don't speak like that. We can't... feel this way for each other."

Dan lets out a short and cruel laugh, his voice velvet. "Tonight, on your date, let him touch you where I just did.

Then, come and tell me if it feels anywhere near as good as what we've just done." He brings his fingers up to his lips, the ones that were just inside me, and sucks every last bit of my wetness off them. "You and I might be wrong for each other. But trust me, Ally, no one has what we have."

CHAPTER NINETEEN

ALLY

This is why I left for Paris, because my attraction to Dan brings out the worst in me. What the fuck is wrong with me, letting him finger me within such close proximity to our family.

I get dressed for my date, telling myself that tonight when I'm with Liam, I *won't* think about Dan. I *will* enjoy my time with Liam. I *will* be present with him. We'll pick things up right where we left off, with good conversation, laughs, kisses, and if he does end up touching me, I'm sure I'll enjoy it as much as I did with Dan. Perhaps I'll enjoy it more since there's nothing wrong about me and Liam being together.

When I return downstairs an hour later, everyone has relocated to the living room, dried off from the pool and back in their clothes, chatting among themselves and grazing on a charcuterie board. I don't look at Dan, though I feel his eyes on me.

A text message arrives from Liam, letting me know his band has finished their gig here in The Hamptons and he'll be at my house in fifteen minutes to pick me up. I send a reply, telling Liam I'm excited to see him, and to message me from his truck when he arrives and I'll come out to him.

While I wait, Daxton insists it's time for our piano competition. Though I'm all nerves and jittery about being in the same room as Dan, I agree, thankful for any excuse to not talk to Dan. Daxton and I sit together on the piano stool and race through scales while everyone continues their conversations.

For the first time ever, Daxton beats me at scales.

Everyone in the living room notices.

Of course they do. I'm the annoying family member who, at fifteen, made them all watch me play advanced scales with ease while blindfolded.

"Nerves about tonight." I try to laugh my failure off, using the date as an excuse.

"Sure, blame the nerves," Daxton teases.

Everyone returns to their conversations, spread out among the couches. I glance at Dan. He's sitting by Killian and is already looking at me—at my body, more accurately —while mindlessly shuffling his neon cards. I glare at him, sending a warning not to look at me like that around our family.

"On a serious note, you look beautiful." Daxton's words draw me back to the moment. "If Liam does anything to hurt you, I've got a shovel."

"What's your plan for getting home tonight, honey?" Mom adds, stepping up to the piano. "Have you organized a car service to drive you back here?"

"Yes, all sorted," I say.

"Don't leave too late. I don't like the idea of you being on the road late at night with such a long journey back here. Maybe you can stay at Dan's place for the night. I'm sure he wouldn't mind having you. Dan, is that okay?"

"I'd love to have her stay with me," he answers from across the room in such a casual tone. "We'll find some way to have fun."

I bite my cheek, working hard not to blush at the hidden meaning behind his words. I don't know whether to take Dan up on the offer. I agreed to give him all my firsts. The quicker we have sex, the quicker I'm able to move on from this obsession with him. On the other hand, it feels wrong to be on a date with Liam then immediately get naked for Dan.

"I don't want to impose on Dan," I say. "I won't be late."

The doorbell rings. I shoot to my feet, panicked that Liam didn't stay in the car like I asked. "Okay, bye, everyone."

"Don't be silly," Josh says, joining my mother beside the piano. "Bring Liam inside for us to meet."

"Ah, no. It's okay."

"Ally, darling," Mom adds. "I'd like to know who my daughter is dating."

Ugh. "Fine. This will only be a quick introduction."

I leave everyone in the living room and answer the front door, shutting it behind me to block out any curious eyes from the family.

Liam grins at me and weaves our fingers. "Hey, gorgeous." He's dressed in jeans, a white tee, and an unbuttoned navy-blue shirt rolled to the elbows. His lips brush against mine in a gentle kiss, which I'm sure would feel nice if I could relax right now. Liam looks me up and down in my baby blue dress and whistles. "Man, am I one lucky guy. Mozart would be jealous."

"Mozart?" I laugh.

"I've been reading up on your kind of music. Turns out, Mozart was quite the ladies' man. I even listened to a podcast about him. It mentioned some movie about him called *Amadeus*, which won eight Oscars. I need to check it out."

"I *love* that movie!" My words come out an octave higher as a sudden burst of excitement takes over. "Will you watch it with me? I've seen it more times than I can count but that's beside the point. Mozart is my favorite composer and I need someone in my life who appreciates his genius ways."

Liam's grin stretches wider. "We'll definitely watch it together. You like him that much? Maybe *I* should be the jealous one."

"He holds a special place in my heart. I see aspects of myself in Mozart. The man was said to have social issues and was misunderstood as a person. It's theorized he had Tourette's or maybe OCD. Not that I have those disorders but..." I cringe, realizing I'm going into far too much detail and am most definitely freaking Liam out. "Okay, wow, that was a weird thing to say. It's just that I have anxiety issues —" Jesus Christ, can I shut up already before making this worse.

He doesn't lose the grin. "Not weird at all. I like learning about you. Though, I'm surprised to hear those things. You always seem pretty relaxed and easy to talk to."

By some miracle, it seems I've made a good impression on Liam. I take a steadying breath, telling myself to calm down. This is nice with Liam, talking to him about my music passion. "You're actually one of the few people I'm able to talk to with ease. You know, I've been listening to your kind of music too. I think I'm becoming a fan of smooth jazz."

There were a range of jazz styles played at the club Liam took me to last weekend. It was a fun night that I've barely had a chance to reflect on, considering how tied up I've been with Dan. The jazz club was a free-spirited place, thriving with energy from the musicians and audience and nothing like the meticulous classical performances I'm so used to attending. During my odd moments of spare time throughout the week, I listened to some of the music from that night and have started forming an appreciation for it.

"If you're getting a taste for smooth jazz, I've got a whole list of songs to share with you," Liam says. "Come on. You ready to hit the road?"

"Uh, my parents want to meet you. Is that okay?"

"Sure. Lead the way."

I return inside with Liam's hand in mine. When we arrive in the living room, I retrieve my hand, feeling awkward about the intimacy in front of my family and especially Dan. All eyes are on us and it's daunting, to say the least. Before I have a chance to introduce Liam, Josh holds out his hand to shake.

"Liam, nice to meet you. I'm Josh Blackwood. This is my wife, Amabella, and our four sons." He names each one of them, introducing Harper, too, and finishes with Daxton and Jordan.

Felix nods at Liam. "Some of us are already acquainted. Liam's band often plays at my cocktail lounge."

"Oh, lovely," Mom says, not aware of the speakeasy. "Liam, we'll have to organize for your band to play at one of the upcoming Forever Families benefits."

"Definitely. We're always looking for gigs."

Liam wraps an arm around my shoulder, continuing to engage in polite conversation with everyone. My hands fidget behind my back, my palms sweating from Liam's stance. To make matters worse, I can feel Dan's eyes boring into me. I steal a glance at him, but he doesn't notice, too busy glaring at Liam.

"Ally tells us you play the double bass," Mom says. "It's so lovely she's found someone with similar interests as her."

Liam winks at me, teasing. "Yes, except Ally knows nothing about jazz other than a few artists from her coin collection."

"Oh, The Greats of Music." Mom gives an excited clap. "Did Ally tell you she almost has the complete collection?"

"Yes. I'm dying to see it. I have all the jazz artist coins except Gershwin."

"Ally, bring your collection downstairs to show Liam."

This whole interaction with my parents is downright humiliating, like I'm seven years old and they're proud of showing me off. I'm bright red in the face, I can feel it, and escape for my bedroom immediately. When I return, Liam is sitting comfortably in an armchair. Without a word, I place my folder of coins on the coffee table for Liam's viewing.

"Incredible." He flips through the folder, pausing on the George Gershwin coin. "Man, I'm jealous."

Mom has a gushing smile. "We spent years searching for Gershwin."

Dan coughs. My eyes dart to him, and I realize he's trying to hide a laugh. He mouths the word *sorry* to me, then distracts himself with his phone. A moment later, I receive a text.

DAN

> You sure you don't want to stay at my place tonight? I'll give you something real to blush over.

I delete Dan's message, not wanting any evidence of this secret between us, and send him a blunt message in response, telling him not to send me texts like that.

DAN

Okay. I guess I can make a promise too.

My eyes flare wide at his reference to the promises I made, naked in the back seat of his car. I shove my phone in my purse, hearing another disguised laugh that gets beneath my skin, and close the coin folder. "We need to leave now. Long drive back to Liam's home in the city. Mom, can you please put the folder back in my bedroom?"

"It was lovely meeting you all." Liam rises to his feet. "And don't worry, Mr and Mrs Blackwood, I'll take good care of your daughter."

"What the fuck is with that dress? Her tits are bursting out of it. They look like they're about to suffocate her."

I laugh into Liam's chest, wrapped in his arms as we watch *Amadeus* on his couch. His commentary of the eighteenth-century style corset costuming is hilarious.

Cuddling with him is nice. He rents a place in Williamsburg in Brooklyn. The apartment is small but cozy, decorated with various jazz instruments strung on the walls. We finished dinner half an hour ago. The lights went off and *Amadeus* on, and Liam hasn't let me out of his arms since.

"I know bigger is supposed to be better, but those tits are way too big for my liking," Liam continues, stroking my hair.

"Are mine to your liking?"

He chuckles. "That's why you wanted us to watch

Amadeus together, isn't it? To get me thinking about your tits."

"Stop." I swat his arm, laughing. "You don't normally think about my breasts?"

"I think about them a lot, actually. And to answer your question, they're just to my liking."

I try to resist a smile. So far, this evening has been one flirtatious thing after the next. While dinner was simmering on the stove, Liam taught me some basics about how to play the double bass. He stood behind me, with his chest pressed to my back and his lips against my ear as he instructed my fingers over the instrument's strings. It was a sensual lesson that ended with kisses while the food boiled over on the stove. I can see myself being with him in the long run if I can manage to get Dan out of my head.

I snuggle closer into Liam, resting my head in the nook of his neck and disregarding the movie. It's nice being in his arms. He kisses my forehead and I can tell that he too has stopped paying attention to the movie, enjoying this moment between us. We're quiet yet it's comfortable. There's no need for conversation.

"Hey." I break the silence, peering up at him. "My parents are hosting a Forever Families benefit in the gardens of our beach house tomorrow night. Would you like to be my date?"

Dan won't be in attendance. He's never at Forever Families events, which will give me a good opportunity to spend quality time around Liam without the distraction of my stepbrother. As for my parents, they were embarrassing today when meeting Liam, but I'm hoping the more they see me with him, the less they'll think of me as their little girl.

The skin around Liam's eyes tightens with concern. Not

quite the reaction I was hoping for when asking him to be my date. He twirls a lock of my hair around his finger, contemplating something. "I'd love to be your date but I already have plans."

"Oh, no worries."

"Ally." He strokes my cheeks, his voice gentle. "I've been meaning to speak with you about something. You said you're willing to give an open relationship a try. I'm glad, because I really like you. Honesty is the only way these kinds of relationships work, and while I know we're not in a relationship yet, I'll always be one hundred percent honest with you. I'm seeing someone tomorrow night."

"Oh. Okay. That's all good." My words come out on autopilot before I have a chance to absorb the information Liam dropped on me.

"How does that make you feel? I know you're new to this style of dating. I want to make sure you're okay with everything."

He's being very caring toward my well-being, which I appreciate, along with the honesty. I take a breath, trying to navigate my feelings. Liam going on a date does feel a little weird but only because I'm new to open relationships. Overall, I don't have an issue with him seeing someone else. I knew this was a possibility right from the first time we met.

The two of us have fun together. I enjoy our conversations and his kisses are nice. All I want is to go with the flow and not overthink.

"I'm fine with you seeing someone tomorrow night. I wouldn't have agreed to see you again if I wasn't."

The light from the TV flickers across his face as he studies me. "You sure? I'm happy to talk through any feelings you may have about this. Any questions."

I shrug. "I don't have any issues."

"You'll tell me if anything changes?"

"Of course."

Liam's arms tighten around me. "Good. So, tell me about this benefit. You're pretty involved with Forever Families?"

"From an appearance standpoint, yes. Our family is the face of the organization. All I have to do is smile for the cameras and give the occasional interview. Be on my best behavior. I'll be performing a piece on the piano tomorrow night. Funnily enough, a piece by Mozart."

"I miss out on you performing? Damn. I'm still hanging out to see you play."

"I'll play something for you on our next date."

His fingers weave with mine and he brings the back of my hand to his lips. "I'll be out of town for ten days performing with the band. When I get back, I'm holding you to your word. As for tomorrow night, since you'll be performing Mozart, I must insist you wear a dress like that one and send me a photo." Liam nods to the TV screen, at the actress in her corseted dress with life-threatening cleavage.

I laugh again, my amusement cut short by Liam's lips pressing against mine. The kiss is gentle and sweet and warms me. I sink into his embrace, my lips moving in time with his.

"Your laugh is beautiful," he murmurs. "I really like you, Ally."

"I like you too."

A few weeks ago, I could barely talk to a guy. Now, I'm making out with one on his couch. I'm so... *pleased* with myself for getting here. Pleased that I have the ability to be attracted to someone other than my stepbrother.

Dan's words return to me from earlier in the day. *Tonight, on your date, let him touch you where I just did. Then, come and tell me if it feels anywhere near as good as what we've just done.*

Dan is wrong about us and I'm going to prove it.

I deepen the kiss, attempting to lose myself within Liam's touch and chase away all thoughts of Dan. My hands slide up his chest and into his hair. Liam pauses the movie, then guides me onto my back and hovers above me, grinding between my legs. My hands trail down and I gasp when my fingers run over the large bulge in Liam's pants.

"You sound so good," he groans.

"I should let you know I've never... slept with a guy."

His grinding stops. "Fuck, that's hot."

Whoever knew my virginity was such a turn on for men. Here I am, trying to get rid of it like it's the plague.

"Let's slow down," Liam says. "I don't want to rush into anything. Sex too soon can ruin something good. I think we could have something good, Ally."

"So do I."

"All I want to do tonight is please you, if you'll let me. Can I take your panties off?"

I nod, my throat tight, realizing I'm actually about to do this with someone other than Dan. It's what I want, but... this feels a little confronting now that the opportunity is here. New and unknown. Dan always instructs me and gives commands. It's what gives me confidence and turns me on. I know it's a little fucked up but I like how he doesn't ask for permission. He knows what I want. He pushes my limits and I get off on doing anything he asks.

With Liam, I'm unsure how I should be acting. His style is different to Dan's. I wouldn't have the confidence to do any of those dirty things in front of Liam even if he instructed me like Dan does.

"What kind of... sex are you into?" I ask between kisses, my voice thin.

"Uh... normal sex."

I tell myself that's a good thing. I need normality. The things Dan and I do are unhealthy, even if they excite me to no end.

Liam's fingers slip beneath my dress and hook into the hem of my panties. He guides them down my legs and drops them to the floor. I'm on display and it feels... procedural. The silence in this apartment is suddenly deafening and my thoughts are too loud.

I hear things in movies and TV shows, that it's awkward when two people first get together and are learning each other's bodies. But I thought... I don't know what I thought —that I'd be more responsive to Liam's touch.

His fingers glide over the slickness between my thighs, and I shiver from the contact, the feeling not entirely pleasurable. Nerves flood me, making my body seize up.

Liam kisses my lips again while slipping his fingers inside me just as Dan did earlier in the day. But the pleasure isn't there. It feels like a medical examination, with awkward poking and prodding, and not because Liam is doing anything wrong. He's kissing me the same way he has all night, and yet his face suddenly feels too close to mine and his lips are smothering.

Maybe I need to warm up to Liam's touch.

I didn't need to warm up to Dan's touch.

Panic hits me, that I won't adjust to Liam's fingers and I'll have to pretend like I'm enjoying myself. Even fake an orgasm. It's wrong to pretend, but the alternative is asking Liam to stop, and that would be the most awkward moment of my life. It would bruise his ego and damage any chances of us moving forward in a relationship.

I want to enjoy his touch. This is what I've wanted for so long, to be intimate with a guy. A *normal* guy who is suited to me.

No one has what we have.

An unexpected ripple of pleasure spreads through me when Dan's words repeat in my mind, making me quiver. A proud grunt leaves Liam's mouth as he kisses the base of my neck. I try to be present with Liam, but Dan enters my mind again. It's the same issue I faced during our date at the jazz club, unable to stop thinking about Dan, despite wanting to focus on Liam.

My brows pinch with frustration. I feel like I've been jinxed. The more I try to focus on Liam, the more memories I have of Dan at the outdoor shower, pinning me against the wall and fucking me with his hand.

A moan slips from my mouth.

Shit. I'm a bad person. I've found a guy I like and I'm self-sabotaging. But the thought of Dan builds an ache low in my tummy, tightening my muscles, and I realize this is the only way I'm going to escape this situation without faking it. I need to get this over with quickly. Liam will be none the wiser. No harm done.

I grind against Liam's hand, chasing my peak. He says something to me, encouragement, I think, but I'm too consumed with thoughts of Dan fingering me at the outdoor shower to hear. The memory of Dan's commanding voice sends me closer to the edge. The sordid memory brings on another wave of bliss, making me cry out.

I keep bucking my hips, growing closer and closer. So many fantasies run through my mind. Dan being here with me right now and *him* being the one fingering me. Dan fucking me. Dan coming *inside* me.

That last fantasy is the one that tips me over the edge and sends me into a spasming mess. My ass lifts off the couch and I'm bursting at the seams with my release.

Once the orgasm is over, Liam's kisses on my neck bring me back to the moment and the reality of what I've done—thinking about Dan while being with another guy. Guilt replaces all pleasure.

"You are so fucking hot when you come, Ally."

"Um... thank you."

He chuckles, and I feel like a bit of an idiot for my response. But most of all, a terrible person.

The truth dawns on me in this moment, one I don't want to admit, but there's no escaping it: Liam doesn't turn me on because there's nothing wrong about us being together.

Dan was right. No one can give me what he does. I was confused as to why he'd been so willing to let me go on this date. Now it makes sense. This was his plan all along, knowing I'd come to this realization about us. He manipulated me again, and yet I can't bring myself to be mad.

Dan is the one person who makes me feel alive and this date reinstates how much I want him. Just him. I'm tired of being ruled by shame over something that feels so good. I'm tired of running and I can't do it anymore.

CHAPTER TWENTY

ALLY

A flurry of cameras flash as my photo is taken. I stand from the piano and soak up the praise, loving the high that fills me every time I perform. Guests are scattered through the garden in tuxedos and gowns, all applauding me. The night has a whimsical feeling, like we're in a scene from a fairy-tale. The garden is lit up with string lights draped from trees and floating lanterns in the fountains.

My mother has always taken great pride in the beach house and its land. There are several gardens within the property that she hires full time staff to maintain year-round. Tonight, she's hosting in what she calls her French Provincial Garden. The design was inspired from a visit to Versailles on her honeymoon with Josh. It's constructed of low hedges planted in symmetrical patterns, along with water fountains and statues.

To the right of this garden, a tall hedge maze looms over the guests. It's been here since before Mom met Josh. She's never liked the maze and often talks about demolishing it, but Felix, for some reason, has always insisted it remains. Dan knows its layout like the back of his hand.

The few times I've entered the maze, I found it eerie and lost my way, and have since made it a habit to stay clear of.

My applause fades. The hum of voices grows louder as the benefit carries on, now with a string quartet playing background music.

"Incredible performance."

I turn to the sound of Violet's voice, finding her with Principal Sinclair. I didn't know my boss had been invited. They both greet me with a smile, though the principal's is less welcoming. From the desperate look in Violet's eyes, I'll take a guess that she's been stuck socializing with Principal Sinclair longer than comfortable and has come to me for an escape.

"Beautifully played, Alexandra. Mozart is perhaps the most incredible composer to have ever lived."

"I couldn't agree more." I smile, pleased that for once I'm having a conversation with my boss that isn't about curriculum and where I don't feel like a student myself. "His *Rondo Alla Turca* is what made me fall in love with classical music."

"Ah, yes, his *Turkish March*. An incredible piece of music history. Alexandra, this evening is delightful. I'm pleased to see the fine image you and your family are bringing to Sacred Heart. Enjoy the rest of your night."

Violet pulls a cringy face and laughs as soon as the principal leaves us. "Glad she's gone. I was stuck in conversation with her for ten minutes and it was dry as anything. So, no Liam tonight? I was hoping to meet this guy."

"I invited him but he's seeing someone else tonight."

Her eyebrows lift, creasing her forehead. "You're okay with that?"

"I'm fine." I shrug, not wanting to talk about Liam or

even think about him after the awkward sexual encounter last night.

He asked the same question. It seems as though I'm supposed to be upset about his dating habits.

"Hey." Something else comes to mind, an important question I've been meaning to ask Violet. Nerves get the best of me, and I stutter through the question. "Have you g-got plans for this upcoming five-day weekend?"

Violet and I have grown friendlier over the last few weeks with work interactions, our morning jogs with Killian, and the occasional times she helped me pick outfits for my dates, but I've never asked her something of this magnitude, and I keep thinking she'll laugh in my face. It's an irrational fear, I try to convince myself. She's nice. I've had so many bad experiences with girls in the past, but I'm pushing myself to attempt more of a friendship between us.

"No plans except catching up on sleep," she says. "You want to do something together?"

"Yeah, if you're interested. My uncle bought ballet tickets for him and his fiancée, but they can't attend anymore due to work commitments. They offered them to me for this Thursday night. It's a New York City Ballet production of *Sleeping Beauty*. Would you like to come with me? I know you used to dance with that ballet company, so I understand if you'd rather not attend."

Violet's face lights up. "That sounds like so much fun. I'd love to go to the ballet with you."

I sigh a breath of relief. "Great. It's showing in the city. I'm staying at my uncle's place for the long weekend. He owns this incredible penthouse on the Upper East Side. I'm sure you'd be welcome to stay the night."

"Oh, fun. I love that."

My attention catches in the distance behind Violet, and

I barely hear her response, surprised by the sight of Dan. I can't help but smile, my chest suddenly warm, wondering if he came tonight for me.

He looks so sleek and handsome in his tuxedo. His dark hair is slicked back and he's holding a flute glass, grinning and talking to someone. I want to pull him aside to a private area in the garden and tell him he's right about everything, that no one has what we do, I won't find anything close, and that I'm tired of being ashamed of myself for the way I feel about him.

The smile drops from my face when I realize the person he's talking to is a woman. She's a brunette in a short, black dress. Dan told me not to doubt his attraction to me, but I can't help this ugly feeling that's creeping up my throat. Women are always so eager to drop their panties for Dan and I hate witnessing it even if there's no sexual intention on his behalf.

"What's got you so heated all of a sudden?" Violet glances over her shoulder, searching for the source.

"Nothing," I say too fast, panicked that she'll see who I'm glaring at and piece everything together.

"Wow." She laughs, turning back to me. "Is it a guy?"

"No. It's nothing."

"Doesn't seem like nothing. Who is he?"

"No one. Just..." I sigh, feeding her the least amount of information possible in the hopes that she'll drop this conversation. "I saw him talking to a woman."

"You don't like him talking to another woman?"

"It's complicated."

She presses her lips together, watching me with a knowing look in her eyes. "It doesn't seem complicated at all. You don't give two shits about Liam sleeping with other people, yet here you are, glaring at a guy for merely talking to another woman."

It does sound ridiculous when she states it like that. I should be thinking about Liam non-stop, eager to see him again after we became more intimate. Yet Dan is still the only one on my mind. I tried to convince myself that last night with Liam was awkward because it was our first time doing anything sexual. In all honesty, I really like Liam, but I think he might only be a friend.

After last night didn't go to plan with Liam, I've decided to stop hating myself for the things I like and want. It doesn't mean Dan and I can be together in the long run. People would eventually find out about us and we'd never be accepted as a couple. We'd be a scandal that would impact too many people around us. But I'm going to stop worrying about the future and enjoy what I have now.

"Ally, honey," my mother calls. She's standing by the maze with Josh and a bunch of photographers, waving me over. "Family photo."

I excuse myself from Violet's side and weave through the crowded garden, arriving for the photo at the same time as Dan does.

"Sis," he greets, stepping alongside me into the shot with our parents. I'm right in the middle, with my mother and Josh to my right and Dan on my left.

Ignoring his smug greeting, I smile for the cameras. On the inside, I'm purring over the tone he used with me. Thankfully, no one else heard him over the noise of the reporters calling out to us and the cameras flashing.

"Beautiful, as always." Dan looks me over in my champagne satin dress. The hem is short, sitting mid-thigh length. To keep warm, I have a faux fur white jacket on. My hair is pulled back from my face with a pink ribbon.

"I'm glad you could make it tonight, son," Josh says from the far right of the group.

"Got to make an appearance at these things every once in a while."

"No Felix, Tyler, or Killian tonight?"

"Just me," Dan answers him, leaning in a little closer and placing his hand on my ass.

I stiffen from his touch, knowing I should pull away, but I don't see how I can in such a public setting. The hedge wall offers protection so no one can see us from behind. I just hope no one gets a side view.

"You okay?" Dan asks, his voice concerned but the look in his eyes amused. "Smile for the cameras. Happy family, right?"

His hand slips beneath my dress, to my bare ass in my thong. I maintain my cool exterior, though I'm panicking and... *throbbing*. A rush of arousal soaks my panties. Jesus. He's touching my ass right beside our parents and in front of the press. I even spot Principal Sinclair in the crowd, watching us.

"Ally, incredible performance tonight," a reporter calls out to me. "Tell us about your studies at the Paris Conservatoire."

"It was—" My words cut short as Dan pulls my thong to the side and strokes my clit. "Um..." My voice wavers and I'm trembling. My legs clamp, trying to ward off his hand, both loving and panicking over every second of this torture. He leaves my clit alone but pushes a finger inside my pussy. I bite my tongue to prevent a moan, working hard to keep the smile on my face. "I had a... good year."

"Dan, your father says you were the one who sent an audition tape on Ally's behalf."

He starts thrusting in slow strokes. "What can I say,

we're a tight family. I'd do anything to make my little sister happy."

My pussy grips Dan's finger, seeking out an orgasm when I hear his label for me.

The focus shifts to my mother as a reporter asks her a question. Dan leans down and whispers in my ear. "Fuck, you're actually getting off on this."

I nod, knowing if I speak, I won't be able to maintain my composure. I squeeze his finger again.

He groans, his eyes dark upon me. "You're mine in the maze. *Now.*"

Dan pulls his hand out of my panties and leaves my side, slipping by guests unnoticed, disappearing into the maze entrance. I'm in such a state of shock and arousal that I remain in place for the next few minutes, smiling on cue for the cameras before leaving my parents and following Dan.

As soon as I step past the hedge opening, the mood of the night shifts from a whimsical party to an eerie, lifeless night. All is dead still in the maze. Visibility is low other than scarce specks of moonlight. The tall hedge walls absorb all sound of the benefit, blocking it out and creating silence in here. A breeze rustles through the leaves, bringing gooseflesh to my skin.

"Dan?" I cling to myself for warmth and glance around.

When I don't receive an answer, I step deeper into the maze, my heart pounding with nerves. I'm not one to easily spook, but when I'm alone in a dark and caged in place like this, it's easy to let my mind wander.

"Dan, come on, this isn't funny."

Something brushes past my foot and I scream, jumping back and bumping into someone's chest. I spin around, barely able to make out Dan's features in the dark.

"Relax," he says. "It's only a cat."

"You know I don't like it in here, especially at night."

"You sure about that? There's a whole lot of people out there. In here, it's just you and me. You can scream as loud as you want from the orgasm I'm about to give you, and no one will hear." He steps forward, cocooning me between the hedge wall and him, resting a hand high above my head and leaning into me. His free hand finds my thigh, tracing patterns over my skin. "You never stop surprising me, Queen. The things you let me do to you. The fact that you *like* them."

My breasts swell with each shallow breath I take. Though the maze is dark, I see the exact moment Dan's jaw tenses, along with the anger that flashes into his eyes.

His voice lowers to something smooth but dangerous. "You and I have a *lot* to talk about. He touched you last night. I can sense it in you."

"You told me to let him touch me."

"I did, and I've been in hell every moment since, knowing someone else has had their hands on you. But I needed to prove a point, that he can't give you what I can."

I well and truly learned that lesson. I open my mouth to tell him so, but remember the punishment he served me yesterday at the outdoor shower and how I've never experienced anything so euphoric. "I don't know if your lesson worked," I say. "Liam gave me an orgasm. It felt good."

"Ally, if you're fucking with me right now—"

"I'm not fucking with you."

"I think you are. I think you like being a brat and teasing me. Tell me exactly what you did with him."

"The same things I do for you," I say, my smile sweet and my voice innocent. "I let him watch me while I fingered myself. He asked me to bend over so he could watch me from behind. I did that. I did anything he asked. Then he took over and made me come. If we're done here, I'm going to return to the garden."

I turn to leave, but Dan grabs my jaw and shoves me firmly to the maze wall. His body presses to mine, his erection digging into my stomach, making me moan. He's not delicate with me at all. This is a side to Dan I've recently discovered, and it makes my heart race with a kind of fear that heightens my arousal and need for him, not knowing what he's capable of but trusting completely that he won't harm me.

Dan's mouth traces along my cheek before his hot breath caresses my ear, his voice a vicious whisper, "Ally, I'm not anywhere near done with you. For your sake, I hope you're lying." He lets go of me and steps back. "I suggest you get to the center of the maze before I catch you."

My chest tightens with unease. "Or else what? There's nothing you can do that I won't want."

"Another lie. If I catch you, I'll get you right on the edge of an orgasm but refuse to let you come, no matter how hard you beg. You'd hate that. Such a needy girl. I'll take your clothes too and won't return them. You can be the one to explain to everyone why you're naked in a maze with your brother."

My breath shudders, uncertain if he's playing with me. "I don't know the way to the center."

"I've taught you before."

"I don't remember, *and* I have heels on."

"Not my problem. I'll give you a one-minute head start."

My God, he's actually serious. He wants me to run through the maze in the dead of night. A maze I have no clue how to navigate.

"Fifty seconds."

"Okay, I was lying. Liam touched me but it wasn't like when I'm with you."

"Doesn't lessen the consequences. Forty seconds."

Goddammit. I take my heels off and rush in the opposite direction from Dan, my bare feet tender on the rough gravel. Though my eyes are a little more adjusted to the night, visibility is still low. It's almost impossible to find any distinguishing landmarks in here. I take the first left turn, vaguely remembering Dan teaching me the route.

"Wrong way, baby. Fuck, I'm going to enjoy getting you naked," he calls.

His footsteps start leisurely, as he knows I have no chance to find the heart of the maze. Regardless, I push myself to run faster.

"He didn't feel good at all," I shout, already breathless, hoping the truth will make Dan call off this game. "My clothes stayed on. I didn't bend over for him."

Dan's only response is an increase in pace. His footsteps grow louder, pushing me to run faster now that I know he's chasing me. My feet ache but I ignore the pain, taking so many corners that I lose all sense of direction. The walls appear identical at every turn. Hopelessness sinks in when I pass a statue I swear I ran by not long ago. I'm going round in circles like a mouse in a cage.

"I thought of you during it," I pant, trying to reason with Dan again. There's still no reply, just the sound of the gravel beneath his feet. His footsteps are so close that there must be only one hedge wall separating us. "The only reason I came was because I was thinking about you. I'm going to end things with him. I've decided to stop feeling so ashamed for wanting you."

Dan's footsteps come to a standstill. I smile to myself, catching my breath as I slow down to walk.

"You and I are wrong for each other," I say between breaths. "But that's what makes us so perfect, even if no one else understands. You're my person."

I turn a corner, arriving at a crossroad. My heart jumps when I spot Dan a few feet to the left, standing still with his gaze boring into me like he wants to fuck me this very second. To the right, by some miracle, the center lies waiting for me with a trickling water fountain sparkling in the moonlight, less than one hundred feet away.

"We *are* perfect, Ally," Dan finally speaks, drawing my attention back to him.

I bite my bottom lip, grinning, and make a run for the center opening, not sparing a glance behind me but hearing Dan's footsteps turn into a sprint, gaining heavily. I push faster, the goal so close, but not close enough, and scream as Dan's hands tighten around my waist.

With little effort, Dan pins me against the wall with his mouth hot against mine. I cling to him, needing his kisses despite the punishment he threatened for being caught. Dan growls and lifts me off the ground, wrapping my thighs around his waist and pressing me firmer into the hedge. Twigs dig into my back, but I don't care about the pain. All I want is for this man to devour me. Fuck me. Use my body in every way he can. I want to be completely at his mercy.

CHAPTER TWENTY-ONE
DAN

She said it. I can't believe she finally said the words out loud, admitting we're perfect together. I carry Ally to the heart of the maze, kissing her every step of the way. She's so tiny in my arms. So fucking delicate and pretty.

The moon shines brighter here, the clearing spacious. I can see the flushed color of Ally's cheeks and the want in her eyes. Keeping her legs hooked around my waist, I sit on a stone bench by the fountain. The maze is silent all but for the sound of our kisses and the trickling water.

"You caught me," Ally whispers, making to stand from my lap, but I hold her tight.

"I'm not letting go."

"There's something I want to do. Something... new." Her voice is soft. Even shy. I search her eyes, surprised to find she's nervous.

"Tell me."

This time when she tries to stand from my lap, I let her go. She takes a few steps back, never taking her eyes off me, and drops her fur jacket to the ground. Next, she unzips her dress. The fabric slips down her body, pooling at her feet.

My dick is fully hard, watching my stepsister strip in front of me. She's not wearing a bra, but her breasts are concealed by the curtain of her hair.

"Push your hair back. Take the thong off. Let me see all of your body."

She steps out of the thong and brushes her hair behind her shoulders, revealing peaked nipples in the cold night breeze. I can think of a couple of ways to warm her up.

She's risking a lot by being naked with me right now. Though, I hardly think there's a chance of us being caught. The maze, especially at night, isn't enticing for people. Even if they did stumble upon us, we're surrounded by darkness. They'd struggle to identify us from afar.

"Love the sight, baby, but this isn't new."

She doesn't say anything in response. Her lips twitch with a hint of that nervousness again. She's never like this. I'm curious to know what's on her mind. Most of all, I want to put her at ease.

"Come here," I say.

She holds my gaze with each step forward. I expect Ally to climb back onto my lap. Instead, she removes the pink ribbon from her hair and rips it in half, then takes my right hand and spreads it along the backrest of the bench, tying my wrist down with her ribbon. Fucking goddess. She does the same to my other hand. Of all the times I've considered bondage, I never thought I'd take the submissive role. But there's something so fucking hot about being tied up in Ally's pink ribbons.

"You'll let me do anything to you, for once." She returns to my lap, straddling one thigh. "Teach me how to make you come."

A deep groan rises from my chest, filled with urgency.

"This is what has you nervous? You do realize you'll barely have to try."

She laughs softly. "I want to learn how to please you. I want to make you feel as good as you make me feel."

"Are you going to hate yourself afterward?"

"No." Her hips roll against my leg, and she lets out the tiniest moan. "I told you, I'm through with feeling so ashamed of myself. You don't understand how much I need this. I've needed it for so long. I need to know what sounds you make. What you look like when coming. I need to know that *I'm* the one who made you come."

"Since I met you, Ally, thinking of you is the only thing that makes me come."

Ally kisses me, moaning into my mouth as her naked body presses to mine. Her heart pounds against my chest. She grips my shoulders tight and keeps grinding, her slick heat soaking through the fabric of my pants. Ally's eyes flutter shut, and a soft whimper leaves her lips as she continues to seek out an orgasm on my leg.

"Fuck," I growl, remaining still and watching in awe. A thin trace of sweat glistens on her forehead. I can already see the tension building in her muscles. "You're going to come on me, aren't you?"

"Not before I make you come."

Ally undoes my belt and fly, pausing for a moment at the sight of my cock straining against my briefs. Her hand strokes along the shaft, over the fabric, making my dick twitch, and draws out a groan from me.

She pulls the waistband down, freeing my erection. Her eyes widen as she stares at my hard length, seeing it for the first time ever.

"I want it inside me." Ally smears a thumb over the tip,

watching curiously and spreading my pre-cum all over the head. Already, her hand feels incredible.

Then she brings her thumb to her lips, tasting me.

Fuck. This girl.

Her innocence and inexperience is such a turn on, how desperate she is to learn and please me. Her hand wraps around my cock and I groan at the contact through gritted teeth. Ally works her hand up and down slowly, her lips parting as she watches herself jerk me off. I lean back, enjoying the show, admiring her naked body and the way her tits swell with each breath.

"Tell me what you like, and I'll do it," she says.

"The sight of you enjoying my cock is all I need."

Her speed increases a little. I hiss at the rush of pleasure, barely able to take it. Her gaze flicks up to my face, watching my reaction.

She smiles a little. "It feels good?"

"Yes," I choke out.

"What are you thinking?"

"That it's a good thing you've tied my wrists to the bench. Otherwise, my self-control would snap. I'd grab your hips and shove your pussy straight onto my cock. You're so wet you would slide onto me with ease."

She grinds against my thigh, wincing with pleasure at my words, her pussy clenching on my leg.

"That's it, Queen," I encourage. "Don't stop grinding. Your pussy is tight, but I know I can make my cock fit in it. I'll train you to take it. Every fucking day."

"Every day?" Her voice is pinched with pleasure as she continues rocking on my leg, her hand pumping me in a steady rhythm. "We're only meant to do it once."

"But you want it more than once, don't you?"

"Yes," she whispers, her breath hitching as her fingers

tighten around my cock, making my hips buck against her hand, helpless to the pleasure coursing through me. "We can't do it more than once. I'll never be able to stop."

"Why fight what feels natural?"

Ally's brows draw together as she sucks in a hiss of pleasure. "Your hands are tied. There's nothing stopping me from sliding onto your dick right this second."

Her hips lift from my leg and she drags the tip of my dick along her wetness. My eyes burst wide, an electric current spiraling through me at the torturous feel of her pussy hot against my cock. No barrier between us.

"Fuck, Ally. Don't you dare. Not like this. Not while my hands are tied."

She laughs softly and kisses me, returning to her seat on my thigh. I bite her bottom lip hard, scolding her.

She yelps and pulls back, touching her fingers to her lips. When she lowers them, they're tinged red. "You drew blood." Her chest rises with unsteady breaths, then she launches forward, crashing her mouth to mine.

Her kisses are metallic with the taste of blood. My cock strains in her hand, aching to come, which only adds to how fucked up I am over this girl, that even her blood turns me on.

Pain shoots through me when she bites my lip in return, drawing *my* blood this time. I kiss her harder, groaning into her mouth as our blood mixes as one. This girl is literally running through my veins and I'm in hers.

"Fucking little freak. Don't ever change. I am so fucking obsessed with you, Ally. Go faster," I order.

She follows my instruction perfectly, looking down and watching the work she's performing on my cock. Her hips continue riding me, matching the speed of her hand.

I grunt, my hips thrusting. "You're going to make me come. Faster. I'm right there."

Out of nowhere, her wrist stops moving, along with her grinding. She looks me directly in the eyes, her voice breathless. "I'll let you come if you promise me something."

The corner of my mouth tugs into a grin. She's playing with me, but there's nothing manipulative in her voice. "I promise."

"You're not going to ask me what the promise is?"

"No."

She licks our blood from her lips and leans in, her laugh brushing my ear. "Last chance to rethink your answer. You'll regret making this promise."

Doubtful.

I will do anything this girl asks of me.

When I don't back out, she grinds on my leg again and her hand continues working my cock up and down at an achingly perfect pace.

"Dan," she winces my name, her face tight, like she's struggling not to come. Her voice is a beg, telling me she can't hold off much longer.

"Let me watch you come," I tell her. "Watching you is what's going to make me spill everywhere for you."

She doesn't need to be told twice. Ally moans and her body shudders with an orgasm as she rides my leg. And just from that one sound Ally makes, she draws the cum out of me, heat bursting all through my body, my hips bucking violently up from the bench. I groan, trying to not be too loud on the odd chance someone hears. The cum is pouring out, shooting all over Ally's stomach and dripping down to her pussy. I feel it on my pants, right where Ally is grinding. It's mixing with her own wetness. She realizes too, and her moans grow louder, her orgasm intensifying. Just knowing that my cum is smeared all over her pussy and that she likes it makes me come harder. The hardest I've ever come. Five years of pent-up sexual tension spills out of me.

Finally, Ally's body gives out on her and she falls into my chest, limp and panting.

"I know you're wrecked, baby. You've worked hard. But untie these ribbons. I need to hold you."

She loosens the knots and I wrap her in my arms, cradling her to my chest. Everything is perfect as we hold each other, catching our breaths beneath the moonlight in this maze. I stroke her hair and run my fingers along her damp skin, savoring this moment while I get to live in the delusion that she's mine forever. She brings her lips to mine, and when she kisses me, it's gentle and slow. It's like she's my girlfriend and we've just made love. It's a dangerous fantasy to embrace when I know she isn't truly mine, yet I can't bring myself to crush it.

"We've kept this a secret for so long, Ally. We can continue just like this. No one will find out."

She leans back, looking at me. "They will find out. You had your fingers in me while we were posing for a family photo. My mother has almost caught us several times." She glances around us at the maze. "Our meeting spots aren't exactly private."

"We'll meet at my place only."

"For how long? You plan to live in secrecy for the rest of our lives?"

"Yes, if it means having you."

She smiles at me, but her eyes are riddled with sadness. "Let's talk about this later. I don't want to ruin this moment. You have no idea how much I needed this." Her lips graze mine, the metallic taste gone. I push our issues aside, not wanting to tarnish this moment either.

"Let me find you something to clean up with," I say, zipping up my fly.

"I'm not wiping your cum off me, if that's what you're implying."

"You're a mess. It's all over your stomach and between your thighs. You're going to return to the benefit like that?"

"Yes. I won't shower tonight either."

I grin, having no objection, and brush my lips along her naked shoulder. "So, what promise are you holding me to?"

When she doesn't reply, I meet her gaze. She bites her bottom lip and a flash of nerves enters her eyes. "We're spending your birthday together, *every* year from now on."

My jaw hangs open and I groan, instantly on the defense. "Ally... fuck. That's too much."

"You promised."

"Yeah, because I thought I was promising something of a sexual nature, given the circumstances the promise was made under."

"Your birthday is important, Dan. *You* are important. We won't do anything over the top, but I want to be with you."

"Fine." I scratch my jaw, irritated with her. Yet I have no one to blame but myself. "You win, Ally."

CHAPTER TWENTY-TWO

ALLY

My five-day weekend arrives and I'm catching an early lift with Josh Thursday morning as he drives to Manhattan for work. We were busy talking about plans for Daxton and Jordan's wedding until I received a text from Dan, linking an audition application for Juilliard.

I sigh with mixed feelings. Dan believes in me and knows me too well to trust when I say I'm content with teaching. I love that about him. But there's also disappointment and fear inside me over Juilliard, knowing I'm not good enough based off my time at the Paris Conservatoire. Even if I were good enough, I can't audition without breaking out in a panic. I want nothing more than to fill out the application form, but I can't bring myself to do it.

"So, you're attending the bridesmaid fittings with Jordan this weekend." Josh's voice draws me back to our conversation. "What else is on the agenda while staying in the city?"

I put my phone away. "I'm attending the ballet with Violet tonight."

"And the boyfriend? Are you spending time with Liam?"

My shoulders clench. "Liam isn't my boyfriend. We've just been on a few dates."

I've wanted to officially end things with Liam since our date last weekend but he's out of town with his band. I don't know much about dating, but what I do know is that I like and respect Liam and he deserves an in-person explanation.

Josh glances at me for a second, smiles, then focuses back on the road. "Your mother and I like Liam a lot."

Yeah, I can tell. They ask me about him every other day. "I'm also spending Dan's birthday with him."

Josh's eyebrows knit. "How did you talk him into that?"

A flush of heat hits me between my thighs at the memory of me grinding on Dan's leg with his cock in my hand. "Um... I won a poker game against him and this was the prize."

Worst lie ever. I've never won a game against Dan in my life.

Josh's brow remains furrowed as he drives in silence. I don't know how to read his expression. Frustration or disappointment. A rumor surfaced in the media on Tuesday about Dan winning a million dollars in a poker game. It's brought negative press to Forever Families and has been a stressful week for Mom and Josh. I'm tempted to ask Josh what he's thinking, but Dan is a sensitive topic for him that I'm not game to broach.

After minutes of driving in silence, Josh speaks quietly. "Out of all my sons, Dan is the one I've struggled with the most. He rebels the most. He frustrates me. I can't get through to him. I don't know how to talk to him anymore. But none of that stops me from loving him. I'm glad Dan has someone like you in his life and that he won't be alone on his birthday. Thank you, Ally."

"I... um..." I don't know how to respond. While I've always seen Josh's affectionate, fatherly side, I've never witnessed him be so vulnerable in front of me. "You don't need to thank me. We're family and I care a lot about Dan." Wow, this is weird. "I've never liked him being alone on his birthday."

"I do need to thank you, Ally. You don't know it, but you and your mother are the glue to this family. My boys see you as a sister and Amabella as a mother. After their mother passed away, I struggled to be the father my sons deserved. I made mistakes I wish I could take back. But I love them all very much. I love you and Amabella for bringing them back to me, even if my relationship with them is tarnished. I think the reason I cling to you and your mother so tight is because I messed up with my sons and I don't want to repeat the same mistakes with you two."

"Have you told them this?"

He shakes his head. "I don't know how to when Dan barely speaks to me. The other three aren't much better."

"Maybe you could write them a letter, or I could say something to them on your behalf."

"No, Ally, I appreciate the offer, but I don't want you in the middle of this. My boys are something I have to figure out on my own."

"Okay. I understand."

His face softens, his voice warm again as he glances from the road to me. "Speaking of family, your mother mentioned you were asking about a photo of your father."

"Yes." I sit a little taller, hoping good news is about to follow. "It's a photo of us from when I was born. I haven't seen it in years, ever since we moved in with you. Mom said she was going to search for it."

"I've been thinking maybe you could ask Daxton about

the photo. He stored a couple of your mom's boxes at his place during the move. I thought we received them all but perhaps a few got left behind."

I sink back with disappointment. At least I have a potential lead on that photo. Daxton owns the hotel he lives in, and after all the terrible things that went down with Mom's ex, Daxton housed us in the same building, a few floors below and free of charge. The photo could definitely be in Daxton's penthouse.

"You make a good point. Thanks. I'll ask him."

"So, do I get any more details about this mystery guy you ran off with at the benefit?" Violet asks while applying mascara in the mirror.

We're both getting dressed for tonight's ballet in the guest bedroom Daxton and Jordan always give me when I stay at their place. The room is fancy, like the rest of the penthouse, with a glass wall that looks out to the private rooftop pool and has a stunning view of Central Park.

I sit on the edge of my bed, buckling my heels and acting oblivious. "What are you talking about? I didn't run off with anyone."

"Oh, come on. You were glaring at some guy for talking to another woman. Then you excuse yourself for a family photo and that's the last I see of you for the rest of the night. You were totally sneaking away with whoever that guy was."

"I was busy socializing and talking to reporters."

Despite the awkwardness of her questions, there's a little ball of happiness burning in my chest because I've never had a girlfriend like this before. Someone to discuss boys with. There's Jordan, but she's a lot older than me and I never know if what I tell her will get back to Daxton and my mom.

Something inside me wants to open up to Violet and tell her everything about Dan but leave his name out. I could never live with myself if anyone finds out I've been fooling around with my stepbrother. But the slight risk of Violet placing two and two together holds me back from saying anything.

"Nothing happened with that guy."

She sinks onto the bed with me, blowing out a huff of air. "Well, that's disappointing. I was hoping to live vicariously through your sex life."

We both laugh. "What about you and Killian?" I ask. "I can see potential with you two. If you repeat this to him, I'll deny it, but sometimes I catch him looking at you."

She smiles, ducking her head. "Your brother is very... handsome. I could see myself with him. But we're friends and colleagues and I know neither one of us wants to cross the line of professionalism. You've seen what Sacred Heart is like."

Yeah, I do know what Sacred Heart is like, which only confirms my decision to remain quiet about Dan.

"So, is Liam amazing with his dick or something?"

I snort, caught off guard by the question. "What do you mean?"

"I'm trying to figure out why you're with him."

"I'm not *with* him. I'm going to end things with him—" A knock on the bedroom door interrupts me. "Come in."

Daxton steps inside, handsome in a black suit and about to head out for the night with Jordan. "Hope I'm not interrupting anything."

"Not at all," Violet says. "We were only talking about boys."

"Only?" Daxton teases. "That's the *best* topic of conversation. I'll let you girls get back to it. I just wanted to let you know there's a car service waiting downstairs to take you two to the ballet."

"Okay, thanks." I rise from the bed and grab my purse. Daxton turns to leave, but I call out to him before he closes the door, remembering my conversation in the car with Josh. "Hey, Uncle Dax?"

"Yeah, kid?"

"I've been looking for a photo of my father that I haven't seen in years. Josh mentioned that when Mom and I moved out of here, you stored a couple of her boxes and might still have them. The photo could be inside one of them. Do you know if you have those boxes?"

Daxton sucks his bottom lip, thinking about the question. "It rings a bell. I might have those boxes buried at the back of my closet. I'll see if I can dig them up later tonight."

The ballet is beautiful. I enjoy Violet's commentary on the performance and all the ballet knowledge she shares with me. Tyler's girlfriend, Harper, is a principal ballerina in the show, and it turns out Violet knows her from her own time in the New York City Ballet.

The two of us stay up all night talking and laughing out by Daxton's rooftop pool and it's the most fun I've had with anyone other than Dan. Come Friday morning, she returns to The Hamptons, and a stack of boxes are waiting for me in Daxton's living room. I spend the morning sorting through them.

There's no photo of my father inside.

I blow off my frustration by playing Daxton's piano. My afternoon is occupied with Jordan and the bridesmaid dress fittings. By evening, I'm ready to curl up and watch something in their home theater, tired from the day, but a phone call from Liam stops me. I return to my bedroom, pacing around the room in a cold sweat as I answer.

"Hi, Liam."

"Hey, beautiful, I've missed you. I've been thinking about you all day long. All *week* long."

His words are flattering but I find them hard to believe, considering there's another person he's seeing.

"I'm back in town earlier than expected. You said you're in the city. Can I see you tonight?" he asks.

I'm about to turn him down with the truth, that I'm tired. I also don't want to deal with the awkward and tense encounter of ending things with him, which I plan to do the next time we see each other. I hate confrontation. My mom's ex hit her for trying to leave him. I know this is a different situation and I don't believe Liam will turn violent over me wanting to just be friends, but it's still a stressful conversation to have.

Dan is the one thing that gives me courage. It's his birthday on Sunday and I don't want this issue with Liam lingering over my head. Dan deserves my full attention on his birthday, especially with it being such a difficult day for him.

"I can make tonight work." My throat strains and there's a sharpness in my stomach as I push myself to be honest. "There's something we need to discuss. Can we meet somewhere public?"

Silence lingers on Liam's end of the phone. He sighs. "Shit. I know those words. What's wrong?"

My stomach clenches tighter. "Um... I'd rather talk in person."

He swears under his breath. "Tell me now. I can take it."

"I'd rather see you—"

"Ally." His voice is firm but level. "If you're ending this, just tell me. I don't want to wait. You have me sweating like mad over here."

I wipe my own sweaty palms on my dress and swallow hard, afraid of his reaction. "Okay, um, I like you a lot and I mean it, but just as a friend."

He sighs, staying silent for so long that I have to ask if he's still on the phone with me. "Yeah, I'm here. I'm just processing everything."

"We can meet up if you want to discuss this further," I tell him, jittery and bouncing on the spot, my words coming out fast. "You're a good guy. I really would like to be friends but I understand if you're not interested. In terms of dating, I think we're just too different. I thought I would be okay with an open relationship but I'm not. I understand you have your way of doing things. I just want one person. One guy and—" Shut the hell up with the nervous talking, Ally.

Liam sighs again. "I really like you, Ally. I'm sorry this didn't work. Maybe we can talk in a few days. Tonight is probably not the best idea. I need some time to think."

"Sure. Whatever you need."

"Goodbye, Ally."

CHAPTER TWENTY-THREE

DAN

Persistent knocking at my door. That fucking promise I wish I could erase.

My phone says it's nine a.m. Way too early. I'd been hoping to sleep through the majority of my birthday to make this day go faster. I drag myself out of bed and pull a shirt on, forcing myself to head to the door. For the first time since Ally's return from Paris, I'm not in the mood to see her. To see anyone. But I never go back on my word.

"Yeah, I'm coming—" My mouth pauses mid-sentence as I open the door, finding what's waiting for me.

Blood rushes to my cock and I've suddenly forgotten what day it is. Ally isn't wearing her usual bows or ribbons or pastels. She doesn't look like her cutesy self at all. I don't know where to look first, at her blood-red lips begging to be kissed or the indulgent shape of her cleavage. Her dress matches the shade of her lipstick. The top is tight and low, shaped like a heart across her breasts and with velvet straps that fall off her shoulders. There's so much skin exposed. I've never seen her wear anything so revealing and suggestive and I'm obsessed.

The skirt of her dress is short, not even mid-thigh length, and flares out, making her look like a doll. She's wearing beige fishnet stockings and red heels. Her hair is in long, blond finger waves that must have taken hours to create. They'll be ruined the first second I get my hands on her.

A smug expression rises on those perfect red lips. "Happy birthday. I see you like the first part of your present."

Knowing that Ally dressed up like this for me sparks all kinds of primal urges. She has an overnight bag in one hand. I take it from her and place it inside, then pull her into my apartment, locking us in and stealing that kiss I've been thinking about. Not wanting to ruin the effort she's put into her appearance, the kiss is slow and delicate. She smiles against my lips.

"What's the other part of my present?" I ask.

Ally places her fingers on my lips and meets my eyes, looking up at me with raw heat and desire, her voice low. "Just for today, we get to pretend we're together for real. I'm your girlfriend. There's no fear about the future or what others might think of us."

Sex enters my mind and the thought of finally indulging in all of Ally's body. Fucking her without a care in the world of being caught. Truly being free with Ally and as loud as we want. The same thoughts are reflected in her eyes, and it sends me feral.

I kiss her again, struggling to be gentle as I walk her backward, pressing her against the closed door. "My girlfriend," I whisper the words with pleasure while resting my forehead against hers, taking a breath to calm myself. This day can't be so bad under those circumstances. "That's a dangerous thing to pretend. I might get used to it."

There's a look in her eyes that doesn't fight against the idea of us getting used to this pretense. "I want you to know I ended things with Liam. So, I truly am yours today."

My fingers twine with hers. More good news, not only because I hate the thought of Ally being with another guy, but because Liam isn't right for her. Ally is special and deserves a man who is so infatuated with her that he doesn't even notice other women walking by.

"How are you feeling today?" she asks. "I've planned a few things for us to do, but I want to know where your head is."

I huff a laugh. "I've got shit on my mind, but you dressed like this is doing a pretty good job at distracting me. I hope Daxton and Jordan didn't see you leaving for my place looking like this."

She rolls her eyes and smiles. "I wore a coat. So, would you like to stay in or are you feeling up to going out for the day?"

"Ally, I can't go anywhere in public with you." I place her hand on the raging hard-on in my pants.

"I can take care of that problem." She strokes her hand along my length.

A deep groan comes from my chest, and my dick presses into Ally, chasing the feeling of her hand. But I want something more—the true turn on—of making *Ally* feel good. Our moment at the benefit, alone in the heart of the maze, has been living in my mind non-stop for the past week. I need to hear those sweet sounds leave her lips again and see the look on her face as she climaxes. If I'm careful, I can do it without ruining her hair and makeup.

Ally's hand moves to stroke me again, but I grab her thighs, eliciting a surprised gasp from her as I hoist her legs around my waist. I carry her to the closest surface, sitting her on the kitchen counter.

"Dan, what are you—" She gasps again but catches on quickly when I slip off her heels and trace kisses up her legs, over the fishnets, and arrive at the top of her thighs. She leans back on her elbows, adjusting the angle of her hips, allowing me to remove her stockings and panties.

"Fuck." I spread her thighs. My throat works as I stare at her wet pussy, deciding what I want to do with it. My dick is dripping with pre-cum, growing harder at the thought of her pussy clenched around it. But that's tonight's treat, I've decided, one I am going to indulge in for hours.

I bend down, brushing my lips against the soft skin between Ally's thighs, her legs trembling at my touch. And then I go in for what I really want, licking a trail from the base of her wet opening all the way up to her clit.

She trembles and her head falls back with a moan. "Dan, I'm supposed to be making *you* feel good today."

"Believe me, baby, this is making me feel *so* fucking good." I groan at her sweet taste, having jerked off countless times over the years to the thought of eating Ally out and feeling her come on my tongue.

"I know, but—"

I take another lick, and this time, my lips linger on her clit, kissing and sucking. She gasps my name, and her breath comes out in shorter and sharper bursts.

"I know how needy you are for orgasms. You'll let me make you come, and you won't object. Isn't that right?"

She nods and lets out a desperate moan of agreement as her hips begin to move in sync with my mouth. My gaze trails up to watch Ally's face while I'm licking her out. She's already watching me, struggling to keep herself upright on her elbows but fascinated by the sight of my head between her legs. She claps a hand to her mouth, muffling a moan.

"No need to be quiet," I say. "Let the neighbors hear. None of them know I'm in here with my sister."

She releases her hand, panting as I continue sucking her clit. The sounds she makes are so fucking hot I have to brush a hand along my dick to relieve some of the ache. She's still holding back on me, though, so used to us needing to be quiet. I slip a finger inside her tight opening and watch Ally lose herself in pleasure, her elbows giving way as she cries out and collapses on the counter.

"That's my good girl." I add another finger, finding her G-spot with ease and teasing it, causing Ally to arch her back and grip the countertop.

She's working toward an orgasm. Her muscles continuously clench and release around my fingers, building the pleasure, like I taught her to do. Her moans are growing louder and more frantic.

"That's it, baby. You can do it. You're almost there."

She tightens around my fingers and her body quivers as she begs me, "Dan, don't stop, please. I'm so close."

I can't resist her pleas and suck her clit deeper into my mouth. Her pussy clenches my fingers so incredibly tight and finally she surrenders, her body convulsing. Her hips jerk as she lets out a high-pitched moan, coming on my fingers and tongue.

Fuck, she's delicious.

Ally's breaths are ragged as she comes down from her orgasm. Her face is flushed, and her eyes dazed. The best birthday present ever.

It's not long before she sits up, resting her hands on my chest, and kisses me. "Now it's your turn. Teach me how to make my boyfriend come with my mouth."

I've spent so many goddamn nights thinking about this, beating my dick to the thought of Ally sucking me dry. I want my cock between those luscious red lips and my cum spilling out of her mouth.

She steps down from the counter and lowers to her knees in front of me, releasing me from the waistband of my pants. Ally remains still for a moment, staring at my erection with curiosity. I smirk, wondering what she's thinking. This is the first time she's getting a proper look at me. Quite possibly, it's the first time she's seen any man naked in real life. Last week in the maze, when she had her hand wrapped around my cock, the night was too dark to see much.

"You want to stop?" Before I can finish asking the question, she licks the pre-cum from the tip of my dick.

I hiss as a ripple of urgency spreads through me, already knowing this is going to be the best head I've ever received. Ally won't have to work hard to get me off. "Take it in your mouth," I instruct.

She does as I say, eager to please, and slides her tongue from base to tip before forming a tight seal around my cock with her lips, her cheeks hollowing out with suction. I grasp the countertop for support, groaning at the intense pleasure of her warm mouth. Her tongue swirls around the tip as she gazes up at me.

"So pretty with my cock in your mouth, sis."

She moans, aroused by my words. I stroke her cheek then thread my hand through her hair, withdrawing my cock then slowly feeding it back between her lips.

She continues the pace, worshipping my dick with her mouth. I watch every second of it, loving the way her lips slide along me, so perfect and tight.

"Fuck, baby, that's it. Just like that. You're a natural at pleasing your man."

Her lips part, and she takes me deeper, causing my cock to hit the back of her throat.

"Shit." I pull out to prevent myself from coming. My little virgin tried to deep-throat me. So eager to please. I won't last a second if she tries it again.

Ally licks her lips and smiles, deeply satisfied by her effect on me, then gets right back to blowing me, increasing her speed. My legs can barely hold me up, she feels that incredible. I lean over her, bracing myself with my free hand against the kitchen wall as I continue watching Ally beneath me.

"You've got my dick feeling so good. I'm not going to last."

She moans, the vibrations traveling up my cock and pushing me closer to the edge. Unable to hold back, I start fucking her mouth.

"That sound you just made. Do you like this, Ally, sucking my dick?"

She nods, sucking harder, so determined to please me.

"Fuck, the sight of you with my dick between your lips. I'm about to come. If you don't want my cum in your mouth, you need to stop right this second."

She sucks harder, her lips forming an even tighter seal around my cock. I grit my teeth, trying to hold back. I want to last longer and prolong this moment I've waited years for, but I'm a lost cause.

My control slips and I'm gasping Ally's name as I spill into her mouth. My cock jerks with each spurt. When I see her throat work, swallowing me down, I come harder, the sight almost too much to process. She keeps sucking and swallowing, trying to get every last drop out of me. I can barely breathe, the high is so intense.

Slowly, she pulls back, releasing me from her mouth. I can't think straight, stunned by the intensity of the orgasm. My heart is pounding in my chest, my body pulsing with a rush of adrenaline.

I pull her up and wrap her in my arms, kissing her deeply as I hold her close. "You're incredible," I whisper, pushing a few strands of hair from her face. "You swallowed. You didn't have to."

"I wanted to. I liked it." She kisses me softly. "I already want to do it again."

I laugh against her lips, enjoying her line of thinking. "Come on, let's take this to the shower."

CHAPTER TWENTY-FOUR

ALLY

I'm living in delusion and it's the happiest I've ever been.

I don't let myself dwell on how this is for only one day. I'm Dan's and he's mine, and I've never experienced this level of emotional intimacy with another person, not even with Dan, until now. He's let me be with him on his birthday when he could have turned me away. There was a promise involved, but he could have broken it.

I like that I'm the one who can comfort him on this difficult day, with my words as well as my body. I loved taking him in my mouth and locking eyes with him as I sucked his cock; the way his teeth clenched and the sharp hisses that left his lips, like he was almost in pain; the way he tasted when he came in my mouth and I swallowed him down; the kisses that followed. I love how he stripped my clothes off and took me into the shower, then pressed me against the wet tiled wall and slid his fingers back inside me.

The lunch reservations I made for us went unattended. The movie tickets I pre-ordered were wasted. We haven't left Dan's apartment all day. My lips are bruised from all of

Dan's kisses and the make out sessions on his couch. I'm tender between my legs from the number of times Dan insisted on fucking me with his hand.

And I have no complaints.

At five p.m., I convince him to leave the apartment with me for an early dinner since we skipped all meals throughout the day. We do our best to ignore paparazzi when dining at a boutique French restaurant. Afterward, we attend another showing of the movie we missed, where we can be away from prying eyes.

In the dark theater, with no eyes on us, he pulls my legs across his lap and holds me in his arms. My head rests on his shoulder as we watch the movie. For once, Dan and I are able to be affectionate with each other in public, and it feels so perfect. Everything is a dream, until the movie ends, and I realize Dan is acting quieter than usual.

"You okay?" I ask as we return to the street, standing beneath the marquee lights of the theater's entrance.

"Yeah. Just... the movie was the first time I've stopped all day. My mind started drifting to bad places."

"Maybe a movie wasn't the best idea." I check the time on my phone. It's only eight p.m. We could return to Dan's apartment, but I don't want to do that when he's feeling off. One of my backup plans for the day comes to mind. "Will you take me to The Scarlet Mirage?"

His lips twitch with surprise, then rise into a teasing grin. "You aren't scared of tarnishing your reputation?"

"If this speakeasy is so secretive, shouldn't my reputation be safe?"

"Fair point. But I'm curious as to why you want to go there."

"It's Felix's baby and you're always hanging out there. I

want to see what all the fuss is about. Plus, I was thinking I could have another 'first' with you and order a cocktail."

Amusement fills Dan's eyes. "Jesus fuck. How can you be twenty-one in a month and never have tried a cocktail?"

"Shut up." I push his arm, laughing.

"Okay, I'll take you to The Scarlet Mirage."

Midtown Manhattan. Felix runs a sophisticated cocktail lounge, modern in interior and with New Age Electronic music. We don't linger in the lounge area. Dan leads me to a busy corridor filled with multiple doors leading to restrooms and staff quarters. He stops at an unmarked door, where a man dressed in a black and red striped suit stands guard. The man lets us enter after sharing a knowing glance with Dan.

Inside, we're met with a powder room. Dan steps up to a floor-to-ceiling mirror gilded with old-world embellishments that clash with the modern style of the venue. He slips his hand behind the frame. I'm about to ask what he's doing, but my question is answered when the mirror unlatches from the wall, swinging open as a doorway to someplace dark.

"Impressive."

"Wait till you see what's downstairs," he says. "Ladies first."

As soon as I step through the hidden door, darkness engulfs me, all but for the red neon signs on either side of the wall, illuminating a narrow staircase leading to the basement. The distant echo of smooth jazz travels up the staircase, along with a hum of voices.

I pause for a moment at the top of the stairs, my heart

thumping. The dull red glow of the neon lights makes it look like sin down there. Entering this speakeasy is the first time I'll have purposefully done something illegal, and while I have confidence my presence will remain unknown, being here is still a little nerve-wracking.

But I can't deny the allure of The Scarlet Mirage. A spark of excitement burns in my chest, the idea of doing something wrong, and I follow that lure, slowly descending each step.

As I make my way down, the music grows louder. The hum of voices becomes more distinct, mingling with laughter and the clinking of glasses. The air is filled with the scent of cigar smoke and liquor.

Finally, I reach the basement and turn the corner, finding myself standing at the entrance of a hidden paradise, transported back in time to the Roaring Twenties.

Everything captures the essence of the era, from the jazz band on stage to the Art Deco furniture and paintings. Even the people are dressed like they're from the Prohibition era, the gentlemen in three-piece suits and the ladies in sparkly flapper dresses. I'm out of place in my pink sun dress. The sexy red dress I wore at Dan's apartment would be more appropriate, but he made it clear that dress is for his eyes only.

"Incredible, huh?" Dan must see the amazement on my face.

"Now I understand why Felix makes a fortune off this place. It's amazing."

"Should we order that first drink of yours?"

I nod, and we make our way to the bar, through the many chairs and tables and people lounging on velvet couches. Dan passes me a drinks menu. I skim through it, seeing a list of cocktails with names I've never heard of.

Chicago Fizz, Gin Rickey, Southside, Hanky Panky, and many more, all in the theme of the 1920s, no doubt.

"I'll get a whiskey on ice," Dan orders from the bartender. "Sis, what would you like?"

My gaze flicks to Dan's, hearing the smug tone in the way he calls me his sister. The two of us have a silent conversation, Dan fucking me with his eyes, knowing I like how wrong the name sounds coming from his lips. I'm sure that's why he said it.

"I don't know what any of these drinks are. Will you order me something that tastes nice?"

He nods at the bartender. "And a Bee's Knees."

"Cute name. What's it taste like?"

Dan leans against the bar, grinning at me while the bartender mixes our drinks. "It's sweet, with honey, like you. You'll like it."

"Baby sis." I hear Felix's name for me cutting through the buzz of voices and a saxophonist improvising on stage. The name is endearing when Felix says it and holds none of the filth present in Dan's voice when referring to us as siblings. "Never thought I'd see you here."

Felix steps up to me, fitting right into the atmosphere with a pinstriped suit. He'd be intimidating, if I didn't know him better, looking like a 1920s gangster. Tattoos poke above his collar and his blond hair is smoothed back. His eyes shift to my left, noticing Dan for the first time, and his forehead creases with surprise.

"How on earth did you get Dan out of his apartment today? It's good to see you, bro." He pats Dan on the forearm and nods his head to the side, gesturing to a row of booths along the back wall. "You're just in time for a little brotherly bonding. Killian and Tyler are here too. You two should join us."

Surprise gets the better of me, and I blurt out a question I probably shouldn't. "You're here with Tyler?" Felix raises an eyebrow at the question, and I realize it was perhaps a little rude of me. "Sorry, I just thought you two didn't—"

"On a day like today, Tyler and I can put aside our differences."

I still don't understand what the issue is between Felix and Tyler. Before I can ask anything, Dan speaks, not sounding thrilled. "I guess we can sit for a bit."

Our drinks are placed on the bar and Dan passes my cocktail to me. My drink is a tone of soft yellow, served in a stemmed coupe glass, broad and shallow, and is absolute decadence. The cocktail touches my lips, a delicious balance between sweet and citrus.

Dan watches me, pleased by my reaction, and places a hand on my upper back, guiding us through the crowd and to a booth where the three brothers sit with playing cards and poker chips scattered across the table.

Killian and Tyler look as shocked as Felix was to see Dan, but they brush off their surprise and greet us casually.

"We're about to start a game. You two want in?" Tyler asks us, lighting the end of a cigar.

"No. We're not staying long." Dan nods for me to take a seat. I slide into the booth and he follows, the two of us alone on one side.

With the seating a little cramped, my thigh presses against Dan's, and I hold back a gasp when feeling his hot palm on the inside of my thigh, hidden from view beneath the table. The tiniest smirk curls his lips, and he raises his glass to disguise it.

The poker game begins with each brother placing a tower of poker chips in the center of the table. "What have you two been up to today?" Killian asks, and I almost choke on my drink.

"Dinner. Movies. Not much," Dan answers.

"You receive the same copy and paste text from Dad as we all did this morning?"

"He knows not to message me today."

"What did it say?" I ask, not wanting to overstep my boundaries, but also feeling bad for Josh.

Killian rolls his eyes, drawling an answer. "The same old crap. *I'm proud of your many accomplishments. Your mother is looking down on you and would be proud.*"

Dan groans.

"Maybe we should change the subject," I say, wanting to keep the conversation positive.

"It's fine, Ally."

"Josh *is* proud of you. *All* of you," I offer. I know none of them want to hear it, but I want them to know Josh is genuine. "He loves you all. He told me so when I mentioned spending Dan's birthday with him."

Tyler leans back, sucking on his cigar and puffing smoke hoops into the air. "It's generic bullshit, Ally. Even if he was being sincere, it's too late. It doesn't make up for the years of abandonment while we grew up."

The situation is complicated, and I understand their side too. I only wish I knew how to mend things between them all. "I told Josh I wouldn't get involved, and I won't. But he knows he messed up. I don't think he knows how to fix it. I won't say anything else."

"As I said, the damage is done," Tyler replies. "We only hang around because of you and Amabella."

It's a nice sentiment, that my mother and I have found such a good family. But it makes me sad for Josh.

The boys move on to the next stage of their game. As

another round of betting takes place, I sip my drink, my gaze wandering out of the booth, admiring a lady wearing a dress of fringe tassels, the woman beside her with a fur wrap and—

A man sitting in an armchair, glaring at Dan.

"Why is that man looking at you like that?" I ask.

All four brothers peer out of the booth to see who I'm talking about. The man is older, perhaps thirty. Tall and lanky and with a thick, dark, beard.

Felix laughs. "That's Phillip Jones. He's a regular here. The C.E.O. of a software company. He played poker with Dan earlier in the week and lost a million dollars."

"That rumor is true?" I gasp.

Dan shrugs, like it's no big deal.

Felix laughs again, twirling a poker chip between his fingers. "Man, Jones is *pissed* off. How did Dad handle the rumor?"

"I don't know," Dan says. "I've got a bunch of missed calls from him. Don't plan on returning them."

Killian deals a card from the deck, and while he, Felix, and Tyler contemplate their next move, I speak quietly with Dan. "What do you plan to do with all this money you win?"

"Spend it on you," he answers low enough for only me to hear, sliding his palm a little higher up my thigh.

My breath catches. I tell myself to concentrate. "Seriously. You have a few luxuries in life. A nice car. Expensive suits. But it's not like you're living an extravagant lifestyle, buying yachts and private jets."

"I like the thrill of the game and the strategy involved. Money is a nice extra."

"So, would it kill you to donate some of it? The money could go to a really good cause. You could help people who are in dangerous living conditions like me and my mom used to be. There are loads of charities. Plus, it would get Mom and Josh off your back about the bad image your poker games bring to Forever Families."

Dan's jaw tenses with displeasure.

"What? I'm only saying how I feel," I tell him.

"It's not that. I hate picturing what your life with that bastard used to be like. And perhaps you're right. When you pitch the donation idea like that, it does sound appealing."

The music on stage fades to an end. "Ladies and gentle-man," a man speaks into the microphone with a saxophone strapped around his neck. "For this next song, we're opening up the dance floor for a little swing dancing."

Upbeat music resumes and people make their way to in front of the stage.

I bring my cocktail to my lips, gulping down the last of the sweet alcohol, feeling a pleasant dizziness and in the mood for some fun. "You want to dance?"

Dan laughs. "Neither of us know how to swing dance."

"So? It will be fun."

He shakes his head, still laughing. "Fine. Let's go."

Dan slides out of the booth, taking my hand and helping me to my feet.

"Bro," Felix says before we walk off, and from the serious look in his eyes and the sincerity of his voice, I know he has something important to say. "I won't push it, but Mom would be proud, you know." Dan's throat strains as he holds his brother's gaze. "I have few memories of her, but I remember her pregnant with you, and she was so happy."

Killian finishes his drink and adds on, "I wish you wouldn't feel so guilty about what happened. None of us really remember her. Think of it this way—shit happens, but now Dad is happily in love with Amabella and we have Ally."

Dan nods, pensive about Killian's words. I'm not sure swing dancing is the best idea anymore. Before I can tell Dan it's fine if he just wants to leave, someone bumps into me. I'm knocked forward, only managing to stay upright due to Dan steadying me.

"Oh, pardon me," a man says. I look up, finding the man who was glaring at Dan moments ago. Phillip Jones, Felix called him. He smiles at me, yet there's something sly within his eyes that leaves me unsettled. The guy also reeks of liquor, and I question whether he's drunk. "Such a pretty little girlfriend you have here, Blackwood."

"Watch the way you speak about her," Dan warns.

"What, I can't compliment your girl?"

Muffled laughter comes from the brothers in the booth, not realizing how perceptive this Phillip guy is.

"Jones, is there something you want?" Dan asks, bored by their interaction. "Or are you still licking your wounds over the one mill you lost fair and square?"

"Yeah, there is something I want. You have my money. I think it's only fair I take away something precious from you."

Phillip lunges forward with eyes set on me, and before I can react, there's a flash of silver slicing through the air, heading my way. Dan pushes me behind himself. My other three brothers launch out of the booth and tackle Phillip, but they're not fast enough.

I look down at the sharp, hot pain in my left arm, finding a stream of blood trailing down to my wrist.

"Fuck, Ally." Dan grabs my injured arm, out of his mind with panic.

"I'm okay. The cut isn't that bad." And it isn't. The fright is worse than anything.

He keeps swearing and grabs a bunch of napkins from a nearby table, pressing them to the wound on my forearm. All around us, people are gasping and watching Phillip struggle on the floor. The band has stopped playing. No one is dancing.

"Go, Dan," Felix orders. "Get Ally out of here and take care of her. We'll handle Jones."

Dan takes me by the waist, shielding me with his body as he pushes through the crowd. "Shit. I'm so sorry, Ally. How deep is the cut?"

"Don't apologize. Everything is fine."

"Everything is *not* fine. You nearly got stabbed. If I hadn't pulled you out of the way in time—" He cuts himself off with a groan and a whole lot of self-hatred. "None of this would have happened if it weren't for me."

CHAPTER TWENTY-FIVE
ALLY

Dan sits me on his couch, kneeling in front of me with a box of first aid supplies. He takes hold of my injured forearm, being delicate as he disinfects the wound. The apartment is filled with a heavy silence, broken only by the distant sound of traffic. Through the dim glow of his red neon lights, I watch his face contorted with guilt.

He hasn't spoken much since we left The Scarlet Mirage, other than to ask how my arm is feeling. But I've felt the self-loathing within him every second of the journey back here.

"Tell me what you're thinking," I whisper.

He finishes with the disinfectant and searches through the first aid supplies, avoiding my gaze.

"This day, every year, is horrendous. A reminder of what a fuck up I am."

"Dan." I rest my good hand on his, forcing him to stop rummaging for medical equipment and listen. Though, he still won't look at me. "Having you in my life is the best thing that has ever happened to me."

"I almost got you killed." His hand slips out from

beneath mine and he dresses my wound, taking care as he winds a bandage around my forearm.

"You're the first real friend I've ever had. You make me feel like I'm not alone in this world. You believe in me during times when I don't believe in myself. When we met, I was having frequent panic attacks. You were the only one who could help me. You're my person."

He breaks at my last words, his head hanging between his shoulders. I place my hand on Dan's cheek, feeling him tremble beneath my touch. My heart aches, seeing him in this much pain.

He takes a breath and finally meets my eyes, cupping my jaw in his palms. "Ally, if anything were to ever happen to you, I don't think I could live with myself. You're all that is good in this world. You're everything to me."

"Nothing will happen to me."

Dan closes the distance between us with a soft but desperate kiss. His hands move from my jaw to the nape of my neck, his touch feather-light yet electrifying. And then the gentleness is gone and he's clinging to me like he's afraid I'll vanish. I slide forward on the couch, spreading my legs around Dan's waist, inviting him in closer.

Our kisses grow deeper and more urgent as I press my body to his. Dan's breath comes in ragged gasps, hot against my lips as his hands slip down my waist and up beneath my dress, grabbing my hips and ass. His fingertips dig into my skin, and I'm sure they'll leave small indents in their wake. Maybe even slight bruises. I need his mark on me. Only his. I want to look at myself in the mirror after all this is over and see evidence that reminds me of the passion from this night.

I tilt my head back, exposing the column of my throat to him. He takes advantage, pressing open-mouthed kisses to my skin, each one sending a jolt of desire straight to my core.

Dan's lips draw back, leaving an unwanted coolness to my skin. I meet his gaze, and though guilt still lives within his eyes, he's overpowered by pain. The same pain I feel in myself, knowing this will be over between us tomorrow. We can't continue sneaking around. But I told Dan we have this one day together where the future isn't our concern. I won't dwell on the heartache. Tonight, I'm his.

Tomorrow is a different story.

"Take me to your bed," I whisper.

With a newfound urgency, Dan lifts me off the couch and carries me to his bedroom where everything takes on a blue tinge from the neon lights. The neon is so him and I love being in his space.

My heart pounds, knowing I'm about to be with Dan in such an intimate way that I've always wanted but never thought possible. He lays me beneath him, and his kisses become more fervent, almost aggressive. His hands find the zip on the side of my dress, and after a few moments of attempting to pull it down, Dan rips the fabric, tearing it straight off my body.

"I'll buy you a new dress." His dick grinds between my legs and we both groan. "I'll buy you anything you want."

Dan fists my lace panties, ripping them off me too. My bra comes off in the same manner. I'm not mad about the ruined clothes. His urgency to get me naked only heightens my arousal.

Dan's tongue finds my nipple, his thumb pinching and stroking the other, and I clutch his shoulders, gasping as pleasure bursts through me. His hands roam my body, hungered to explore every curve, every contour as if trying to etch me into his memory. The way his touch makes me feel is like nothing I could have ever imagined. I want him to take me further, to make me his completely. And I want it now.

I press up, sitting with Dan on his bed, my fingers trembling as I undo the buttons of his shirt, exposing his bare chest. His skin is warm beneath my fingertips, and I marvel at the strength of his muscles, admiring his body in the dim blue light. He pulls his shirt off and steps out of his pants, standing naked in front of me.

I stare at the thick length of his cock, a little nervous at the size of it. I've always assumed my first time wouldn't hurt because of toys I've used, but none of them were the size of him.

"I'll be gentle," Dan says, seeing my thoughts reflected in my eyes.

I shake my head, meeting his gaze. "I don't want you to be."

I've been shameless in front of Dan with the things I've done. Unrecognizable to even myself. So often, I've performed sexual acts in front of him that were about pushing the boundaries and seeking the thrill of doing something wrong. But tonight, with Dan right now, none of this is about thrill-seeking. I'm wholeheartedly in love with this man.

"We have one night together. I want no barriers," I tell him. "Don't hold back on me just because it's my first time."

His eyes darken with possession. "Don't say that, Ally, or I'll truly lose control."

"I mean it."

"Then open your legs. You're about to get fucked." Dan returns to the bed, climbing over me and laying me flat with kisses.

His dominance is always my undoing. I follow his command, gasping when Dan grabs my thighs and yanks them around his waist. The tip of his cock strokes a line up the entire length of my wetness, making me whimper from how much I need him.

"Slow at first," he says, hovering above me on his hands. "I'll need to get you adjusted to my dick before I can fuck you how I want to." His words send a spark of arousal all the way from my clit to my toes. He strokes his dick along my wetness again. "This will hurt a little. But then it will start to feel good. *Real* good, I promise."

I angle my hips, in search of the head of his cock. His hardness presses at the opening between my legs and inches in. My breath quickens and I shut my eyes, trying to work through the initial sting.

"Fuck," Dan groans, the sound filled with obsession. He pushes in more, and it's too much.

"Stop," I gasp. I'm stretched so tight around him, I need a moment.

His tongue returns to my nipples, drawing out an unexpected cry of pleasure that helps with the pain.

"That's it. Good girl," Dan praises. "I know you can take more. Your little pussy is so fucking tight, but it was made for my dick."

I nod, signaling for him to give me more. His cock sinks deeper, all the way until our hips are locked tight with each other. This time, I cry out with both pain and bliss, my spine arching off the mattress at the feel of him hitting my back wall. Dan shudders above me, continuing to kiss and brush my nipples, worshiping my breasts to lessen the pain.

"Breathe." He lowers my back to the bed, his breath

heavy and his eyes dark, monitoring my pain level. "Are you ready for me to start moving?"

I shake my head. I'm stretched so tightly around his cock that it hurts, but in the best way possible. I don't think I can take more, but I don't want him to stop being this deep inside me. My legs wrap around his waist, keeping him in place.

"Trust me." He releases my legs and pulls out, all the way to the tip, the emptiness making me crave him again.

Dan slowly thrusts back inside, as deep as the first time, and the feeling is so intense that I can't help myself from moaning.

"I know, baby. I know," he rasps, tilting his hips. His dick flexes inside me, drawing out another gasp from me. "Fuck, Ally. You are so tight. You're doing so well. You feel incredible."

He thrusts again, this time a little faster, and the movement is easier for me to take. We find a slow rhythm, my hips working in time with his. I watch him move above me and try to memorize every little detail about this moment, the way his jaw begins to tighten and his muscles strain. The blue light cast upon us and how I'll think back to this moment every time I see a neon light from now on.

"Look at you, taking my dick." He watches where his cock pumps into me, shuddering. I love having this effect on him, knowing he's enjoying my body. "You're so good at it, Ally. Such a fast learner. Your body was made for sex. Made for me to fuck."

Dan's praise, along with his hands roaming my body, sends shivers down my spine.

On his next thrust, his teeth clench and he sucks in a sharp hiss of air. "I've thought about this every day, Ally. Every single day for years."

"Me too." I can barely form the words, I'm so overcome by the connection we share in this moment.

"You told me to not hold back on you. I can't keep this slow pace much longer. You have no idea how hard I want to fuck this little body of yours."

"Do it. Please."

Dan's hands, once gentle, now grip my hips fiercely, pulling me onto his cock with each thrust. I whimper as he hits a spot inside me that makes my toes curl. My back curves, trying to get him deeper.

I can feel myself slipping away from reality, overcome by the pleasure he's giving me. His thrusts are now ragged and desperate, his moans growing louder with each one. He's not holding anything back, only taking me harder and faster, and I'm lost in the connection of our bodies, finally becoming one. Lost in the dizzying pleasure that spreads through my entire body. Dan has taken control of me, and I'm loving every second of it. The feeling of his cock filling me up and the raw power of his movements drive me wild. This is all I've ever wanted, to be Dan's to fuck.

Our bodies slap together in a perfect unison, our sweat mingling as we both reach a state of complete surrender to the moment. The way we move together is raw and primal. Dan's eyes are locked onto mine, never breaking the connection as he thrusts deeper and harder, creating a low, guttural moan that echoes through the room.

He leans down, nipping at my neck and collarbone, a mix of pain and pleasure. His lips return to mine, each kiss more consuming, our breaths mingling as we continue to fuck with an intensity that's both exhilarating and terrifying, because I know I am going to be broken for life after this.

The sensation of his dick sliding in and out of me is

driving me wild, every thrust rubbing against my clit and eliciting a new cry of pleasure.

"You're taking my dick so well," Dan grunts. "I knew you would."

I nod, too overwhelmed to speak.

"You're getting close. I can feel your pussy growing tighter. Clench your muscles around my cock on purpose."

I follow the instructions, squeezing my inner muscles, and an unexpected rush of pleasure shoots through me, making my neck arch.

"That's it. Good girl. You like that, huh? Do it again. I'm going to make you come on my cock."

I squeeze, the heat growing in my pussy, pulling me close to my climax.

His lips brush along mine and he murmurs, "You and I are perfect for each other. Never forget it."

Hearing Dan speak those words makes my muscles tighten around his cock involuntarily, and I can't hold back any longer. I grip his shoulders, digging my nails into his skin as I reach my peak. My orgasm arrives in an explosion of mind-numbing ecstasy, every nerve ending in my body alight.

"Fuck, Ally. I need to fill you with my cum."

"Yes, *please*," I beg through my orgasm, my legs tightening around his waist, locking him deep within me so he can't pull out even if he tries.

His thrusts become erratic, each one impaling me deeper, harder, until finally he groans the most incredible sounds I've ever heard, filling me with his release. I feel his hips convulse, his cock twitching inside me as he floods me. Every inch of my body is tingling, singing with bliss. This is what I've always wanted, needed, to have Dan come inside me. To be marked by his cum. Claimed and owned.

Dan's rhythm slows down to a gentle pump, and he kisses me through the movement until we find stillness. We lay here, spent and panting, sharing breath in the blue light, his cock still inside me. The moment is perfect, everything I imagined it would be and more.

"Thank you," Dan murmurs against my lips. There's vulnerability in his voice again, like when he kneeled in front of me on the couch, tending to my wound.

"For what?"

"Giving this day a new meaning. There'll always be sadness, but now, this memory of you overpowers everything else."

DAN

Mid-morning, Ally potters around my bedroom, blissfully humming a song while packing her belongings. My eyes never leave her as I sit on the edge of my bed, shuffling my neon cards and admiring the shape of her as she changes into a dress. The flashbacks of last night are non-stop. I've owned that tight little body of Ally's in ways I never should have, and instead of the sex quenching my thirst for her, it's made me more addicted.

Nothing compares to feeling Ally coming on my dick.

Me, coming inside her.

Fuck, it was the most incredible moment I've ever experienced.

Also, the most irresponsible moment. I always wrap it up with girls. With Ally—the girl I should have been most cautious to use a condom with—I wasn't thinking, too caught up in the moment. Too fucking obsessed with finally having her after all these years.

"We didn't use a condom last night."

My words are calm despite the foolishness of my actions. She's calm too, and I have to wonder why. Ally is the kind of girl I imagine to be meticulous about birth control, especially given the public disgrace that would come with getting pregnant by me. I think back to the way she begged me to come inside her last night. Perhaps she's on her own form of birth control and there's no issue at all.

Ally's humming stops. She zips up her bag, smiling to herself. "I know."

That's it? That's her answer?

"Are you on birth control?" I ask.

"No." She finally looks up at me, still at ease, her gaze focusing on the cards in my hands. "I'm not worried. I should have mentioned this sooner, but my period is due in three days. It's like clockwork every month."

"Not a great birth control method."

She shrugs, her soft smile never fading. "I know how a female's cycle works. We gave ourselves one night together. I didn't want any barriers."

"Neither did I," I speak quietly.

She mistakes my tone as something negative, and joins me by my bed, straddling my lap and kissing me softly. I place the deck of cards in my pocket and hold her close.

"You're freaking out that I'm pregnant."

The complete opposite. Of course, I don't want Ally to be pregnant, but if she is, some part of me thinks it wouldn't be such a disaster. It would cause a shit show with our family. The media would go wild and Forever Families' reputation would be severely damaged. But I'd find some way to keep her. Make her mine. She'd be tethered to me for life.

"I'm not freaking out." I return her kiss. "Just tell me as soon as your period arrives."

"I will." Her forehead rests against mine and she sighs heavily. With that one sigh, I sense her mood shift and all the happiness we shared last night draining from her. "I should go."

"Ally, we can find a way to make this work. You're afraid to go public, I get it. We can keep this a secret—"

"We've spoken about this. Sooner or later, it won't be a secret. Please don't ruin how amazing last night was."

I close my eyes, clinging to her for our last moments, realizing I've gone about everything wrong. Since Ally's return from Paris, I've been fighting for her, for us, every step of the way. We've made progress. She's learned to indulge in what she wants and not feel ashamed of it. Yet at the core, she's still the same timid girl who lives her life by the rulebook to please everyone else. Ally wants us, she's just not ready, and there's nothing I can do to convince her that we should be together. She needs to come to this decision in her own time and way.

Ally rises from my lap and grabs her overnight bag. I walk her to my front door, hating every second that is slipping away from us. How can I experience such an extreme high one second, to now this, where I feel like my heart is being ripped from my chest.

Before Ally reaches for the handle, she turns to me with her gaze on the ground. "I think we should spend some time apart to make this easier on ourselves."

Her suggestion only intensifies the ache within me. I lift Ally's chin, holding her gaze so she can see how serious these next words out of my mouth are. "You're it for me, Ally. There's no one else and there never will be. You'll be back. I don't know when. It could be days. Months. Years. But you'll be back, and I'll be here waiting for you. Go do what you need to. I won't hold it against you. I've waited this long for you. I can wait longer."

I retrieve the deck of cards from my pocket, sifting

through them until I find the Queen of Hearts with Ally's handwriting on it. *You'll always be my person.*

"You gave this back to me when you left for Paris, but it belongs to you. You'll always be my person, Ally. No matter what. My Queen of Hearts."

She takes it from me and nods, her bottom lip trembling and a stray tear falling down her cheek as she gazes at the card then back up at me. "I shouldn't say this, but I love you. I never stopped."

"I know. I never stopped loving you either." I press my lips to hers, trying to live in this moment forever as I hold her tight in my arms. Her kisses are desperate, mixed with soft whimpers. I could take her again, right here against the door. Ally knows it and I can feel she wants it as badly as I do.

But she has more self-restraint than I do and pulls back from the kiss, her chin trembling as she speaks her last words to me. "Please don't wait for me. You deserve more than I can give you."

She disappears out the door and everything is suddenly so quiet. So empty and lifeless. I don't know what to do with myself. I'm hollow.

Not even a minute after I've closed the door, my phone rings. Hope ignites within me that Ally is calling to tell me she needs more than one night of being my girlfriend. I race to grab my phone from my pocket, all hope vanishing when I see Amabella's name on the screen.

The second I answer the phone, Amabella's panicked voice erupts. "Dan, please tell me Ally is all right. It's everywhere in the news that she got stabbed last night. I haven't been able to get ahold of her."

Shit. "Yes, she's fine. And she didn't get stabbed. It was a shallow knife wound."

"Why is there a knife wound at all? What situation was she put in?"

The self-hatred returns. "A man was drunk and tried to attack her because... I won a game against him."

Amabella's shocked gasp is overpowered by my father's stern voice, and I realize I've been placed on speakerphone. "Daniel, when are you going to learn how irresponsible your actions are? I can deal with your defiance against me but now you're putting Ally's life at risk? I can't understand you."

No rational conversation can be held with my father when he's in a mood like this. I don't have any fight within me today and hang up the phone. Though, for once, I'm not at odds with the man.

CHAPTER TWENTY-SEVEN

DAN

My arms ache as I punch the boxing bag over and over again. Sweat drips off me. I'm out of breath. Everything burns. But I don't stop.

"Man, what is *up* with you today?" Felix laughs.

Only now do I realize Felix's friends have left and the two of us are alone in his apartment gym. "What do you mean?" I take a breather, removing my boxing gloves to wipe my face with a towel.

Felix leans one hand high on the gym's squat rack, watching me curiously. "I've never seen you so... aggressive."

"I've got shit on my mind."

"Yeah, like what?"

"Nothing."

He laughs again, the sound smug. "Since when have you ever had girl issues?"

"What are you talking about?" I glare at him and gulp down water.

"Dad pisses you off, but you never let him get you this

riled up. You've lost hundreds of thousands of dollars in poker and never cared. So, it's got to be a girl."

Goddammit. "Fine. Yes, it's a girl."

"And?"

"And nothing." I place the gloves back on and resume punching.

"Wow." Felix laughs harder. "She must have really done a number on you."

I growl, punching the bag once more before giving Felix enough information to shut him up. "There's a girl who's off limits to me. End of story."

He shrugs. "So, what's the issue? Unless she's dating your brother, I don't see why she's so off limits."

I glance at Felix, surprised that he's mentioning Harper. For a while now, I've known he's had a thing for Tyler's girlfriend but she's not a topic we ever discuss. Felix and Harper rarely speak to each other. When they do, it's forced pleasantries at family events. I caught him looking at her a few years back, longer than a guy should ever look at his brother's girlfriend and realized there was something unspoken happening. When I asked him about it, he didn't say much, but made me promise to not tell anyone else.

"Bro, what's going on?" Felix pushes. "You clearly need someone to vent to."

I take a seat on a nearby bench and catch my breath. These last three days have been the most agonizing of my life. Not only am I going out of my mind unable to talk to Ally or hold her in my arms, but I still haven't heard news on whether her period has arrived. If there's one person I can trust with this secret, it's Felix. He won't like what I have to say, but given his situation with Harper, he's the least likely to judge.

"I gave you my word I wouldn't mention your Harper

situation to anyone. Do I have your word you'll do the same for me?"

"Of course."

"Blond, blue eyes." I start listing Ally's features, hoping Felix will catch on, like it somehow lessens the severity of my situation if I don't speak her name aloud. "Incredible piano player. Turns twenty-one in a month."

I see the exact moment realization hits Felix. The smug look washes off his face and he turns still. "Oh, fuck, man. You and Ally?"

I don't answer the question. His shock only reinforces the deep shit I'm in.

"Now I see your issue. I mean, look, that's... really fucked up."

"I *know* it's fucked up." I groan. "And to be clear, there is no *me and Ally*."

"Nothing has happened between you two?" he asks.

I shoot Felix a glare, which answers the question for me.

Felix sits down to absorb the information, scratching his jaw irritably. "I knew you two were close. I thought it was just friendship because of how difficult her past has been." He wipes a hand over his face in contemplation, then sets stern eyes upon me. "What Tyler said on your birthday is true, that we only remain a part of this family because of Ally and her mom. You might not see Ally as family, but we do, and I need to know you're not just fucking around with her to piss off Dad."

"This has nothing to do with Dad. I've kept my distance from Ally for years because I wanted to do right by this family. She went to Paris because she was trying to fight her feelings for me. I'm in love with her and always will be. But she won't be with me because of what others will think."

"Okay. I just needed to understand your situation. Not

that I *do* understand. But I needed to know you were doing right by her." Felix scrunches his eyes shut and pinches the bridge of his nose. "Wow, man, you're playing with fire,"

I rake my hand through my hair, pulling at the ends. "You don't know the half of it. I didn't use a condom."

"Shit." His gaze whips to me. "What the *fuck* were you thinking? I thought I taught you to always wear—"

"I wasn't thinking."

"Clearly. Is she pregnant?"

"I don't know. She's not worried. She says her period is due today, but I haven't heard from her yet."

Felix looks at a clock on his gym wall. "Six p.m. Fuck, man, you better hope you hear from her soon. I need a drink to deal with this. I can't imagine how *you're* feeling. Come on, we're going to The Scarlet Mirage."

Thursday night and Felix's speakeasy is fairly quiet. A solo female vocalist sings a melancholy song on stage, matching my mood perfectly. Felix and I sit at the bar, both nursing a whisky, though I've barely touched mine. I can't focus on anything other than getting confirmation that Ally isn't pregnant, and decide it's best to stay sober in case confirmation never arrives and I need to drive to Ally to support her.

"This whole thing with Ally is a lot to wrap my head around," Felix says. "But maybe she's been good for you. She got you to come out on your birthday."

"I've been thinking about a lot over the last couple of days. What I'm about to say is pretty fucked up. That comment Killian made about Mom on my birthday—*shit happens, but now Dad is happily in love with Amabella and we have Ally*—I don't want to admit it, but he's right. If Mom was still here, I never would have met Ally. Maybe everything happens for a reason. Maybe I'm finally okay with letting go of the issue around my birthday."

Felix side-eyes me, laughing in disbelief. "I've spent twenty-two years trying to convince you of this, and yet Ally is the one who gets the message through to your head. Okay, she *is* good for you. But could you just imagine if Dad and Amabella found out? You'd have corrupted their innocent little girl and brought disgrace to the Blackwood name and Forever Families."

"Oh, they would never forgive me." I spin my crystal whiskey glass in mindless circles on the wooden bar top, then check my phone. No messages. The silence is driving me insane. If I don't hear from Ally by the end of the night, I'm calling her, regardless that I agreed to not contact her. "I need to get off the topic of Ally. Tell me what's with you and Harper. You two were friends as kids. I remember you and Tyler used to spend a lot of time at her home growing up."

Felix sips his whiskey, chewing on ice. "The short version of the story—Harper and I used to sleep together before she started dating Tyler."

My eyebrows rise at the news, though it's not a total shock. I knew there'd have to be some explanation like this to warrant the tension between them all. "Does Tyler know you slept with her?"

"He certainly does." His answer is bitter. Felix downs the remainder of his drink and orders another one.

"I'm going to need more of an explanation."

"Growing up, Tyler was always Harper's best friend. I was close with her too until high school when I started getting in trouble with the law. Harper was my opposite.

She had strong morals, took pride in her education, had insane focus on ballet, and was proudly saving herself for marriage. She didn't approve of my choices and distanced herself from me. We barely spoke again until my senior year."

Felix's new drink arrives. He thanks the bartender and gulps half of the glass down. A moment later, he laughs under his breath, shaking his head at what I can only assume is some sordid memory. "Let's just say she changed her mind about a lot of things. About me and waiting for marriage. Whenever Harper and I were alone... The girl was... Well, I imagine it was like what you and Ally have. *Had.*"

His laughter has to be a coping mechanism. If Harper means to Felix what Ally means to me, and he lost her... I know how bad that hurts. After all these years, he's still hung up on the same girl. It's like looking at a reflection of myself and where I'll be in several years, still in love with Ally but watching her with another man. I asked to hear this story as a distraction from my own shit. Now I feel worse.

"So, where did it all go south?" I ask, knowing from experience there's nothing I can say or do that will offer Felix any relief.

"She wasn't just mine. Tyler and I used to share Harper."

I pause, not shocked that my brothers would share a girl but that Harper is the kind of girl who would be into that. "How did she end up with just Tyler?"

"I haven't had enough drinks to retell that part of the story."

"Do you still want her?"

Felix gulps down the rest of his whiskey. "It doesn't matter what I want. She made her choice and it was Tyler."

My phone vibrates. I pull it out from my pocket, my heart racing when I finally see Ally's name on the screen.

ALLY

I got my period.

I should be relieved. I *am* relieved. But now, I have no reason to talk to Ally. Now, I have to find some way to get on with my life without Ally by my side.

CHAPTER TWENTY-EIGHT

ALLY

Over two weeks have passed since I returned to the beach house after Dan's birthday, and I have never felt more smothered by my parents in my life.

To say they freaked out about the knife attack is an understatement. I can't blame them for their behavior when the media exaggerated and made the attack sound like a stabbing. I suppose what happens in The Scarlet Mirage isn't a complete secret after all. Although, the speakeasy itself was never mentioned in all the news articles, and from the photos that were leaked, nothing within the images distinguished the location.

Regardless, Mom and Josh are treating me more like a child than before, asking to be informed everywhere I go. They're not pleased with Dan, even though I told them the attack wasn't his fault.

Sacred Heart was not impressed with the news reports either and had harsh words to me about my image and how I shouldn't be placing myself in situations where a knife attack is in the realm of possibility.

It's been a tough two weeks. Tougher without Dan to

talk to. I think about that night we shared non-stop. About how he said he would wait for me. He's so perfect in every way, except that he's my stepbrother.

I've since gone on the pill, not because I intend on having sex anytime soon, but it seems like the sensible thing to do.

Wednesday night after work, I'm alone in the living room, practicing the piano, when Mom interrupts me. "Ally, honey, you have a visitor at the front door."

"Who is it?" I stand from the piano stool, surprised anyone would visit me unannounced.

She doesn't answer my question, just moves into the next room with a grin. Not suspicious at all. When I arrive at the front door, my mother's happiness all makes sense.

"Liam. Hi."

A nervous smile plays on my lips, as I'm not sure how to approach this encounter. Liam and I haven't spoken in two and a half weeks. In all honesty, I've barely thought about him, being consumed with Dan. But it's nice to see him. From the soft smile on Liam's face, I'd say he's pleased to see me too. Perhaps a little nervous from the way he shifts back and forth on his feet.

"Ally, hey. My band just finished playing at the local jazz club. I thought I'd stop by and see how you are. We never got a chance to speak properly about us."

I nod to the veranda swing gently swaying in the evening breeze. "Would you like to sit and chat?"

We take our seats on opposite ends, the swing long enough that there's a fair gap between us. I tuck my legs beneath me and turn to face Liam as we rock back and forth.

"I heard you playing the piano when I arrived," Liam says. "It sounded beautiful. *Moonlight Sonata*?"

"Yes. I'm impressed you know it."

"Most people know the *Moonlight Sonata*."

"Not the movement I was playing."

We laugh, and it's nice. Talking to Liam is like talking to a friend. And I realize I miss him, not in a romantic way, but because of all the good chats we had about music. He taught me things about jazz I didn't know I'd be interested in and gave me new experiences.

Our laughter fades, leaving us with a moment of silence. The mood between us is awkward, and I know we're both tiptoeing around the topic of our last phone call. I decide to speak first, seeing as this is a less sensitive issue for me.

"Liam, I hope we can still be friends. I genuinely mean it. How have you been since we last spoke on the phone?"

He rubs the back of his neck, his face a little strained. "Not good. I told you I needed some time. The truth is, I haven't stopped thinking about you."

His throat bobs as he searches for something else to say. I feel terrible, seeing him like this and knowing he's been struggling.

I slide closer to Liam and take his hand in mine before he can say anything further. "I'm sorry I've caused you pain but I'm not right for an open relationship. Even if I were, I see you as a friend, which means a lot since I don't have many friends."

His warm hand squeezes mine as he searches my eyes with softness. "Ally, I never shared with you the reason why I do open relationships. My parents had a bad marriage and as a kid, I witnessed them constantly arguing. They divorced when I was ten. After that, my father told me marriage is a lie people are tricked into. That being with one person forever sounds romantic at first, but the romance fades and one person can't fulfill all our needs. I took his word for it. But then... you ended things with me and... I know this will sound crazy, but I've spent the last two weeks thinking about a moment you and I shared in my apartment."

"Oh?" I draw my hand back from Liam's, unsure where he's going with this explanation.

"I was sitting on the couch with you in my arms and there was a stretch of silence between us that was so comfortable. I didn't feel the need to fill it with conversation. We were just together. I've never had that with anyone. The girl I went on a date with the following night... she was nice but... my mind was with you and how it felt when we were on the couch."

"Liam..."

"Please just let me finish. What I'm trying to say is I've come to realize we're all living our own lives, having our own experiences, and this jaded idea of monogamy is just my father's experience. When you ended things with me, I spent days missing you and questioning why I need anyone else. I want to be exclusive with you, Ally. I know you said you see me as a friend, but you didn't give us a chance to be anything more. I want that chance."

I bite my bottom lip, stunned by Liam's declaration. For a moment, I'm speechless as my mind tries to process Liam's words. They're beautiful but are a lot to take on board.

"I know that moment on the couch you're talking about. It was nice." I'm surprised I was able to have a moment like that with anyone other than Dan. Liam is right that I didn't give us a proper chance. It would be convenient if I could switch off the side of me that is in love with Dan, but my feelings for him aren't going anywhere.

"Couples start off as friends all the time," Liam continues, seeing my hesitation. "It's what makes their connection so strong."

It's flattering how determined Liam is to be with me, especially since I've lived my whole life without any guys being overly interested in me other than Dan. I sigh, wondering if there's some merit to his argument. Dan and I started as friends. This was the original plan for me and Liam, to see if down the track we could be anything more.

"Maybe we can hang out as friends and see if this goes anywhere." Something in my gut doesn't sit right as I speak the words. But I'll never move on from Dan if I don't at least entertain the idea of letting another man into my life. "I'm not in the right headspace to jump straight into being your girlfriend."

He smiles at me and tucks a piece of hair behind my ear. "So, let's do it. Let's see where this goes."

CHAPTER TWENTY-NINE

ALLY

"Happy birthday, honey!"

Mom pulls the curtains open, blinding me with sunlight. I roll over in bed, silently cursing her for being so cheerful at this early hour on Saturday morning.

"Wake up. Liam is downstairs."

"Already?" I rub my eyes, checking the time on my phone. I've asked Mom not to plan a celebration for me—knowing a celebration would mean interacting with Dan—and instead told Liam we could spend the day together, but I didn't expect him here so early.

We've hung out a few times in the last ten days since he came to my house, asking me to give him another chance. He took me back to the jazz club one evening. We went out to dinner another night. It's been nice. He hasn't tried to kiss me, which I appreciate. He's giving me my space like I asked, being my friend.

"Trust me, honey, Liam's present for you is incredible. You'll want to get out of bed."

My mother loves the idea of me being with Liam. Over-all, I think she's just pleased that I've started socializing outside of the family. She always tells me how well-suited Liam and I are with our interests and what a polite young man he is every time he stops by the house. She's already organized for his band to perform at the next Forever Families benefit in one week's time.

Mom passes my dressing gown to me and kisses my cheek. "I'll see you downstairs. Josh and I have a present for you."

As soon as she's gone, I sit up in bed and check my phone, the zero messages and zero missed calls carving a hollow space in my chest. Dan and I used to always spend my birthday together. My God, I miss him. I told him we shouldn't speak for a while. I never stated how long but it doesn't feel like enough time has passed, not when that night with him is still so fresh in my mind.

Yet it feels weird not talking to him today. Dan would always go above and beyond on my birthday, spoiling me with the most incredibly thought-out gifts. For my sixteenth, the first year we met, Dan decorated the ceiling of my room to resemble the night sky and all its stars that can't be seen from the city. It would have taken him hours to create. We stayed up the entire night, in the dark and side by side on our backs, gazing up at the beautiful ceiling and talking till sunrise.

My birthday last year in Paris was so lonely without him. This year feels even more unnatural, but this feeling is something I need to get used to.

Leaving my phone behind, I pull on my dressing gown and head downstairs. When I'm halfway down the stairs, my feet come to a stop and I'm laughing at the sight of Liam in the entry hall, dressed like a nobleman from centuries ago. He wears an olive-green velvet coat that extends down to his knees, a waistcoat and cravat beneath, and breeches on the bottom.

"What on earth are you wearing?"

He grins at me. "An eighteenth-century costume. You have one too."

"Why?"

"You'll need it for where we're spending the day. Happy birthday, beautiful." He holds out two tickets.

I step beside him and read the tickets. *Classical Age Music Fair.*

"Okay, I actually love this." I hug Liam, smiling. "This is an amazing present. Thank you."

"I'm glad to hear it. Here's your costume. A dress with a neckline just like the one we saw in *Amadeus*." He winks, passing a garment bag to me.

I laugh, remembering how full the actress's cleavage was and swat Liam's arm. "Give me a minute to get dressed. I'll be right back."

Liam and I arrive at the fair midmorning, held in Manhattan at the Lincoln Center for the Performing Arts.

Right where the Juilliard campus is.

I try not to let the Juilliard part be a hindrance on my mood. Liam doesn't know that for years I had my heart set on attending Juilliard. He planned a perfect day for us and I'm going to enjoy it. And honestly, the fair looks incredible. It's held out in the open, in the plaza. The weather is cool, being mid-November, but I have this massive ballgown and cashmere wrap to keep me warm.

All the attendees are dressed in costumes much like ours. Everywhere I look, there's some attraction luring me in, from the many market stalls selling Classical composer merchandise, to musical artefacts from hundreds of years ago on display. Spread all throughout the plaza are performances of chamber music and solo performances. There are demonstrations of instruments being crafted from scratch. Antique instruments are available to play. Tonight, there will be a banquet and masquerade ball.

Everything about the event is exquisite.

Which leaves me confused when out of nowhere, my throat starts to ache. My chin wobbles and my eyes water.

"Where would you like to visit first?" Liam asks.

"Um." My voice breaks. Embarrassment hits hard over how emotional I suddenly am. What the hell is wrong with me?

Liam taking me to this fair is a thoughtful gift and I'm so excited to be here. But there's a feeling within my chest I can't explain. I don't know if the reminder of Juilliard has triggered a stress response in me, or if this is something else.

I work hard to make my next words sound strong. "Maybe we can get a bite to eat."

"Yeah, I'm starving. Let's check out what food they have."

My jaw clenches. I wipe my eyes, trying to ward off the tears. The last thing I want is for Liam to see me crying, especially after all the effort he's gone to today.

While Liam passes our entry tickets to an attendant, I readjust my hair, pulling it forward to hide my face. I take a deep breath, attempting to calm myself, but the weight of my ballgown and how tightly strung it is around my waist makes it hard to breathe. My skin itches. I'm suddenly hot. Too hot. My neck feels like it's burning up. My arms stiffen, locking at my sides.

This *can't* be happening right now. I haven't had a panic attack in months, since before returning from Paris. I need to get a hold on myself. I cannot start crying and lose control just because I'm feeling out of sorts.

But knowing I'm on the brink of a panic attack makes my emotions more rampant and harder to keep under control.

"So, food." Liam takes my hand and starts walking, turning back to me with concern in his eyes. "Wow, you're clammy. Are you feeling all right?"

I wipe my hands on my dress and continue forward, not letting him see my face. "Just hot."

The sounds of the fair grow louder as we walk deeper into the plaza, a jumble of voices and instrumental music. I recognize one of my favorite tunes, but it does nothing to calm me. All of the surrounding noises are too overpowering. People are cluttered in the walkways, bumping into me. I'm in complete sensory overload and feel trapped, like I need to push my head out of a window and gasp for fresh air.

"Oh, Italian. Feel like eating pizza?" Liam points to a nearby food stall.

"I... need to find a restroom. I'll be back soon. Just... enjoy yourself." I rush off, pushing my way through the crowd in search for a quiet space where I can have a moment alone to compose myself.

Liam calls after me with alarm. I don't look back. Perhaps I'm being rude, but I don't want Liam to see me like this. It's humiliating and I wouldn't even know how to explain any of these feelings to him when I don't understand them myself.

With Liam out of sight, my tears fall free. I continue nudging through the crowd, heading to the edge of the plaza, relieved when I spot a nook within the buildings up ahead.

Finally, I lose the crowd and enter the nook, finding myself in an isolated crevice where the blaring noise of the fair is dampened. I loosen the drawstrings on the back of my costume and slump against the brick wall, closing my eyes and attempting to center myself with deep breaths.

With each breath in, I think back to that night when I was sixteen, having a panic attack at a party and where Dan was able to calm me. I visualize him in front of me now, holding my shoulders and telling me to maintain eye contact while I take deep breaths as he counts to four.

My phone vibrates in my cleavage. I tell myself to ignore it and focus on the counting. But the vibrations distract me. I reach into my bra to switch my phone off, stopping when I see Dan's name on the screen.

I answer his call without a second thought. "Dan, hi."

"I know we're not meant to be talking, but I had to wish you happy birthday, Queen."

Hearing the warmth in Dan's voice and his name for me destroys all the progress I've made toward calming myself, and I slide to the ground in a silent cry.

"Ally? Where are you? It sounds loud."

"I'm..." My first instinct is to tell him my location. But I'm close to where Dan lives. He'll drop everything and come to me without hesitation, and I can't have that. "It doesn't matter where I am." My voice cracks and this time I can't keep the sobs to myself.

"Fuck. What's happened?"

I try to answer Dan but all I can do is cry.

"You're having a panic attack. Shit. It's okay. I'm here with you. Just breathe. Focus on my voice." He starts counting in that deep and soothing voice he always uses in these moments, instructing me through my breathing. I follow along, and it's a few minutes before I'm stable enough to have a conversation with him.

"Thank you," I whisper. "I'm sorry for answering the phone like that."

"Don't ever apologize for the way you're feeling. Tell me what's happening."

"I don't know. It's just a feeling I have. It's my birthday and the day doesn't feel right. You're not here and I miss you. I know it's a pathetic reason to have a panic attack."

"Tell me where you are. I'm coming to get you."

"I... No." I take a breath and wipe my wet cheeks. "Thank you, but you're not coming to get me. I need to deal with this myself. I *can* deal with it myself. I spent an entire year without you."

Silence lingers on the phone. When Dan speaks again, he's gentle with me, yet I can hear an edge of annoyance in his voice. "I spoke to Amabella just now. I hear you're back with Liam. You're spending your birthday with him?"

My chest tightens as I broach this topic with Dan. "He's taken me somewhere for my birthday. We're not together. It's going to take me a long time to be with anyone after you. We're just hanging out as friends."

"I think he has a little more than friendship on his mind with you."

"Dan..."

"It's okay, Ally." His voice is deep and smooth. "I'm not mad. I told you to go off and do what you need to. Why isn't he with you right now, taking care of you?"

"He shouldn't see me like this. Liam went to all this effort for my birthday." I clear my throat, knowing this conversation needs to find an end. "And I don't need taking care of. I'm not Liam's problem or yours. I'm sorry I broke down on the phone. I'm going to find some way to pull myself together and enjoy my birthday. I should go."

"Ally..." His tone softens and he sighs. "I'll be worrying about you all day."

"I'll text you with updates, okay?"

He scoffs, frustrated with me. "Your updates aren't great. Three days I spent in radio silence, wondering if I'd gotten you pregnant."

My face is instantly hot. I can't tell if it's due to the possessiveness in his voice and how much I like it, or the way he scolds me. Perhaps both. "I told you not to worry about that. And I told you the second I got my period."

"You don't get it, Ally." He groans and backs off, even though I can tell he wants to say something more. From the pain in his voice, it dawns on me that this shift in tone isn't about Dan panicking I was pregnant. It's about the emotional and physical intimacy we've shared and how abruptly it's been cut off.

"Yeah, I do get it," I say quietly. "We're not meant to be talking to each other and this is why. There are too many feelings involved. I'll be fine today. Trust me, okay?"

With reluctance, Dan agrees and we both hang up. At the same time, Liam steps into view, towering over me sitting curled up on the ground, and sighs with relief.

"Come here. You poor thing." He helps me to my feet and draws me into a hug. I'm stiff in his arms, embarrassed and confused over his reaction. "Your parents warned me about this."

They did? That's even more embarrassing. "I'm sorry. I've ruined everything. Sometimes I get overwhelmed. The Juilliard school is here which brought up negative feelings." Though, in all honesty, I can't one hundred percent say this outburst was caused by Juilliard. "You went to so much effort—"

"You haven't ruined anything. Come on, I'll get you back to the truck and drive you home."

"No. I want to be here with you. I just had a moment but I'm feeling better now. I'd like to stay, if you're not scared off."

"Scared off?" He laughs softly, cupping my jaw in his palms. "You can be vulnerable around me. I won't run away or judge you."

My God. He's being a dream.

Liam takes the heel of my palm and raises it to his lips. The gesture makes me smile a little. The weirdness of the day hasn't worn off, but after having my moment of weakness, I can push through this.

CHAPTER THIRTY

ALLY

The work week starts off a drag, even more so than usual. I'm mentally drained from the panic attack on my birthday and it shows when even my students ask if I'm all right. I can't bring myself to wake up early to join Killian and Violet for our runs. Each day when work finishes, I remain behind, having no energy to act happy around Mom and Josh. I tell them I'm busy with work.

Instead, I stay cooped up in my classroom, playing the piano late into the evenings because I miss the feeling of transcendence it gives me. But most of all, because it occupies my mind and I don't have to think about anything else, especially the one man who refuses to leave my head.

Come Wednesday at five p.m., Violet knocks on my classroom and enters. "I have a date tonight."

My fingers stop mid-song and I smile. Other people's dating lives I can be excited for. Mine, not so much. "Nice. With Killian?"

She gives me the middle finger and laughs. "A guy I met on a dating app. I need to ask a massive favor. Can I please raid your closet for something cute to wear?"

"Of course." I cuss inside my head, knowing I'll have to return home earlier than usual. But I'll do it for Violet.

I close the piano and pack up my belongings. As the two of us head to Violet's car, she gushes about all the conversations she's had with this guy, but as soon as we pull out of the parking lot, the focus shifts to me.

"How was your birthday with Liam?"

I sigh and tell her the truth. "It was nice aside from the panic attack I had."

"Shit. What happened?"

"I don't know. I was just... over stimulated."

Violet chews her bottom lip. I can tell she wants to say something, so I ask her to spit it out. "You reckon you would have had a panic attack with this other guy?"

"What other guy?"

"You know, the one you had sex with at the benefit." Her grin is filled with mischief. I jab her ribs and she squeals.

"We didn't—" I sigh, avoiding that topic. To answer her question, the absence of Dan on my birthday definitely didn't help the panic attack situation. "I know you don't like Liam because of the open relationship thing. But he's changed. Can we focus on your date tonight? What do you want to wear?"

We talk about potential outfits for the rest of the drive home. When I step through my front door, I head upstairs, guiding Violet to my room, wanting to avoid my parents. But I'm not quick enough. By the time I reach the fourth step, I can already hear Mom approaching.

"Honey, is that you?" She enters the hallway, looking far more fancy than she should for a random Wednesday night. Her hair is perfected with long golden curls, and she has the most gorgeous floral dress on. I assume she's having a date night with Josh. "You're home in time for dinner. Oh, and you've brought Violet. Excellent. Why don't you help me set the table? Violet, are you staying for dinner?"

"She has a date," I answer. "I'm helping her find an outfit. I'll be down soon."

"Honey?" Mom rests a hand at the bottom of the staircase railing, watching me with a concerned look. "Are you feeling all right? You haven't been yourself recently. Ever since the knife attack."

Since the night I slept with Dan.

I force a smile. "Just tired and overworked. I'm okay."

"Well, it's a good thing I've cooked your favorite dinner." Mom climbs the staircase and takes my hand in hers, guiding me back down to the ground.

"Mom, what are you doing?"

Violet chuckles, following the two of us.

"Mom, seriously."

"Come on, darling. I promise you'll feel better once you have some food in you."

She pulls me from the entry hall, through the living room and kitchen. As soon as we enter the dining room, a bunch of voices shout, "SURPRISE!"

A massive *Happy Twenty-First Birthday, Ally* banner hangs above a banquet table covered in a feast. Dozens of balloons filled with sparkling confetti float at the ceiling with gold ribbon hanging down. There's even an overflowing champagne tower.

Scattered throughout the dining room is all my family. The brothers. Harper.

Dan.

He's smiling at me and I can't look away. My heart is beating so incredibly fast at the sight of him. Our phone call on my birthday ended badly, but I realize I'm smiling too, having missed him so much during this month we've been apart.

Mom wraps an arm around my shoulders. "I know you asked for no party, and I'm sorry if you hate it. But we all love you so much and there's no way we could let your twenty-first go by without celebrating."

The initial shock of the surprise party hasn't worn off yet. Maybe I should be upset with my mother for going against my wishes, but Dan is here and that's all I care about. I could cry, I'm so happy to see him.

"I love the party. Thank you." To my surprise, the words aren't a lie. Despite the mental exhaustion I've been feeling these last few days, the effort my mother has made to celebrate my birthday, plus everyone showing up for me, does make me happy. "Wait, Violet, you have that date."

Violet laughs, shaking her head. "I needed some excuse to get you away from work. Oh, and on the topic of work, we've organized for you to have the day off tomorrow. So, party hard tonight."

"Sacred Heart approved this?"

"It took some sweet talking, but yes."

My eyes land on a side table with a mini grand piano on top. "Jesus Christ." There's a cake knife beside it, along with plates and spoons. "Is that piano a cake? Mom, that's incredible."

Josh steps out from behind all the guests, laughing, and draws me into a hug. "Your mother and Jordan organized an amazing party but the cake was my idea, and I'm taking credit for it."

"Best cake ever."

The moment I step back from Josh, someone's hand slips into mine, weaving their fingers with mine, and they kiss my cheek. "Happy birthday, beautiful."

It takes me far too long to realize it's Liam. I hadn't seen him standing among everyone and feel awkward about his intimate greeting, especially in front of Dan. I sneak a glance at Dan to gauge his reaction, finding his gaze on Liam, his jaw tight. Definitely a situation I wanted to avoid.

Felix places a hand on Dan's shoulder and squeezes. I'm no lip reader, but it looks like he whispers the word *easy* in Dan's ear. Dan breaks concentration, starting a conversation with his brother.

I hug Liam and thank him for the happy birthday wishes. "Hey, I thought you had a gig in the city tonight?"

"I do. Starts at midnight. I'll get there in time. I didn't want to miss your party. Come on, let's say hi to everyone."

"A classical music fair. What a perfect gift. It sounds like you and Ally had a good day together," Jordan says in response to Liam's recount of my birthday, having left out the panic attack part.

Small groups of conversation take place at the table as everyone finishes their meal. I'm seated in the middle, with Liam and Dan on either side of me. It's awkward as hell. Dan and I have barely exchanged words. Daxton and Jordan are seated across from us, listening to Liam.

"The fair was great fun," Liam says.

Dan gives a ridiculing laugh. "Yeah, a panic attack sounds like real fun."

My eyes whip to him. It's the first thing he's said in ten minutes. He's words were quiet, and among all the chatter at the table, I'm hoping I'm the only one who heard.

"Ally was feeling a little off," Liam says. "But she recovered quickly."

Daxton pours himself another drink. "Still getting those nasty panic attacks, kid?"

Great, I guess everyone heard.

"I get them occasionally. It's not that bad." I glare at Dan for bringing up the topic. He holds my gaze, not backing down.

Mom stands from the head of the table. "Okay, everyone, the night is getting on and I know Liam needs to leave early for his gig. Let's clear the table and open the presents."

Everyone helps clean up, stacking plates and carrying them through to the kitchen. Within five minutes, we all return to our chairs and there's a mound of presents in the center of the table.

"Okay, open your present from me and Josh first," Mom says, leaning over the table to hand me an envelope. They gave me a present on my actual birthday. It was an expensive bottle of champagne with a Mozart label, imported from his hometown. I suppose its purpose was achieved, to prevent any suspicion of an upcoming party.

Inside the envelope, there's a gift voucher for a weekend away at an island resort, along with two plane tickets. "Wow. Thank you. I love it."

"So romantic." Violet winks at me. "I know the perfect guy for you to take."

I shake my head, laughing at the meaning behind her words only I understand.

"We thought you and Violet could have a fun girls weekend away," Mom says. "But of course, you can take whoever you please."

More presents come my way. I open each one, receiving athlete grade running shoes from Killian, theater tickets from Tyler and Harper, a bottle of absinthe from Felix, which he insists we'll drink together now that I'm legal, and sheet music from Daxton and Jordan. Violet passes me her gift, and I give her a massive hug when seeing she's bought us ballet tickets to an upcoming production of *The Nutcracker*.

"Liam's present is next." Mom slides forward a tall and narrow present, about two feet in height.

I glance at Liam, shocked. "The fair was your present. You didn't need to get me anything else."

"I know I didn't need to. I wanted to."

I unwrap the present and the box inside, pulling out a bouquet of roses constructed from sheet music. "Liam, this is incredible." I give him a quick hug, beyond impressed. Since inviting Liam back into my life, he's done one thoughtful thing after the next, crafted to my interests. "What song is this?"

"A serenade by Mozart."

"Did you fold the roses yourself?" Harper asks.

"Yeah," Liam laughs. "Took a while. Got a few paper cuts."

"It's amazing. Thank you," I tell him.

"Liam, you are so sweet." Mom passes me a small box. "This is the last present. Dan, I'm guessing this one is from you?"

"Yeah," he mutters beside me.

I feel strange opening Dan's present, given our situation. We haven't had a chance to speak much. Things are tense between us, regardless of how pleased I am that he's here tonight.

Dan's gaze softens. "Happy birthday. You going to open the present or just hold it?"

I glance around the table, realizing everyone is waiting on me. I unwrap the present, finding a small velvet box, and when I open it, there's a gold necklace with a heart pendant inside.

"Dan… it's beautiful. Thank you."

"The heart is a locket. Open it."

As soon as I unclasp the heart, a lump forms in my throat and tears well in my eyes. Staring back at me is a copy of the misplaced photograph of my mother and father holding me as a baby, shrunken down to fit inside.

"Oh my gosh, Dan, how did you find this photo?"

"What photo is it?" Mom asks. I turn the box for her to see. She raises a hand to her mouth and her eyes become pools of tears. "We have been searching for years. Dan, this is the most thoughtful present."

"You did good, son," Josh says, wrapping an arm around Mom. Everyone sits in silence. The party is so quiet that all I can hear are the waves crashing in the ocean beyond this dining room.

"Where did you find the photo?" Mom asks.

Dan rubs the back of his neck, his voice low and reserved, like this is an awkward conversation to be having with an audience. "I took a day trip up here recently while you were all at work and searched the attic for hours. I'd already turned the Manhattan apartment upside down searching for the photo. The only other place it could have been was here. I made a copy for the necklace. I can get the original back to you."

Tears fall down my cheeks. "This is the most amazing present anyone could have given me. You don't know how much this means to me."

"I do." His voice drops even lower, almost to a whisper, just for me. "I spent ages thinking of something meaningful I could get you for your twenty-first. Nothing felt right except for this. I knew you'd been searching for it over the years."

You'll be back. I don't know when. It could be days. Months. Years. But you'll be back, and I'll be here waiting for you.

My chest tightens as I gaze into Dan's dark eyes, remembering his parting words from our one night together. Breathing becomes painful, just as it did at the fair.

"Um, I'm going to take the presents to my room." I stand from the table, collecting all the gifts in my hands, using them as an excuse to escape, when what I really need is privacy to get a hold on myself before I break out with another panic attack.

"Do you need help with the presents?" Mom asks.

"No, it's okay. I'd like a moment alone if no one minds."

CHAPTER THIRTY-ONE

ALLY

By the time I arrive at my bedroom, my face is a wet mess. I place the presents on my bed and lie back, sobbing uncontrollably. All my emotions flood out and it hurts to the core of my soul.

My entire life is a wreck. I think back to when I first returned from Paris and got stood up on my date, how I was at the lowest point of my life and knew changes needed to be made to find happiness.

I've made changes, and yet, this massive void still lays inside me.

I had this picture-perfect idea of what happiness would look like for me. I'd be in love with a perfect guy who treats me right and isn't my stepbrother. Dan and I would be a thing of the past.

Since that night of being stood up, I've found the textbook perfect guy. Liam is everything I should want. He's eager to commit to me. We have fun together. He's caring and attentive.

And yet nothing feels right with him.

I said I'd give Liam a proper chance. But after receiving

this locket, it's pushed me to my breaking point and I'm done fighting the one thing in this world that makes sense to my heart.

The risk of being caught with Dan won't ever go away. Tonight, right now, I've decided it's a risk worth taking. My parents' opinion of me, my public image and job, Forever Families... *Everything* is worth risking if it means being with Dan.

When my breathing calms and the tears stop flowing, I check the time on my bedside clock. It's almost nine and I've been absent from the party for ten minutes. Far too long to not raise suspicion. I head to the bathroom with the heart locket in my hand, needing to see the damage this emotional outburst has done to my makeup. My eyes are red, but surprisingly nothing has been smudged or washed away. Thank goodness for waterproof makeup.

"Kind of the opposite reaction I was hoping for with my gift."

I spin around in fright, finding Dan leaning a shoulder against the doorframe.

"Tears of joy, maybe." His voice is deep and slow. Intimate. His gaze traces my body, down and back up to my eyes, heating every inch of me. "But I didn't expect you to leave your own party upset."

"I'm fine. I love the necklace. I'm just overwhelmed."

"I knew you'd love the necklace," he murmurs. "When you opened the present, you looked at me in a way I've never seen before. It was a look you shouldn't have given me in public. Not in front of our family. Our parents. Especially not in front of Liam. Even now, you're giving me the same look. I want to know what it means."

His gaze bores into me, holding me in place. I lick my lips, my heart beating so incredibly fast as I speak my next words. "It means I'm back, just like you said I would be. But this time, I'm back for good. I don't know how, but we'll find a way to make this work. We'll be together in secret. This necklace you gave me—" I hold it up in my hand. "I want you to be the one to clasp it around my neck, and then I'm never taking it off. I'm yours forever. Let everyone see your mark on me, even if they don't realize the meaning behind it. We will."

A flicker of disbelief crosses his face as my words register in his mind. Dan wastes no time closing the distance between us, and within a few swift strides, his lips are hot upon mine and his hands are tangled through my hair. I moan into his kisses, clinging to him. Nothing has ever felt this good, having his body against mine and knowing there's no expiration date on what we have. I don't care if we have to continue our relationship in secret. I'm taking what I want. He's mine and every part of me belongs to him.

Dan lifts me up by the backs of my thighs and places me on the basin, pushing his hips between my legs, right where he belongs.

"I'm sorry it's taken me this long to see the truth," I say as Dan's kisses move down my throat. He takes the necklace from my hand and secures it around my neck. "I'm sorry about every time I ran away from you."

"I know, baby. I don't care. You're here with me now."

I unbuckle Dan's belt, working fast to get his thick, hard length free. We're at a party with all our family nearby, but I don't care. I need to feel Dan inside me. I need him to come in me.

He hoists my dress up and pulls my panties to the side, pushing the entire length of his dick into me in one quick thrust. I cry out at the sharp and sudden stretch. He covers my mouth with a kiss, muffling my sounds from the party downstairs. My legs wrap around Dan's waist, locking him to me as my muscles adjust to his size. Our foreheads press together and all I can hear is our panting.

"We shouldn't be doing this again without a condom." He pulls out and thrusts back in, ignoring his own words. Dan repeats the pattern, fucking me slow but desperately, his muscles trembling.

"I went on the pill right after we had sex. I need you to come in me. *Please*."

I barely get the words out before Dan groans, the sound filled with possession and urgency. He grips my hips tighter and pulls me onto his dick with each slow but harsh thrust. "Hearing those words... I can't hold off, Ally."

"I don't want you to." The act of reuniting with Dan and finally giving myself completely to him already has me close to an orgasm. "We don't have much time before everyone wonders where we are."

He growls through clenched teeth, pumping fast until losing control and spilling into me, repeating the word *mine* over and over in a deep and breathless groan. My orgasm hits, spasming around Dan's cock, drawing his cum deep within me where I need it. I pant his name, trying my hardest to be quiet, but it's a difficult task when he makes me feel this complete.

"Ally?" my mother calls. Her footsteps approach from the far end of the corridor outside the bathroom.

Panic flashes through me. Dan and I quickly pull apart from each other and straighten our clothes. He sits on the rim of the bathtub, pretending like we're in the middle of a conversation. I fix my hair in the mirror, lightheaded and still tingling from my orgasm.

Mom enters the bathroom. "There you are, honey. I

wanted to check up on you." She joins me at the mirror and kisses my forehead, her attention catching on my new necklace. "Oh, Dan, you really are so incredible for finding this photo. Ally, how are you feeling? You look flushed."

"I... was crying over the photo of my dad. Happy tears," I say, feeling Dan's cum seeping out of me.

She smiles, convinced by the lie. "All right, you two. Come downstairs so we can cut the cake."

Dan follows her out of the bathroom first. I catch up, hooking my pinkie finger with his. He side-eyes me, glancing down at the necklace then back at me, the two of us sharing a secret smile.

I press up on my toes and whisper in his ear, "I can think of a whole list of things you still have to teach me."

As soon as Mom, Dan, and I return to the party, Liam stands from his seat and slips an arm around my waist. "Hey, beautiful. I wish I could stay for the cake, but I need to get on the road to make it to my gig in time."

"Of course. I'll walk you out to your car."

Liam says a quick goodbye to everyone, we exit the dining room together, and I walk with him out to the side of the house where his truck and all the other cars are hidden for my surprise party. Each step of the way is awkward, knowing the conversation we're about to have.

"Your family is really nice," Liam says as we arrive at his truck. There's a chill to the night air, but I barely feel it, prepping myself for the bad news I'm about to deliver. "I had a great time tonight. I hope you enjoyed your party." He strokes my cheek. A look enters his eyes like he's thinking about kissing me.

I duck my head, leaning away from his palm. "Liam, I need to say something."

"Okay." There's a brightness to his voice which makes my stomach clench, knowing what I'm about to say will be harsh.

"I said I would give us a chance. I meant it at the time, but... I can't be your girlfriend. I'm sorry. My heart isn't in this."

His brow creases. He's utterly shocked. "I thought that was the whole point of giving us a chance. Not rushing into anything and giving us time to form a bond. We only just started—"

"I know. I'm sorry."

"I thought things were going well." Liam rubs both hands over his face, groaning into his palms. "I stopped seeing other girls because I like you so much. I don't do shit like that for just anyone, Ally."

"I know. Again, I'm sorry. My mind has been a mess recently. I wanted this to work between us."

He lowers his hands, the look in his eyes both hurt and anger. "What did I do wrong?"

"You didn't do anything. You're amazing. It's... there's..." My hands clasp behind my back and I bite my cheek, nervous and unable to speak a proper sentence.

"Stop dancing around the truth and be honest. I can handle it."

"Really, Liam, it's not you."

"I don't see what you could possibly have to hide unless there's some other guy you're seeing and are trying to protect my feelings."

My shoulders tighten at his sharp tone and how perceptive he is. Liam has been nothing but genuine and honest with me throughout our entire time knowing each other, and I feel terrible that I can't do the same in return. I want to offer him somewhat of the truth, but then he could piece everything together, and I can't have anyone find out about me and Dan.

"There's no explanation other than it doesn't feel right. I'm sorry."

"This is bullshit." Liam enters his truck, slamming the door shut behind himself. The ignition roars to life, he reverses down the driveway, and I watch as he speeds off into the night.

Well, that went pretty bad.

I do feel awful for hurting Liam. At the same time, there's a massive sense of relief in me. Liam was a great guy who I could have been with in another life, but we weren't right for each other, even if it took me too long to learn so.

I head back through the house, to the party, walking in on a discussion about bedrooms and where everyone is sleeping.

"Oh, good, Ally, you're back," Mom says. "Will you please convince Dan he needs to sleep here tonight. It will be so nice to have the whole family under one roof. Like old times."

"You offered Dax and Jordan the room I used to sleep in. All the other bedrooms are taken," Dan says, leaning back at the table while mindlessly shuffling his neon cards. A soft smile tugs at my lips, seeing him with those cards and knowing I have the Queen of Hearts.

"We can set up the couch," Mom tells him.

"The couch?" Dan laughs. "You're not really selling the idea of me sleeping over, Amabella."

I return to my chair beside Dan, not saying a word, my thoughts still with Liam and the tense scene that went down between us. How he drove off in anger.

"Honey, tell Dan he has to stay for your birthday. We're going to play board games after the cake and need correct numbers for each group."

I look at my mom and shrug, my mind distant, hoping Liam is safe on the road.

"Ally, darling, what's wrong?"

"Liam and I got into an argument. I don't think I'll be seeing him again."

"What?" she gasps. All eyes whip to me, and I'm met with a million questions. *What was the argument about? Who started it? Am I upset?*

"I'm fine." Liam's anger wasn't nice to experience, but with each passing second, I'm feeling a greater sense of freedom and... I'm *happy*. I don't think I've ever been this happy, knowing I can finally let myself be with Dan. "I'm actually better than fine. I told Liam we weren't right for each other."

"You only just started seeing him," Josh states in confusion.

"We weren't seeing each other. We were only... It doesn't even matter."

"How did he take it?" Violet asks with the biggest grin on her face.

I roll my eyes at her reaction, resisting the urge to laugh out of respect for Liam. "Not well. He'll be fine, though."

Felix tosses a balled-up napkin across the table at Dan. "Now you have to stay the night. Baby sis needs her family around for comfort." There's a teasing grin on his face, and he finishes with a wink at Dan, to which Dan scowls back. I have no clue what any of that is about. "Come on, bro. I'll take the couch. You have my old bedroom."

"Fine," Dan says, grabbing my thigh beneath the table. "I'll stay."

CHAPTER THIRTY-TWO

DAN

The night draws close to eleven o'clock. Violet has gone home, and now the family is scattered among the couches in the living room, drinking champagne and playing board games.

My phone vibrates in my pocket.

FELIX

I know you, bro. You snuck off after the presents were opened to fuck her, didn't you? Tell me I'm not sleeping on the couch tonight for nothing.

I shoot him a look, sitting all the way across the room, and find him laughing quietly to himself.

FELIX

One of us deserves to enjoy the night.

I read the hidden meaning in his words, directed at Harper. I've sensed the tension between the two of them tonight more so than usual. Not because anything between them has changed, but I have a greater awareness of their situation. They've stayed far away from each other during the party, barely interacting, other than anything that is required of them.

I now have a new appreciation for how difficult these family gatherings must be for Felix, not only because of Dad, but being forced to watch Tyler and Harper together. The way she's sitting on Tyler's lap right now, and him stroking her hair. Knowing that Tyler takes Harper to bed each night. I could barely stand watching Ally and Liam together earlier in the evening.

I'm back, just like you said I would be. I've never been more relieved than when Ally spoke those words.

I would love to have Ally in my bed with me tonight but doing anything with her while so much family is around is a dangerous move. We shouldn't have had sex in the bathroom earlier. Amabella was seconds away from catching us. I've risked a lot by sneaking around with Ally. Now that something real is happening between us, I can't keep risking us being caught.

Ally's laughter pulls me out of my deep thoughts. She's just rolled the dice and landed double sixes. I haven't heard her laugh like that in... maybe since before Paris. She moves her piece on the game board and jumps up, heading back to me with a glass of champagne now that her turn is over. The game goes on with Killian's turn next. The volume in the room is loud with everyone chatting.

Ally sits beside me on the couch with remnants of that beautiful laugh lingering on her face. She looks at me, and her eyes are bright, so full of life. Fucking perfection.

"What is this?" I nod, gesturing to her whole demeanor.

"Me having fun."

"Yeah, I see that. But right after a tough conversation with Liam? How are you feeling? *Really* feeling."

"Happy. I know that makes me a bitch—"

"It doesn't."

She raises the champagne to her lips and turns to watch the board game. Her voice drops to a whisper. "You *know* why I'm happy."

I think back to our moment in the bathroom. Our reunion was quick and cut short. I need to be with her again, away from the eyes of our family, even if it's just to talk. I have questions for her. She says she's mine forever, but what happens if people discover we're together. She's prepared to deal with the consequences?

"Do you want to take a walk on the beach?" I ask.

"You two can't leave during the game," Jordan calls from the next couch over.

Fuck. There are eyes and ears *everywhere* in this house.

Ally types something on her phone. A few seconds later, I receive a message.

ALLY

Later, when everyone is asleep.

The last light turns off at one in the morning. I'm in Felix's old bedroom, down the hall from Ally's room, wide awake and wondering how long I should wait before it's safe to leave and see Ally. I send her a text, asking her to meet me on the beach.

When five minutes pass and there's no response, I weigh up the risks of sneaking over to her room. If someone saw me, I could pass the visit off as some kind of friendly encounter. After all, it's been common knowledge among the family that Ally and I had movie nights in each other's room when we were teenagers. No one ever thought anything odd of it, just that we were really close friends.

I head for the door, but it opens before I arrive. "Dan?" Ally whispers.

Her silhouette sneaks inside and she quietly shuts the door behind herself, clicking the lock into place. She tiptoes, meeting me halfway across the room, and presses her lips to my mouth, her whole body against mine, and weaves her fingers through my hair. I groan at the feeling of her lips, and grab her ass. Her satin nightdress bunches in my hands as I crush her hips against my instant hard-on. She gives an approving laugh, the sound quiet but a reminder that we need to be careful.

"We should go to the beach," I whisper. "It will be safer away from everyone."

"No, the beach is a public space. As long as we're quiet, no one will know I'm in here with you." Her lips find mine again and her hands slide beneath my shirt, her cool fingertips like ice against my hot skin. She pulls my shirt up and I slip it over my head. Next, she's working on lowering my pants.

I grasp her wrists, placing a pause on her advancements. The moonlight filters through the bedroom window, casting a glow upon us and illuminating the same spark of happiness I've been seeing in Ally's eyes this evening. God, she's so beautiful. For the longest time, *I've* been the one chasing *her*. Now, she's pushing for us to have sex every chance she gets and I love it.

"Slow down." I bring the backs of her hands to my lips, kissing them. "I just got you all to myself. I'm not fucking you here and risking anyone discovering us."

"Okay, but what if I fuck you?" she teases, pressing up

on her toes to brush her lips against mine. "I can be quiet. I need to have you inside me right now."

My chest purrs at the way she needs me. I maintain my ground: we're not having sex. But there are other ways to enjoy her body. I lift her from the floor, wrapping her thighs around me. Ally's hands knot through my hair as I carry her to the bed and lower her beneath me to the mattress. Her thighs tighten, making me grind against her.

The springs in the mattress squeak and we both go still.

"How loud was that?" she whispers.

I don't think anyone in the surrounding bedrooms would have heard. Even if they did, it was a one-off sound. But it can't happen again, especially not in a rhythmic pattern.

"This is why we need to wait till we're back at my apartment." I loosen Ally's legs from around me and tease her with my mouth instead, trailing kisses down her neck while savoring every inch of her skin as I make my way lower.

When my lips arrive at Ally's stomach, I bunch her night dress up over her hips, and she moans as I place soft kisses above the waistband of her panties. My hands creep up beneath her dress, my dick pulsing harder when I feel the curve of her breasts and her tightened nipples. She places a hand over her mouth, muffling another moan when my tongue flicks the sensitive pink flesh.

"I swear to God, Ally, when we're back at my place, I'll be fucking you so hard, giving you so many orgasms, you'll be begging me to stop." I trace circles over her nipples with my tongue, paying attention to her every breath and how she writhes beneath me.

"I'll never beg you to stop." Ally reaches down, attempting to lower her panties.

I pull back and watch, smirking as she undresses her bottom half. Her panties are off, and I have to choke back a groan when she pulls my waistband down, stroking my cock.

"Take these off," she begs, tugging at my pants.

"You know, I'm loving this, seeing how desperate you are to be fucked." My lips graze against her other nipple and I suck hard, making her squirm beneath me.

"*Please*. We'll be quiet." Ally's neck arches up from the pillow. Her hips rise, searching for the tip of my dick. Her wetness brushes against the head, warm and feeling so fucking incredible that I nearly push into her right this second.

"Such a needy thing, aren't you?" I slide my dick over her pussy, along her clit, earning myself another moan from Ally. "Don't worry, Queen, I'll be taking care of that. I'm going to teach you to take my dick multiple times a day. I'll fuck you in every position. Every hole. You'll be so full of my cum it will be dripping out of you."

The sound she makes this time is more desperate.

"You like the thought of me having your ass?"

She nods. "I want you to have all of me."

I nearly come from those words and the thought of how tight she'd be in that position. "Your ass was made for my dick."

I slide against her pussy again, pushing into the entrance just enough that the head of my cock sinks inside her. Ally's legs lock around me. She's so wet, leaving no resistance for my dick. Without meaning to, I plunge deep into her.

The sudden rush of pleasure consumes me and takes over all logical thought. My lips are desperate against hers, way too forceful, and create another loud creak from the bed frame. I should stop, but I'm addicted and need to fill her with my cum. Ally smiles when I push her nightdress up over her head, knowing she's finally getting her way. I'm just as quickly out of my pants, and take her to the floor with me, away from any furniture that can create sounds.

I make a move to get Ally beneath me, but she climbs on top of me, the two of us sitting upright as she straddles my thighs. "I told you—" Her lips graze mine. "*I* want to be the one doing the fucking tonight."

Ally reaches down between us, positioning her pussy to the tip of my cock, and sinks onto me. I hiss at the burst of pleasure that shoots through me. She works slow, her wet heat covering only the head, and I can tell from the tension in her muscles, she's still not adjusted to my size and needs to brace herself.

My thumb finds her clit, stroking with encouraging circles. "Just breathe. You can take it. Nice and slow. We'll make it fit again."

She gasps, her pussy stretching to accommodate me as she sinks a little lower.

"You're doing so good. I know you can take more. You took it so deep the first time."

I watch the space between us where our bodies connect, where my dick disappears into her pussy. She slowly rises up and back down, stretching a little more.

"That's it. Fuck. Look at you riding my dick. Now, sit all the way down on me."

Her pussy lowers again, taking all of me this time, and when my cock hits her deepest point, I grab her hips to gain leverage and push my dick deeper. She covers her mouth just in time to smother the moan.

I grit my teeth, working hard not to come inside her this very second. "You're always so fucking tight."

Her forehead is pressed to mine and she's panting, her inner muscles rippling over my dick as she adjusts to my depth and size. "You're deeper than the other time."

"You like this position?"

She nods, trying to control her breathing. Her blue eyes lock on me, and a thrill races through my entire body.

"My little stepsister. Look at you. You're going to come on my cock."

Ally's face tightens with pleasure right as her pussy grips me, all due to my words. That's my good girl.

Still holding her hips, I guide her movements, up and down, until she takes over, slowing riding me, her pussy massaging my cock in a perfect rhythm.

I lean back against the edge of a nearby armchair, watching and marveling over the sight of Ally fucking me, if that's even the right way to describe what she does to me. This is deeper than sex. She's taken over my entire mind and body and owns every part of me.

Her hair cascades down her chest, acting as a curtain over her breasts. Wanting to see all of Ally, I push her hair behind her shoulders and bring her nipple into my mouth. Her quiet moans fill the room as our bodies rock against each other, our skin meeting in the most intimate ways. Every inch of her wetness grips me. She trembles beneath my hands, the two of us fighting to remain quiet. Her pace is so agonizingly slow that it intensifies every sensation.

A floorboard right outside the bedroom creaks. We both go still, glancing at the door.

The hallway light turns on, creeping beneath the door, and I hear my father's voice. "Amabella, are you okay? What are you doing out of bed?"

"Checking I turned everything off in the kitchen."

"You always do. Come back to bed, honey."

The light switches off and their footsteps fade away.

Ally and I look at each other. She laughs quietly then attempts to rise from my cock and resume her pace, but I hold her hips firm to mine.

"Tell me you're mine, Ally."

"I already did—"

"No, I mean *truly* mine. You're mine in private but what happens if people find out about us. Will you stop being with me to please them?"

She frowns. "Dan... I don't want to think like that. They won't find out about us. They can't."

"If they do?"

She's silent for a moment, her gaze tracing my face. And then she leans in, caressing her lips to mine and whispers, "I can't give you up. Nothing will stop me from being with you."

I deepen the kiss, overcome with possession now that I know Ally is in this with me no matter what. She's mine completely. My hands tighten on her hips, pressing her down onto my dick even farther. She sighs with pleasure as she clings to me, her nails digging into my back. I let her ride me again. Her breaths are ragged now, her teeth sinking into her lower lip as she fights to maintain her composure.

I'm struggling along with her. I can't believe we're finally here. That she's mine.

Her inner muscles squeeze my cock, and she winces, clutching my shoulders as her forehead returns to mine. "I'm so close."

"So am I."

Her pussy clenches my dick again, so tight that her delicate muscles give way and flutter around my cock. She gasps against my mouth, and the contractions of her orgasm suck the cum right out of me with slow, intense pumps. It's only been three times now that we've had sex, but I'm addicted to coming inside Ally and marking her with my cum.

Her body buckles and I hold her tight as we both come down from the high, breathless and exhausted. She's flushed from working hard and glistens with sweat. Her golden hair sticks to her face. Utter perfection. The best part is knowing that come morning, I don't have to say goodbye to her. There's no end to us.

"You're not working in the morning," I whisper. "Take Friday off too and come back to the city with me for the weekend."

Her mouth opens like she's about to tell me she can't, but she stops herself and gives another smile. "Okay, I'll call in sick. But I have to return on Saturday night. I'm playing at the Forever Families benefit."

"As long as I have you to myself for the next few days that's all I care about."

CHAPTER THIRTY-THREE

ALLY

I wake late afternoon to the sound of voices from another room. The sun is almost set and it takes me a moment to gain my bearings, in a blissful daze from having spent the last two days being fucked senseless by my boyfriend. I'm alone in Dan's bed, naked beneath the sheets. My body is bruised and tender from overuse in the best kind of way, with Dan's cum still inside me.

I wrap the sheets around me and peek out the door, scoping the apartment for who Dan is speaking with. I'm a little surprised when I find him over by the far wall wearing nothing but black track pants.

"That's perfect right there. Thanks for delivering this," Dan says to two men standing by an upright piano.

I'm smiling from ear to ear. As soon as Dan says goodbye to the two delivery men, I leave my hiding place, entering the living area with the sheets clutched to my body. "You bought a piano."

Dan spins around to the sound of my voice, grinning at me. "For you, Queen. I want you to have everything you need here."

I lift up onto my toes, brushing my lips against his. "I love it."

He smiles against my mouth, holding me in his arms. "This place is yours, you know." He's spent the last few days proving so, making sure I feel at home. Dan cleared out space in his walk-in for my clothes. He's done the same with the bathroom medicine cabinet. He's even given me a set of keys. "I'm going to struggle sending you back to The Hamptons. You belong here, with me."

I don't let myself think about the logistics of our relationship. Living here with Dan would raise questions from our family, not to mention the long commute I'd need to make every day to Sacred Heart. We can sort those issues out later. All I want right now is to be lost in this happy place I've finally found with Dan.

Dan takes my hand in his, lowering me onto his lap in front of the piano. "Play something for me."

"While your dick is poking at my ass? Kind of hard to concentrate."

We both laugh. Dan kisses my bare shoulder. "You shouldn't have come out here wearing only bedsheets. Play something. I miss watching you at the piano."

I perform a simple waltz because it's all I'm capable of when I can feel how hard Dan is. Upon finishing, I turn in Dan's lap, placing a soft kiss on his lips. "Happy?"

His gaze drops to my mouth in a total daze before meeting my eyes. "Audition for Juilliard."

My stomach knots, removing me from the intimate moment. "What? Dan, no. I can't."

"We'll work through the panic attacks together. You don't have to audition this year. Just... make it a goal. I know you want to study there."

I shake my head. "It's more than the auditioning part that scares me. If I get accepted, it will be so competitive."

He kisses my neck, the warmth of his breath tickling me, and I feel its effects between my thighs. His lips lower, tracing a path down to my breasts, and I'm suddenly finding it hard to think about anything other than him.

"Dan..." I laugh between words. "If this is some way to... distract me or coax me into agreeing to audition, it won't work."

"Yeah, but I can always try." He unties the sheet from around me, letting it fall to the ground, revealing my naked body.

Dan repositions my legs around his waist so that I'm straddling him. His gaze roams down my breasts, my hips, all the way to my pussy. I flush with heat, loving the way he stares at me, the way his jaw tics and how his gaze darkens.

His fingers brush against my wetness and a guttural sound leaves his chest. "My cum is leaking out of you from the last time."

I bring his fingers to my mouth, sucking them clean.

Dan's eyes flare. He kisses me while returning his fingers between my thighs, gliding them over my clit then pushing them deep inside me.

I moan, arching into his touch. I'm so tender that this is the last thing we should be doing right now, but I can't stop chasing the pleasure his touch gives me. Dan's fingers thrust in and out of me. The sensation is raw and exhilarating, sending shocks of heat through my entire body.

"I love playing with your body like this," he murmurs. "Using it how I want. Making you come. I want to watch you come on my fingers over and over again."

Dan's fingers curve, hitting my G-spot, making me buck

my hips involuntarily. From the corner of my eye, I spot movement, and catch the sight of myself in a nearby wall-mounted
mirror. My pussy clenches around his fingers as I lean back
against the piano and watch my reflection while Dan fucks me
with his hand. It's the hottest thing I've ever seen—him,
working his fingers inside of me, sucking my nipples.

Dan chuckles. "Ally, are you watching us in the mirror?"

I nod, breathless.

"Keep watching as I make you come."

As soon as he rubs my clit, the heat building in my core
expands and I lose control, shuddering as I watch myself
having an orgasm.

"That's it. Good girl," Dan praises. "Such a good little
slut letting me work your body so hard." His fingers keep
thrusting inside me, slowing down as the pleasure fades.

I collapse into him, panting and flushed. "If that was
meant to change my mind about Juilliard, the answer is
still no."

Dan laughs. "I'd forgotten all about Juilliard. I have
something else on my mind right now." He carries me to his
bed and I lay back on the mattress, watching as he strips
out of his pants. My eyes travel straight to his erection.

Before I can get a word out, Dan flips me over onto my
stomach. I cry out with bliss, clutching the bedsheets as he
thrusts into me from behind. His grip on my waist is firm
and possessive. I push back, thrusting with him. He groans,
entering me hard. Faster. I come again, shouting his name.
Dan doesn't stop. He keeps fucking until another orgasm
ripples through me.

Finally, he slows down, and I laugh, limp beneath him.
"What are you doing to me?"

"Getting your muscles relaxed." His dick remains in me,
and he continues to thrust with slow but deep strokes. I

gasp as his finger traces a line down my backside, to that forbidden place where no one has ever touched me before. "You have no idea how badly I want to fuck this tight ass of yours, Ally."

A shiver of arousal travels through me at those words. Dan must feel my muscles tremble around his dick, because he groans, pulling out of me quickly. I love how much he worships my body and wants to experience every part of me.

"Do it."

"You're sure?" he whispers, brushing kisses along my shoulders.

"I've told you before that I want it."

He reaches across the bed while I catch my breath and grabs lube from the nightstand.

"How do you want me?" I ask as he applies the gel to me. "I've never done this before."

He smirks at the obvious knowledge and climbs on top of me. "Stay as you are."

Dan grabs my left knee and bends it out to the side, then glides the head of his dick along my behind, teasing me, making me want it even more, despite being a little nervous of the unknown.

His hand slides beneath me, playing with my clit. I feel his breath hot at the nape of my neck as he whispers, "Breathe and try to relax. You're going to love this, I promise."

Dan strokes himself along my slick ass once more before pushing forward, taking his time as I try to ease into this new sensation.

"You okay, baby?"

I nod, taking deep breaths and trying to relax as I feel the tip of his cock press against my entrance. He continues stroking my clit while his cock slowly pushes inside, stretching and working me open.

"Fuck, Ally." His voice shakes, like he's already struggling not to come. The sound of Dan taking this much pleasure from my body is the biggest turn on.

He eases farther into me, until my ass is pressed flush against the base of his cock. I hiss at the foreign pleasure, gripping the sheets as I rise to my elbows to give myself more leverage for movement. I'm so full, so needy and urgent to feel him pull out and thrust back in.

Dan is still teasing my clit, and the pleasure combined with his heavy breath right above my ear has me begging for more. "Please make me come like this."

His dick starts moving, back and forth in slow thrusts for my body to adjust to the new sensation. "Ally, you're so fucking tight," Dan groans.

With each thrust, I feel more stretched and full. Every time he enters me, a new wave of pleasure arrives, and I'm unable to control the moans escaping my lips, enjoying every moment of being taken in such an intimate way.

"Fuck, you take my dick so good." Dan kisses my neck. My cheek.

I peer over my shoulder to watch him, almost finding my orgasm at the way his muscles strain and his abs flex with each thrust. I reach up to kiss him, and his tongue enters my mouth with such heat and urgency. The pace of our movements increases. I'm now pushing my ass back against his hips, needing to feel more of him, craving this sensation that I didn't know I'd been missing.

"Slow down," Dan murmurs at my temple. "I don't want to hurt you."

"I can't. I don't want to. It feels too good. *Please*, go faster."

I arch my back, craving more. The head of his cock hits a sensitive spot inside me and I gasp, feeling my ass clench around him. He gives me what I want, his fingers working faster over my clit and his cock thrusting harder to build my orgasm. It's too good. Too intense. I work with him, my ass pushing back, slapping against his thighs.

I scream as the orgasm consumes me. My body shakes and my ass grips Dan's cock as I come hard. The tightness of my orgasm triggers his own, and I feel his hot cum spill into me. He groans so loud, the primal sound one I've never heard from him.

Once he's finished, Dan pulls out and I collapse beneath him, dazed and euphoric. I feel his kisses at my shoulders, his breath labored as he strokes my hair back from my face.

"That was the most intense sex has ever felt for me," he murmurs along my skin. "Fuck, you are... *everything*, Ally."

I smile, so relaxed I can't even bring myself to talk.

He frowns, interpreting my silence the wrong way. "I hurt you."

I draw his lips down to mine. "No. I liked it a lot. I'm just tired now. You worked me hard."

"I know. I couldn't help it. That's what years of pent-up sexual tension over you does to me." He laughs softly. "Let me run you a warm bath and take care of you."

CHAPTER THIRTY-FOUR

ALLY

Saturday night arrives and I've returned to The Hamptons for my performance at the Forever Families benefit, held in the old museum. The whole family is here, under Josh and Mom's request. A lot of important press is at the event and my parents said it would be a good opportunity to display our blended family united as one. The brothers only agreed, I'm sure, because Mom asked them, insistent that we get a photo taken for the public that includes all the family.

I've barely spoken a word to Dan all night. It feels odd distancing myself from him after the last three days at his apartment where his hands never left my body. It was constant kisses. Constant orgasms. A secret smile plays on my lips, thinking back to how we pulled over on the side of the road during the drive up here because we needed each other's body again.

I steal a glance at Dan from across the crowded room of suits and gowns, finding his eyes already on me. I blush and pull out my phone.

ALLY

You can't look at me like that in public.

DAN

Sorry. I can't help myself. Your ass looks
incredible in that dress.

"What are you smiling at?"

My eyes snap up from my phone and I wipe the look off my face the second I hear my mother's voice. "Nothing."

"Is there a new boy?"

"Of course not. I was smiling at something Violet sent me."

"Relax, sweetie." She sips from her champagne flute. "All I'm saying is you seem happy. Happier than I've ever seen you. I was sad to hear you ended things with Liam, but clearly you're doing well. Speaking of Liam, have you spoken to him tonight?"

"Tonight?"

"His band is performing next. Did you forget?"

My eyebrows lift in shock. The news of his presence fills me with unease. I'd forgotten all about Liam performing here until this very second. "Why didn't he cancel?"

"You expected him to cancel because you broke things off with him? That wouldn't be very professional of Liam."

"I suppose you're right. Have you spoken to him? How does he seem?"

"Flat. He hasn't bounced back as well as you have, that's for sure."

Makes sense, considering the way he sped off after our last conversation.

"Oh, here he is now." Mom nods at the stage.

I turn around, clenching my teeth with nerves when I find Liam and his band setting up their equipment. They tune their instruments and ease into the start of gentle background music. The crowd continues to chat among themselves. My mom moves on from me to a conversation with Tyler and Killian. But I watch Liam, wondering how he is. He's not the right guy for me but that doesn't mean I don't care for him.

I've seen Liam play his double bass a few times, and during each of those occasions it was clear how deeply he felt the music. He would put himself into the music, expressing the beat and rhythm with his body. There was always a smile on his face.

Tonight, there's none of that. Mom was right. He does look flat.

Liam's eyes scan the audience, pausing when they land on me. Not knowing how else to respond, I smile and wave. He glances away and shakes his head with frustration denting between his eyes.

I gulp hard, feeling the sting of guilt. I tried to not lead him on. I was honest when he came asking for a second chance, telling him we'd hang out and see where things go between us but that I wasn't ready to jump into a relationship.

I really like you and I don't want to rush into anything. Those were the words he spoke on our date when he cooked dinner for me at his apartment.

Then on Wednesday... *I stopped seeing other girls because I like you so much. I don't do shit like that for just anyone, Ally.*

He gave that whole speech about how comfortable he is with me and how he's never felt that way with anyone.

I pinch the bridge of my nose and sigh. Maybe I fucked up and didn't realize things were more serious between us than I thought.

I send Liam a text, asking if we can talk when the band finishes performing.

The song ends and another starts. Despite wanting to be by Dan's side, I keep my distance for appearances' sake and make my way to Felix, knowing it's safer this way. When I arrive, I realize Felix isn't alone. He's talking with Harper, which is a sight I've rarely seen. Whatever they're discussing has Harper worked up. Her face is as red as her scarlet hair. Their conversation comes to an abrupt stop the second they notice me. The brutal looks they're giving each other smooth out.

"Ally, hey." Harper smiles at me, though I can tell the smile is an act. She's distracted by whatever she and Felix were talking about.

Felix leaves the two of us, muttering, "This family photo better make Amabella happy," before disappearing into the crowd.

I nod in his direction. "What was that about?"

"Nothing. What song are you performing tonight?" Harper's subject change is anything by subtle. I don't push with the many questions I have about her and Felix. She clearly doesn't want to talk about it, and I don't have a good enough rapport with her to ask. Instead, I answer her question, and we settle into a conversation about music.

An hour later, after chatting with Harper about her job in the ballet company, Tyler's busy work schedule in hotel development, and how they hope to take a vacation within the next year if they can get time off, the band announces they're taking a break.

Surprisingly, Liam approaches me.

Harper gently squeezes my arm. "I should see what Tyler's doing. I'm not far if you need me."

As soon as she's gone, Liam digs his hands into his

pockets. The look in his eyes is a long way from pleasant. "You wanted to talk?"

Nausea creeps over me. My mouth turns dry and it's hard to swallow. "Yeah. I'm sorry again for hurting you. I have little experience with relationships, not that that's an excuse. I just wanted to see how you are. So... how are you?"

"What kind of a question is that?" Liam's voice is harsh. He sighs, attempting to cool his frustration, and scratches his jaw. "Something has been playing on my mind. You said there isn't anyone else, but it feels like a lie. Things were good between us. I can't see why you would end it unless there was another guy."

My chest tightens, nervous over what to say. If I answer *yes*, not only does it hurt him but also leads to the question of *who*.

"There's no one, Liam. You're a great guy—"

"Don't give me that generic crap. Fuck, you girls are all the same."

He groans and walks off, and I'm left hot and flustered, my muscles seizing up at his anger. That sick feeling in my stomach intensifies, and I'm in more of a panic when I realize I have to perform on the piano in ten minutes.

Harper returns to my side. "Hey, that sounded pretty nasty. You okay?"

"Not really. I need a moment to calm down. I'm going to find somewhere quiet."

"Do you want company?"

"No, thank you."

I rush off, slipping through the crowd and out of the main hall in the museum. This doesn't feel like a panic attack, but I need silence and somewhere private to center myself and focus on my breathing, otherwise I'll be a wreck playing the piano.

The first few doors I try to escape into are locked. The fourth one opens and I rush inside, finding myself in a small office. I shut the door and switch the light on, then lean against the desk, closing my eyes and taking a few deep breaths to calm myself.

The door opens, and when I look up, Dan is standing in front of me with concern. "You all right? Harper told me you had a rough conversation with Liam. I saw you come in here and wanted to check up on you."

I brush my hands through my hair, pulling at the nape of my neck. "I'm fine, I'm just worked up and stressed because I don't know how I'm supposed to perform in this state of mind."

Dan locks the door and steps right up to me, stroking gentle patterns along my arms. "Maybe I can help you calm down."

I let out a long breath and close my eyes again, focusing on the light sensation of his fingertips running up and down my skin. His lips brush along my jaw, making me shiver. I laugh softly.

"I know, I'll stop," he whispers.

"No. It's helping." I look up at Dan, at his lips, and suddenly don't feel so tense. "How am I going to survive this next week without seeing you?"

"I have no fucking clue." He lifts me onto the desk and pushes himself between my thighs.

I grab Dan's collar, pulling his lips to mine. The kiss is soft at first, and I lean into his embrace, taking comfort in the feel of his body against mine. When I feel his erection between my thighs, I lose myself in memories of our last few days together, how Dan has claimed my body in every possible way, and how I've never known someone could take me to such extreme physical and emotional heights.

My legs tighten around his waist, forcing his dick to grind against me. This is the last thing I should be doing right now, but the door is locked, and my God, I need this to calm down.

Dan groans into my mouth, leaning forward and resting his hands behind me on the desk. Our kisses turn fevered. His mouth trails down my neck, to my cleavage. His fingers skim up the front of my panties, making me gasp, and then they slip beneath the fabric, straight into my wetness.

"This is what you really want, isn't it?" Dan whispers against my ear. "An orgasm to calm down. I know you, Queen."

I nod, and Dan slides my panties down my legs, dropping them in a pile on the floor.

"How long do we have before your performance?"

"Long enough."

"Ally looked upset." I hear Harper's voice from beyond the office door. "I saw her enter that room."

My mother answers. "Oh, I hope she's all right. We need to get this family photo taken."

Shit. A streak of panic rushes through me. The door handle rattles. Dan locked the door and I know we're safe, but we don't have long to compose ourselves.

A door opens, not the one we entered through, a second door on the opposite wall I wasn't aware this office had. Dan and I push away from each other, but not fast enough.

It's not only Mom and Harper at the door, witnessing everything. We have the entire family as an audience, all of them catching me with my dress hoisted around my hips and Dan's shirt untucked. My panties are on the floor.

Photographers are crowded in the hallway for this family photo Mom is so desperate to capture. Cameras start flashing in my direction, dozens of them, blinding me.

All I can hear are shocked voices. *Disgusted* voices, gasping at the sight of Dan and me. I'm on display, with humiliation and dread striking me hard in the chest.

Dan steps in front of my body, shielding me from everyone's sight. But it's too late. My deepest secret has already been caught on camera and eternalized for the world to see.

CHAPTER THIRTY-FIVE

DAN

"What is going on here?" my father shouts.

I've done many things in life to earn my father's disapproval, but never have I seen him this furious. He's quick to shut the office door and lock it, blocking out the photographers. What good that will do, I don't know. They've already got their shot of Ally's legs around me. Within an hour, those images will have hit the media and will be plastered across all news outlets. Amabella wanted a photo to show how united our family is. The public is about to see how united I am with my stepsister.

Now that it's just me, Ally, Dad and Amabella in the office, Ally steps far away from me, her face red hot and her shoulders tight. I reach for her hand, but she shakes her head. She won't look at me. She won't look at anyone. Her eyes are on the ground and she's clutching her body.

She's beyond embarrassed and ashamed, I get it, and let her have her own reaction. Unlike Ally, I don't feel as shameful as I expected to now that the truth has come out. In fact, I don't feel shame at all. I stand by what I said to

Ally the first time we slept together, that the two of us are perfect for each other. I don't care how wrong the world thinks we are. It's far from ideal how people have found out about us, but it doesn't change anything for me. I still love Ally. She's still mine and I'm not letting her go.

"Get away from Ally," Dad demands. "What on earth were you doing to her?"

"Do I really need to explain it?" I answer.

"Is this another one of your defiance games? Well, congratulations, you have successfully humiliated me and Amabella in the public eye, as well as privately. Not to mention the damage this will bring upon Forever Families. This is low, Daniel, even for you, to defile your sister—"

"She's not my sister," I cut in, unable to listen to another word. "None of this is about defiance."

"I have never been more disgusted in my life," Dad continues. "Ally, did he force you into anything?"

"No. Of course not." She shakes her head, continuing to stare at the ground. "This isn't Dan's fault."

"I don't believe that for a second."

Of course he doesn't. My father's opinion of me is that low. I look at Amabella to gauge her reaction. Her silence is far worse than my father's anger. Her bottom lip quivers as she looks between me and Ally, too horrified to talk.

"Amabella, I care about Ally." Making her see the truth is somehow more important to me than with my own father.

"Dan," Amabella speaks for the first time, her voice quiet and filled with disappointment. "I can't talk rationally with you right now. Ally, get in the car. We're going home."

Ally nods and walks for the door.

"You don't have to do what they say," I tell her. "You're an adult, regardless if they treat you like one or not."

"I know," she whispers. "I want to leave with them to explain everything. I need to fix this."

What does that even mean, that she's fighting for us? I can't tell. She's so shellshocked by being caught, I can't read where her head is regarding us.

Ally obeys her mother's instructions, following her to the door. I want to grab Ally by the waist and hold her close, promising her we can work through this. We can work through anything. I need to see her look at me just once, to see a look in her eyes that tells me we're still in this together. The night of Ally's birthday celebration when we were alone in the bedroom, Ally told me she wouldn't give me up, even if people found out about us.

The heart locket I gave her. *I'm never taking it off. I'm yours forever.*

I want to believe her, but now that we've been discovered, I'm not sure she'll hold true to her word. She's always been such a people pleaser, wanting to do the right thing by our parents and Forever Families.

I call Ally's name, but she shakes her head, still unable to look at me. "Let me handle this," she mutters. "I'll call you."

Fuck. I want to believe she can handle this. I swallow hard, my chest aching at the sight of her leaving. She's left me so many times before. I hope this time is different.

The moment Amabella opens the door, the cameras are flashing again. I get a glimpse of my brothers, Harper too, all of them in shock, except Felix who is in damage control mode, trying to clear out the photographers.

"Do you see this mess I have to clean up because of

you," Dad says as soon as the door shuts, leaving the two of us alone in the office. "Why are you so set on defying me? What have I done?"

"I'm not set on defying you, but if you want to talk about all the ways you've fucked me up over the years, how much time do you have?"

He paces in front of the desk. "You're angry with me, fine. I've made mistakes. But stop trying to destroy this family with your reckless behavior. When are you going to get serious about your life?"

"I *am* serious."

"Fucking around with Ally to punish me is not serious. You know how delicate that girl is. First, you almost get her killed by a drunk man because of your poker habits. Now this. I've seen the way you move through women. When you're done with Ally and throw her to the wayside—"

"Dad, I'm in love with Ally." My words are firm and I hold eye contact so he can see how serious I am. "I've been in love with her for years."

"Enough." He spits the word, disgusted. "I have heard absolutely enough from you. You will stay away from her. Now, if you will excuse me, I have to clean up a public mess you created."

He walks out of the office to deal with all the photographers and reporters. With the doors open again, Liam slips inside, glaring at me.

"Are you the reason she ended things with me?" He stalks up to me like he's looking for a fight.

For fuck's sake. I cannot deal with him right now, not when I have doubts whether Ally will ever speak to me again. I head past Liam to get out of this building and back to my car.

"Hey, I'm talking to you." He grabs my shirt but I shove him away.

The next thing I know, splitting pain shoots through me as his fist crushes into my jaw. There's a roar from the press as they all rush into the office with their cameras.

Fan-fucking-tastic.

CHAPTER THIRTY-SIX

ALLY

My mother refuses to talk to me throughout the entire drive home from the benefit. I don't hear a single word from her until the two of us step through the front door of the beach house.

"Explain yourself, Ally."

My mother is a calm woman. I don't think I've ever heard her raise her voice, especially not at me. Yet I can tell from the sharpness in her tone how furious and disturbed she is right now. I can see it in her eyes. I'm not her little girl anymore. She's disgusted with me. I'm living in a nightmare, having news of my relationship with Dan come to light in this manner. The embarrassment and shame is something I don't know how to deal with. But out of all the things I've done wrong, I know loving Dan isn't one of them.

"Help me understand why you would do something like this."

My throat feels as if there's a huge ball wedged in it. "I love him," I whisper, my entire body shaking as I stare at my feet.

"Oh, Ally, please tell me you are not foolish enough to believe whatever this is between you and Dan is love. And please, for the love of God, tell me you haven't slept with him." I don't say anything, and she reads my silence perfectly. "I am *sick*. Were you sleeping with him behind Liam's back? I thought I raised you to know better."

My shoulders rise closer to my ears, and I clench my eyes shut, whispering, "I didn't cheat on Liam."

"How long has this been going on behind *my* back?"

"Since I first met Dan. We fought our feelings for each other from the start. I know Dan is like a son to you, but he's not my brother. He's never been a brother to me."

"*Six* years," she gasps, furious. "You've been lying to me, doing God knows what right beneath my nose, for *six* years? Who even are you? Certainly not the daughter I thought I had."

My vision grows blurred with tears, hearing her talk like this to me. I wipe my eyes before they start leaking and try to remain strong.

"This... *thing* you have with Dan stops now. Do you understand me? It's wrong. I don't want you around him again, at least not until Josh and I have figured out how to deal with you two. He's a bad influence on you. Do not call Dan. Do not text him—"

"Mom, you're treating me like a child." Somehow, I find my voice, but she's quick to cut me off.

"Because you're acting like a child. Tomorrow, there will be photos everywhere of you with your dress around your waist, looking like a whore, and with your brother, of all people. You know how hard Josh and I have worked to make Forever Families thrive. I've poured everything into it, and for what? We'll be ruined when this hits the media. Did you ever stop to consider how your actions would impact those around you, even yourself? You'll be fired from Sacred Heart, for sure."

I'm vibrating, burning up over the way she's speaking to me. Maybe I'm expecting too much of her in this moment, considering the bombshell of information that's been dropped on her about me and Dan. But it would have been nice to have my mother's empathy considering I've been caught on camera in such a vulnerable position.

"I need a drink to deal with this." She hangs her coat and purse on a hook by the front door and sighs, heading out of the entry way.

I watch the back of her head as she leaves, wondering if it's best to give her space. She's not in any state to have a reasonable conversation with and I'd like to avoid being labeled with more derogatory terms. I don't know if I can express myself adequately even if I try speaking with her about Dan. But there's one thing I'm certain of.

"I won't stop seeing him," I say before she disappears around the corner.

My mother pauses, listening to my words but not turning to face me.

I'm holding back tears. My voice is weak, but this she needs to know. "I didn't come home with you tonight because you ordered it. I came here because I love and care about you and thought we could talk about this properly. I understand this is a lot for you to take on board. When you're ready to talk, I'll be in my bedroom."

She doesn't respond. The house is deathly silent, all but for the sound of my mother's high heels on the marble floor as she walks away from me.

Now that I'm alone, I let the tears fall down my cheeks. My emotions run raw, wishing I could rewind time and have chosen to stay in the city with Dan this weekend, where I was so stupidly happy.

I reach for my purse to call Dan and tell him I'm sorry for not being more careful tonight, that I love him and despite the nightmare we're in, I'm not running away this time. But only now that I'm alone and have a moment to breathe, do I realize my purse isn't on me.

I left the benefit in such a hurry, I must have left my purse in the office where Dan and I were discovered. I never even had a chance to put my panties back on. They're still there in that office, probably having been photographed a hundred times already, solidifying the proof of what Dan and I were doing.

Without my phone, I don't have any means of contacting Dan. I don't know his number off the top of my head, and he doesn't use any form of social media. What a perfect end to this horrendous night.

CHAPTER THIRTY-SEVEN

DAN

Someone is banging on my front door. Paparazzi, I assume. I don't know how they got into my building, but they've been having a field day ever since this scandal hit the media last night. They've spent the entire day on the street, staking out my building in the hopes they catch me leave and can get another photograph.

I made the mistake of looking at the news earlier in the day and had to stop when I saw how much coverage this story is getting. I can't look anywhere without seeing photos of me and Ally or gossip columns about us. As expected, there are dozens of articles questioning the credibility of Forever Families.

To make things worse, Ally won't answer my calls. All I've received is a text early this morning from her that said *Please stop trying to contact me. I need space from you after everything that happened.*

Reading those words fucking hurt.

They feel wrong, especially after the last few days we spent together at my place.

The declaration she made on the night of her birthday

party: *I don't know how, but we'll find a way to make this work. I'm yours forever.* I want to believe Ally meant every one of those words. That she's changed from the girl she was before Paris and won't run away from her feelings and desires just to please the people around her. We've been through so much together these last few months. Grown more intimate, physically as well as emotionally, than I ever knew possible between two people.

But she's cut off communication between us before. It's what I've been so afraid of for months, ever since I got her back from Paris, that she'll run off again.

I can't help but feel like it's happening again now.

I've tried phoning Amabella but she won't answer. My father is the one person who picks up the goddamn phone. We spoke this morning, and it was only to give me strict instructions to not speak with the media. Like I'd want to anyway. My only care is Ally and when I asked how she is, if he'll hand the phone to her so we can speak, he refused, telling me she's upset and to stop calling her.

I'm tempted to drive back to The Hamptons and barge into the beach house so I can figure this all out with Ally because it's fucking agony not knowing what she's thinking. I've spent the entire day shuffling through my deck of neon cards, hoping to find the peace of mind it always brings me. Hoping that however bad Ally is feeling, she's back in her bedroom, holding the missing card from this deck and remembering everything the Queen of Hearts represents between us.

"Bro, come on, open up," Felix calls. I let out a breath of relief to hear it's him banging at the door.

I answer, finding all three of my brothers. They'll no doubt want an explanation from me. I'm not in the mood to deal with their judgment, but no time better than now to get this shit over with. Stepping back, I invite them inside. Only Felix and Tyler enter. Killian remains in the hallway, preoccupied with a phone call.

Felix removes his suit jacket and makes himself comfortable on my couch, reclining with his ankle crossed over his opposite knee. "Your jaw looks fucked. Liam got you good."

"I'll live."

"You and Ally are... how should I phrase this... *together*, since the last time we spoke about her?"

"We *were* together," I mutter. "I don't know what we are after last night. I can't get in contact with her."

Tyler stands with both hands in his pockets, observing my living room, his attention pausing on the piano, then on a pile of lingerie I stripped off Ally before fucking her on the table. I grab the garments and toss them out of sight, into the bathroom.

Tyler scratches the back of his neck. "This is fucked up, man."

"If that's all you came here to say—"

"Easy," Felix cuts in, the word authoritative but spoken in the relaxed, smug manner he always has about him. "We're here because you have two very pissed off brothers. Killian in particular. Thought I'd help facilitate a mediation session so they can move past their issues and offer their support."

Tyler glares at Felix. "I'm not supporting anything. She's our—"

"Yes, Ally has come to feel like a real sister to us. Not to Dan," Felix says. I've never been more grateful to have him as my brother. "The word *sister* doesn't get spoken again during this conversation. You may not approve of this relationship, but it has nothing to do with you as long as they're both happy. Tyler, you said you understood this before coming here. You can leave if there's still an issue. Run back to daddy and take his side in all of this."

"Asshole." The muscles in Tyler's neck strain. I'm surprised when he maintains his composure and returns his focus to me. "I know what you're like with women. You're not just messing around with Ally?"

"No."

"Then I'll keep my opinions to myself. But I need more time to process this relationship before I can even attempt to accept it."

Before I can say anything further, Killian barges through the front door scowling at me. "Do you realize how much shit you've gotten me into at work? I have been on the phone all afternoon with Sacred Heart, being interviewed over you and Ally and having my own professional reputation questioned. They've already fired Ally. The school want to get rid of me too because I'm connected to Forever Families."

The news about Ally being fired isn't a shock, though I do worry for her emotional state, knowing she'll be crushed by this turn of events. The rebound effect onto Killian is what has me alarmed.

"The school can't do that to you," I tell him. "You have nothing to do with this."

"This isn't just about you. All of us Blackwoods are the face of Forever Families. Sacred Heart can do whatever the fuck they like."

"Shit. Man, I'm sorry. I didn't mean to drag anyone into this mess."

"If this is only some kink about fucking Ally because she's off limits to you, then stop it right now. You're screwing with my career," he says.

"It's not. We kept this a secret for so long because we knew it wouldn't be accepted. But I'm serious about her."

Killian slumps onto the couch with Felix, groaning as he rubs both palms over his eyes. Silence creeps over the four of us. Unless they have questions for me, I'm not about to waste time trying to make them accept what they clearly can't.

"Has anyone spoken with Ally?" I ask. "She's not answering my calls."

"We've tried," Felix says. "She's not answering any of our calls."

Fuck. Staying put in this apartment, without any communication with Ally, feels like a prison cell. "I need to go to her. Something isn't right. She wouldn't—" My throat closes up. My chest twists at the possibility of Ally shutting me out. "Ally loves me."

"I know," Felix says, his eyes firm on me, his words heavy with empathy for the pain I'm feeling. "But going to Ally isn't a good idea. I'm sure she has a lot to process right now and just needs time to move through it on her own. She's not like us. Never been the defiant kind. Never publicly done anything to feel ashamed of. She'll be dealing with a whole lot of shit from Dad and Amabella, along with Sacred Heart."

I groan, biting my fist, and start pacing. "I can't stay away from her."

"I spoke to Dad on the phone this morning," Felix continues, "and he's livid. You showing up will make it ten times worse. Trust me, you want to avoid Dad at all costs right now. Not only that, he says the house is swarmed by the media. No one is leaving or entering the property. Give everything a couple of days to die down. Let things cool off with Dad and Amabella. Ally will call you when she's ready."

Perhaps Felix is right. Doesn't make the situation any easier. I'm sick to the pit of my stomach, knowing the last time I gave Ally space like this, I came home to find nothing but a goodbye letter, the Queen of Hearts, and had lost her to a year in France. If she returns the Queen of Hearts to me again, *her* heart, I don't think I can recover this time.

CHAPTER THIRTY-EIGHT

ALLY

Moonlight streams down on me in my bay window, shining on the Queen of Hearts card in my hand. She's been the only thing keeping me sane these last twenty-four hours. Neither of my parents have spoken to me, other than a warning to stay in the house, away from the reporters that have set up camp in front of our gates. I told Mom and Josh I'd like the three of us to speak about me and Dan, but they turned me away, saying they're too busy in damage control mode with Forever Families.

It's part of the truth. They've been locked in the home office all day taking non-stop video meetings and giving statements to the public. This step sibling scandal, along with the regular bad press Dan's poker games bring to the organization, has the public demanding an audit of the charity's credibility.

The other part of the truth is that my parents don't want to entertain the idea of Dan and me having real feelings for each other.

Their reaction is beyond upsetting, but not a shock. This is why I tried to keep me and Dan a secret. But now the whole world knows and I'm being punished for loving him. I lost my job this morning. No surprise there. Principal Sinclair was able to reach me on the home's landline. The conversation between us was humiliating but is so small in the grand scheme of all my issues. I haven't bothered searching my name on the internet, knowing I'm better off without seeing the photos or reading what's being said about me.

My bedroom door creaks open, letting in a trail of light to the darkness I'm sitting in. "Knock, knock."

I glance at the door, finding Daxton's head poking inside. I had no idea he was visiting. Ordinarily, I'd be happy to have his company. But I don't think I can handle seeing him right now if he has anything negative to say. Nor can I deal with him, of all people, thinking less of me.

"Hey, kid. Can I come in?"

"Only if you don't hate me now too."

"No one hates you. Certainly not me."

I squint when Daxton turns the light on. He steps inside, closing the door behind himself, and joins me at my window seat.

I slip the Queen of Hearts into the pocket of my pajama pants. "Mom called you here for support, I guess. How did you get through all the paparazzi at the gates?"

"Your parents hired security."

It's that bad out there? Jesus.

I stare at my hands, fidgeting with them in my lap. "You should have seen how angry Mom and Josh were with me last night. They struggle to look at me, their perfect little girl who is not so perfect anymore."

He contemplates my words, silent for a long moment before nodding. "I've never told you this, but I messed up really bad when Jordan and I first started dating. So bad that she broke up with me and I thought I would never see her again."

I look up at him, a little surprised. Curious, even. But I don't pry.

"The point I'm making is that I'm not perfect. No one is. And I'm the last person who should be judging anyone. Your entire life, Ally, you've always worked so hard to be the perfect daughter. Perfect student. Perfect musician. You've never stepped a toe out of line. Perhaps you think people will like you more if you're perfect. Whatever the reason, I can't imagine how tiresome the pressure would be. You don't need to be this perfect girl that other people might want you to be. You need to do what will make you happy." He stops with the spiel and smiles at me. "Dan makes you happy."

I lower my head and sigh, fidgeting with my hands in my lap. Daxton might be my favorite person in the world, second to Dan. He always knows the right thing to say. "Can you repeat all of that to Mom and Josh?"

"I'm working on it. But they need time to process you and Dan."

"You're a really good guy, you know that? Jordan is so lucky to be marrying you."

He chuckles. "I remember when Jordan first met you. You were fifteen. She told me and your mom that you had a crush on Dan. Your mother was convinced Jordan was mistaken. She said you were such a lonely child and just happy to have a friend in Dan. The evidence has always been in front of your mother's face. Perhaps she didn't want to believe it because she's had such a rough past and was so set upon having a picture-perfect family for once."

Daxton again with all the insightful wisdom.

"I wanted a picture-perfect family too after what

happened with Mom's ex. I tried really hard to keep Dan as a friend. A... brother." I cringe, using that label for him. "But he's not. I won't stop seeing Dan. At the same time, I care about Mom and Josh's opinion of me, and I want to fix this family. I don't like that I've caused so many issues for them with Forever Families."

Daxton takes my hand in his, giving it an encouraging squeeze. "Tell them everything you've just said to me."

"I've tried. They don't want to talk."

"They'll come around. Give them time." Daxton stands from the window seat. "In the meantime, come downstairs and eat ice cream with me."

I smile, about to take him up on the offer, but something more pressing comes to mind. "Ice cream sounds good. Would you mind if I borrow your phone first to call Dan? I left mine at the benefit and haven't been able to contact him since." Nor have I been game to ask Mom or Josh if I can borrow their phone to make this call.

"Sure. I'll be downstairs when you're ready." Daxton hands me his phone and steps out of my room.

The moment I'm alone, I'm left staring at the screen, wondering how I plan to contact Dan when I still don't have his number. I scroll through Daxton's contacts, hopeful to find Dan's name. It's not there, nor can I find anyone else's name who would be able to pass Dan's number to me. Goddammit. I don't know why I thought this would work.

I take a long shot, calling Jordan in the hopes that she can help me find Dan's number. When she doesn't answer, I give up, knowing I'll have to resort to the dreaded option of asking one of my parents for their phone. I'm betting they'll turn me away when I explain I've lost my phone and would like to use theirs to speak with Dan. But I'll take my chances.

I head downstairs, straight for the office, a ball of nervous energy as I knock on the door. Nobody answers. My palms are sweating, anxious over disturbing them in a meeting. I knock a second time, and when there's still no answer, I open the door, finding the office empty and... my phone laying in the middle of their desk.

My purse is there too. A slither of pink lace peeks out from the zipper and I realize it's my panties I left behind at the benefit.

Jesus Christ. My parents have had these items the whole time? What, did Josh grab my belongings at the benefit, realizing I'd left them behind? And now they've kept them here in secret, knowing that without my phone I can't contact Dan.

I don't care how much stress they're under, how disappointed and even angry they are in my choices, keeping my phone from me isn't right.

My blood pumps hot around my body with frustration. I live under my parents' roof but it's not because I'm reliant on them. *They* were the ones who were so eager for us to live together when I returned from Paris. I have my own money. I pay for this phone myself. Yet they've kept the phone from me like I'm a rebellious teenager instead of a fully-grown adult. Just because they don't like me being with Dan doesn't mean they can act like this.

I lean against the desk and hold my head in my hands, wondering if it's all my fault they've kept my phone from me. They believe they're doing right by me. They're treating me like a child because I've always let them treat me this way. *My* behavior needs to change.

With a heavy exhale, I unlock my phone to call Dan,

finding our text message conversation already open. There are a bunch of messages from Dan, asking if I'm okay and why I'm not returning his texts or phone calls. Then I see the last message from me.

ALLY

> Please stop trying to contact me. I need space from you after everything that happened.

My hand tightens around the phone, my blood pressure rising.

I never sent that message.

Someone sent it. Who?

I'm riddled with disbelief, not wanting to face that my parents could have sent Dan a message, pretending to be me. They wouldn't... They're mad with me but...

I grow hotter by the second, *seething*, not seeing any other possibility when they're the ones who have been in possession of my phone. If they did send the message, this is crossing the fucking line. Do they think they're protecting me? Whatever the answer is, I don't care. There's no acceptable excuse. Sending this message is deceitful and an invasion of privacy.

I storm out of the office, searching for Mom and Josh. Voices come from the kitchen. I search there first, finding them in a conversation with Daxton, the three of them sitting on stools around the island counter.

"You hid my phone from me?" I interrupt, my voice revolted but level.

The three of them turn my way, startled by my tone.

"Yes," Mom admits. "We didn't want—"

"You sent Dan a message, pretending to be me."

She falters, looking to Josh for support. "We did what we thought was best—"

"How *dare* you," I shout. I'm shaking, having an out of body experience, never having raised my voice like this in my entire life. I always speak to my parents with the utmost respect, but I'm too angry to care right now. They don't deserve my respect when they don't respect me.

They're sitting wide-eyed, stunned by my outburst, Daxton especially. He's the first one to move, his gaze shifting in confusion between me and my parents. "Ally, take a breath."

I ignore him, unleashing myself on my parents. "Do you even care about Dan in all of this and how that message will impact him? You say you don't recognize me anymore. I don't recognize you two either. I stayed with you last night instead of going to Dan because I love you and thought you deserved an explanation about my relationship with him, but you don't want to talk. You want me to fall into line and take orders. I am *not* a child. And I am *not* staying here another night."

"Ally, you're upset," Josh says carefully. "There's a lot of high stress going on in this household right now and you're not thinking properly."

"For the first time, I'm thinking properly."

"You have no car," Mom adds. "Not to mention all the press outside."

"I don't care about the press. And I don't care if I have to walk to Dan. I am leaving this house."

"Ally, enough," her voice cuts through the air, trying to discipline me.

"No. I'm an adult and you don't get to treat me like this. You don't get to tell me who I can and can't love. You don't get to tell me I look like a whore."

Silence rings between all four of us, broken only by Daxton in disbelief. "A... whore?"

My mother sighs, holding her temples. "I was speaking in reference to the photographs of Ally taken last night and the bad image they would cast upon her and Forever Families. I said they would make her look like a whore, not that she is one."

I scoff, finally understanding Dan's issue with the organization. "That's all you seem to care about, saving Forever Families, instead of talking to your children and mending relationships."

"Ally, that's not true," Josh says, trying to cease fire and hush me with his hands. "Your mother and I care about you very much."

"How? Because I can't see it. You won't talk to me. You send a message to Dan, impersonating me, trying to destroy my relationship with him. God knows how terrible he's feeling right now. I thought you wanted to fix things between you and Dan. You've just made everything a million times worse for yourself. He's a good person and deserves so much better than this treatment."

Daxton digs into his suit jacket, retrieving keys. "I think it's best for everyone if you all have space to calm down. I'll take Ally back to the city to be with Dan."

"Absolutely not," Mom snaps. "That will only encourage—"

"Amabella, you are driving your daughter away from you right now. Trust me in this decision before you lose her for good."

CHAPTER THIRTY-NINE
DAN

Midnight and I'm lying in bed, empty inside as I stare at the ceiling with the room drowned in a dull neon blue glow. I'm startled out of my blackhole of thoughts when someone knocks on my door again. For fuck's sake.

"Dan, are you home?"

I sit up instantly, recognizing Ally's voice, and rush to the door. Before I get there, keys rattle in the lock and Ally steps inside with Daxton right behind her. She's in her pajamas and her eyes are red from crying. The moment Ally sees me, she runs into my arms, and I've never been so relieved.

I hold Ally tight, lifting her from the ground and burying my face in her hair, inhaling her sweet scent. She clings to me just as urgently, murmuring over and over again that she's sorry. What she's apologizing for, I don't know. I don't care. All that matters is she's here with me, in my arms where she belongs.

"It's okay, baby," I whisper, stroking her hair. "Everything is going to be all right."

"I love you. I wanted to talk to you but didn't have my

phone. Our parents..." Her voice breaks and she starts sobbing into my chest. "Dan, it's been horrible."

"I can only imagine. We're together now. Nothing else matters."

I'm so wrapped up in Ally that I forget we're not alone until Daxton places a suitcase inside the doorway and clears his throat. "Things got messy between Ally and your parents. I brought her here because I could see everything turning far worse if she stayed."

"Thank you." I nod at Daxton.

"I should be on my way. Ally, I know your mom and Josh didn't behave right, but they're good people. You know they love you both very much."

Didn't behave right? That's a big statement, coming from Daxton. "What the fuck happened?"

"It's late. I'll give you two some privacy and let Ally fill you in on the details. Ally, just remember they're processing the news of you and Dan in their own way, but they'll come around to accepting you two. Take the space from them you need, whether it's a week or a month or however long it takes until you can all have a civilized conversation."

Ally turns in my arms to face Daxton. "Thank you. I really appreciate everything you've done for me."

"Anything for you, kid. If you two need anything, I'm only a phone call away."

She sinks back into my chest the moment Daxton is gone. "I left my phone at the benefit. I didn't know how to contact you for an entire day, and then I found that not only did our parents have my phone and were hiding it from me, but they'd sent you a message, pretending to be me, asking you to stay away."

I lean back from Ally to look her in the eyes, astounded

by her words. Deep down, I knew that message couldn't have been genuine.

"I confronted them and we got into a fight. I was yelling and..."

"*You* were yelling?"

Her lips twitch and she gives the softest laugh. "Yeah. It felt kind of good."

I can feel myself smirking. "I would have loved to have witnessed that."

She returns her head to my chest. "I should have stayed by your side last night. I'm sorry. I was in shock and wasn't thinking straight. Mom and Josh were so angry and disgusted and... I thought I could try to explain things to them. I was embarrassed I'd been caught with you and... I'm sorry. Dan, I'm so sorry. I'm not embarrassed anymore. I'm proud to be yours. I'm through with trying to please them and being the girl they want me to be."

"You don't need to explain yourself to me. We're together and that's all I care about." I kiss her forehead. "You belong here with me, Ally. Let me run you a warm bath to relax."

"Only if you're planning on getting in it with me."

I grab her ass and press her hips to mine. "Obviously, Queen."

CHAPTER FORTY

ALLY

While Dan runs the bath, I make myself comfortable on the couch, taking a moment to check my phone. It died shortly after Daxton and I left The Hamptons, giving me no chance to call Dan. Now, with my phone on charge, I see all the missed calls and messages I've received over the last day. A bunch from all my stepbrothers. Killian, telling me how much shit he's in at Sacred Heart, then sending a follow up message asking if I'm all right. Tyler and Harper also ask if I'm okay, making no comment about me and Dan.

FELIX

I'm proud of you, baby sis. Didn't know you had it in you to piss off Dad. You're officially one of us. Also, nice going with Dan ;)

I scoff at the message, laughing a little.

"Apparently Felix is proud of me," I call out over the sound of the running water.

"He's had more time to process us than everyone else." Dan steps into view, leaning one shoulder against the door frame. His body is washed in purple neon light seeping from the bathroom. "I told Felix about us a few weeks ago. It was when I thought you could have been pregnant. I needed someone to talk to and knew I could trust him. He's been good about everything."

I'm too busy admiring the sight of Dan to care what he's just said, shirtless and with the elastic of his track pants low, barely concealing his dick. It's a sight I'll never tire from. The thick muscles in his arms and torso. His dark hair is a mess from lying in bed. He's my boyfriend and everyone knows it now, that I get *this*.

I fold my legs, squeezing them tight. Earlier in the day, I was still embarrassed about people knowing I've slept with Dan. Now, I just think screw them all.

Dan laughs, smirking. "What the fuck are you thinking about to be looking at me like that?"

My attention rises from the bulge in Dan's pants up to his face. "That everyone knows what you've done to me, and I don't care. Maybe I even like that they know."

His eyes darken, smug over my confession. "You like people knowing that I've fucked you. That you're my slut."

There's no denying I've always gotten off on being a slut for Dan and no one else.

"You really never told anyone about us?" Dan asks.

"I wanted to tell Violet, but I couldn't risk it."

There are a bunch of missed calls and texts from her on my phone too. I open her texts, relieved to find she feels much the same as Felix.

VIOLET

THE OTHER GUY IS DAN?!?!?!? YOUR STEPBROTHER!!!! Girl, that's hot. Call me right this second! I need details!

Shit. I just heard Sacred Heart fired you. Seriously, call me back. I hope you're ok.

There are a few more messages from her in the same vein. It's such a relief she hasn't turned against me. I check the time, seeing it's past midnight, and send Violet a quick text, letting her know I'm fine and that we'll talk tomorrow. Jordan has sent supportive messages too. I reply with a thank you message, knowing Daxton will fill her in on all the details.

"Bath's ready," Dan says.

My eyes flick up from my phone, landing on his naked body in the doorway. My stomach tightens with a delicious kind of anticipation. I lick my lips, a smile lifting the corners of my mouth. Discarding my phone, I slip out of my pajamas and head through to the neon purple bathroom, brushing my lips against Dan's as I walk by. He pulls me back and deepens the kiss. Warmth fills me as our bodies press together, skin to skin.

We slide into the hot, bubbly water together, and I lean back against Dan's chest, trying my best to relax in his arms after all the chaos that's gone down today. It feels so strange to be in this bathtub with him, in our own cozy little world at last, when all hell is breaking loose with our parents, Forever Families, and the media. Mom and Josh would be fuming right now, knowing I'm here with Dan.

"You're so tense. Let me help you relax." Dan rubs my shoulders, massaging me with soap.

His hands feel incredible. I'm trying my hardest to be present, but it's difficult, considering everything going on outside the sanctuary of this apartment.

"I'm sorry about your job."

"Sacred Heart is the least of my problems right now. But thank you." I let out a shaky breath. "I want to believe things will resolve with Mom and Josh but... It got so ugly,

Dan. Neither of them would talk with me. Mom forbids me to see you. She said... I looked like a whore."

His hands pause on my shoulders, and I feel him tense. "I'm sorry. I know how much that must hurt, coming from your mother." Dan turns me around to face him, wrapping my legs around his waist. He washes the bubbles from his hand and strokes my cheek. "We'll do as Daxton said— separate ourselves from our parents for a while. It will be best for everyone, at least until all the high emotions have calmed down. We'll go on living our lives, doing our best not to think about them. I'm not going to let all of this drama stop me from being happy with you."

I press a soft kiss to his lips, deciding I won't let it stop me either. "I hate that the truth has caused such a rift. I wish it hadn't come out this way and caused so many issues. But I'm glad the truth is out there. You're the one person who makes me feel alive, and now we can be together without any secrets."

Dan's dick twitches between my thighs, bringing a smile to my face. I tilt my hips, gliding along his hard length, drawing a groan from low in his chest.

"You said you get all my firsts," I whisper, moaning as I drag my clit along his dick again. "We've never done it in the bath before."

Without warning, Dan grabs hold of my hips and shoves me down onto his cock, filling every inch of me. I gasp and arch my back at the sudden rush of pleasure that consumes me. The length of him, stretching me. His mouth takes one of my nipples, and I clench around his cock as his tongue brushes over the sensitive flesh.

"You always know what I need." I grab either side of the bathtub and slowly start to move up and down, massaging Dan's cock with my pussy.

The water laps around us, even spills over the rim of the tub. Neither of us care about the mess we'll need to clean up later. Groaning, Dan grips my hips and guides me, helping me ride his dick with slow strokes.

"I thought I was losing you again," he murmurs. His gaze latches onto mine and I see so much pain within his eyes.

"Never." I brush a hand over the heart locket, reminding him of the declaration I made when he clasped it around my neck.

Dan's hot breath against my lips sends a shiver throughout my body, and I start to pick up the pace, bouncing faster on his cock. I can't help but feel a sense of defiance in this moment, as if we're saying *fuck you* to the world. The defiance only makes everything feel better, having everyone know I belong to Dan.

My body tingles with anticipation as an orgasm grows within me. I can feel it, the tension in my muscles, the rising heat between my thighs. I begin to ride Dan faster, not chasing my own orgasm, but trying to build his, desperate to have Dan's cum inside me.

His breath quickens. Dan clenches his teeth, hissing through the pleasure. I can see the muscles in his neck and shoulders flexing. And then Dan groans, his body tense. He slams up into me, releasing a loud grunt. The moment I feel his cum spurt into me, I let go of my own control and come hard on his dick. My orgasm bursts through me, the feeling so intense I almost black out.

CHAPTER FORTY-ONE

DAN

ALLY

I love the dresses. You're amazing.

DAN

Which dress have you decided to wear?

That's a surprise you'll have to wait for. See
you tonight.

I reread our messages from earlier, smiling as I return my
phone to my suit jacket, waiting at the street front for Ally's
arrival. The hour is eight p.m., and she should be here at the
restaurant any moment. It's a strange feeling, going on a
date with Ally and finally being able to act affectionate with
her in public. On top of that newness, I can't deny feeling
nervous, having never asked a girl on a date before. At least,
a date that means something.

Ally deserves the world and I want this to be a memorable occasion for her. While she was out today with Jordan
at another wedding dress fitting, I purchased two dresses
for Ally and wrapped them in a box, leaving them on our
bed for her to find when she returned home. I took off to

The Scarlet Mirage for a game of poker, leaving behind a letter for Ally to find with the details of tonight.

Two dresses. Choose the one that makes you feel the most beautiful and wear it tonight because I'm taking you on a date. A car service will pick you up at 7:30.

I straighten my jacket and readjust the bouquet of red roses in my hands. It's been a week since our relationship became public news. We've mostly stayed inside to avoid being hounded by paparazzi. The few times we ventured out, it was chaotic, with photographers following our every move, shouting questions about our relationship and Forever Families. We did our best to ignore them and made no comments.

The third time out of the apartment wasn't quite so intense. The photographers were still around but lurking at a distance. I have no clue what the tabloids are saying about us, nor do I care. Neither does Ally, which is impressive.

Violet, on the other hand, is thoroughly invested in the gossip articles and visited us mid-week, proudly insisting we see the paparazzi shots and how happy we look together in them. She showed us several supposed viral images. Me and Ally sharing an ice cream. Kissing in the street. Walking hand in hand. Laughing. There are even photos of me with my hand unapologetically on Ally's ass. We look good together, I won't lie. I'm glad Ally has a friend in Violet.

A Lexus pulls up in front of the building and the driver opens the back passenger door. I see Ally's smooth, bare legs first, as she places a jeweled stiletto on the sidewalk. The question runs through my mind of which dress she chose, both polar opposites in style. The first one is full of bows and ribbons, a pastel pink, as she's always loved.

The second is black satin, more sophisticated and with a deep thigh split. If she doesn't feel comfortable wearing it in public, no issues here, I'll enjoy the dress on her in private.

The driver steps out of the way, and I have to work hard to keep my thoughts under control when I get a full view of Ally standing in front of the car. I fail terribly and blood rushes to my cock.

She chose the black dress and she looks so goddamn fuckable in it.

My girl's lips are a bright red, her hair is styled in loose waves, and she has a thick shawl wrapped around her shoulders for warmth in the cold night. Staring at her, I can't form a single word. A camera flash goes off somewhere nearby. If that photo finds its way onto the internet, I can only imagine what the public will say.

Ally smirks, stepping up to me and planting a kiss to my lips, her mouth lingering on mine. "Cat got your tongue?"

"I didn't expect you to choose this dress. You're getting fucked senseless when we return home." She giggles when I place a soft smack on her ass before raising the bouquet of roses between us. "For you. A perfect match to your lips."

Ally grins and takes the flowers, bringing them to her nose. "They're beautiful. Thank you. I love them."

I grab her hand, weaving our fingers, and lead her inside the building for the elevator. When we arrive at the enclosed rooftop restaurant, Ally gasps at the 360-degree city views.

The restaurant is an intimate setting, with soft chandelier lighting cast over the dining area. Each patron is dressed in formal attire, sipping on champagne and engaged in quiet conversation at their table. A pianist sits in the corner playing background music. A seating hostess guides us to our table, taking our drink order before leaving us to read the dinner menu.

"How's the wedding prep coming along?" I ask as Ally places her roses on the table.

"Jordan looks so beautiful in her dress. Just over two months till the big day." She thrums her fingers on the table, silently watching them. "I've been thinking... This wedding will be awkward if we haven't cleared things up with Mom and Josh by then."

It will be. Despite Ally's angst toward our parents, there's a touch of sadness in her eyes. We haven't attempted to speak with Dad and Amabella in a week. Nor have they contacted us. We've barely spoken to Tyler and Killian either. It feels weird, considering Thanksgiving is in a couple of days.

I place my hand over Ally's. "Don't stress too much about the wedding. All we can do is take things one day at a time."

"I know. You're right." She watches our two hands, quiet for another long moment. I'm about to ask where her thoughts have traveled to, but she clears her throat and beats me to it. "I made a decision today." A nervous smile accompanies the words. "I'm going to start seeing a therapist again so I can... eventually audition for Juilliard."

I suck in a quick breath. My eyes widen and I'm suddenly smiling from ear to ear. "Fuck, Ally, I'm so proud of you. This is what you want?"

"Yes." She meets my gaze, laughing softly. Any sadness that she felt a moment ago has vanished from her beautiful face. "I lost my way for a while. These last few days have made me realize that I *can* have what I want, even if it seems unattainable. There'll be a lot of hard work ahead of me, but if I get into Juilliard—" She stops herself and smiles again. "*When* I get into Juilliard, it will be competitive but I'm letting go of this idea that I need to be the best and always perfect. I won't let fear and panic attacks hold me back. You believe in me and so do I."

I slide my chair around the table, positioning myself right next to Ally. We're dining in a fancy restaurant, but I can't resist kissing her just a little, not when she's glowing with happiness right in front of me like the most brilliant fucking creature on this planet.

"You'll get into Juilliard," I murmur against her lips. "You'll have everything you've ever wanted. I'll make sure of it, my Queen of Hearts."

CHAPTER FORTY-TWO

DAN

2 MONTHS LATER

"I can't believe you two are getting married in a week," Ally says.

"I can barely believe it either," Jordan gushes and giggles as she leans into Daxton, the two of them sitting on the opposite couch from me and Ally in the living room of their penthouse. "The date has always felt so far away, and now it's right here."

Daxton, too, has a buzz about him. They both look happy and in love, full of pre-wedding bliss.

"So, run us through the plans again," Ally says, sipping a Pina Colada that Jordan insisted on making for all of us. We've been invited over for dinner and drinks. I don't know what they plan on serving for food, but it smells incredible cooking in the oven.

"We're flying the wedding party to California on Thursday, which will give us time to settle in at the vineyard before the big day. There'll be a rehearsal dinner Friday night. Then the wedding is Saturday afternoon."

"So exciting. I can't wait."

Daxton shifts, spreading his arms along the backrest, and clears his throat. "So..." That one word has a change in mood to something I can tell he's treading carefully around. "Amabella tells me the two of you are meeting with her and Josh tomorrow."

I'm not surprised she's mentioned it to him. Daxton has been good about everything over the last two months, acting as neutral territory between us and our parents. Jordan has too.

Ally responds with an awkward smile but remains quiet. Her gaze drops to her lap.

"Yes," I answer for the two of us. "It should be... interesting."

Our parents contacted us shortly after we broke off communication with them. It was a phone call to me from my father. When I didn't answer, he sent a text addressed to me and Ally, explaining that he and Amabella were regretful over what had gone down between all of us and that they'd like us to speak. Ally ended up replying, thanking him for reaching out but that we needed space.

They respected our wishes. We didn't hear from them again until a couple of days ago, a text letting us know they're living back in the city at their apartment on the Upper East Side. They asked if we would visit them. Ally and I had our reservations, but in the end decided enough time has passed that we can all be civil toward each other.

Ally looks up from her lap and takes another sip of her cocktail. "I won't lie. I'm nervous about seeing Mom and Josh."

"Don't be nervous. They want to reconcile things with you both," Daxton says, like that really adds much comfort.

We'll be walking into our parents' home blind, with no indication of what their vision of a reconciliation looks like. Will they embrace our relationship or brush it under the rug, wanting to mend the fallout between us as long as they can ignore that Ally and I are together? I've been fucking their daughter and they know it. I can't see how they'll be accepting of us. Perhaps their idea of a reconciliation means an attempt at convincing me and Ally out of our relationship.

"They miss you and often ask what you're both up to," Daxton continues. "Ally, I told them you're pursuing Juilliard again. They're pleased to hear it."

She's doing well, attending weekly therapy sessions and practicing the piano a lot. Ally hasn't tried to get another teaching job. Even if a school manages to overlook all the recent negative press, Ally feels it would be a job steering her in the wrong direction. She has money saved and can afford the luxury of taking time off work to find herself. I've told her multiple times I earn more than enough money from poker to pay for anything she needs, but she says I spoil her enough as is.

It doesn't get lost on me how Daxton hasn't mentioned to the parents what I've been up to. I cough, attempting to hide my laugh. "And the update you gave them on me? I bet they're pleased to hear I'm still playing poker."

Daxton laughs at my sarcasm. "I don't need to update them on that. They see it in the media enough. But they constantly ask about how you are, your father especially. I've told them you're well and happy. The happiest I've ever seen you. Both of you. I tell them every time we talk how good you are for each other."

Ally speaks up, clasping her hands in her lap. "This sounds great in theory, but I can't see how they will be accepting of my relationship with Dan."

"Just hear them out, okay?" Daxton says. "Go in with an open mind. I know you don't like this rift between you and your family. And I, selfishly, want everyone to be united at my wedding. I don't want family drama there."

"I second that thought," Jordan says, bringing her cocktail to her lips and curling into Daxton's arms. "Please try to find some kind of common ground between all of you."

There won't be any drama with my brothers at the wedding. Tyler and Killian have come around in the last few weeks, accepting me and Ally. I assume a lot of Killian's acceptance had to do with Sacred Heart easing up on him now that Forever Families has stopped making news headlines every day. Tyler isn't enthusiastic about us as a couple, but then again, he's never enthusiastic about anything. He's just learned to be okay with us.

As for our parents...

I rake a hand through my hair, tugging at the ends in silent frustration. Perhaps finding common ground with Amabella will be manageable. It's my father that's the real concern. I can barely stand to be in the same room as him. The issues between us go far deeper than his disapproval of me sleeping with Ally. It's a lifetime of being angry at him for the way he abandoned me as a child, and this isn't a one-sided issue. He hasn't been happy about my lifestyle for years. I don't see how one conversation tomorrow will fix anything or even give us common ground.

"You know, you're right," Ally finally says. "You both have been so good to us throughout the last few months. I'll do this for you, because I don't want to bring this tension to your wedding. And because... despite everything that's happened, I love Mom and Josh. I miss them."

I can see it in Ally's eyes how much fixing things with our parents means to her. I've seen it every day for the last two months. She tells me this has been the happiest two months of her life, and I know she speaks the truth. We've been so incredibly connected and free to finally be us. But I see her sadness peek through from time to time, wishing our family wasn't so divided.

"Dan, you'll make an effort too?" Daxton asks.

I bite the inside of my mouth, groaning quietly. My mind is set when I notice Ally's eyes have turned glassy. I'll make an effort, not for Daxton and Jordan, even though they've been good to me. Not for my parents' sake.

I'll do it for Ally.

I'll do *anything* for Ally because I love her and want her to be happy in every aspect of her life. Which means showing Dad and Amabella that I'm good for Ally and...

Fuck.

I wipe a hand over my face and sigh, knowing what else needs to happen. This family divide won't ever truly be resolved unless my father and I work on these life-long issues between us.

Ally slides her hand into mine. "Dan, you okay?"

"Yeah," I murmur, lifting her hand to my lips. "I'm going to make things right. I promise."

CHAPTER FORTY-THREE
ALLY

My palms are sweating. I take a deep breath, trying to calm my racing heart.

Dan kisses my forehead. "Relax. We've got this."

"I hope you're right. You ready?"

"Yeah." He squeezes my waist. "We'll get through this together."

Dan raises his hand, not even getting a chance to knock before the door opens and we're face to face with Mom and Josh.

"Hi," I say, taking in the sight of them.

They look how I suppose I do. Nervous smiles. Yet there's no mistaking the relief in their eyes. Their focus shifts to Dan's hand at my waist. My cheeks flush, feeling awkward. I won't hide my relationship with Dan just because it makes them uncomfortable, but that doesn't mean I want to flaunt our physical affection in front of them when everything is so uncertain between all of us.

Being on the same page as me, Dan drops his hand. I press my lips together, rocking back and forth on my feet, wondering if some harsh comment is about to come our way.

"Dan, Ally, it's good to see you both," Josh says with genuine warmth. "Thanks for visiting us this afternoon. Come inside."

Dan clears his throat. "It's good to see you too."

I let out a breath of relief and we enter the front door, into the penthouse living room. It's been about eighteen months since I've stepped foot in this place, since before Paris. Despite the circumstances, it's nice to be back in the home I used to live in. Mom and I moved in here when I was fifteen and it's the first home I ever felt like I had a real family to live with.

"Take a seat. Can I get you two anything to drink? Cake?" Mom asks. It's so formal and unlike us. I don't like it at all.

"Mom..." I start, not having planned to delve straight into this speech, but I can't stand all the pleasantries. I swallow hard, forcing myself to remain strong. I won't crumple and hide like the girl I was a few months ago. "You don't need to tiptoe around us. I know we haven't spoken in a long time and the last time we did speak it was ugly, but it's still me. It's still Dan. We just want to have a calm and honest conversation with you two. No cake needed."

She nods. "I know it's still you, honey. It's just... I've been sick over this. It means a lot to me that you two are here today. Josh too."

Josh gestures to the couches. "How about we all take a seat and chat."

Dan and I sit together, not too close—again, wanting to be respectful. Mom and Josh take the opposite couch.

An awkward silence lingers between all of us before Josh opens his mouth. "I'd like to start by saying—"

"Wait." The word escapes me, nervous and high in pitch. "If you don't mind, I'd like to say something first."

"Of course. Go ahead."

I look at Dan and he gives me an encouraging nod that calms me. "Dan and I have spoken a lot about what we hope to achieve with this visit. We're both sorry about the way our relationship came to light and the damage it's caused. We know things will take time to mend but we've come here today to make peace with you both and work toward some kind of normality. I want to be upfront and clear, though, that nothing you say will stop me and Dan from being together."

Josh takes Mom's hand. I can't read either of their expressions, other than they don't look angered over my words, which I'll take as a win.

Dan leans forward, resting both elbows on his knees. "I want you two to know how serious I am about Ally. Given my past reputation with women and poker and God knows what else, I'm sure I don't appear to be a good fit for Ally. It's never been stated, but you both know my poker games haven't been exactly legal. I've gotten into some shit over them and have thrown shade on Forever Families. It's going to stop, to prove to you both that I have Ally's best interest at heart and that she's safe with me. I've been beside myself with guilt since the night Ally was attacked over a game I won. From now on, I'll only be playing professional. And I've decided I'm going to donate a percentage of my winnings."

Dan finishes speaking, and I feel good about all that we've said. If our parents aren't happy with this, I don't know what more we can do. I gauge their reaction, relieved to find them both nodding with what looks like approval.

"Thank you, both, for everything you've said. We truly

appreciate it." Mom brushes out the skirt of her dress. Despite telling her to relax with us, she's jittery. Her chin is trembling. She's more nervous than I am. "I think Josh and I are the ones who need to do most of the talking. We haven't acted right toward you two and we're appalled at ourselves. That night at the benefit was such a shock. Then there was the pressure of the media. But it's not an excuse. You were right, Ally, when you said Forever Families was our priority over you and Dan. We both knew as soon as Daxton took you from the house that we'd messed up. I spoke terribly to you. I wasn't treating you like an adult. I'm beyond embarrassed over what Josh and I did with your phone. I'm so sorry."

"We both are," Josh adds. "We've had a lot of time to reflect on everything. It's taken us a while to get here, but we're going to do our best at embracing your relationship."

"Really?" I'm shocked and yet comforted by their words. It doesn't fix the pain they caused but it's the foundation needed for us to move forward. "That means a lot to us. Thank you."

"Dan," Mom says. "You've always been a son to me. I'm sorry I haven't acted as more of a mother to you recently."

"Hug it out?" Dan rises to his feet, bringing a much-needed touch of lightheartedness to the conversation.

She smiles. "I'd like that very much."

I watch, pleasantly surprised as Mom stands from the couch and hugs Dan.

"I'm feeling left out, Ally. Get over here," Josh says.

I laugh, and the next thing I know, Josh has me wrapped in his arms. My eyes water from how relieved I am, but I hold onto my tears. I'm no idiot to think things will immediately be back to normal in the family. Seeing me and Dan together will be an adjustment for everyone, but we're taking positive steps forward.

"Dan," Josh says with me still in his arms. "I know I'm pushing my luck to expect a hug from you, but I'd like to have a word in private to make things right between us. Step out to the balcony with me? We'll give the girls some time to catch up with each other."

Dan nods, his jaw stiff, his shoulders even more so. "Yes, I'd like that."

CHAPTER FORTY-FOUR

DAN

The sun is low in the sky as I step out to the balcony, pulling my jacket on. It's snowing lightly, being late January. My breath comes out in a visible plume, though the temperature of the balcony is comfortable with an outdoor heater already running. A roof shelters us from the snow.

Dad shuts the glass door behind us, giving us privacy for what is guaranteed to be a difficult conversation. Resting my forearms on the railing, I glance over my shoulder at Ally and her mother in the living room, talking and laughing over something. The sight of them warms me. I'm pleased for Ally and that I have Amabella's affection again.

My father joins me at the railing. "I can see you love her very much."

"I do." I glance back out at the city. Talking about Ally with my father feels odd. I don't know if it will ever feel normal. "That's why I'm here today, for her. I told Ally I'll work on the issues you and I have. I don't know how I'm meant to find a way to stop being angry at you. But I will. For her."

The city sounds of car horns and engines fills the silence between us for what seems like minutes, though I'm sure it's less. My father is contemplating how to respond. I'm wondering if I should dive in headfirst by mentioning all of my childhood trauma.

"You know, Dan, right before your birthday, I had a conversation with Ally about you," he speaks first, calm and even sounding... caring. I can't remember the last time he's taken this tone with me.

I remember Ally mentioning something about this to me and my brothers when we spoke with them at The Scarlet Mirage, and wonder if this is the same conversation he's referencing. At the time, I didn't care much for whatever their chat involved. Now, I'm intrigued.

"I told Ally that she and her mother are the key to holding this family together. That we all come together because of them." Dad pauses, letting out a troubled sigh. "It shouldn't be that way. We should be a family even without them. I realize it's my fault we never have been. But everything you've just said confirms what I told Ally that day. *She* is what keeps you in my life. *She* is the reason I haven't completely lost you. And for that, I've come to realize there's no way I can stand against your relationship with Ally. It's taken me a while to realize this, but she's good for you."

For the first time throughout this conversation, I turn to face him. "Thank you," I say, genuinely meaning it. "What can you and I do to work through our issues?"

"How about this—we'll talk about anything from the past that you need to. I know I've been absent for a lot of your life. It's my biggest regret. I've been harsh on your decisions. You've shown me today that you're making better choices, and I'm proud of you. I know that when I got remarried and tried to be more family-orientated, it was too little too late. But I'm here now, telling you that you are my son and I love you, and that you and your brothers are the most important thing to me in this world. Nothing will fix our past, but I'm determined to fix our future. I know mending our relationship will be a long process. It means the world to me that you're willing."

I'm sure he's said *I love you* to me at some point in my life, but I can't remember a time. Hearing it now is healing. Everything he's said is progress. Perhaps there's hope for us yet.

I hold my hand out, not being the hugging type with my father, but wanting to show him that his words have resonated with me. He looks down at my hand, hesitating before pulling me in for a hug.

I stiffen in his arms, the physical contact strange and unnatural for us, until I let go of my reservations and hug him back, accepting that this is all part of the journey of forgiveness and letting go of my anger.

In an ideal world, if I could rewrite history, this is the kind of relationship I would have wanted to have with my father. Maybe I can still have that relationship one day.

CHAPTER FORTY-FIVE

ALLY

"You good to do this, baby?"

"Yeah."

"And you're sure Liam will be here?"

"His band performs at this club every Wednesday." I reach across the center console of Dan's car and kiss him. "Wait here, okay. Thanks for driving me. I shouldn't be too long."

He taps my ass as I climb out of the car. I squeal and shut the passenger door, slinging my purse over my shoulder as I glance back at him, finding a smirk on his handsome face.

It would have been ideal to get confirmation from Liam that he'll be here before driving all the way to The Hamptons, but when I tried calling him, his number had been disconnected. Perhaps he blocked me. I don't blame him.

After the way Dan's and my visit went so well with Mom and Josh at the start of the week, I decided there's one more person I need to fix things with, and I wouldn't feel right if there's never any closure between me and Liam.

I've been to this jazz club with Liam a few times. It's a

casual place, welcoming to everyone. During the two occasions when I visited, it was bustling, but the club is almost empty when I step through the entrance, the hour barely being evening.

There's one bartender on duty. A couple of customers are sitting in front of the stage, watching the band perform slow jazz. I gulp, seeing Liam on stage. Surely enough time has passed that this interaction will be civil. Pushing my nerves aside, I step up to the stage, right in his line of sight.

Liam sees me, his body stiffening as he plays his instrument. He looks away, avoiding my gaze for the rest of the song. Not a great start. Perhaps civil is still asking too much of him.

When the song comes to an end, he groans and rubs the back of his neck. "Ally, what are you doing here?"

"Hoping we can talk."

"I'm working."

"I know." I smile softly, hoping he sees the gesture as a peace offering. Even an apology. "I didn't know how else to contact you. I won't be long. I just want a minute of your time."

He thinks about my request for a moment. I can see it in his eyes that he wants to turn me away. If he does, so be it. At least I've tried.

"Fine," he finally says. "Let's head out the back."

I follow him through the venue to a quiet room where the band's equipment is stored.

Liam leans against a desk, crossing his arms, his tone blunt. "I asked you if there was someone else."

"I didn't know how to tell you the truth. I didn't want to risk anyone finding out about Dan. You and I weren't ever in a committed relationship, but I know you were ready to commit and I'm sorry for hurting you. I wasn't trying to waste your time."

Liam remains quiet with his arms folded. I get it. He probably feels used and thrown to the wayside.

"I know my words might not mean much to you, and I don't expect forgiveness," I continue, getting to the whole point of my visit. "But I want to give you something that will show the depth of my apology."

I retrieve the George Gershwin coin from my purse and hold it out for Liam to take. He stares at it, his mouth opening and shutting, no words coming out.

"Here. This is for you."

"Ally, what? No, I can't take the coin from you."

"I want you to have it."

"This was a birthday present to you from your mom. Not to mention how rare this coin is."

I shrug, smiling. "I know. Which I hope symbolizes how sorry I am."

Finally, he drops the harsh stance and smiles in return, a *true* smile, and shakes his head. "Okay, Ally, I accept your apology. But I can't take this from you."

I grab his hand and place the coin in his palm. "I insist. And now, I'm leaving so you can't give it back to me. Goodbye."

I walk out the door, through the club, and out to the car park. When I'm halfway back to Dan's car, Liam calls my name. I turn back to the club, finding him jogging toward me.

"Liam, I'm not taking the coin back."

"I know." He catches his breath, joining my side. "Look, I have these opera tickets I bought a while back and was going to surprise you with them. Mozart's *The Magic Flute*. Why don't you take the tickets. Otherwise, they'll go to waste. It's the least I can do after you've given me George Gershwin. They're for this weekend."

"Thank you, but I'll be out of town at my uncle's wedding." I take a few steps back. "I should go now. My ride is waiting."

Liam's focus switches to Dan's Aston Martin. To my surprise, he waves at Dan, then says one last thing to me. "I'll see you around, okay, Ally."

"I'd like that."

CHAPTER FORTY-SIX

ALLY

"You and I have never had a common interest. No father-son hobby to bond over. Let's say we find something." Josh raises his voice for Dan to hear over the wedding reception music.

The night is getting on, with the three-course meal and speeches behind us. All the guests are partying, mingling throughout the dining area or on the dance floor. The three of us are gathered around an upright wine barrel table, each with a flute glass in our hand. Mom's among the guests somewhere, dancing and having fun. I'm pretty sure she's tipsy. Josh too. It's a sight I'm not used to, but I'm glad they're enjoying themselves at Daxton and Jordan's wedding.

I've been to this vineyard a few times in my childhood. It first belonged to Daxton's parents before his brother took over the family business a few years back. The vineyard is beautiful. Rustic and timeless with a Mediterranean feel, like we're partying in an Italian villa. The weather isn't too cold either, being in California. It's the perfect place for a wedding, with the most perfect bride and groom.

I've spent the entire day consumed with bridesmaid duties, puffing up Jordan's dress and holding her bouquet, pampering her in the morning when we got our hair and makeup done. She went for a princess ballgown style wedding dress and looks stunning. All the bridesmaids are in champagne satin dresses.

"I could teach you how to play poker," Dan says to Josh, the suggestion sarcastic and a joke.

To my surprise, Josh laughs, patting Dan on the shoulder. It has to be from the alcohol. "You know what, let's do it. But absolutely no money involved. All right, I'm off to find Amabella. Have fun, you two."

I watch Josh leave before making a comment. "Things are going well between you two, by the looks of it."

"So far."

Felix, Tyler, and Killian join our side, looking handsome in their suits. "Bro, becoming best friends with Dad. Have you painted each other's nails yet?" Felix taunts, laughing a little. "Is this an act to please him so he'll approve of you and Ally?"

Dan shrugs the comment off, lifting his drink to his mouth. "Dad and I had a long chat. He seems genuinely sorry about a lot of shit that happened in the past and is trying to be a better father. He'll probably try to speak with each of you soon about the same thing."

Killian laughs. "Oh, God. Something to look forward to."

Beyonce's *Single Ladies* starts playing over the speakers and guests are suddenly cheering. All the unmarried women flock to the dance floor.

"Isn't this your cue to join the bouquet toss?" Tyler asks me, hands in his pockets.

"I'm happy to sit this out. I've always found it embarrassing to be in the crowd, fighting to catch the bouquet. Oh... *shit*. Hide me." I step back, trying to get behind Dan when I see Mom and Harper heading in my direction.

"Not a chance," Felix chuckles, nudging me forward. "Join in, baby sis. You and Dan could be the next ones getting hitched."

My cheeks heat up at the suggestion. I glance at Dan, finding a smug grin on his face over Felix's comment.

"Ally! Come on! You're not getting out of this," Mom shouts over the rabid women on the dance floor. Both her and Harper grab my hands and pull me along with them.

I give up the fight when grinding my heels into the floor gets me nowhere, and follow, calling back to Dan over my shoulder, "You're in trouble later."

"Looking forward to it," he calls back, and I pray to God my mother hasn't heard.

My relationship with her is doing well, but I don't want to push my luck. She's been acting her normal self with me again, minus the babying, which I'm grateful for. Most importantly, none of the recent family tension has been brought to the wedding.

"Go catch the bouquet, girls," Mom says, leaving me and Harper at the outskirts of the crowd.

I stand beside Harper, waiting for this to be over, glad I'm not in the thick of the group where everyone is squished together and being pushed about.

"You and Dan look good together," Harper says as we wait for Jordan to step up to the stage and toss her roses.

"Thank you. I know it must be weird seeing us together."

"I've dealt with weird. You two are not weird when I can see how happy you make each other."

"You've dealt with something stranger?"

"Let's not get into the specifics." She rolls her eyes, not at me but at the topic, which sparks my intrigue. I couldn't even guess what she's referring to if I tried.

The cheering grows louder. I look over the heads of all the women in front of me, realizing Jordan is now standing on the stage with her back to the dance floor. She tosses her flowers into the air, and it's as if I'm watching in slow motion, mortified as the bouquet travels in my direction.

Being with Dan has felt impossible for so long that I've never entertained the idea of marrying him. In these last few months, it's become clear that we're in this relationship for the long run. We wouldn't have gone through all this pain if we weren't. Dan is my forever. But I could seriously do without the whispers and strange glances that are bound to happen from the guests at this wedding if that bouquet lands in my hands.

I let out a breath of relief when Harper catches the bouquet. Everyone turns to look at her, clapping in applause. She smiles but it doesn't touch her eyes.

"You and Tyler are next!" Mom appears out of nowhere, wrapping an arm around Harper and kissing her cheek. I try to slink away unnoticed, back to Dan, but Mom wraps her other arm around me. "The garter toss is next. Let's watch together."

I oblige my mother and clear out of the way with her and Harper as the crowd disperses. A chair is placed in the center of the dance floor and single men gather around, including all the Blackwood brothers. I get that same smug glance from Dan as before, and laugh in return, grinning back at him.

Jordan sits in the chair, smiling, laughing, and blushing as Daxton kneels in front of her, sliding her dress up her thigh. The look he gives her is so playful yet intimate that I feel like I'm intruding on a private moment of theirs.

The noise at this wedding grows even more hectic as Daxton takes the garter between his teeth and slides it down her leg. He tosses it into the crowd of men without looking and presses his lips to Jordan's. The kiss is tender, and I can see the two of them laughing against each other's lips. My God, they are perfection. I could melt from watching how cute they are together.

Mom cheers, so loud in my ear I flinch. She's not tipsy, I've decided, but totally drunk. "The Blackwoods are on fire tonight!"

Scanning the crowd, I search for the man who caught the garter and find it in Felix's hands. I scoff. Yeah, right, like he's getting married anytime soon. He's like Dan used to be, going through women but never having a girlfriend.

The crowd scatters and the celebrations continue with more music and dancing. Mom finally releases me from her grip, busying herself with another guest, letting Harper and me return to the brothers, the four of them gathered around the same barrel table as before.

Dan wraps an arm around my waist, pulling me close to his side. I smile at him, knowing there'd normally be something more between us like a kiss, but that neither of us want to be too affectionate in front of our family. I'm not complaining. We've been sneaking around for years and it's hot thinking about what he'll do to me when we get our next private moment.

Dan leans in and whispers in my ear, the deep tone of his voice and tickle of his breath sending shivers down my spine and tightening my muscles. "Whatever you're thinking right now, get that look off your face. We're in public and the last thing I need is those little *fuck me* eyes making me hard. Wait until we get back to our room."

My stomach coils at his words, the tension traveling to my clit. I lick my lips and turn into him, whispering back, "What's waiting for me in our room?"

Dan's gaze dips to my mouth. "That ribbon on your dress, wrapped around your waist—I'm going to tie your naked body up in it then strap you to the bed so you're at my mercy to fuck however I please."

A gasp slips out of me, aroused by the visual. I clear my throat, attempting to disguise the sound, hoping no one heard. Dan chuckles, his fingers tracing soft swirling patterns at my waist, teasing me.

I try to distract myself with the current conversation at the table, but whatever Harper and the boys are talking about is stilted and tense. It's all generic chit-chat and one-word answers.

I shrug, trying to bring some humor to the group. "So, Harper and Felix are the next ones to get married."

Killian doesn't seem to think anything of my comment, but there's no missing the way Tyler, Harper, and Felix's eyes all flick to me.

"I didn't mean you'd marry each other. Just that—"

Dan squeezes my waist, quick to whisper in my ear again. "Touchy subject. Don't say anything else. I'll explain later."

Clearly, I've put my foot in my mouth. I have no concept of how, unless perhaps Harper wants a proposal from Tyler, but he isn't keen on getting married. Or the same situation but in reverse.

"Anyone need a new drink?" Tyler asks, the tone of his voice cold. Tyler never seems to be in an overly happy mood, but this is drastic, even for him.

I caused this by joking about marriage?

Dan and Killian take Tyler up on his offer and he leaves the group without another word.

"Harper," Felix sounds just as cold. "Your boyfriend has a large drink order. You should help him."

She scowls at Felix, and then she's gone, muttering *jerk* beneath her breath as she follows Tyler through the crowd. Seriously, what the hell is going on between those three?

Killian is the only one who doesn't seem aware of the tension, busy texting someone on this phone and grinning at the screen. "Violet says hi."

"You're texting Violet?" I ask, perking up. I don't care what either of them say, there's definitely something happening between them. "You know, you could have invited her to the wedding as your date."

"I don't know how many times I have to tell you, it's not like that between us."

"Sure. Whatever. Any romantic prospects for you, Felix?"

He side-eyes me with a look of amusement. "Baby sis, I'm flattered you're taking an interest in my love life, but it's non-existent."

Dan laughs. "No romantic prospects for Felix. Just a lot of sexual prospects."

The similarities between Dan and Felix resurface in my mind. Dan used to sleep around a lot without committing to anyone, but that was because he only wanted me and I was off limits. I laugh under my breath at the thought of Felix being in the same position, in love with a girl he can't have.

Yeah, right. As if.

Dan slips his hand into mine. "Okay, enough chat. I'm stealing you away to the dance floor. See you boys later."

I walk alongside Dan, speaking freely now that it's only the two of us. "What was all that between Felix, Tyler, and Harper?"

His arms curl around my waist when we arrive at the dance floor. "I don't know the full details, just that Felix and Tyler used to share Harper."

My eyebrows lift in surprise. "She slept with both of them at the same time?"

"You can't tell anyone."

"I won't. I'm just shocked. I mean, *wow*." She said she's experienced something stranger than Dan's and my relationship. I suppose two brothers sharing her could be what she was referring to.

My hands rest on Dan's shoulders as we sway to the music. He spins me out wide, and when he pulls me back in, my back is pressed to his chest. Dan holds me tight, kissing my cheek.

"Enough talk about them. Let's dance and enjoy this moment," he says. "You know, this will be us one day, having our own wedding. Let's give everyone a few more years to get used to the idea of us."

"You want to get married?"

"To you, I do. My Queen of Hearts."

I smile and kiss his lips, keeping it respectful in public. "I have to say yes, first."

"Like that will be hard to get out of you. You've been trying to get me out of your system for years and look how that ended up." His voice dips for my ears alone. "Perfect, desperate little slut. Just the way I like you."

I bite my bottom lip, resisting a smile, but there's no hiding how happy Dan makes me. "Your slut and no one else's."

"Exactly. There'll never be anyone else who owns my heart but you."

CHAPTER FORTY-SEVEN

DAN

2 YEARS LATER

Ally walks through our front door right as I pour us two glasses of wine. Perfect timing. I've prepared her favorite meal of roast chicken and have it cooking in the oven, ready to eat in thirty minutes.

"Oh my goodness, Dan. What is all this?"

I step out of the kitchen, greeting Ally with her wine. "A romantic, candlelit dinner for my queen."

She smiles, giving me a kiss. "What's the occasion?"

"Do I need an occasion to spoil you?"

"Good point." Ally places our wine on the table and her lips return to mine. Her hands slide around my shoulders, up into my hair.

Two years on and this need we have for each other is more consuming than ever. My girl needs sex and orgasms every day to be kept happy. My perfect little slut and queen that I will give the world to.

Her hands travel to my cock. I'm going to enjoy fucking her tonight if all goes to plan. There's an envelope from Juilliard sitting on our bed, which I'm hoping has an acceptance letter waiting inside. Afterward, I'll get down on one knee and ask her the most important question of my life. Dad and Amabella have already given their blessing.

We've turned a real corner with them in the last two years, especially me and my father. We're still working on our relationship but he's more of a positive presence in my life now. He reinstated my trust fund, which I assured him I don't need, but he insisted, saying he's proud of the life choices I'm making. I'm playing professional league poker now, which has no reflection on Forever Families and its reputation, and eliminates the dangers that my old gaming habits evoked. Forever Families took some time to recover from the scandal of my relationship with Ally, but it's back on track now.

Ally's fingers work to unbuckle my belt. I smirk, loving how much she wants me, but I can't get sidetracked with her needy hands just yet, and pull them away from my fly.

"Before we get too carried away, how was your day?"

"Good. The audition went well."

"Glad to hear it."

Today was an audition for an orchestra. This is all part of the therapist's plan, for Ally to attend as many auditions as she can. Exposure to the fear. The panic attacks haven't completely disappeared, but Ally has a better grip on them now. She was able to get through her Juilliard audition without breaking down. And now, the outcome of that audition is only moments away.

My fingers twine with Ally's. "Something arrived in the mail. It's waiting on the bed for you to open."

She gives me a curious look, then takes my hand,

leading me into our bedroom. The moment Ally sees the envelope, she gasps, clapping a hand to her mouth. "It's here. What do I do?"

I laugh, hugging her from behind and kissing her neck. "Open it."

She grabs the envelope, tearing a slither of the seal before stopping herself and taking a deep, calming breath.

"You all right?"

She nods. "It's okay if this is a rejection letter. I'll keep working toward my goals and audition again next year."

"I know, because you're strong and determined. I'm proud of you, whatever the outcome of this letter is. You've made so much progress to have even auditioned in the first place."

She kisses me. "You're the most incredible boyfriend ever."

"I try. Okay, enough stalling. Open the letter."

Ally tears the envelope and her hands shake as she unfolds the letter. I'm holding my breath, watching Ally's eyes skim across the paper as she reads. Seconds tick by. Her chest is rising up and down with rapid breaths. And then I see the exact moment her eyes widen.

"I got in," Ally whispers. She looks up at me in disbelief, with the most beautiful smile stretching across her face. "Dan, I got in."

As soon as the news sinks in, she starts jumping, she's that excited. Not little jumps, either. Ally bounces all around the room, continuously shouting *Yes! Yes! Yes!* It's the most magnificent sight to watch. She bends forward, bracing her head between her knees and with a sob escaping her. She's so happy she's crying.

I stand back, smiling and giving Ally space to have her own reaction. This moment is just like the time she received her acceptance letter to the Paris Conservatoire, only with heightened joy.

"I'm so fucking proud of you, baby."

She wipes her eyes and stands tall, laughing to herself. "I did it. I actually did it. I can't believe it."

"You better believe it because you're incredible."

She starts jumping again and launches herself onto me, wrapping her legs around my waist. I lose balance and stumble forward, bracing myself as I fall onto the bed with Ally beneath me. I'm hit with déjà vu. The events of this moment are just like the first kiss we ever shared. She laughs. The sound is so beautiful it spreads chills through my body.

Everything about this moment is perfect.

I'm so in love with this girl that I can't hold back from what I planned to ask later tonight. "Marry me."

She stills beneath me, registering what I've said. But that gorgeous smile goes nowhere. It only grows wider.

"Maybe I shouldn't be asking at a moment like this, but seeing you this happy… It's so beautiful and—"

"Yes, Dan."

My lips twitch. "Yes?"

Ally's laughter returns and she presses her mouth up to mine. "This is the *perfect* moment to ask. Yes. I'll marry you."

Join my newsletter to stay up to date with future book releases in the Playing Favorites series. You can sign up at www.skylasummers.com or scan the QR code below.

If you haven't read Dan and Ally's prequel novella yet, **My Favorite Girl**, you can find it on Amazon and in Kindle Unlimited.

Follow me on Instagram: @authorskylasummers for teasers and all the latest updates on my next book release.

REVIEWS AND SPREADING THE WORD

Book reviews are invaluable to an author's success. If you enjoyed this book, leaving a written review and star rating on the *My Favorite Sin* Amazon and Goodreads page will be much appreciated. Spreading the word via any social media platforms you may have is also greatly appreciated.

BOOKS BY SKYLA SUMMERS

Celebrity Fake Dating series
Fake Dating Adrian Hunter
Fake Dating Zac Delavin
Fake Dating Daxton Hawk

PLAYING FAVORITES
My Favorite Girl (Book 0.5 Prequel Novella)
My Favorite Sin (Book 1)

ACKNOWLEDGMENTS

Dan and Ally's story nearly didn't make it to publication. TWICE! I'll spare you the details of why, but there were outside forces working against this story.

The first time it happened, I took a break from writing, literally broken hearted that I wouldn't be able to tell Dan and Ally's story. I tried to forget about these characters and cut my losses.

Long story short, I couldn't forget about Dan and Ally. Hopefully, after reading this story, you've fallen in love with these characters too and understand why I couldn't give up on them.

The second time this book ran into a roadblock was very recently, and I'm so glad I had the support of my hype team to encourage me through the drama. Thank you to everyone in the team for always supporting me and my books and sharing the love for Ally and Dan.

To all ARC readers, thank you for taking the time to read and review My Favorite Sin and for supporting this book in its early stages.

Thank you to everyone who fell in love with Dan and Ally in My Favorite Girl and shared their excitement for My Favorite Sin.

Thank you to my husband who always encourages me to keep writing.

ABOUT THE AUTHOR

Skyla Summers is an Australian author who lives with her husband and daughter in the sunny state of Queensland. Her favorite part of story telling is making characters fall in love. She always enjoys talking with her readers. You can message Skyla through her website www.skylasummers.com or find her on social media using the link below.

instagram.com/authorskylasummers

Printed in Great Britain
by Amazon